MW00387196

A Barbarian
in
Rome's Legions

A Barbarian in Rome's Legions

Mark L. Richards

CopyRight Page

For my late cousin,
Pamela Grosschmid,
who never had the opportunity
to realize her dreams.

Contents

PART I

Chapter I
Spring

West Bank of the Rhine
Military District of Germania Superior
44 BC

With his heart thumping wildly, Alderic edged painstakingly slow through the forest glade. He was part of a small vanguard, advancing in a chevron formation—the scouting party for a larger force of combatants positioned several hundred paces behind them. Alderic stood near the front right side of the wedge. He could sense rather than see the others, as most of them were beyond his line of sight. They were being led by Caldor, a veteran of many battles positioned at the apex of the formation, about twenty paces ahead of the others.

Alderic and the other eight warriors of the reconnaissance force had been tasked with exploring the road ahead. The main body of German raiders—about fifty men—waited silently for word that it was safe to proceed. He had been informed by his fellow warriors that the road ahead was considered a danger point and thus, warranted cautious advancing. After all, he didn't know such things himself. He had witnessed but eighteen summers, and this was the first time he had been allowed to accompany the fighters of his small Germanic tribe. Their purpose was to raid the Gallic settlements on the opposite bank of the Rhine or—as the Romans called the river—the Rhenus.

The party glided forward stealthily, their footsteps no more than a whisper. Each man placed his heel cautiously on the forest bed. No heavy footsteps. No sudden movements. No noise. No nothing. The men, clad in drab woolen garments, blended with the shadows that

3

obscured their presence. Their tracking skills had been instilled since they were boys. It was second nature to them—a craft they knew well.

Alderic was a striking figure: he was tall, standing well above the others in his tribe. His face featured a rugged, square jaw-line, offset by piercing blue eyes and light brown hair. He was oblivious of the effect he had on the fairer sex, which was perhaps for the better. If he knew, it could get him into all kinds of trouble in the small village, for many of the ladies—both married and single—gave him many an appraising, sidelong glance, and not out of idle curiosity.

The clan of sixty-odd fighters of the Tencteri nation had crossed the Rhine early this morning in their crude makeshift rafts. They sought to pillage the Gallic villages in the vicinity, and the loot—the gold, silver, foodstuffs, and iron tools secured from these forays—would ensure the prosperity of the village, especially during the harsh winter months.

The Tencteri had raided beyond the river once earlier this spring with paltry results. The foray was made against one of the poorer Gallic settlements and had yielded a meagre plunder. To make matters worse, one of the boats carrying the captured loot had capsized and sunk in the turbulent river, taking with it two of the tribe's warriors and their booty, never to be seen again.

There had been much debate among the warriors against going across again so soon after their last incursion. Some of the elders had cautioned them about an impulsive counter-raid. Danger lurked in wait on these excursions, perhaps doubly so now. Those opposing the second raid had argued that the Gauls would be on high alert. In the end, greed overruled caution, and the tribal council decided to go on another incursion despite the endangerment. They didn't fear the Gallic warriors who inhabited these settlements—they were weak and no match for the Tencteri warriors; what they did fear, though, was the nearby garrison of Roman soldiers, located a short distance down the Roman-constructed thoroughfare, thus warranting the high level of vigilance when approaching the road ahead.

Alderic continued to pad slowly through the silent forest. His senses heightened, he could smell the rich loamy scent of the woods, see the colors and shapes of the foliage around him, and hear even the slightest rustle of the leaves. The forest glade was eerie this spring morning; even the birds and insects were hushed. Ghostly wisps of fog swirled about the ground in an ethereal embrace, obscuring the landscape. He halted briefly and brushed aside a large, thorn-laced bush in his path. An ill-advised action, for one of the supple limbs viciously sprang back upon him. Some thistles from the offended bush pierced his leggings, making him slightly stumble. He caught his balance, but not before his foot made contact with a twig. The dry stick snapped, sending a piercing sound echoing through the silence of the woodland. His face flushed almost instantaneously. Wincing, he stared straight ahead, not wishing to see the reproachful frowns he knew were being directed at him.

Sigivald, his best friend and fellow novice-at-arms, sauntered up to his right and—as only good friends can—smirked at Alderic for his indiscretion. This was a rite of passage for Alderic and Sigivald, their first raid into Gallic territories; and both were excited as could be to join the other men from their clan on a fighting expedition.

Days earlier, Widogast, their chieftain, had informed Alderic and Sigivald that they were to accompany the adult warriors. This, however, came with the strict condition that they weren't to take part in any of the fighting or the ensuing plundering. The two inexperienced youths were to be observers and nothing more.

Widogast had stared sternly at the two young men after informing them of the conditions, ensuring that there was no misunderstanding about the role they would be playing in the day's endeavor. He had stated in no uncertain terms that there would be severe consequences if they disobeyed him. He had no desire to inform their mothers— both widows, and toward whom Widogast, as chieftain, felt a certain protectiveness—that their sons had perished in their first raid.

For their first responsibility, Widogast had assigned the pair to Caldor, the senior leader of the scouting party, to patrol the terrain ahead. They would halt where the Roman road traversed the wooded glade. Widogast was of the firm opinion that they faced no more threat than usual, even returning so shortly after the last intrusion. He reasoned that it would be a good experience for two young men and shouldn't be too dangerous either, given the clan's past successful excursions into Gallic territory. Alderic and Sigivald had followed the veteran warrior, Caldor, like eager puppies. This was the adventurous quest they had but dreamed of. So here they were, waiting for what would unfold before them.

Caldor, at the tip of the formation, raised his arm for all to halt. Alderic obediently crouched amid the bushes, concealing his tall form. He inhaled deeply, attempting to dispel his nervousness. *They must be near the road that's directly ahead.* A puff of breeze swayed the nearby trees, rustling the leaves ever so slightly, and a few slender beams of sunlight suddenly penetrated the dense forest. The mist eddied, then dissipated, allowing them a view of the area before them. Using a slow and deliberate motion—for sudden movements were more easily spotted by both men and beasts—Alderic parted the thick foliage and peered ahead, gasping at the sight.

So this is what they looked like. Dressed the same. He had heard much about them but never seen these highly feared warriors. They were Roman legionnaires. Even though the soldiers were not big men (Alderic easily towered over them), what was imposing about them was their armaments. Every legionnaire wore an iron helmet, with iron suits encasing their torso. A large number of men paraded on the road before the Germans' concealed positions. Each Roman soldier carried several spears in addition to their *gladii,* the Roman short stabbing swords hanging on military belts fastened around their middle. Strapped to their left were large rectangular wooden shields painted in bright red with the golden figure of a bull embossed in the center. He wondered how one could possibly kill these beasts. Tasting the bile that had unexpectedly risen in his throat, he grimaced. The Romans were not supposed to be here. The raid planned by his tribe was supposed to be an adventure, a lark, which had now turned into something entirely unexpected.

The Tencteri had every reason to fear these Romans. A little over a decade ago, when Alderic was just a young boy, their arch enemy, the Suebi tribe, had pressured the Tencteri to vacate much of their ancestral lands as the Suebi Empire expanded and dominated. In search of new lands, the Tencteri had crossed the Rhenus into the Gallic province in search of a home. They were met by the Romans and their feared leader, Caesar.

The Romans had recently conquered Gaul and wanted to demonstrate the benefits of being under Rome's protection to their new client state. Caesar had refused to parley with the Tencteri, for in his eyes, they were weak and, thus, of no profit to him. His army, subsequently, slaughtered the unfortunate Tencteri who had crossed the river, including Alderic's father. The warriors who survived had to flee back across the river. The Tencteri tribe was marginalized and forced to subsist on meager pockets of land that were empty of game and unsuited for tillage

Alderic studied the armored Romans, and then considered his own meagre armaments. He carried a long wooden spear with an iron point plus a short-bladed iron knife. He carried on his left arm was a small wicker shield. He had on plain woolen trousers and a sleeveless deer hide vest. To his right, Sigivald seemed as mesmerized as him by the appearance of these conquerors, his mouth agape in awe and his gaze fixated on the figures.

Alderic couldn't contain himself. Leaning close to Sigivald, he said in a hushed tone, "Just look at all that armor and the weapons!" He was rewarded with a harsh glance from Caldor. He mimed with his fingers to his lips, silencing him. Before them, commands were shouted, which resonated down the Roman column. Promptly, the Roman legionnaires, acting as one, spread out and faced the forest where the band of Tencteri hid. Alderic felt an icy feeling spread in his bowels. *What was this all about?* He gripped the shaft of his spear tight and crouched even lower.

It felt as though every Roman soldier was staring directly at him. How could the Romans sense they were hiding in this forested grove? They couldn't possibly spot the German band at this distance through the intervening foliage thick with trees and heavy brush. They were over fifty paces away. His fear was heightened by the Romans' next move. Further harsh commands were issued, piercing the quietude of the forest. All as one, the soldiers dropped their marching packs and spears and drew their swords from the scabbards attached to their right. The blades made an ominous hissing sound as they slid out from their sheaths. Within a single instant, a solid wall of shields and glistening steel faced the wooded enclave where Alderic and his brethren hid. The legionnaires began shouting and banging the flat edge of their swords upon their shields. He looked to Caldor for guidance, but his leader's eyes were wide with fright, and his body static with indecision.

Why were the Romans making such a ruckus? He didn't have to wait long to find out. Alderic heard a rising clamor behind him, and then angry shouts and the sounds of iron swords clashing amid the shrieks of dying men. Turning around, he witnessed more of the iron-suited creatures charging into his comrades. *The uproar was a diversion! Clever bastards.* Sigivald let out a cry as his neck was pierced by a sword. His shriek was cut short as a fountain of blood erupted from where the blade had punctured his neck. Collapsing to the ground, he looked at his friend pleadingly for help. Alderic could not comprehend the horror he had just witnessed. He was immobilized as more Roman beasts slammed into them.

Issuing forth a great roar, a swarthy legionnaire with a short, dark beard charged at Alderic. Instinctively, he side-stepped the attack and slammed the butt of his spear into the side of the man's face. The legionnaire collapsed with a groan as Alderic spun about, unsure of what he could do next. He couldn't go forward; the road was sealed off by the wall of Roman shields.

Then, as if the gods had intervened, he noticed a gap in the line of soldiers who had attacked from the rear. He bolted through the breach, his heart thudding in panic, rushing forward to escape the trap sprung by the Romans. In a brief moment of clarity amid this escalating terror, he realized that he had to reach the main body of warriors if he wished to survive. He had no way of knowing that the bulk of the raiding party was also surrounded and under assault at the moment. So, unable to think any longer, he ran.

He didn't get far. A cavalryman materialized out of nowhere in front of him, thrusting a long-bladed sword at him. Alderic made no attempt to parry the blow with his spear. Instead, he ducked under the blade and between the horse's legs. Uttering an oath, the Roman swung his weapon again, but couldn't reach Alderic. Before the rider could strike again, Alderic deftly slid to the rear of the horse and stood up. Employing his long arms and tremendous strength, he seized the rider's armor from behind and yanked him off his mount before attempting to leap into the saddle himself. The horse, however, panicked at the unfamiliar German and reared on its hind legs, forcing Alderic to try and mount once again. As he twisted sideways to get in position, he sensed some movement to his right. Turning his head toward the threat, one of the heavy wooden shields employed by the Romans smashed into his face. As darkness descended, his last thought was that his short life had come to an abrupt end. But this was not his end, for the gods had other plans for him. This was just the beginning of his new life—one that would help shape an empire.

Later that morning, Centurion Marcus Verres, cohort commander, stood on the raised Roman road, slightly above the fallow field where his legionnaires had gathered. He watched as his victorious cohort of nearly five-hundred men fell into ranks.

Verres was a large man in his mid-forties. His bulk was not of fat but solid muscle. His face, browned by the sun and hatched with several whitish scars, bore testament to his years of service within the legions. His men not only respected him, they feared him as well. His intimidating presence caused even the toughest legionnaire to quicken his step or double his efforts in the task assigned. When describing the centurion, only the words brutal, menacing, and demanding would come to mind—the term compassionate being absent.

As commander, the *primus pilus* of the fifth cohort, Fourth Legion, he was satisfied—if the emotion could ever be ascribed to Verres— with his troops' performance today. They had interdicted the German raiding party that had crossed the Rhenus and put a serious hurt on them. The centurion smirked silently. "Interdict"—that was the term his legate had used to describe the purpose of their mission. The centurion didn't even know what the fancy word meant; what he did know was how to slay Germans. He was good at it. The legate of his legion, General Claudius Lucius Placidius, would be pleased with today's outcome; and if he was pleased, there was no doubt that the governor would be pleased as well, which meant that they would lay off his ass about putting an end to these German marauders who insolently crossed the Rhenus to raid Rome's Gallic provinces.

The centurion had deployed his full cohort today, including an *ala* of cavalry. On the surface, using five-hundred men to combat around sixty poorly armed Germans would seem like an excessive use of force; but in cases such as this, it was necessary. At the first sign of danger, the Germans typically bolted like rabbits flushed from the high grass. His legionnaires were heavily armored and would lose a foot-race pursuing the fleet-footed Germans every time. Thus, this time he had used his entire force to surround the raiding Germans and ensnare them in an inescapable trap. So, yes, he had made the right decision to position his full cohort. Besides, he reasoned, his men needed some action; they were getting soft from their life in the garrison. His strategy had been executed to perfection.

A single figure detached from the assembled troops and strode toward Marcus. His second in command, Centurion Gnaeus Cattallus, was about to report the results of today's skirmish. Gnaeus strode within several feet from Marcus and stopped. He consulted his wax tablet, squinting at his scribbled notations, and said, "It was a good day for the legions, Marcus. We sent those barbarian bastards packing. My tally shows forty-five of the filthy barbarians slain with another eight captured. It is believed that a handful escaped back across the river. No men in our forces were killed and four were wounded, although none are believed to be serious." Gnaeus looked up from his wax tablet and proffered a triumphant grin. "Did those bloody barbarians really believe they could venture into our territory with impunity? The dumb fucks. They had no idea we were reconnoitering the river. They traversed the body of water in broad daylight and fell right into our trap." He paused for a moment, then continued, "What would you have me to do with the prisoners? Crucify them to set an example?"

Marcus contemplated the question for a moment. "No, I don't think so. Who is there to witness it? Can't make an example if none of the bloody fools are around. The few survivors have fled back to their lands." He thought for a moment. "When we return to camp, notify the slave merchants. We can make some coin from their sale. There will not be a great sum for only eight men, but every little bit will help when we join the ranks of the elderly."

"We live in uncertain times, Gnaeus. Those cowardly senators murdered our beloved Caesar two months ago. Yet you know he was one of us. Caesar ate the same rations and slept as we did. He always took care of the legions. Who knows what we will get in the name of leaders now. I have no faith that our new sovereigns will look out for those who serve and protect Rome. We need to get our hands on as much coin as possible to fund our retirement, right Gnaeus?"

The second in command grinned broadly. "Right you are, Marcus."

What Marcus didn't add is that he would alter the figures Gnaeus had reported to reflect no surviving Germans. That way he wouldn't have to split any of the monies made from the sale of the captives with the legate. Besides, the general, who Marcus despised and considered an aristocratic prick, had enough money to buy half the province if he so desired. What were a few more coins to him?

Alderic roused from his stupor to find his arms bound tightly behind his back. He was amid the seven other captives from his village. It took his addled brain a moment to realize that he was not dead, though he reasoned that his present circumstances were equally dire. They were watched over by a number of stern-faced legionnaires, their gazes unsympathetic and cruel. Alderic's head ached intensely. He sat up to get a better view of his surroundings. His head swam and he promptly felt violently ill, spewing bile onto his fellow captives. The man next to him, Detlef, a veteran warrior of his tribe, uttered an oath and howled at Alderic, pushing him away. His disposition was already sour, as he had been one of those tasked with carrying Alderic's inert form from the battlefield to the assembly location in the fallow field. The guards guffawed at the incident, gesturing with glee at the slime-coated Detlef.

Alderic scooted farther away from Detlef. He heaved again, and then again. His head was pounding. He glanced up briefly at his captors, then bowed his head. He understood that his life hung in the balance. He had heard of the awful things that these Roman beasts did to their captives and hoped his end would be mercifully quick. He recounted his village life. He would never see his cherished Ealdgyd again. Although she wasn't the most beautiful woman in the village, she always managed to make him laugh with her comic expressions and glib tongue. She was tall, like him, and lithe with brown hair and blue eyes. She seemed drawn to Alderic as well, and they both basked in playful banter. His sad musings were interrupted as the guards shouted at the captives, kicking them and gesturing for them to stand up. Alderic rose, attempting to blink back the tears that clouded his eyes.

Alderic stood upright, swaying. He placed his hand on Detlef's shoulder to steady himself and only received a snarl His hand was brushed away. The line of captives was prodded forward, and they began moving down the paved Roman road to who knew where. They journeyed for a short period before arriving at a small ridge overlooking the Roman camp. Alderic gaped in awe at the spectacle before him. A vast fortress made of earth and wood, with towering turrets at either side of the entrance gates, rose from the earth. The parapets were much taller than an average man. Beyond them lay a sea of tents that looked like a dense cluster of trees in the forest. As he stood there, still spellbound, he received a sharp blow on his back delivered by the butt of a spear, urging him to move forward.

Alderic awoke the next morning feeling somewhat better. His headache had subsided. He and his fellow captives had been put in a sunken mud pit, which now coated the Tencteri warriors from head to foot, surrounded by a hastily constructed, crude wooden corral. They were guarded by several legionnaires and had not been given food or water since they arrived. Beyond the barricaded enclosure were the legionnaire's tents. The soldiers were up early, conversing in their strange tongue and strolling along the tented avenues. They didn't spare even a glance at the prisoners huddled together in misery.

He gazed up at who he assumed to be, based on his uniform and his bearing, a Roman officer—he later learned that they were known as centurions—escorted by two tough looking legionnaires. Accompanying them was a corpulent civilian with weasel-like eyes and a rotund body clad in a filthy tunic. The small group of men treaded into the mud enclosure and approached the captives. The two escorting legionnaires began shouting commands in their strange language, motioning with their cudgels for them to stand and line up.

The ragged group of prisoners understood the message and rose to their feet. Alderic, last in the row of captives, watched as the Romans moved down the line and inspected each man. They peered at their arms and legs and even into their mouths. He wondered what they could be doing. The Roman officer appeared to be quarrelling with the civilian over something. They bantered back and forth in their foreign tongue, punctuated by animated motions and gestures. Finally, reaching the end of the file of prisoners, the two men regarded Alderic.

Centurion Gnaeus Cattallus, second in command of the fifth cohort, the unit that had captured the Tencteri, turned toward the civilian. "Well, Balbus, you thieving bastard," he started. "Here's the last of the lot. Look at the size of this son of a bitch. He caused half of our casualties in yesterday's skirmish. Only a young man, but already a fierce warrior."

The unkempt civilian turned his dark eyes to Alderic, staring him up and down as though he were some farm animal. He didn't respond to the centurion, continuing his appraisal in silence. At last, he spoke: "He appears to be a bit on the slim side."

Gnaeus stroked his chin in thought. "Aye, it's true. But look at him. His beard is not yet fully grown. He will fill out nicely as he matures. It would be a shame to waste such a figure toiling away on some farm. This man is destined for the arena. He belongs in a *ludus*. With proper training, he has the potential to be a star attraction. I will only sell him to you at a hefty premium, not the standard fare of one hundred silver denarii as the others."

Gnaeus stopped speaking, hoping Balbus would agree to a steep price for this Tencteri. If he returned to Marcus Verres, his commanding centurion, with an amount below the expected return, the senior centurion would chew his ass out. Not something Gnaeus wanted to face. Although he was friends with Marcus and would share the occasional cup of wine with him, there was still a breach between commander and subordinate. Marcus did not hesitate to voice his displeasure or assign him the lowest assignments in the cohort. Besides, it was his in his self-interest to extract the largest possible sum; as part of the proceeds would fund his retirement.

Balbus silently continued to assess the young German. He motioned for one of the legionnaires. "Remove his bonds." The guard hesitated, looking to Gnaeus for instruction. The centurion shrugged, "Go ahead."

Alderic rubbed his wrists as the ropes securing him were untied. Not knowing what to expect, he warily eyed the civilian figure in front of him. His instincts told him that something was off. Why was he being unbound? Unexpectedly, the man launched a fist at Alderic's face. With incredible deftness, Alderic raised his left arm and grabbed the man's wrist, squeezing as tightly as he could. The man gasped in pain and sunk to his knees.

The two legionnaire guards raised their cudgels, and the Roman officer shouted something in his peculiar tongue. Alderic released the civilian's arm and ducked the strike of a club to his left. He grabbed the off-balance legionnaire who had missed his strike and sent him hurtling into the other legionnaire. As both men tumbled to the ground, Alderic pivoted to face the next threat. He was met by the Roman officer pointing a sword menacingly at his face. Alderic dropped his arms to his side in submission, knowing he wouldn't prevail. The two legionnaires, who had now recovered, raised their truncheons.

The centurion shouted something, and the pair cautiously lowered their weapons. The Roman officer gestured for Alderic to place his hands behind his back, so he could be secured once more. The centurion smirked; the prisoner had unwittingly made his point to the slave trader. This German had the makings of a gladiator.

Balbus stood rubbing his injured wrist. "All right, I will pay you three hundred denarii for this one. And that is my final offer."

Gnaeus beamed. His commander would be pleased. "Excellent. Balbus, now that this is settled, let's get some wine to celebrate our transaction. Of course, you'll be buying."

Alderic watched the cluster of men depart. He was relieved, for he now knew that, at least, he would not be executed. He reasoned that the only purpose behind the Romans' close inspection of the captives was to sell them, and that they surely would not have gone to all this trouble if they were to be killed. He had heard the Roman officer mention "ludus." He didn't know what the word meant, but he guessed he would find out soon enough.

The next day, the slave trader returned to the huddled group of prisoners, who sat chilled and damp from a night spent on the open ground. The slave merchant and his two helpers yelled at the men and motioned with their clubs for them to spread out. The slaver went directly to Alderic, singling him out from the others. His two assistants stood guard against any possible interference from the others. Alderic's feet were untied and he was prodded to stand. He numbly followed his new master, shooting one last forlorn glance at his German comrades.

For the remainder of the day, Alderic walked with his wardens. From the position of the sun, he reckoned that they were traveling south. Around twilight, they reached a waiting caravan that held other bound strangers and a bevy of armed guards; the wagon was drawn by two oxen. One of the men, a large commanding figure who seemed to have a certain authority, strode over to him and began to speak in heavily accented German: "Listen very carefully and don't interrupt me. You are now a slave and will be transported to Rome, where you will be sold to a ludus who will train you in gladiatorial combat. We have a journey of many weeks ahead of us. During the day, you will walk without shackles, with your arms tied behind your back. At night, your legs will be placed in iron fetters along with the others. If you attempt to escape, you will be severely punished. If you disobey any command, you will be severely punished. Don't cause me any trouble. If you understand what I just told you, nod your head."

Alderic nodded.

"Good. Go, get in line with the other slaves. We begin our journey to Rome in the morning. It will be a long one."

The next day, the entourage of slaves and overseers continued to trek south. The five captives walked in silence, as they were forbidden to talk while marching. Alderic, last in the line of tethered prisoners, stared at the man in front of him the entire day. His throat ached with thirst, and his face, swollen from the shield blow that had knocked him out, was a throbbing mass of pain. The men plodded along the dusty road that soon morphed into an avenue of paved stones. They passed through villages and hamlets, and the people they encountered stared curiously for a few moments, then broke away to go about their businesses, thankful that they didn't share the plight of these prisoners. Wherever they were going, it was most likely to a brutal life.

Toward the evening, the captives' restraints were removed, and they were issued water along with some coarse porridge to eat. Starving, Alderic wolfed down his rations. He decided to seek some solace in the company of his fellow captives. "Hello! I'm Alderic from the Tencteri tribe. I see that you already know each other and are in the same ill-fated plight as me."

There was silence among the other four men. Finally, one of them, a huge brute with broken teeth, glared at him and snarled. "We are from the Marcomanni clan and don't care what your name is, you Tencteri swine. Mind your own business and stay away from us."

Alderic was taken aback by the rudeness and was not sure about how to respond. After a few moments, he spoke. "I was simply introducing myself. That's all. No need to display such ire."

The huge Marcomanni figure growled. "Did you not listen to what I just said? Don't speak to us. Stay away." To underscore his point, he shoved the surprised Alderic to the ground.

Alderic leaped to his feet, surging toward his antagonist. Before he could get his hands on him, three of the captors intervened, pulling the combatants apart. The figure in charge hurried over.

"What the fuck is going on here?" he growled.

All four Marcomanni pointed at Alderic. "He's the one instigating trouble. Get him away from us."

The burly figure roared at Alderic, not waiting for a response. "What did I say about not following commands and acting out? You don't listen well." He smashed Alderic in his already swollen jaw, knocking him to the ground. Pointing at Alderic, he said to the guards, "This man gets no food for the next three days. If he steps out of line one more time, I will whip him within a handbreadth of his life."

Amid the sneers from his fellow captives, Alderic sat dejectedly on the ground, staring off into the distance. His current circumstances were beyond what he could have ever imagined for himself. Life could be harsh back in his village. Plagues regularly claimed many lives especially the old and the infants, and many died at the hand of marauders from other tribes. Yet, there was always the hunting and fishing with friends, the love of women, and the kinship of family among his people. All of this was gone now. He was alive, but his future looked dim amid these Roman beasts.

His moping was interrupted by a sudden burst of optimism, and his self-pity immediately transformed into something else. A flame burned within him. He wanted to live. He wouldn't give up; that was not his way. He silently vowed to survive whatever adversities awaited him and be free once again. His improbable journey into the Roman world was about to commence. The question to be posed here was whether Rome was ready for the likes of him.

Chapter II
Rome, Two Months Later

The captives shuffled through the paved streets of Rome, past tenements, taverns, temples, and other edifices. Alderic gawked at the scale of it all. The size of these massive, dazzling, stone buildings was beyond his most vivid imagination. *How is it possible that men constructed these structures? There's nothing like this in my homeland.* And then there were the people—huge numbers crowding the streets, rushing to and fro, anxious to get somewhere. The din of the teeming horde was overwhelming. Vendors shouted out declarations of the quality of their wares; children cried and women shrieked, as the mob ebbed and flowed. Carts drawn by oxen and mules were everywhere to be seen. Alderic hurriedly hobbled forward the best he could, encumbered as he was by the heavy iron shackles on his wrists and ankles. The captives were also tethered by their necks with a heavy woven rope. When they had reached the city and were amid the swarming crowds, extra precautions were put in place to ensure there would be no possibility of escape.

The horde suddenly thickened, blocking their progress, and the five prisoners halted. Alderic's attention was drawn to his right at the sound of a female squeal. A woman stood in a stall along the avenue with her face painted and a breast exposed. She met his eye and seductively began rubbing her crotch. Alderic gawked at her, never having seen such a public display. The group pushed its way through the crowd, moving forward, all except Alderic, who continued staring in wonder. One of the guards smashed him in the face with the butt of a coiled whip, saying, "What's the matter? Never seen a harlot before? Get moving now!" The women squealed in laughter, and the guards smirked.

The men plodded onward through the crowd. Eventually, the mass of people dissipated, and the streets became more navigable. Alderic ignored the burning pain around his neck from the chafing of the rope. Besides, there was nothing he could do about it; the guards would show him no sympathy. He sensed that they were nearing their destination. Whatever his future held, it had to be better than the eight weeks he had spent in these shackles. From what he could gather, he was to be taken to a place called a ludus, where he would be trained to fight. He didn't understand why and what for, but he supposed he would soon find out.

They arrived at an enclosed fortress. The brick walls were twice as tall as an average man. Two guards stood at the portal. The captives entered through a gate of thick iron bars into a rectangular compound. It featured a central courtyard surrounded by colonnaded buildings. They were directed to the shade of the parapet, and slaves rushed forth and began unfastening their fetters.

A large figure holding a coiled whip and attired in leather muscle cuirass emerged from one of the outer buildings and strode toward them. He had a cruel face, and a small dark beard adorned his lower jaw, adding to his menacing appearance. He was being trailed by a powerful-looking man clad in a rough, woolen tunic. The five captives stood in a line rubbing their chafed ankles and wrists. They ceased their ministrations as the intimidating figure stood before them. He walked along the front of the captives, pausing in front of each man, examining him. His face was clouded with fury, and an angry scowl formed on his lips.

He began to bellow in their strange language. The tunic-clad man who had accompanied him translated his words into German: "My name is Macro Sestinius. I am the *lanista,* in command of this ludus. As of today, you are the property of this establishment. You will do everything I say. You will not ask questions. You will obey instantly without hesitation. You are the dregs of society. Here, you have no rights. If you don't obey as commanded, you will be brutally punished or worse yet, sold to the mines. You will be trained to fight other men to death. If you attempt to escape, you will be executed. There are five of you. Three will likely be dead within the first two years. The first fights in the arena are the deadliest."

The man paused, carefully eyeing each of the new arrivals, inspecting his new property. He continued, "You will be fed and clothed well and while you are here. Once again, the rule is simple: you will do everything I say. If you follow my orders, we will get along just fine."

They heard a creaking, groaning noise. One of the doors in a large rectangular building, perhaps fifty paces away, opened. Approximately two dozen muscular men, clad in various kinds of armor, trotted out onto the parade ground. When they spied the newcomers, whistles and shouts were directed in their general direction. Although Alderic could not make out what they were saying, he could tell from the tone of their voices that they were not welcoming terms.

A second figure emerged from the large central building, also carrying a large coiled whip. He barked out a command, and the men immediately went silent and paired off against one another with their wooden weapons. The five captives stared in awe as the distant figures began trading blows with their swords and shields.

Macro bellowed at the new recruits to get their attention. "Look at me, not them. You will be drilling soon enough. We will train you hard, unlike anything you have ever experienced. We will mold you into skilled fighters who do not fear death and are willing to die with honor in the arena. At the end of every training session, you will declare to the heavens, 'DIE WITH HONOR.' I am handing you over to Lothar, your interpreter. He will show you to your quarters and tell you how things work around here." The lanista turned about and marched toward the drilling gladiators.

Alderic watched the figure of the lanista stride away from the group. He wondered why he appeared so angry; they had, after all, done nothing wrong. Was he always this irate? As he would learn later, the answer was no, he was not always this enraged; and although his ire was directed at the new arrivals today, it had nothing to do with what they had done—he was seething at the impoverished condition of his five new recruits. They were emaciated, and the rope burns and shackle marks from their captivity stood out starkly. As lanista, he was in charge of training the gladiators. These men needed to be in top physical shape so they could compete successfully in the arena. His agent in Germania, who acquired new recruits for him, was derelict in his duties. It was his responsibility to ensure that the men arrived in a reasonable condition. These captives were substandard, hardly fit for the rigors of their initial training.

Lothar motioned for the men to gather around. He offered a brief smile to the group before speaking: "I'm just like you in that I also belong to this ludus and train as a gladiator." He held up his hand, displaying five open fingers. "I have survived five contests in the arena." He thumbed toward the retreating figure of Macro. "You should understand that it would be extremely unwise to disobey that man. Besides not pissing off the lanista, the other rule is to never let any other inmate disrespect you. If you permit that to happen, your life will be worse than if you are in Hades. Now, having said that, most of the men drilling here are of a decent sort, but there are a few deranged assholes who might test you. Under no circumstances should you ever back down. It will be perceived as weakness, and the ensuing torment will never cease. Although, on a cautionary note, please remember that there are strict rules about fighting one another, so don't begin a brawl with your antagonist."

Lothar paused to look at each man. "I know some of you are probably feeling sorry for yourself," he began, "questioning the life you have been thrust into. In truth, the odds are that you will die in the arena." He paused for a breath before continuing. "But there is some hope. There is a chance you may survive and be awarded the *rudis*—the wooden sword symbolizing your freedom. You are fortunate to not have been sent to the mines or the big crop farms, where you would have toiled to a slow death. There would be no hope for you in those places, only death. So, my advice is to train well and perhaps you will find freedom if you become a skilled gladiator. The food is half-decent, and you have a roof over your head. Every now and then, they let some women in to visit our cells. If you become a successful gladiator like me, you may even be permitted the liberty of enjoying a night out in the town. Now, if you will follow me, I'll take you to your cells."

Alderic sat alone, gazing at the confines of his cubicle. Each man had his own small room. They were all identical, all equally dismal. The walls were made of sturdy red brick, with an unforgiving barred iron gate extending from the floor to the ceiling. Each chamber had a straw pallet for sleeping, a chair and a small wooden table, a small clay oil lamp, and a waste bucket. That was about it. His accommodation looked like it had been recently occupied. He noted a few trinkets on the table, and the oil lamp appeared to have been used recently. Alderic quivered: he could only guess the fate of the last occupant, probably slaughtered in the arena, but decided not to dwell on the subject. This was his future. He would do what he could to survive.

He contemplated his lot. He had no friends and couldn't speak or understand the strange Roman language. The four other German captives were insufferable, and they let him know at every opportunity that they wanted nothing to do with him. The group stuck to themselves and completely ignored Alderic. The antipathy they had exhibited at the beginning of the journey had not lessened over the last eight weeks.

His gloom was interrupted by shouting from down the hall, but he couldn't understand the language. Lothar appeared in the hallway outside his room. "Come on," he smiled. "It's dinner time. Follow me. I'll lead you to the dining hall."

As they made their way down the narrow corridor, Lothar continued. "You know, I'm not the shrewdest judge of human nature, but I picked up right away on the animosity your fellow inductees showed toward you. I heard them bragging about being of the Marcomanni. Let me guess. They don't want anything to do with you."

Alderic emitted a bitter laugh. "That aptly describes their sentiment. I am a Tencteri, an outsider."

Lothar scoffed. "I have encountered their kind before. They think their shit doesn't stink. They are going to learn quickly that they bleed just like the rest of us. Back in Germania, I was of the Cherusci clan. We hated the Marcomanni. Let me tell you, once you are here, your tribal affiliation doesn't mean squat. You are no longer a Tencteri, a Cherusci, or a Marcomanni. You are a Roman gladiator, property of this ludus, trained to fight in a Roman arena. You stick with me, Alderic. I could use a fellow German for a friend. Your life is going to be extremely unpleasant for the next several weeks. I will help you get through it."

Alderic grinned. "Fine with me."

The pair entered a large rectangular room filled with tables and benches. Shouts and boisterous laughter reverberated in the room as nearly thirty men crowded the dining hall for their evening meal. A queue of men was forming at the far end of the room, where slaves handed them clay drinking cups, wooden bowls, and spoons. Farther down the line, another slave ladled gruel in heaping portions into huge bowls, as one issued large rolls of bread. Alderic was famished. They had been fed very little on their journey, and the gruel smelled delicious. Lothar turned to Alderic and said, "Follow me through the serving line, and we'll find a place at one of the tables."

As Alderic moved through the line hesitantly; he had lost sight of Lothar. He exited the serving area, and craning his neck, he looked for Lothar at one of the tables. He spotted him and ventured toward him, balancing the porridge with the bread perched atop in one hand and a cup of sour wine in the other. He was halfway to his destination when a brute of a man rose from a nearby table and collided with Alderic, spilling the porridge and bread onto the floor.

The brute began howling at him in a language he didn't understand. The dining hall suddenly turned silent. Alderic was befuddled. Where had the man suddenly appeared from? He stared at his dinner splattered on the floor. The man he had crashed into pointed at the mess and burst out in laughter. A few others joined in. Alderic surmised that the collision had been no accident, and this was one of the people Lothar had warned him about. He was being tested. Shit, why did this have to happen to him? His eyes blazed in fury. He remembered Lothar's advice about such situations, but he was at a loss of what to do. His antagonist stared back at him with intensity, daring him to take action. Alderic reasoned that he could not risk a confrontation. He was the new man here, and if he engaged in a fight, things would not go well for him with Macro. Still, he couldn't allow this slight to go unchallenged.

Turning his back on his tormenter, Alderic slowly and deliberately scooped up his dinner from the floor. He heard muffled laughter in the background as he walked over to where Lothar was seated. Conversation resumed to its normal din in the hall as Alderic took his seat. Speaking softly, he asked, "Who is that nasty shit, and what did he say to me?"

"His name is Draxir, a Thracian," Lothar replied. "He is one of those deranged assholes I told you about. He cursed you and called you 'another one of those German pig-fuckers.' Did you not hear what I said about someone treating you with contempt? You cannot let this go—"

Alderic held up his hand. "I know what you said about not letting anyone disrespect me, but you also said that anyone caught fighting with another inmate outside the training regimen would be severely punished. Yes?"

Lothar nodded in acquiescence. "I said those words, yes."

"Lothar, really, what could I do? Start a brawl? I'm not afraid of him, but if I had started fighting him, I don't think things would have gone well for the new guy. So, where would that get me?" Alderic picked up his bread and bit a large chunk. He chewed silently, directing his gaze to the farthest wall. He took another bite and put the bread down. "Lothar, is it possible to sneak this bowl of mush out of this dining area?"

"If you're very careful about it, it can be done. But why would you want to do that? I hope you aren't going to eat that after it was on the grimy floor."

"I never said I was going to eat it." Alderic bit another piece off the bread. Between mouthfuls, he inquired, "Which cell belongs to this Draxir, and can you somehow stall him from returning to his room?"

"Alderic, what are you planning to do with that spoiled gruel?" A look of comprehension dawned upon him. "Oh! What a splendid idea. It'll serve the prick right. Send him a message." He smiled at the realization. "Alderic," he continued, "you are going to do well here. Draxir's cell, let me think…The fifth cell from the end of the hall…Yes, the fifth one from the end is his, I'm certain. Let me know when you're leaving so I can detain him in the event he decides to venture to his quarters. Now go, do your mischief."

Alderic finished his bread and exited the dining hall, unobtrusively carrying his bowl of fouled gruel along his right side, hidden by his arm and hand so no one would notice. He hurried down the corridor until he reached the end before pausing to look around and ensure no one was observing. There was no one. He grinned gleefully as he counted the cells from the end of hallway with his fingers and scooted inside the fifth one. He dumped the cold bowl of spoiled porridge on the straw pallet, leaving the incriminating bowl under Draxir's bed. His heart thudding wildly, he exited the cell and, as casually as he could, sauntered back down the hallway to his own cell.

A while later, one of the caretakers of the ludus shuffled down the corridor, locking the cells for the night. Alderic sat on his pallet, his hands trembling slightly. His confrontation with Draxir had been troubling, not something he had ever encountered back in his homeland. No one there would ever think of deliberately provoking a confrontation. The bumping into had not been meant for the sake of humor but for humiliation. What kind of a person would even contemplate doing that? Sure, they all played practical jokes on each other back in his village, but what had occurred in the dining hall was a mean-spirited, malicious act.

He recalled his own pranks back in Germania. He remembered the time he had told Sigivald that the village beauty, Clarimond, had made it known to Alderic that she desired Sigivald. Trotting after her like an eager puppy, the encounter with Clarimond had not gone according to Sigivald's expectations. She had rudely dismissed his advances. When a dejected Sigivald returned to speak to a smirking Alderic, he realized the hoax foisted upon him. Sigivald had chased him all over the village, swearing to exact a terrible retribution. But in the end, the two laughed, with Sigivald promising to get back at Alderic some day.

When news of his trick reached the ears of Ealdgyd, Alderic's female companion and friend, she chastised him to no end. How, she wanted to know, could Alderic have played such a cruel prank on his best friend? She had emphatically stated that she never wanted to speak with him again. Alderic remembered her stalking off in anger, pointedly telling him that a true friend would never play such a prank and that he should be ashamed of himself. Alderic, bewildered by Ealdgyd's anger, sought her out alone and profusely apologized. After much groveling on his part, Ealdgyd erupted into uncontrolled laughter. Then, as if on cue, Sigivald emerged from his hiding place, a huge smile plastered on his face. It's not every day that you get to see your best friend grovel so extensively, and he had said some embarrassing things, trying to win Ealdgyd back. Alderic had momentarily been angry for having been played for a fool, but soon, all three of them roared with mirth at the whole sequence of events. Alderic had vowed retribution on Ealdgyd for her role in the joke, but he never took it.

Alderic frowned in sorrow and felt his heart sink in despair: Sigivald was dead, and he would never see Ealdgyd again. He would never be able to lie with her and experience bliss as only couples do. She probably thought him dead.

His musings were cut short as a terrible roar of anger erupted from down the corridor. It could only be Draxir. He guessed the gist of what he was screaming about. Alderic grinned in satisfaction. *Served that shit right for messing with me.* He extended his tall form on his straw pallet, his feet hanging uncomfortably over the edge. He wondered what was in store for him tomorrow. Exhausted, he drifted into the arms of Morpheus.

Alderic and the other four German novices stood in a line as Macro spoke, with Lothar interpreting by his side: "We are going to strengthen and train you until you puke, and then train you some more. If you can't measure up to our standards, we will sell you to the mines where they will work you to death. You will be hardened and drilled in the ways of individual combat. No one from my ludus, and I mean *no one,* will be sent to an arena for mortal combat until they are fully trained. The rest is up you. This school is renowned for the fighters we produce, so train well and make me proud. This ludus is one of four in Rome. We are small, with only about forty gladiators, but we are by far the best. To fatten their purses, some of the other schools train *venatores,* the animal hunters. They pride themselves on killing beasts in the arena." Macro snorted in derision. "They are a bunch of lame-asses and will never train in my ludus. My gladiators are trained to kill *men,* not pathetic animals. Now prepare yourselves for some serious pain."

The five men were sent to the armory to be fitted with their training armor. It was a combination of leather and metal that weighed heavily upon them. They were all issued a metal chest armament and an iron helmet. Leather sleeves and gaiters protected their legs and arms, and long studded leather straps hung from their chest to protect their groins.

The strengthening and conditioning began. The group of five ran circles in their heavy armor around the periphery of the compound. Tulo, Macro's assistant, stood observing them from the shade of the portico. He wore an aloof expression while the men ran in a single file. Alderic soon began gasping and sweat poured down his face. He had believed himself to be a good runner with decent stamina. He had tracked game in the northern woodlands for days in the heat and cold without tiring, but this was different. The unaccustomed weight of the armor and the blazing Roman sun drained his body and soul. There was no end in sight. They couldn't halt until Tulo was satisfied, and he gave no indication of being so anytime soon. As they continued running in the rectangular courtyard, each man wondering who would be the first to collapse.

Alderic retched several times but didn't dare stop. He pictured Tulo standing over him with his coiled whip, or worse, informing him that he was to be sent to the mines because he was not deemed tough enough to be a gladiator. He continued shuffling along with the others. By now, all the men were wobbly in the knees, some staggering. After several more laps, the inevitable happened: the man directly in front of Alderic—he thought his name was Leutwin—stumbled to his knees and then sank to the ground, immobile. The other four men hesitated at the sight of one of their fellows prone on the ground. Tulo came charging from his shaded alcove, yelling at the men and urging them to keep moving. He uncoiled his whip menacingly, which urged them all to keep going.

The bedraggled group ran another circuit, casting sidelong glances at Tulo, who seemed to be kicking and prodding the figure on the ground. They completed several more circuits before Tulo commanded them to halt. He gestured for the men to pick up Leutwin and move to a shaded area where they were given water. But this was not to be the end of their day; in fact, it was far from it. After they were sufficiently revived, including the unfortunate Leutwin, they were trooped to an area with wooden posts as high as a man pinned into the ground.

Each man was issued a wooden training sword that had been filled with lead to increase its weight. Under Macro's direction, the men were commanded to endlessly strike the wooden posts. If Macro believed they were not using sufficient force, the whip was brandished to strike the unfortunate trainee.

At first, Alderic struck the post, the *palus,* with great enthusiasm, reveling in the punishment he was inflicting upon the wooden sentry. This didn't last long. The weighted sword took its toll on his arm and shoulder muscles. It seemed to increase in heft with every swing. Many repetitions later, Alderic struck the piece of timber weakly. It's not that he wasn't trying; his right arm was simply no longer functioning. *WHACK.* Again, he forced his entire body to direct the force of another blow. He gritted his teeth for one more blow, when he heard the most blissful word he could have: "Halt!"

Macro peered at the men in disdain. "You have completed another session of your training. Upon my command, you will shout the words *'Die with honor.'* Ready? Let's hear it."

"DIE WITH HONOR!" the five men shouted raggedly.

Macro wasn't pleased. "Yell so I can hear you. One more time."

"DIE WITH HONOR!"

He grinned. "That's better."

The group moved on to its next undertaking, which would prove to be yet another painful experience. Macro stood before the weary men, his eyes devoid of pity. The ever-present Lothar translated: "Your next task will be to form a single line, right here." He pointed with his whip to an area about ten paces to his left, where a pile of stones, each the size of a large melon, lay strewn. "You will pass each stone in that pile down the line and form a new pile, at the end of your line. It is a simple enough task. I want to see stones constantly in motion. No resting between lifts. I have seen this exercise enough times to know when people are slacking. I will have none of it. Begin."

Alderic grunted as he cradled the heavy stone and passed it to the next figure. At least this time he knew when the exercise would end—after the pile had been moved and none remained. The task was no better or worse than the others—it was hard, arduous labor, stretching every man's reserves to the limit. He attempted to let his mind wander to better times and places, but that lasted only a few moments. He almost dropped one of the heavy rocks on his foot. The glaring sun scorched his face, and his tortured muscles screamed in agony. After they had finished moving the pile, all men stood there with their aching arms hanging limp at their sides. But that was not to be the end of it.

Macro roared at them: "Did I order you to stop? You aren't finished. Now, do the reverse. Move the pile back to where it was. Begin!"

The recruits looked at Macro in dismay, but knew better than to protest or even emit a groan. After several more cycles of moving stones from one pile to another, they ended the grueling exercise with another "die with honor" pledge. The men then graduated to the logs; it was explained to them that the purpose was to lift the heavy wooden object as part of a three-count movement. At the count of one, the log was lifted to waist height; at two, to the chest; and at three, over their heads, where they would hold it in position until told to drop it. They performed what seemed like endless repetitions of lifting. They were far from done; on the contrary, they were just beginning. The recruits endured several more rotations of running, wooden sword, stone pile, and log drills. At last, they were dismissed for their evening meal.

Macro faced the men. "One more time, with gusto."

"DIE WITH HONOR!"

They were then allowed to wash off the grime from the day's activities in a wooden trough. Alderic, his arms and legs aching, entered the mess area of the barracks and stood in the serving line. He kept out a wary eye for the presence of Draxir, for he knew it was not over between them. He couldn't see him and let out a sigh of relief. Alderic received his food, which comprised porridge mixed with vegetables and meat, a hard, flat loaf of bread, some olives, and a cup of sour wine. He found a spot next to Lothar, who smiled in greeting.

"You survived the day in one piece?"

"Let's just say I've had better days, but I'm determined to survive this." Alderic promptly dug into his porridge and gulped it down. Wiping his face on the sleeve of his coarse wool tunic, he munched on his bread. "I hope the training gets easier than the Hades I've experienced today." he remarked.

Lothar proffered a knowing grin. "Don't worry. We all go through this. It will get better, but the first couple of weeks here are, well, brutal." He lowered his voice to a whisper. "Listen, I don't mean to alarm you, but I heard Draxir talking. He has it in for you. That stunt you pulled with the porridge was a perfect response to his aggression, but you have humiliated him. The whole barrack is aware of what happened, and almost all are in favor of what you did. But he is livid. So, be on guard."

"I will. Thanks for the warning."

Alderic munched happily on his bread, taking an occasional sip of wine. He was about to ask Lothar about his initial training days, when he sensed a presence near him. He turned to see the looming figure of Draxir with two of his cronies.

Draxir spoke, and Lothar translated, although the meaning was quite obvious from his tone: "You pig-fucker German. I know it was you who put that gruel in my bed last night. You are a dead man. You hear me? A dead man!"

Alderic nonchalantly dusted the crumbs off his palms. Finally, he lied, "I don't know what you're talking about."

The denial infuriated Draxir even further. His face reddening, he bellowed loud enough for the entire hall to hear him. "It was you. Don't you *dare* deny it. I know it was you, pig fucker. I am going to tear you apart right here for all to see. Nobody gets away with humiliating me. No one."

Macro stormed into the room and to the table with his whip. "What the fuck is going on in my mess? Draxir, you are creating a disturbance, which does not please me in the least. Now what in Hades is happening?"

Draxir, spittle flying from his lips, responded, "This stinking German put gruel in my bed last night, and I am going to tear him a new asshole."

Macro peered at Alderic. "You're one of those who came in the other day. What do you have to say?"

"I don't know what his problem is," Alderic replied, gesturing toward Draxir. "Maybe he just fouled his bed." Lothar translated his words.

This sent Draxir into a howling rage. "I'm going to kill you and I'll do it *slowly* in front of everybody."

Macro stepped in swiftly, his tone menacing. "You are not going to kill anyone, Draxir, unless it's in the arena. You understand me? If I hear of any violence by you directed at this man, I will have you flogged. You know the rules: No fighting. End of discussion. Now, everyone go to your cells. The dining area is closed."

Alderic rose from his seat and ventured out of the hall, but not before Macro caught his eye to give him a warning glance. He entered his cell and thumped down on his bed. *To Hades with Draxir and this brutal routine.* He was sick of it. He silently scoffed at the motto, 'die with honor.' What a crock of shit! With that, he lay upon his cot and stared at the ceiling, waiting for sleep.

Weeks passed and they trained even harder. Added to their regimen were agility drills, where they would leap from a standing position over obstacles, hop, skip, and jump through a rope labyrinth, and avoid sword thrusts without moving their feet. Alderic could feel his strength growing, as his muscles swelled. He had been strong and agile before the training began, but now he was a fearsome physical being. His sinewy form had bulked up. He felt as though he could run through a brick wall without sustaining injury. In addition to all this, Lothar spent time each evening tutoring all five German novices in the Latin tongue. Alderic struggled at first, but he soon discovered that he enjoyed his lessons, and that he had a knack for the language. Alderic was, by no means, yet proficient in the Roman tongue, but he could at least understand the commands they were given now.

The recruits entered a new phase of their instruction—weapons proficiency. Every man was to learn the skills of the basic sword drill. Later, they would be assigned their specialties for the arena. Macro addressed the five Germans, all attired in their training armor and holding their wooden swords: "When you are thrust into the arena, the objective is to disable your opponent by whatever means available to you. Once he is on the ground, you are hailed the victor. How you accomplish this is up to you. It may be with a quick sword thrust to a vulnerable area or in some other way. Do whatever you must." He paused to peer at the new gladiators. "Keep in mind that both you and your opponent will be heavily armored. That is why you have been given such extensive strength and conditioning training. You must have stamina, and you must be able to knock your opponent down on his ass. Sheer physical power—that is what you need. You may resort to tripping him, bowling him over, or whatever else—just get his ass on the ground, and your victory will be assured. Our training regimen will focus on strength, agility, and endurance."

Macro picked up a sword and shield. He paused, searching the eyes of the men. "I need a volunteer." Before anyone could respond, Macro pointed to Alderic. "You. Come out here. I want you to attack me with your sword. Show me what you're made of."

Alderic stepped forward, confused about what he was supposed to do. He had never trained with a sword, except for striking the wooden post endlessly. He glanced briefly at his wooden sword as if it were a foreign object, realizing that this was going to end badly for him. As much as he desired to smash Macro's face, he knew he had no sword skills. Back in Germania, the men used spears, and only the very rich or privileged could afford an iron sword. He had observed some of the veteran gladiators in their weapon drills.

They moved with confidence and alacrity. *I can't do that. I'm probably just the scapegoat because of that Draxir altercation. It can't be just Macro's whim. He wants to send a message.*

"Come on, Alderic. I don't have all day. Attack! Now!"

Alderic stood poised with his sword and shield. He deftly leaped forward, his right arm thrusting at Macro's torso. His opponent retreated. Alderic continued his advance and thrust forward again, and then, again. Suddenly, Macro appeared to his right, trapping his sword down and pounding his shield into Aldrich's face. He fell to the ground, tasting blood in his mouth.

"Get up, Alderic. Is that the best you can do?" Marco jeered. This time, Alderic advanced more cautiously, wary of Macro and his shield. It didn't matter. Within a brief moment, Alderic was on the ground again, defeated by a series of thrusts and punches delivered by the shield. Macro had his sword at Alderic's throat. He grinned wolfishly, enjoying his victory. He extended a hand and helped Alderic to his feet.

"I hope you all learned a lesson from this demonstration. Look at Alderic. He is much younger than me, and he is bigger and stronger. You may be a stalwart, even the quickest man alive, but if you are not skilled in the ways of using the sword and shield, you *will* be defeated. And defeat means death. The sword and the shield are used in coordination. Both are weapons that you will use to earn victories and remain alive."

They began their tutelage under Macro's constant scrutiny. He missed nothing, and if ever he thought that one of the men wasn't giving his full measure, the lash was employed to remind the unfortunate trainee. There were endless repetitions of parry and thrust, block and chop. Alderic learned to use his legs for tripping his opponent and his body to topple a man. He was taught how to stab over an opponent's shield, slash a vulnerable limb, and to cut the face and neck.

Several days later, they underwent their first real test. They were to fight each other with the rudimentary skills they had learned. To even the number of men out, Lothar was included with the group of new recruits to make it an even six men. He was paired against Alderic, and they were first up. Both men entered the area cordoned off by ropes secured to posts, which measured around twenty feet each side.

The pair assumed their positions, knees slightly bent, swords and shields poised. Alderic knew Lothar was a skilled swordsman. He had five victories in the arena. He knew he stood little chance, but Alderic also recognized that he had a distinct advantage over Lothar, who was a powerfully built and of medium height, but his reach was far less. Alderic decided to go on the defensive and not be aggressive. He reasoned that he would fall prey to Lothar's experience if he attacked. Macro looked at the two combatants and dropped his arm. "Begin," he shouted.

Lothar advanced slowly and then, in a flurry of moves, thrust forward with his sword and shield. Alderic back-pedaled and then smoothly shifted to the right, away from the menacing figure of Lothar. "Good move," Macro bellowed. Lothar advanced again. Alderic used his long arms to block and parry, and then moved again to his right. Lothar feinted with a thrust to the throat, and then swung his shield in an arc toward Alderic's head. Alderic barely recovered in time, blocking the swing with his shield. Lothar grinned mockingly. "Come fight me, Alderic. Show me what you've learned." But Alderic wasn't about to be drawn into that trap, knowing all too well that Lothar would employ some maneuver to defeat him.

Macro yelled, "Alderic, the arena crowd will be clamoring for your head. You need to attack." Alderic edged forward, thrusting with his sword, but then he quickly backed off again. Lothar advanced, charging forward, his sword a blur of movement. Not willing to engage in offensive movements, Alderic parried the blows, and then retreated. Lothar struck with another flurry of blows, none of which touched Alderic. By now, both men were panting. Lothar engaged once more with a burst of thrust and cuts, all of which were stymied by Alderic.

"Halt," roared a glowering Macro. "Alderic, good defense. But you *need* to attack." Lothar translated the words, some of which Alderic had already understood. "Next pair, advance forward." Alderic stepped out of the small space, noting the curious glance that Macro was directing his way. He wondered whether this was a good or a bad sign.

That evening at supper, Alderic took his usual place next to Lothar, his best and only friend at the ludus. It seemed that the veteran gladiator had taken a liking to Alderic and an aversion to the other German trainees. Alderic quickly glanced around to make sure that Draxir was not lurking nearby. There had been no other confrontations between the two, although the gladiator had continued to direct baleful glances at Alderic. A few of the veterans had approached him, warning him that Draxir meant him ill will if the opportunity presented itself. One of the men had referred to him as "that nasty shit of a Thracian."

Lothar looked up from his meal. "Good show today. You did well for a beginner."

Alderic was pleased with the compliment. "You weren't taking it easy on me, were you?"

"Hades, no! Macro would have me flogged me if he thought I wasn't giving my full effort. I tried my best to get through your guard, but I couldn't no matter what maneuvers I employed. You are a quick one, and those long arms of yours make it nearly impossible to penetrate your defenses. It was a good strategy you employed, to not go on the offensive. I would have had you there. My counter attacks are the best part of my sword-work. Listen, afterwards, Macro questioned me, inquiring whether I had given you my best. I told him that I had. He said to me that you had the makings of a good one. One doesn't often get a compliment like that from Macro."

A few more weeks passed before the five gladiatorial trainees joined the other men of the ludus—a big step, for this meant they were out of their probationary period. They would now partake in the same training and regimen as everyone else. The gladiators had been hacking at wooden posts for the better part of the morning, and it was time to move on to something else. Macro and his assistant, Tulo, stood before the assembled group. Macro bellowed, "Alright, we are now going to engage in mock combat. Tulo and I will begin pairing you up."

Alderic was wondering who he might be paired against, when Tulo grabbed his arm and led him a short distance to where Draxir stood. Alderic noted a knowing glance being shared between Tulo and Draxir. The two had obviously conspired for Alderic to face off against Draxir.

Alderic glanced at his antagonist, who proffered an angry scowl. There was no doubt that the man intended to do him harm. Even with the wooden weapons, it was possible to be severely injured. The type weapons Draxir possessed concerned Alderic. He had a net attached to his left arm and a wooden trident in his right. Alderic had heard that this type of a gladiator was called a *retiarius*. He had no idea how to defend himself against these weapons and what the weaknesses were.

The first two pairs of men were sent into the center of the quad. Tulo and Macro supervised the mock combat. Alderic paid little attention to the ongoing contests, instead staying focused on his upcoming bout. He slid amidst the men until he found Lothar. "Tulo deliberately matched me against Draxir. How do I fight men armed with the net and trident? All of my training has been against men with swords."

Lothar spat on the ground. "Draxir must have bribed him. Tulo is an odious turd. You need to not be too focused on the trident. It is the net that you must be wary of. If he entangles you with that, he will attempt to beat you to a bloody pulp with that trident. Also, watch out for the lead weights attached to the net's edges. He will try to strike you in the face with those. Draxir is an experienced gladiator and has won many times in the arena. He is the best retiarius in the ludus. As you did when you fought with me, stay on the defensive."

Alderic nodded. "I will, but if I get the opportunity, I *will* hurt him."

The initial pairs of combatants were done, and Alderic heard his name called. The next thing he knew, he was facing the ominous form of Draxir. Tulo dropped his arm, signaling for the combat to begin. Draxir feinted with the trident and slashed at Alderic's face with the net. He barely got his shield up in time and heard the menacing sound of the weights clatter off his shield. Draxir advanced, thrusting his trident and twirling his net. Alderic rapidly retreated blocking the trident.

Draxir snarled in rage. "Come on and fight boy. You can't run away in the arena."

Alderic, using his best Latin, responded, "Come get me, fuckwit." He let out a laugh as he danced away from his opponent's thrusts. Most of the other gladiators chuckled at Alderic's remarks, for Draxir wasn't a popular figure with the other men either.

Draxir snarled, then tossed the net in an overhand cast. The net came flying toward Alderic. He deftly knocked it aside, and then thrust hard at the retiarius. Draxir barely blocked the lunge with his trident. Alderic followed with another jab and then another. Draxir retreated. Alderic stopped his advances. "Come on, fuckwit. I heard you're a good fighter. Show me."

In a fury, Draxir charged and thrust at him with his trident. Alderic blocked the blow with his sword, the blade sliding between the tines of the trident. Draxir savagely twisted the trident, forcing the sword to fly out of Alderic's grasp. The retiarius yelled in triumph. He charged at Alderic, but in his overconfidence, he made a fateful mistake of his own. He cast the net with not enough force. Alderic used his long arm to grab the net in mid-flight, while simultaneously blocking the trident's jab with his shield. Alderic heaved the net, causing Draxir to lose balance. Alderic moved inside close to his foe, so the trident couldn't effectively be used against him. Remembering his training instructions to get his opponent prone on the earth, Alderic slammed his adversary to the ground with a tremendous thud. He leaped on to Draxir and began beating his head and face with his fists. Strong arms grasped him, pulling him away from his foe. The bloody-faced figure leaped to his feet. He snarled at Alderic. "I'm going to kill you." He attempted to charge at Alderic, but the other gladiators intervened, preventing him from moving forward.

Macro stepped between the two, his tone menacing, "I will not tolerate this behavior in my ludus. Both of you will be restricted to your cells for the next two days. Consider yourselves fortunate that I'm not having you flogged. He motioned to several of the gate guards. Take them away and lock their cells. No food, water, or bathing privileges."

Several weeks after the incident, Alderic's fate took another unexpected turn. He was reclining on his pallet before the evening meal, exhausted from the day's training, thinking of nothing in particular, when Tulo appeared at the entrance to his cell. "Macro wants to see you. Now. Follow me to his chambers."

Alderic, wondering what in Hades he had done to deserve summons to Macro's chamber, followed Tulo to a separate building, where he was directed to enter a small vestibule. Tulo pointed to a wooden bench, and then disappeared into an adjoining chamber. As he sat there waiting, he heard voices from the other room. Tulo reappeared, gesturing for him to enter. Macro sat behind a wooden table, upon which several scrolls rested alongside a beaker of wine. Lothar stood respectfully at his side. The lanista dismissed Tulo with a wave and then indicated for Alderic to sit. Macro sipped from his goblet, his eyes never leaving Alderic's. "I have been watching you during your training. You have the makings of a good gladiator. At first, I had my doubts, but you have all the tools. The problem as I see it is that you are too damn tall."

Macro continued, "Being tall and having a long reach has its advantages, but it also poses a significant liability. You present too large a target for a sword thrust. Too much vulnerable area, especially if you fight as a swordsman. So, here's what I'm going to do. I'm going to make you a retiarius. Your long reach will be enhanced even further with the elongated trident. You will be able to keep your opponent at a distance. Believe me, this will make you less vulnerable."

Alderic was stunned. He had spent so many hours training with the sword and shield, and now, he was being told that he would have to learn to wield new weapons. "I thought me do well with sword," he protested in broken Latin.

Macro laughed. "You did. You even beat that arsehole Draxir. But listen to me. Your height makes you too vulnerable. I know gladiators, and you, Alderic, are a retiarius. Now I won't hear any more objections. You'll begin training tomorrow. You're dismissed."

Alderic turned to leave, when Macro spoke again. "And Alderic, stay away from Draxir. I know he's trouble, but he's our best retiarius."

Alderic was walking down the hall to exit the building when Lothar hurried beside him. He clapped him on the shoulder. "Don't think too much about it. I agree with Macro's decision. It will enhance your chances of survival, and that's what this is all about."

Alderic stopped. "You agree with Macro's decision?"

Lothar maintained, "I do. I've observed those who fight as a retiarius. The taller, the better. You will be unbeatable with your size."

Alderic shrugged. "I hope this is for the best. It will be strange learning to fight without a sword and a shield in my hands."

"Listen, Alderic. When it comes to gladiators, Macro knows what he is doing. He recognizes what talents each man has and how to train them. I understand you aren't thrilled with this change but give it some time. I would wager that you will look back on this moment and thank the gods for the intervention. Now let's get some food. I'm starving."

The next day, Alderic was washing off the sweat and grime from the day when he looked up to see Lothar and a dozen other senior gladiators attired in fresh tunics strolling to the gateway. They were permitted an evening out in the town to do as they pleased. The men smirked at Alderic and the others who were in the process of washing. "Have fun in your cells tonight. Think of us cavorting with the ladies. Maybe someday you'll be permitted too." Another voice crowed, "Or maybe not." There was more laughter as the group continued out.

Later, Alderic sat pensively on his pallet. His first day of training as a retiarius had been painstakingly slow. Tulo was his instructor, but thus far, he had learned little. Tulo's lessons were desultory and delivered with little enthusiasm. He was told that tomorrow they were bringing a former champion of the arena to the ludus, who would assist in his training. Perhaps that was something to look forward to.

He thought briefly about Lothar and the others, who would now be well outside the gates. He could only wonder what lay on the other side and if he would ever get the freedom to explore the city. Maybe someday he would. He mused about his homeland and his village life. He tried to picture Ealdgyd but couldn't. It had been a long time since he had seen her, and his fatigued mind failed him. He thought of his mother. She was a kind woman who had tried her best to raise him well. What had happened to her? Most of the village warriors had been slain in the ill-fated raid. Did his village still exist? He let out an anguished sigh. That world was far from him now. And what kind of life was this? With these thoughts, he drifted off.

The next day he was introduced to Labenius, the former champion retiarius who had received the symbolic wooden sword, the rudis, for his feats in the arena. He was to be the sole student receiving Labenius's instructions. Alderic was surprised that he was being given this much attention. Labenius was an imposing figure, even in his middle years. The man before him was quite tall, not as tall as Alderic, but a lot more muscular. He had a craggy, almost handsome face, which was marred by several scars placed diagonally across his jawline. The two men ventured to a secluded area of the ludus, away from prying eyes.

Labenius motioned for Alderic to pick up his armor and weapons. He strapped on a large leather sleeve that encased his right arm completely and ended with an upturned flange near his shoulder to deflect strikes to the face. The trident was a wooden pole that was about six feet long, affixed with a heavy metal head and three sharpened tines, each about a foot in length. And then there was the net, which was attached to his left arm by means of a corded loop.

Labenius gestured for Alderic to stand before him. "Forget anything you might have learned about fighting as a retiarius. Give me your trident and net so I can show you the proper form. Watch me." With that he moved into a semi-crouched position, his left arm cocked, ready to throw the entangling net, and his right arm poised with the trident to thrust or parry. "Now you try it."

Alderic attempted to mimic the gladiator's stance.

"Stop. No. Not like that," his mentor rebuked him. "First of all, you're standing flat-footed. You look like a post in the ground and you will be dead as a stone if you don't get quicker on your feet. You must always be poised on the balls of your feet, ready to move in an instant." He moved before Alderic, repositioning his feet and the bend of his knees. He then adjusted his arms. "There. Now you look like a retiarius," he said triumphantly.

"Let's begin again. Relax. You look stiff as a stone pillar." He waited for Alderic to stand down. "Now, adopt the position again. Show me how a retiarius should look."

Alderic moved into the posture, his arm cocked to throw the net. "*Bene!*" Labenius was satisfied.

The next component was the casting of the net. Labenius showed him how to toss the net to entangle or trip his opponent. "Remember," he said, "if you fling the net unsuccessfully, you must retrieve it immediately. If not, your foe will pin the net to the ground and probably you with it." He demonstrated the various throws using overhand, side-arm, and the underhand motions.

Labenius stood with the net folded over his left arm. "I want you to learn this such that you can do it in your sleep. Watch what I do with this net." He flung the net with an underhand motion while snapping his wrist, casting the net in a circular motion. It unfurled, spreading out six feet in diameter.

"The underhand throw is the most effective. You must practice it every day. Now try it."

Alderic draped the net over his arm like he had been shown. He hurled it, hoping to imitate Labenius. It sailed high but didn't open. Tangled rope thudded to the ground. He picked it up and cast it again, with the same results.

Labenius frowned impatiently. "You must learn to snap your wrist to get that circular spin." He demonstrated once again. "Like this." The net opened wide.

Alderic attempted more throws, all dismal. Finally, Labenius halted his efforts. "Enough," he said gruffly, "we will revisit this tomorrow. It takes some time to learn this skill anyway. Let's move on."

From there, they graduated to strikes with the trident and how to use the net and trident in combination with one another. They practiced all morning, using the same repetitive motions. Shift left. Shift right. Cast and thrust. Advance. Retreat. With every move, Labenius constantly bellowed, "Stay balanced. Stay balanced."

After a brief lull and the partaking of a quick mid-day meal, Labenius picked up a wooden sword and shield along with some plated armor. He adjusted the straps, moving his arms about to ensure a proper fit. "Let's see if you've learned anything."

"But I have a trident with a steel head. I could hurt you with this."

Labenius snorted. "Let me worry about that. Now attack as I have taught you. Move."

Alderic crouched as he had been shown, and then advanced toward Labenius. He cast the net sidearm followed by a thrust with the trident. Labenius effortlessly deflected the net and parried the jab. "Is that the best you can do?" he roared. "You must overcome my defenses. Your life is at stake. Move."

Alderic cast the net again and stabbed with his trident. Labenius stomped on the net when it hit the ground, pinning it in place. Then Labenius slammed into him, knocking him to the ground. He hovered over the prone figure, his sword arm cocked for the death blow. "You have much to learn, boy."

The two paired off once more. They sparred throughout the afternoon. The outcome was always the same. Labenius was always one maneuver or ruse ahead and managed to easily defeat Alderic every time. Finally, he called for a halt. "We will do the same tomorrow. Right here. You can become a good retiarius, but it will take much practice."

Alderic nodded dejectedly. His body aching and his mind struggling to come to terms with the difficulty learning the skills of a retiarius, Alderic headed back to the barracks. How was he ever to become proficient in this style of fighting? He felt more confident holding a sword and shield. He stopped at the water trough to rinse off the dirt and grime. He had been on the ground today more times than he could remember. He growled in frustration as he scooped water over his head. He headed to the barracks. May the gods have mercy on anybody who fucked with him tonight.

He was back at it again early the next day and the day after that. Alderic sparred with Labenius, trying to remember all the things he was supposed to be doing. He thrust and heaved his net, then parried his opponent's follow-through. Alderic resumed the offensive, advancing on the ground he had previously retreated from. He scored a hit on Labenius's armor, before retreating under a relentless counter attack. But things were different this time; none of the sword blows touched him. He stopped for moment, panting with exertion, and then resumed his attack with a fury. Labenius retreated, and then raised his sword arm in the air, signaling a halt. A fleeting smile appeared. He grunted a single word, "*Bene.*"

Alderic beamed in return. He had finally stymied Labenius's attack without being slaughtered. Labenius was quick to chide him, "Come on, young pup, you're not that good and still have much to learn. Engage." Once again, the two men began their sparring across their make-shift arena.

The next week marked a significant change in their daily ritual. Alderic was no longer allowed to use the steel version of the trident and was instead handed the heavier wooden training version. Alderic rarely breached Labenius's defenses, but he did on occasion. Even better, Alderic didn't allow Labenius through his guard. Most of their matches ended in a draw. Of course, Labenius was not known for his skill with the sword. He was a champion retiarius, but he still knew all the maneuvers and ruses that gladiators employed with the sword. They sparred all day, even in the afternoon heat, over and over again.

An air of tension surrounded the ludus. It wasn't any one thing in particular, but a number of different signs. The usual jocularity was gone, replaced by tight-lipped frowns. The gladiators didn't linger at the dining table, returning directly to their cells. The men were on edge, irritable at the slightest provocation. The training had to be pared down because of the escalation in the flare-ups among sparring partners.

Alderic missed most of these signs as he was heavily engaged with training under Labenius's strict tutelage. Lothar casually broached the subject at the dinner table. "You know, Alderic, you are lucky. You and your other German friends are exempt from the arena next week."

"What are you talking about? What arena? And just to clarify, those Germans transported with me are certainly not my friends."

"You don't know?" he asked laughingly. "Our ludus is fighting against another from Capua in the arena next week. They are good fighters, almost as good as us. About half the men are scheduled for a bout before the crowd. Consider yourself fortunate that Macro knows when a gladiator is ready for the big show. He has deemed none of the new entrants skilled enough."

"I had no idea. I have spent all my time training under Labenius. When do you think any of the newer recruits will be called upon?"

Lothar grimaced. "I don't really know. Maybe next time."

"What about you, Lothar. Are you fighting?"

He sighed. "I am. I will be one of the first bouts."

"Are you worried?"

"No. I'm carefree as a bird. You dumb turd! Of course, I'm anxious. Who wouldn't? It is something we all need to work through in our own heads. One needs to be confident, yet cautious. Bad things can happen out there, on the arena sand. One simple mistake, one careless move is all it takes to meet your doom."

Alderic was silent, mulling a reply. Finally, he said, "Lothar, what's it like out there?"

"It's hard. You need to control your fear, or you're done for. One must let one's training take over. Fight as you trained and hope everything works out."

"Give me your empty cup, I'll get us some more wine." Alderic carried the bowls and empty clay cups toward the kitchen. He was too preoccupied with the news he had just received to notice Draxir sitting on a nearby bench. Alderic tripped on Draxir's extended leg and went sprawling on the floor, breaking the drinking cups and sending the bowls and utensils flying.

Draxir and his cronies bellowed with laughter. He slowly got to his feet, his rage a blinding flame. He turned away as if leaving the scene, then suddenly spun about and launched himself at Draxir. He heard Lothar's scream, telling him to stop. But it was too late. He smashed into Draxir, toppling him from his perch, and then proceeded to pummel his face. He experienced a satisfying crunch as his fist connected with

Draxir's nose. Hands grabbed him and pulled him off his antagonist, who writhed on the floor, moaning in pain.

Macro entered, yelling, "What in Hades is going on in my dining hall?" He looked at the restrained Alderic and then at the bleeding figure of Draxir. "Get him up," he roared. Draxir was helped to his feet by a few of his friends, all the while holding his nose. Macro pried Draxir's hands from his nose. "Let me see the damage." He examined the man's bloody face and scowled. "Shit, his nose is broken. He is supposed to fight next week." He strode over to Alderic. "Damn you, boy. Look at what you've done. There will be repercussion for this." He glowered in anger. "All of you get back to your cells!" he hollered at the gawking hall as he left it.

The next day, a frowning Macro sat at his wooden table with Labenius seated before him. "What is the status of Alderic's training?"

Labenius seemed pleased as he puffed out his chest. "The boy has done well. He has all of the tools to be a good one. I had to have him switch to the wooden weapon because he was getting through my defenses. He just needs more training. He is still raw talent."

Macro fiddled with a dagger on his desk, clearly uncomfortable. "Time is a luxury we don't have. Alderic injured my best retiarius at dinner last night. Broke his nose. The only other retiarius in the ludus, Brixus, pulled up lame last week. The medicus said it will be weeks before his leg is healthy again. Alderic will need to fight next week."

"But Macro, he's not ready yet. He could be a great fighter one day. A few more months is all we need—"

Macro held his hand up. "I have no choice. You think I don't know that Alderic has the potential to be someone special. I haven't seen someone this promising in a long time, but my contract says that I must field a retiarius next week and he's my only option."

Labenius bowed his head in dejection. "Who is he fighting?"

"A *secutor*."

"Well no shit. But who?"

"Not sure," Macro replied evasively.

"Don't give me that crap. You know who it is."

Macro looked down helplessly. "It's Baladar."

Labenius exploded. "By Jupiter's hairy arse, that's not fair! He is one of the best. How is Alderic supposed to stand a chance against that beast? Not only is he good, he is a sadistic, cruel bastard. You know he enjoys seeing his opponents suffer. He cuts them up into pieces. You must change the match. It'll be no contest. Have you told Alderic yet?"

Macro shook his head. "No, but it's his own fault. He's the one who injured Draxir. He brought this upon himself."

Labenius rose. "Draxir is a shit. He deserved what was coming to him. Probably the majority of the ludus is smirking at his ruined face. Why don't you have him fight despite his broken nose? It'll serve him right."

"You know I cannot put damaged goods out onto the arena floor. The reputation of this ludus will suffer. I do not have a choice. Alderic must fight."

Labenius sighed in resignation. "If you don't mind, can I be the one to inform him?"

"Go ahead. I was kind of hoping you would. Please teach him anything you can between now and next week. I wish to see the lad survive."

In response, Labenius shook his head in disgust and stormed out of the room.

The next day, when Alderic approached Labenius for his daily drill and sparring session, he noticed a scowl on Labenius countenance. His instructor had never been the most jovial of people, but there was something more to his expression today, and Alderic sensed it wasn't good.

Labenius motioned him to a nearby bench. "Sit, we need to talk."

Alderic took a seat. Although he was unaware what was amiss, a feeling of dread crept over him. Labenius began, "Lad, I'm impressed with your progress. You have exceeded my expectations, but something has arisen that doesn't bode well for you. There is no easy way to say this. You are to fight in the arena next week on account of Draxir's injuries. The other retiarius, Brixus, also pulled up lame last week. You will be facing a skilled secutor. His name is Baladar."

Alderic's heart pounded. The fact that he'd be facing another man to death in the arena dawned upon him. Still grappling with his suddenly altered reality, he looked up at Labenius with confusion, fear, and disheartenment etched upon his face. "Do I stand a chance?"

Labenius replied in a reassured tone. "Yes, you have a chance. You are good. I trained you. You can win, but I must caution you that your opponent is extremely skilled. He has won many combats."

But Alderic wasn't reassured in the least. "I have so much to learn. How can I possibly beat him? I'm going to be slaughtered out there."

"You mustn't talk like that. You are a tough opponent. Your speed and long reach make you a formidable adversary. You must be confident. Part of the battle is up here," he said, pointing to his head. "Listen up. We will continue to work for the next several days right up until the day of the arena. I have a few tricks that might help even the odds a bit. Let's get started right now. Time is a wasting."

Labenius continued in an urgent tone. "I will demonstrate some of my maneuvers, and I hope for your sake that you can master them by next week. I was waiting to teach you these later, but there is no time now. First, the backhand net slash. This ploy will not kill your opponent or lead to an instant victory, but it will assist you significantly. Give me your net and trident." Alderic handed them over.

"Here's how it works. The first move is a trident thrust at your foe's legs. This maneuver will force him to lower his shield as he attempts to block your strike. At the same time, move the net to a backhand position across your body, and then slash at his face using the net. Like this." He cocked his left arm holding the net across his body toward his right side, then whipped upward at his imaginary foe. "Your opponent will not be expecting the net from the right and will be unprepared to block your move with his sword. If you are successful with this maneuver, the lead weights of the net will strike your opponent in the face, causing him a great deal of pain, and the blood running down his face will obscure his vision. Again, this alone will not earn you a victory, but it will injure your adversary. Now try it."

Alderic worked on the maneuver for the better part of the morning before he was able to smoothly bring the net into position for the strike while thrusting with the trident.

"By Jove! You've got that maneuver perfected."

"I'll continue to practice it. What else have you got for me?"

Labenius motioned for Alderic to hand him his weapons. "Next, your opponent will have a large shield and armor encasing his torso and part of his arms as well as greaves on his lower legs. This means that his vulnerable areas are his upper thighs, neck, and face. Your adversary will feel invincible with all that armor, and he will be trained to avoid or block your net, as the net is considered the most dangerous part of a retiarius. All the good ones know this and will be wary of your throws. So, what do we do? Threaten him with the net, but jab at the exposed sections of his legs. Your long arms grant you an advantage. You can try going for the face, but that kind of a strike will be difficult to land. Feint to the face and thrust at the legs. You get a good strike to the legs, and those barbed tines take hold, your opponent will be disabled. So, go for the legs!"

Alderic looked at Labenius quizzically, "What about the feet? They are unprotected too. A thrust through the foot will disable an opponent."

"Good question but forget about the feet. I have seen bouts won as a result of wounds to the feet, but it isn't a particularly good play. Let me show you why. Pretend you're going for my feet."

Alderic shifted his trident and stabbed downwards toward the ground a small distance from Labenius's sandals.

"Now hold that position," said Labenius, taking a step back to get a better view of Alderic's stance. "Look at you. Your entire body is exposed because you have your trident angled downward. If you miss with this maneuver, you are a dead man. So, forget about the feet and instead go for the legs."

Labenius paused in his instruction. "Speaking of the feet, there is another ploy with the net, but it has its risks too. On occasion, you can use the net to trip an opponent. Instead of casting the net in the air, sling it at your adversary's feet. You can entangle him or trip him with it. The risks are that an agile gladiator can avoid the net and trap it on the ground with his foot. So be careful if you attempt this."

Alderic spent the entire afternoon perfecting his strikes to the legs. He worked on it repetitively. Labenius had procured a man-sized straw figure, replete with a secutor's armor, and had attached it to a wooden pole anchored to the ground. Under the constant scrutiny of Labenius, Alderic circled and weaved, issuing lightning-fast strikes. Labenius warned him several times to avoid the chest area. It would be effort expended with little reward. By late afternoon, Labenius stood with his arms crossed, observing his pupil, his expression inscrutable. Sweat streamed down Alderic's body as he executed his trident strikes. "Halt!" Labenius called out. A broad smile creased his visage. "By the gods, this Baladar fellow better watch his ass next week or he's going to get skewered. You're ready. We will practice for the next few days before the event to perfect your moves. Now go wash up."

Chapter III
The Arena in Rome

Alderic sat on the cold slab in the subterranean chamber of the arena, tapping his foot nervously waiting for his turn. Small oil lamps set in the recesses of the wall barely illuminated the room. Other gladiators from his ludus were sequestered in adjoining rooms. His bout had been scheduled in the morning, and an officious attendant informed him that he was to fight soon. Labenius sat beside Alderic, speaking words of encouragement: "Remember what you have been taught. Don't think too much, just let your body flow. You are one with your trident and net. Your foe will attempt to distract you with name calling. Stay level-headed. Turn the words around on him."

From the arena above, they heard the clamor of the crowd. Then a scream. Then silence. Alderic rose and retched in the corner. A short while later, Lothar paraded into the chamber in blood-splattered armor, his face dripping with sweat. "I live to fight another day," he crowed triumphantly. "Alderic, you look a little pale."

"I have never fought and killed a man before. I can't seem to calm down. Labenius has been attempting to reassure me, but it's all so foreign to me."

"I was nervous as Hades the first time I fought in the arena," Lothar replied, "but once I was out there on the sand, my training took over. It was nasty business—cold, calculated cruelty. Listen Alderic, I've seen you do your drills these last few days. This Baladar is in for a very rude awakening. I heard the odds are twenty to one in his favor. That's horseshit. You can defeat this bastard. Go after him. Seek him out. Kill his ugly fucking face."

"I'll try."

Lothar was almost shouting by now: "Don't try. Succeed. This Baladar is a heartless bastard. He will seek to humiliate you out there. He will ridicule you. He will call you filthy names—a whoreson and worse. He will attempt to carve you up so that you beg for mercy. You must hate that man. He is evil. Go after him. *Kill* him."

Labenius clapped on his shoulder. "Lothar is right. That man is scum. Feel the rage within you. Show him who you are. You are a German killer, trained to perfection."

There were more cheers and screams from above, and then a sudden quietude. Two legionnaires entered the room, and one shouted at Alderic, "You're next. Better put on a good show. The crowd is in an ugly mood after that last bout."

Alderic swallowed the rather large lump stuck in his throat. *I must do this.* Labenius thumped him hard on his shoulder. "Remember your training. You are bigger than him. Run him over. Get him on the ground. Destroy him."

Lothar slapped Alderic's shoulder as well. "Go out there," he shouted. "And kill the fucker!"

Alderic puffed out his chest and looked at the legionnaires. "Show me the way. I'm ready."

One of the legionnaires motioned him forward to a wooden platform. "Hop on. We will ride with you to the arena floor." Once Alderic was on the lift, the legionnaire yelled, "Up." The platform creaked and slowly began its ascent as slaves hauled on the ropes to lift it. The two soldiers accompanying him callously ignored his presence. He heard then talking about a certain brothel they would be visiting after the games today.

Alderic blinked at the bright sunlight that accosted his eyes after having been confined in the Stygian space below all morning. It was hot up here as opposed the cool air underneath. One of the soldiers pointed to the middle of the arena. "Walk toward that man. He will be the umpire for your bout."

Alderic hesitated, still trying to get his bearings and adjust to the brightness. The legionnaire nudged him in the back. "Go now, or we will drag you there." Taking a deep breath, Alderic strode toward the arena. He was about half way there when the crowd erupted in cheer. Glancing to his left, he noticed his opponent parade into view as though he owned the arena. He lifted his arms to the crowd, rousing them further. There was no doubt in Alderic's mind who the mob favored.

Labenius had emphasized that it was always good to curry the crowd's approval; because if one lost, you were at their mercy. So, it was best to be on their good side. As Alderic was a newcomer, he was not popular with them. Yet there were several things he could do to win over the stands. He recalled Labenius's instructions: *Be bold, embellish any success you have against your opponent, and show no fear.*

Alderic was the first to reach the bout official, who was attired in a white wool tunic and carried a stout wooden rod. He smiled kindly. "First time in the arena, aye?"

Alderic croaked a nervous reply.

The official continued. "I will be officiating. You will do everything I tell you to. When I drop the rod in my hand, the bout will begin. I will gesture if I want you to back off. If your opponent is down, you won't strike your opponent until given permission by me. Now give them a good show. Do you understand everything?"

Alderic nodded again. While waiting for Baladar to make his way to the center, he glanced at the huge crowd for the first time. He heard catcalls and insults hurled his way but quickly tuned them out. He needed to focus on what he had been trained for. His senses were heightened. He stared at the sand, feeling the warmth seeping in through his sandaled boots. The leather thongs were laced tightly up his ankles. On the soles were iron hob-nails for better traction. He felt even the slightest puff of breeze on his face. A rather pungent odor wafted up from the arena sand. He wrinkled his nose in disgust.

The next thing he knew, Baladar was standing across him, his dark cruel eyes glaring at Alderic's. He had a narrow face with a beak of a nose and full lips. He carried an oblong shield and a medium-length sword. His torso and arms were heavily armored, along with greaves on his shins, exactly as Labenius had described. On his head, he wore an iron helmet. As Labenius had mentioned, the exposed areas included his bare thighs, neck, and face. This is where he would strike, especially the thighs.

Before the official could speak, Baladar taunted, "Come meet your doom, boy. I hear you're German. Excellent! I *love* killing Germans. I love the way they squeal when I ram my sword into their guts."

"I see now what they say about you is untrue."

"And what is that?"

Alderic smirked. "You are not as ugly as everyone says you are."

Baladar was foaming with anger, his eyes red with fury. Before he could respond, however, the official interceded. "Enough. Save your wrath for the fight. You know the rules. Now, wait for my signal."

The man gestured for the gladiators to separate from one other. He raised his arm, holding the wooden rod above his head. After confirming that both men were ready, he lowered his arm. The crowd roared.

The official immediately backed away from the combatants, lest he gets caught between them. The crowd thundered in anticipation. Alderic assumed his stance, propped lightly on the balls of his feet, just as he had been trained, immobile except for his left arm, which rhythmically moved the net back and forth along the ground. *Swish. Swish. Swish.*

Baladar peered above the rim of his shield; his right arm cocked, clutching his lethal blade. He snarled, then leaped toward Alderic. The retiarius had tried to anticipate his opponent's moves, but it was futile. In a series of lightning moves, his opponent forced Alderic back. He thrust hard at Alderic's chest, but the lunge was blocked by his trident. There was a clang of iron, then a shower of sparks. Taking a step back, Alderic stumbled slightly on an uneven patch of sand. Baladar pounced, yelling in triumph. He thrust hard with his sword but staggered in surprise to not find Alderic there.

He advanced again. "Quick bastard aren't you. It won't save you."

Alderic gave ground once more as his adversary bounded forward. The crowd hissed, taunting him for retreating. Baladar roused the crowd, urging Alderic to fight. The secutor charged again, and Alderic backpedaled again, shifting to his right, out of harm's way, as the crowd jeered loudly.

Everything seemed to slow down. It was just Alderic and the secutor now. His opponent paused to catch his breath. Alderic remembered Labenius's words: *Move fast when the opportunity presents itself.* In a sudden attack, Alderic sprung forward. With a series of thrusts and net throws, he forced Baladar back. His trident and the net acted as one, compelling the secutor to give ground. As he completed his set of lunges, Alderic employed the trick with the net that he had practiced.

Feinting at his opponent's leg with the trident, he smoothly moved his left arm into a backhand position, then viciously swung the net from the right at Baladar's face. With a sickening thud, the lead connected with his face, slashing Baladar's forehead. Crimson streams flowed down his face and into his eyes as the crowd roared in approval.

Alderic gauged his opponent, seeking another opening; but before he could act, Baladar charged, forcing him to retreat again. The secutor feinted right with his sword, confusing Alderic, then flicked his sword to the left. He felt a stinging sensation on his left arm and noted the blood dripping onto the sand. The arena thundered with cheers for Baladar.

"You got lucky with that net trick, but your ass is cooked, German. You have no chance. I am going to grind you to a pulp. I'll leave you begging for me to finish you." He initiated a flurry of savage thrusts with his sword and buckler, forcing Alderic to retreat once more. Baladar put on a show for the crowd, pointing his sword at his opponent. He attacked relentlessly, thrusting savagely, and this time cutting a deep wound on Alderic's left leg. It was a serious injury that left him bleeding copiously on the sand.

Alderic grimaced as the sudden searing pain tore through his leg.

Knowing his opponent was injured and not a threat at the moment, Baladar turned his back on Alderic in derision and waved his arms in the air to incite the crowd to a heightened degree of blood lust.

"Finish him! Finish him!" the mob chanted. Baladar turned to face Alderic once more, sneering at the wounded gladiator. "Told you I would carve you up, boy." Before he could continue, however, Alderic charged at the Baladar, surprising him. He feinted a jab at his face with the net, and then, thrusting the trident, struck his opponent's left leg with force. The trident raked a gash on Baladar's thigh, but the barbed point did not puncture the flesh adequately. It wasn't a crippling blow, but the blood loss was considerable. The mob roared in approval. Everyone was on their feet cheering, wondering what would come next. The young retiarius was giving everything he had, and the crowd's sentiment was shifting toward him. Remembering Labenius's words about winning the crowd, Alderic lifted his arms with the net and trident, beckoning Baladar to attack.

Baladar looked down briefly at his leg and snarled. "You will pay for this, German pig." Screaming an oath, he charged at Alderic, who could do nothing but give ground under the relentless onslaught. Alderic clumsily retreated, dragging his wounded leg, then circled away. Baladar knew he had the advantage. He wasted no time and quickly advanced again. He moved in close, smashing his shield into Alderic's head. The retiarius staggered back, his legs wobbly. Blood trickled down his cheek from the wound inflicted to his face. Still woozy from the shield blow to his face, he barely parried a series of follow-up strikes from the angry secutor.

The two men separated briefly. Alderic panted, he could feel weakness beginning to creep into his body. He roared in anger. He would not succumb quietly to this piece of shit. He didn't know where the maneuver arose from, but out of nowhere, he cast his net at Baladar's feet forcing his foe to focus his attention to not being tripped. He swiftly slashed the trident sideways as if it were a sword. The last prong on the trident sliced through Baladar's cheek, ripping the flesh open to a gush of blood. The secutor hissed in pain, edging warily away from Alderic and dabbing at his bleeding face with the back of his arm.

Alderic hobbled after him but failed to follow up with a killing blow. Each combatant now had three wounds. The bout was supposed to have been over by now—an easy victory for the champion secutor—but it was not. Baladar advanced once more, glowering with rage. A relative novice in the arena was making him look like a fool. The crowd was in a frenzy. He flicked his sword again and again and once again. Alderic found it increasingly difficult to avoid the thrusts. His wounded leg was slowing him down, and Baladar was well aware of this. Alderic needed to do something and soon, or he would most certainly perish. But his adversary was giving him no chance to do anything. He was relentless, advancing with a series of thrusts and slashes that drove Alderic back.

His vision clouded. He wiped his eyes quickly on his forearm, but that did little good. Reacting to Baladar's advance, he pirouetted to his left, a second too late. He felt the sting of the blade as it made a slit on his chest, near his shoulder. Cutting into tissue and muscle, it was a crippling wound. Now was the time. With a last gasp, he whipped the net sideways to create a distraction, simultaneously bringing his right hand all the way to the end of the trident's shaft for maximum reach. He got down on one knee—whether strategically or because out of need, he didn't know.

Baladar raised his buckler to deflect the incoming net, then raised his sword overhead for a killing strike. Alderic's clutched the end of his trident with his long arm angled upwards and struck with all the strength that he had left. The pointed prongs of the trident slipped below his opponent's shield, which he had raised to avoid the net, and caught the astonished Baladar's unprotected throat. The thrust was weak and would not have ordinarily been an effective blow; but Baladar had chosen that particular moment to lunge forward for the kill. The combined momentum of the forces was fatal. The tines penetrated the soft flesh of the neck, puncturing through his muscles and blood vessels. The gladiator grabbed at his throat, attempting to tear the barbed metal out, which only made things worse. Baladar collapsed, a torrid stream of blood gushing from his neck.

Alderic dropped the net and his trident. His vision blurring, he fell to his hands and knees. He heard the crowd's chants: *Mitte, mitte, mitte.* He didn't understand what the word meant and was only later told that it meant, "Let him go." It was customary for arena officials to kill severely wounded gladiators, and Alderic certainly qualified as one.

Alderic felt strong arms grabbing him. He was supported on both sides by Labenius and Lothar and was half-carried, half-dragged out of the arena. The crowd continued roaring in approval as the surviving gladiator exited the arena. Over the din, he heard Lothar's approving voice. "Good show, Alderic! That was an incredible performance. Listen to the crowd. By Jupiter's arse, I have never heard it so loud. They love you. You survived. Now let's get you patched up."

Labenius applauded, "You beat that nasty shit of a secutor. He deserved to die. Cruel bastard. I don't know where you learned that last move you employed, but by Venus's left tit, I've never seen anything like it. You're a hero, boy. All of Rome will be talking about you."

Alderic lay still on a high wooden table deep in the bowels of the amphitheater. A physician stood over him, closely examining his wounds. He shouted testily to the slaves holding the flickering torches: "More light this way. I can't see in this darkness." The physician patted his shoulder. "Don't worry young man, you will survive. But I must warn you, I need to suture some of your wounds, and it's bound to be painful." He handed Alderic a clay cup. "Here, drink up. It will help with the discomfort."

Alderic shut his eyes as the physician began his work. He opened his eyes several times and noticed the anxious faces of Labenius and Lothar peering down at him. He felt the sting of the sutures and the tight wrapping of bandages. Mercifully enough, it wasn't long before he passed out.

He awoke a while later and felt cool water on his forehead, soothing and reviving his senses. He opened his eyes again and spied the hovering figure of Macro.

The physician washed the blood from his hands, then dried them on a towel. He gestured at the two slaves holding the torches, dismissing them, before moving away and out of the Alderic's hearing range. Macro, Labenius, and Lothar followed the healer across the room and huddled together. "Well, he'll survive this," the healer stated, "assuming there is no inflammation of the wounds. The injuries to his left leg, left arm, and face will heal fully with time. The large cut across his chest, on the other hand, is another matter. In my opinion, he will not regain full function and range of motion in his right arm, if at all, for years as a result of the injury."

Macro frowned in dismay. "Shit! That lad had the makings of a good fighter. What a performance! I've never seen a move as the one he used at the end there." He looked at Labenius. "Did you teach him that?"

Labenius shook his head. "No, I have never in all my years seen a maneuver like that either. I told you. Alderic is a natural talent. You don't find many like him."

Macro turned to the physician. "Are you sure he will not recover fully?"

The healer made a clucking noise of disapproval in his throat. "I have been caring for those wounded and maimed in the arena for years. I have seen injuries similar to this before. As I said, it's a long recovery period and rarely do combatants gain full use of their right arm. You can get another opinion if you like, but you will be told the same thing."

Labenius spoke to Macro: "Don't sell the boy to some farm or mine. He doesn't deserve that."

Macro sighed. "I'm not without sympathy for him, but what would you have me do instead? I can't keep him at the ludus. You know that."

"Give me some time," Labenius continued. "He is going to need weeks to make even a partial recovery. I will make some inquiries and find a place for him. He would make a good bodyguard. I mean, look at the size of him. You can probably make more coin if you sell him as a personal guard than as a worker in a farm. Be patient. Let me see what I can do."

"I will give you some time to figure out an arrangement. A month or two. I hope you can find something for him. I really do. After that display in the arena, he deserves a second chance and a hope for a better future. In all my years of witnessing gladiatorial combat, that was the most impressive performance. Remarkable! Did you hear that crowd?" Without waiting for a reply, Macro gestured to his attendants. "Now, let's get this hero back to the ludus."

Chapter IV

Three weeks later after the bout, Labenius traveled to meet Macro at the gladiator compound. Macro sat at his wooden table perusing several wax tablets and scrolls. He looked up from the clutter and offered Labenius a slight smile. "I trust you have some good news about Alderic's employment prospects. He appears to be getting better by the day, but as the medicus had anticipated, he has limited motion in his right arm. I hope his injury is not catastrophic enough to prevent him from being employed as a bodyguard."

Labenius smiled. "I just looked in on him before coming here, and considering his condition three weeks ago, yes, he indeed seems to be making remarkable progress. I do have some news that may interest you." He paused, letting his words hang for a moment.

Macro looked at him expectantly. "Well? Out with it, man. Do we have a buyer or not?"

Labenius smiled. "Ah, I seem to have piqued your interest. As you know, I have on occasion been consulted by wealthy parties asking recommendations for bodyguards, protectors, or defenders of the hearth—whatever you wish to call them. I only endorse men I believe will serve their masters faithfully, without creating any domestic disturbance from excessive wine, gambling, or some other perversion. I provided this service a few years ago to Senator Titus Junius Cilo, and it just so happens that the person I placed with him served him well, but unfortunately, the man died from the plague a few weeks ago. Cilo values my opinion. I told him I have a candidate that might be of interest to him and that I would be back in touch."

Macro clapped his hands. "Excellent, Labenius! Have you quoted a price to this Senator Cilo yet?"

"Yes, we've had some preliminary discussions. I told him the story about the arena fight and his physical wounds. The senator said he had heard about the clash. The fight had apparently achieved some notoriety; he said all of Rome was talking about it. In the spirit of full disclosure, I also mentioned that Alderic had learned some Latin but needs to improve his understanding of the language. After his acceptance of the transaction after meeting Alderic, we agreed on a total sum of 400 silver denarii, minus my fee of 40 denarii."

Macro grunted. "Why would I pay you 40 denarii? That's...Let me think..."

Sighing, Labenius quipped, "One in ten, and there is to be no quibbling about a meagre 40 denarii. Look, he's damaged goods. You would get less than half this price if you had sold him to the mines or the farms. So, quit grumbling and let's settle this deal. The senator will come tomorrow to inspect his prospective purchase."

Early the next day, Labenius stood outside a renowned inn, the White Dove, which lay near the intersection of two main thoroughfares. As per their arrangement, he was awaiting Senator Cilo and his young son, Lucius. Given his station in life, he arrived early; it would be highly impolite to keep the senator waiting. Despite the early hour, the streets were already bustling with activity. He spied the pair edging through the heavy throng: the senator, a middle-aged man with an aquiline nose and a receding hair-line, was attired in a plain toga, and Lucius, a handsome lad in his mid-teens, wore a plain tunic and a light cloak to ward off the chill.

"Good morning, Senator, and to you too, young Lucius. Are you ready to meet your new bodyguard? I guarantee that you will like him. I trained him myself. He is an imposing physical specimen, and his mind is quick. His grasp of the language improves daily. I know you'll have some questions for him, so I have arranged for Lothar to attend the meeting. He is a German gladiator who speaks both languages fluently. This is to ensure that there is no misunderstanding."

Cilo responded, "Thank you, Labenius. I need a bodyguard in place as early as possible, especially with all the political unrest besetting the city. It's not safe for us to go anywhere anymore, especially for my wife and son. I'm sure you understand my concerns. Caesar had held the gangs under control, but they've reared their ugly heads after his death. The level of lawlessness in the city is appalling."

"Quite true, Senator. I know it's prohibited, but I keep a gladius strapped to my side underneath my garments, and I've had to brandish it on several occasions."

Cilo snorted. "If those ruffians only knew who they were up against, they would probably have shit their tunics before accosting you."

Labenius laughed. "What do you make of the political situation, Senator? You're closer to these things than I."

Cilo frowned in thought. "Frankly, I had never liked Caesar. I always thought him to be a tyrant, but the man represented stability. Rome was at peace. The entire city has been turned upside down after his assassination. New men are vying for power now, with Marcus Antonius, Lepidus, and young Octavius stirring the pot. Caesar's murderers have been exiled. Needless to say, I am concerned for Rome and my family. I don't trust anyone anymore, especially our new rulers."

They continued discussing various subjects as they walked and soon arrived at the ludus. Macro met them at the entrance. "Ah, Senator Cilo, I presume. Good of you to come," he greeted. "My name is Macro Sestinius, the lanista here. I will take you directly to meet Alderic. He is waiting in the compound with Lothar, our German translator."

The senator grinned. "Lead the way. I am anxious to meet this young man. His reputation certainly precedes him." The group walked a short distance to where Alderic stood with Lothar. Cilo drew a sharp breath at the sight of Alderic. The former gladiator had on a short tunic that revealed most of his arms and legs. His sheer size was striking. Not only was he unusually tall, but his muscles were uncommonly sculpted. He noted several angry red welts, which he assumed were the result of his recent combat in the arena. The jagged scar on his face—courtesy Baladar's shield—made his countenance even more imposing. The senator observed his figure in silence for a few moments, and then asked, "What are his physical limitations as a result of his injuries?"

Lothar, not sure how much to reveal about Alderic's injuries, looked inquiringly at Macro, who nodded. Lothar translated the words for Alderic. In response, Alderic raised his right arm, but could only do so to the level of his shoulder. He stopped, grimacing in pain.

Macro, fearing that his potential sale might slip away, gestured to Lothar. "I want you and Alderic to have a contest of strength by pushing against each other."

The gladiators squared off against one another, and both men extended their arms to grip each other's shoulders. The two men grunted, their muscles bulging in strain, as they sought to budge their opponent. Gradually, Alderic began to prevail, moving Lothar back a slight distance, and then, with a tremendous surge of strength, he sent Lothar flying backwards.

Cilo grinned. "He will do. If you don't mind, I would like to talk to Alderic and his German translator alone."

"But of course, Senator." Macro bowed before Labenius and he discretely retreated across the courtyard.

"You will now be my property," the senator began. "Your duty will be to the security of my family—my wife, son, and me—both in the streets and in my house. You must protect us even at the risk of your life. You will address me as *dominus* and my wife as *domina,* and you must obey all our orders immediately. In return, you will be treated well and receive both good food and adequate shelter, certainly better than what you get at this ludus. Do you understand?"

Lothar translated the words for Alderic, who looked at the senator and replied in broken Latin: "Yes, I serve you and family. I will protect you."

"Excellent!" the senator exclaimed. "Let me finalize the transaction with Macro and we can be on our way."

After journeying through the city streets for some time, they arrived at the senator's home. Alderic gawked in awe when he caught sight of the size of the mansion. The main entrance, framed by a pair of fluted white marble columns, featured two magnificent wooden doors, each about eight feet high. As he entered the home, he gaped at the splendor of the new surroundings he found himself in. He had never seen such opulence, nor imagined such luxury. He grew up in a mud daub hut with a thatched roof and a floor of bare earth. At the heart of the stone mansion was a fabulous garden with reflecting pools, bubbling fountains, flowering bushes, and small fruit trees. The walls were furbished with beautiful frescos and hanging tapestries, which gave the home a certain warmth. In colder weather, he was told the floors were heated. He was also informed that the house lay in an area called Aventine Hill.

Even the slaves had a bathing pool to wash themselves along with a chamber from where their refuse would flow into Rome's sewers. There were slaves for cleaning, gardening, cooking, and attending to the senator and his wife, and most were women. He would later learn that the female sex was more suited to household chores and were easier to manage. Alderic's sleeping quarters was a small space sectioned off from the others by a heavy drape.

Alderic was put to work the very next day. He strode in front of the dominus as they walked through the busy streets to their destination, a place they called the *curia*. He gripped a thick wooden stave in one hand to clear the path or, if need be, employ as a weapon. He wore a tunic beneath a thin cloak that he used to conceal a short sword strapped to his thigh. It was to be used only as a last resort. Carrying a sword was against the law of the city and one could be subjected to severe punishment if caught.

Walking down the avenue, he warily eyed those to the sides. He couldn't predict what quarter danger might arise from, so he carefully scrutinized any signs of potential threats. His duty was to protect the senator, and he wanted to ensure that nothing untoward happened on his first day. He caught the furtive glance of a scruffy young man lurking in the shadows. He held his gaze and watched as the man meekly retreated into the gloomy alley.

They meandered through the streets; the senator indicating to Alderic the direction that they were to take. Upon reaching their destination, the senator motioned toward a gathering of individuals clad in similar garb as Alderic. "Wait with them until I return."

Alderic stared briefly after the senator as he approached a magnificent stone building with red-tiled roof. A series of steps led to the massive twin bronze doors that made up the entrance. Gazing at the structure for a few more moments, he wandered over to the gathering of bodyguards, similarly armed with wooden staves. He observed hard bulges in their sides beneath their clothing, obviously weapons of some kind.

They were a tough-looking lot, most of them much older than Alderic. They were big men, and some bore facial scars from long-forgotten battles. He stood at the periphery of the group, apprehensive to engage in conversation, given his limited language skills. A man broke away from the milling bunch and moved toward Alderic. He was a beefy figure with close-cropped hair and clean shaven face. "You new here? Who are you guarding?" he enquired.

Alderic did not understand what the man asked but formulated a response based on what he guessed he might have asked. He pointed to himself and said, "Alderic. Me guard Senator Cilo."

The man smiled back. "Ah, you must be replacing Thrixus. Shame about him dying. How did you become the senator's protector? What's your background?"

"I was gladiator in arena. Got injured and became bodyguard."

There was a brief pause, after which the man continued. "Alderic, aye? Say, are you by any chance the same Alderic who killed Baladar in the arena?"

"I fight and kill Baladar in arena. He nasty shit."

The man gasped, incredulous. "So, you're the one! You slew Baladar, the famed secutor." He turned toward the others. "We have a celebrity among us. This here is Alderic. He was the one who killed Baladar in the arena last month."

The entire mob moved toward him, eyeing him curiously. A fat skin of wine was thrust before him. He knew it would be rude to refuse and took a healthy gulp. He nodded his thanks. He was forced to retell the tale of his bout several times. Thereafter, he tried his best to engage in conversation, not really sure of what people were asking him and whether his responses were correctly worded. The group passed the time, handing around several skins of wine, telling stories and jokes while their masters debated in the senate. Alderic laughed with the others, although in many instances, he wasn't quite sure why. But he was grateful to experience companionship again.

The senator exited the curia with a worried scowl. He looked about till he spotted Alderic, gesturing for him to join him. As they walked, the senator seemed preoccupied, oblivious of his surroundings. Alderic understood nothing of Roman governance or politics, but he intuitively knew that the senator was deeply troubled about something. He surmised that the deliberations under discussion in the senate were clearly worrisome. After a while, the senator stopped. He sniffed in Alderic's direction. "Is that wine I smell on your breath?" he asked.

With a contrite expression, Alderic replied, "Other guards drink, tell stories." He shrugged his shoulders. "I try to be like them."

A Barbarian in Rome's Legions

The dominus glowered for a moment, then seemed to relax. "Not too much. I need you sober." He smiled and gestured using his thumb and forefinger, indicating a small amount.

Alderic, realizing the senator was not angry with him, heaved a sigh of relief. "Understand."

Several months went by, and Alderic found the new life he had been cast into much easier in comparison to the ludus. He spent most of his time escorting the senator or his wife through the city. He was beginning to map in mind the various twists and turns of Rome's labyrinthine streets. Occasionally, he would shepherd young Lucius. When he was not accompanying his masters, he took turns serving as a guard at the entrance of the luxurious home. As of yet, he had not needed to use any of the physical skills he had acquired during his gladiator training. His size alone usually acted as a deterrent to any persons up to any nefarious deed.

Alderic firmly believed that some powerful, higher deity was watching over him. Coming from the perilous and intimidating grind of the ludus, here he was in an opulent home, with good food and adequate accommodations. His new owners seemed to be of the benevolent kind and not all that demanding. The senator, although irritable at times, never appeared to raise his voice in the running of his household. His wife, Lucretia, was younger and outgoing. She was a beauty who had maintained her figure and assisted her husband in household affairs when needed. The young son, Lucius, was a handsome lad, having inherited the dark sparkling eyes and sculpted jawline of his mother.

In another stroke of good fortune, the senator had requested that Lucius's tutor, a Greek named Kyros, who came every day to deliver lessons, devote an hour to assist Alderic in learning the language every day. The senator had explained that if Alderic was to welcome visitors and obey his master's commands, it was important for him to understand the language.

At first, Kyros had been impatient and snobbish in dealing with Alderic. The Greek believed it was beneath him to deliver instruction to a Germanic slave when most of his clients were wealthy aristocrats. But Alderic had been enthusiastic and earnest in his devotion to the

61

lessons, prompting the tutor to accept him after a while. He even seemed pleased with his progress.

~

"Ha!" Alderic yelled as he thrust and slashed with his wooden sword at young Lucius. He forced the young Roman—now a tribune in training—to rapidly retreat across the small paved courtyard in the garden.

Lucretia, the ever-protective mother, sat nearby, observing the swordplay. "Careful, Alderic. He's just learning the ways of a soldier and isn't nearly as strong or skilled as you."

Without taking his eyes off his opponent, he responded, "Don't worry, my lady, he will not come to any bodily harm. In any case, he is no longer a novice. He is getting better every day." Alderic paused to catch his breath. This was good exercise for him. There had been too much sitting around and little in the way of physical demands lately. He needed to get his lazy ass in gladiator shape.

As for the skill level of Lucius, he had a long way before he would be anywhere near Alderic's equal. The young master was more boy than man and had not yet fully developed his muscles and strength. Lucius was four years younger and had only begun his military training several months ago. Alderic decided to ease up on him. There was no sense in destroying his fragile self-confidence, and of more importance, his mother was right—he needed to be cautious with this sword play. They were using wooden weapons and wearing training armor, but the possibility of injury was ever present.

Although Alderic was only a slave, Lucius looked up to him as someone accomplished in the martial arts. He had requested his parents that the former gladiator be his sparring partner. At first, they had said no, fearing for their son's safety, but Lucius pleaded with them, reasoning that Alderic would know how to be careful and that the better he was trained as a swordsman, the better he would be in battle. The last point in combination with his insistent whining had finally swayed them. They reluctantly agreed to permit the sparring sessions with the strict provision that one of them must be present at all times.

Alderic let the boy advance and infiltrate his guard, allowing Lucius's sword to crease his neck. He dropped his sword and shield. "I yield. You win, young master."

"Oh Alderic," cried Lucius. "You cannot fool me. You let me win."

"Not true, you are getting better."

Lucretia, sighed, "Alderic, even I saw you deliberately drop your guard. Don't make my son believe he is an accomplished swordsman when he's not."

Alderic grinned. "Forgive me, Domina. In truth, I was getting a little tired. I'm always cautious to not hurt the young man, but he is improving."

Lucius laughed. "See, Mother! Come Alderic, share some wine with me and tell me your stories again—how you trained as a gladiator and grew up in Germania." The two ventured to a nearby stone bench near the fountain, where a tray holding two goblets of chilled wine was waiting for them.

The pair sat down, and out of deference to his role, Alderic waited until he was offered wine by Lucius, which he willingly accepted. Lucius raised his goblet in a toast, and Alderic did the same. Lucius turned his head to make sure his mother had departed, then tried to say something but hesitated.

Alderic raised his eyebrows. "What is it, young master?"

Lucius' words came out in a rush. "Alderic, have you ever been with a woman ... you know ... ?"

Alderic understood that he needed to respond without embarrassing the lad. He smiled at the young Roman and chose his words carefully, "I have back in Germania." "I take it you haven't."

Lucius nodded. "Many of my fellow tribunes brag about their sexual conquests. Some are beginning to tease me about my ... inexperience."

"Don't believe most of what you hear. Those men not tell truth. It was same in my village."

"But I would like to be with a woman. Would you take me to a ... brothel?"

"Do you know of a place?"

"N–No ..." Lucius stammered.

Alderic frowned. He knew the bordellos could be dangerous. When the elite gladiators were given freedom to visit the whores in town, they always did so in numbers. Violence could erupt at any moment. If he took Lucius to a brothel, and if he were to get injured, it would be his hide that would be nailed to a wall. "Listen to me," he answered, "if you find excuse for me to take you somewhere in Rome in late afternoon, I take you there. Not go at night. Too dangerous.

But first, I must consult with friend Lothar at the ludus about a respectable place."

Lucius proffered a wide smile. "Thank you, Alderic. Let me know as soon as you know of a suitable establishment."

Several days later, Alderic was tasked with delivering some documents to a senator's house. Coincidentally, it was in the general direction of his former ludus. If he could hurry, it shouldn't take too much time and prolong his absence from his master's house. It offered the perfect opportunity to chat with Lothar about a brothel for the young master.

He found the senator's home without much difficulty and conveyed the documents. From there, he rushed toward the ludus and arrived at the walled enclosure. Memories came rushing back, sending shivers down his spine. He sighed in relief when the guards at the front gate permitted him to the compound. They appeared unconcerned that he wished to speak to Lothar. Alderic found his friend lounging in the shade of a portico with several other gladiators, sheltered from the mid-day sun.

Lothar's face split into a wide grin. "Alderic, you have recovered and wish to join the ludus again?"

Alderic paused, then spoke in Latin. "Not likely, Lothar, but I have words with you about a sensitive subject."

"This is a first. Someone wishing to consult me about something. What can I do for you?"

Alderic gestured toward a secluded corner out of earshot of the others. "My master has a son," he started. "About four years younger than me. He wants me to take him to a whorehouse."

Lothar broke into a laugh. "So take him. You can take a turn while you're there. It would be good for your health."

Alderic frowned. "It is not funny. I remember you telling me how brothels could be dangerous places. You said you always go with others for safety. I need to know the name of …" He paused to search for the right words. "a high-quality, safe place. If my master finds out I had taken him, he will punish me severely."

"I see your quandary. Let me think. I don't frequent the expensive places, but I have heard of some…" He paused, and then his eyes suddenly blazed. "I remember someone telling me about a place frequented by the young gentlemen of Rome. Never been there of course. Wait a bit... It's coming to me. Let me think. Yes, I remember the name now, Palace of Venus."

"Where is it?"

"I don't know the exact location, but I think it's not too far from the senate building."

"You mean the curia."

"How did you know that? My, you have come a long way, talking like a Roman now." He offered a wry smile.

Alderic preened, proud of his newfound knowledge. "Where near the curia is it, and what's this place like?"

"It's somewhere west of the forum. From what I had heard, it's a nice place. Clean, spacious rooms. High-class neighborhood. Lighted streets. I usually pay a few denarii for a throw. It will probably cost you some extra at the Venus."

"I do not care. It's not my money."

"Let me know how you make out and how much it costs. I might like to try it some time."

"Palace of Venus, west of senate building. I will find it. Thank you, Lothar. Maybe when I have some time to myself, I will buy you a cup of wine."

"I will hold you to that, Alderic."

"I must hurry back. Thank you again, Lothar." He waved his arm as a departing gesture.

Alderic and Lucius huddled out in the garden, away from prying ears. The splashing and gurgling of a nearby fountain helped masked their conversation from anyone in the household who happened to wander into the vicinity. Alderic related to Lucius what he had gathered from Lothar. "It is called the Palace of Venus," he informed. "Somewhere near the curia. Lothar said it is a highly respectable establishment. Many young lords gather for their pleasures. He said it is expensive."

Lucius grinned. "Money isn't a problem. I will find out the exact location from my classmates. I have a pretty good idea—"

Suddenly, Lucius's mother appeared. "What are you two talking about?" Lucretia stood in front of them, hands on her hips. "Come on, out with it. I know that look. It is about something I'm not supposed to hear."

Lucius attempted to adopt a composed expression. "Oh, Mother, Alderic was just telling me about some of his exploits back in Germania," he lied. "It is not something you would enjoy hearing."

His mother was silent. She shifted her glance from her son to Alderic, then back to Lucius again. "Why is it that I don't believe you, and why do you feel the need to have this conversation away from everyone in the household?" She tapped her sandaled foot in annoyance, then turned her frosty glance to Alderic. "And what do you have to say, Alderic?"

Facing Lucretia's stern gaze wasn't a pleasant experience. On occasion, he had seen her temper flare with her husband, and it was not a pretty scene. Her tongue could become quite shrill. Alderic fidgeted briefly, wilting under her gaze. "It's as master Lucius said. I told him of our hunts and stalking game. You know, guy talk," he blurted.

Lucretia gave him a glacial look, letting him know she wasn't buying any of this. "I don't want you filling my son's ears with talk about your conquests of women or anything related to that. He is too young. Understood?"

Alderic nodded, "Yes, Domina." *If she only knew what we were truly discussing, I would be in a heap of trouble.*

With that, Lucretia did an abrupt about face and swiftly departed.

The opportunity arrived the next week. Lucius and Alderic had conferred about how to best schedule a visit to the brothel. It would need to be in the late afternoon, for houses of pleasure would only open at that time, then remain open for business most of the night. Lucius had made some excuse to his parents that he wanted Alderic to accompany him to visit a friend's house after his military training. He said he intended to spend some time there and wouldn't be home until late.

The next day, the pair eagerly hurried along the city streets. Lucius was able to retrieve a specific location for the brothel so that they would not have to search for it, wasting the valuable time they had in the process. They reached an intersection of two paved thoroughfares, where a modest brick building with a red-tiled roof stood. A small sign proclaiming the name of the establishment, Palace of Venus, was framed above the door. Hanging nearby from the eaves was a flat iron effigy of a voluptuous woman suspended from two chains, leaving little doubt of what this place held.

The two hesitated, then strode through the front door. Several oil lamps lit the interior, and incense burned in a small pot. A burly guard stood in a remote corner, his hands folded across his chest. The room was clean as it had probably just been scrubbed. Several divans sat in the middle of the room. The comforting sound of a lute filled the air. Given the early hour, the place was devoid of patrons. The madam, with a painted face and a huge cleavage that showed out of a low-cut bodice, greeted them. She offered a wide smile. "My name is Freida," she introduced herself. "How may I help you this afternoon?"

Neither of the two men replied. Alderic waited for Lucius to say something, but the young man appeared frozen in place. Lucius, with a beseeching expression, shifted his gaze back to Alderic. After a moment of uncomfortable silence, Alderic finally blurted out, "My master, he needs a woman. It is first time."

Lucius reddened at Alderic's words. "You didn't need to tell her that," he whispered.

Alderic shrugged. "It's true."

Freida walked over and placed her hand on Lucius's shoulder nudged her soft hip against his. "No need to be nervous, young man. Everyone has a first time. Sit down on this couch. Relax. We have the best girls in the city. Would you like to see them?"

Lucius again turned imploringly at Alderic for guidance, who in turn bobbed his head.

The madam walked over to the entrance hallway that led to the rooms at the back and shouted several names. Almost immediately, four scantily clad women appeared. Lucius ogled at the women before him.

The madam spoke to him: "They are all skilled in the art of love. Would you like me to select one for you or would you prefer to choose yourself?"

Lucius gulped hard, staring at the voluptuous women. He continued to gape, not sure what to do. Finally, he pointed at a dark-haired beauty with slim hips and olive skin. "I choose her."

"Ah, good choice. This is Ayda. She is from the East. Now, young gentleman, her fee will be twenty denarii."

Alderic cringed inward. Based on the prices Lothar had mentioned, this was exorbitant; but it wasn't his money, so he stayed silent. He watched as Lucius picked out the coins out of the small purse attached to his waist. Then, the two figures retreated down the hall, Ayda clinging to his master's arm.

The madam pointed to the door and said, "You may wait outside if you wish."

Alderic understood he was being politely asked to withdraw, but he would have none of it. "I am his protector. I stay here," he declared.

Freida shot him an annoying glance, but then surveyed his size. She decided it was best not to make an issue of it. She gave a silent signal to the sentinel to remain where he was and not intervene.

Alderic retreated to a corner, making his appearance less conspicuous, to wait patiently for Lucius to reappear. A short time later, the dark-haired girl appeared, clinging to Lucius, who had a huge grin plastered across his face. Alderic gave her an inquiring look.

Ayda smiled back. "A real stallion," she expressed.

Alderic playfully punched Lucius on the shoulder, relieved that this was over. "Now we hurry back, yes?"

Several days later, Alderic and Lucius engaged in their mock sword-play. It had been a warm afternoon and was now nearing twilight. Off to the side, seated on a marble bench, were the senator and Lucretia. They watched closely as the parry and thrust exchange commenced between the two young men. Alderic blocked the sword thrust and retreated. Lucius attempted to knock his opponent off balance to further take advantage of the situation. He gave a tremendous thrust with his shoulder; it was like pushing against a thick tree. No give. He struggled against the immobile object that was Alderic. Coiling his legs, he endeavored, once more, to forcibly throw his opponent off balance.

Remembering a ploy that Labenius had taught him when in close quarters with an opponent, Alderic swiftly side-stepped the effort. Lucius found himself pushing at empty space and went tumbling into the herb garden.

Lucretia and Cilo gasped at the turn of events, believing their son was hurt. Alderic hurried over and hauled the boy to his feet. Lucius was gasping with laughter. "You fooled me with that maneuver. You must teach me how you did that."

Relieved that Lucius wasn't injured, Alderic replied, "It's trick for gladiators, not young boys."

68

The senator approached and clasped his hand on his son's shoulder. "You have made much progress in your sword drill."

"I still cannot beat Alderic."

"No, you can't, but Alderic is a trained fighter."

"I want to be a trained fighter as well."

Alderic chuckled. "Maybe someday you will. But as your father says, you are becoming more skilled."

Lucretia spoke from her seated position on the bench. "Come sit with us, Alderic, have some wine. My husband and I appreciate the lessons you are providing to our son." A female slave came about and poured wine into the serving goblets. The four people sipped their wine in silence.

"So tell us, Alderic," Lucretia began, "how is it that you came to Rome and the ludus?"

Alderic paused in thought, hoping to draw the best out of his language lessons, which had been going exceedingly well. He spoke in his best Latin: "I was from a small village of the Tencteri tribe in what the Romans call Germania. I was on the opposite side of the large river . . . what you say it?"

"The Rhenus," answered Lucius.

"Yes, Rhenus. I was young man, not yet a warrior. I was invited on a raid on the other side of the river. First time. We cross Rhenus, and the Roman legionnaires were waiting for us. They killed most warriors except for me and a few others. I was captured and sold to a ludus in Rome. You know the rest about my encounter in the arena."

There was a brief silence, then Lucretia continued, "What about your family?"

Alderic frowned and spoke in a wistful tone: "My father died when I was young. Killed by Roman legionnaires. I only have mother and woman-to-be, Ealdgyd. They are gone to me now. Even if I were to go back by some twist of fortune, the village would no longer be there. Too many of the warriors were lost to the Romans. Village no longer sustainable."

Lucretia sighed. "How sad, but we are thankful for your presence here. Lucius adores you, and my husband and I are grateful for the protection you provide us. I must also compliment you on your language skills—your Latin has much improved since you joined us."

Alderic beamed. "Thank you, Domina, and my thanks for the language lessons from the tutor, Kyros. I hope to serve you well. I do anything you ask. You provide good home for me."

"You are such a good influence on our son," she continued. "He looks up to you, you know. I always feel so assured whenever you accompany Lucius in the city."

Alderic shifted uncomfortably in his seat; he could feel his face reddening. *If she only knew.*

Chapter V

The three most powerful men in Rome sat sequestered around a polished wood table in a private residence on the outskirts of the city. The room was furnished lavishly with frescoes and hanging tapestries. A silver vessel of expensive wine—now half empty—sat atop the table. Several scribes sat in the background, recording the words of the men. The three figures were Marcus Antonius, the right-hand man of the late Julius Caesar; Gaius Octavius, grandnephew and adopted son of Caesar; and Marcus Aemilius Lepidus, a patrician and close ally of Caesar. Lepidus had previously occupied the position of *Pontifus Maximus*, the chief priest of Rome. The three men had ruthlessly seized power in the wake of Caesar's murder and now called themselves the "Triumvirate."

Marcus Antonius, the strongest and most influential man present, refilled his chalice once more. He had a commanding presence about him that he had nurtured over the years—an aura that dominated the room. His countenance was handsome, yet, at the same time, brutish. "It is agreed then," he spoke. "We will seek out and destroy those who call themselves the Liberators." He was obviously referring to the men responsible for the Caesar's assassination, those who fled Rome and were now declared enemies of the Republic. The ringleaders are amassing an army of considerable size in the East. We will need to confront them and destroy their legions."

Sipping his wine, he continued, "In order to finance our new government and pay for the army we need to assemble, we will require a source of funds. We have already confiscated the properties of these traitors and will use the proceeds to fund our armies, but we require much more. I therefore suggest that we use proscription, as dictator Sulla did when he was in power. We can use it to seize the assets of those who opposed Caesar's efforts."

His words were greeted with silence. Lepidus, a middle-aged man with an aristocratic face and aquiline nose, spoke in a demurring tone: "That is a drastic step. Not only will their property be seized, their families will be killed as well. They would be declared enemies of the state. Who would you include on the list?"

Marcus Antonius glowered, his tone truculent. "I'm glad you asked. First on my list would be that prick, Marcus Tullius Cicero. You know what he is rumored to have said about Caesar's murder? He said he did not take part, but he wished he had been invited to that superb banquet. Furthermore, that man has mocked me and disparaged my reputation on numerous occasions."

Lepidus agreed. "I'm aware of that. He has gone great lengths to sully your image. But he is a powerful senator. There might be consequences."

Marcus Antonius pounded the table with his fist. "All the more reason to rid ourselves of his meddlesome activities. While we're at it, I would suggest we eliminate his brother, Quintus Tullius Cicero, as well." Antonius turned to young Octavius. "What do you say? You have been quiet all evening."

Octavius, only twenty and the youngest of the Triumvirate, lacked the experience of the two others. He, however, had the distinct advantage of being Caesar's adopted son and heir. He didn't hesitate to respond to Antonius. "I agree. Cicero must be eliminated. He attempted to dupe me with some of his inquiries, but I avoided his ensnarement. He thought me to be a naive boy, and his tone was condescending. I am with you on this, Antonius. Cicero and his brother need to be eradicated."

"Good, Octavius. I am glad to see we are at least in agreement about something. Now gentlemen, let us move on to the others. Next on my list is Marcus Favonius. He has opposed the formation of our government and was a strong critic of Caesar. Any objection to adding him to the list?"

Lepidus fidgeted. "Again, he is a powerful senator."

A fury clouded Antonius's face. "If you don't have the stomach for this, why don't you resign from our council? Harsh measures will be necessary for what we have set out to do."

"That is not what I meant."

"Well, are you in agreement or not? We don't have all day."

Lepidus nodded wearily. "Who's next?"

Several hours later, the list was almost completed. Antonius looked around the room. "Anyone else?"

Lepidus cleared his throat. "I have one more: Senator Titus Junius Cilo."

Antonius peered from the rim of his wine goblet. "Who the fuck is that?"

"He is the cousin of Quintus Antistius Labeo—one of the conspirators who took Caesar's life. Cilo also opposed most of Caesar's proposals. I bring up his name because my spies tell me he has been liquidating many of his properties. He probably has a hoard of coin."

Antonius, the wine slurring his words, replied, "Then, by all means, we shall add him to the list. Gentlemen, I have thought about this at great length, and this is the only way it will work. We will employ the street gangs, the brotherhoods, to do the dirty work. There will be no blood on our hands. Their job will be to eliminate the family members and recover the cash along with other household valuables. Naturally, we will have our representatives on the scene to ensure that the gangs do not steal from us. However, in the case of Cicero, I will send my own personal envoy to deal with him."

"Do we need to kill the women and children as well? It seems rather harsh?" Octavius inquired, concerned.

Antonius scowled at Octavius. "It makes things less complicated, and we must launch the plan as soon as possible." His tone turned grave. "Everyone must die—men, women, children. It makes things less complicated. We will launch the process soon."

Alderic stood in the vestibule of Gaius Statius Sulpicius's house, a friend and fellow senator who his master and his wife were visiting. The encroaching crepuscular shadows in the garden told him it was getting late in the afternoon. He had been waiting for some time now and had anxiously begun pacing back and forth. Despite being a relative newcomer to the city, he knew that the streets were not safe after dark. At last, the couple emerged out of the house, hand in hand, ready for Alderic to accompany them home to the Aventine.

As they descended the steps outside the dwelling, Alderic glanced at the imminent darkness and frowned. It was later than he had anticipated. He led the way, wooden stave in hand, with the couple following close behind him. The residence was about six blocks away. His concern was amplified by the course they would take back to the senator's home. There was no direct route, and the only path involved traversing through several side streets, which were far less safe than the main thoroughfares. He hadn't needed to employ any physical force thus far in his duties, but the encroaching gloom demanded extra vigilance.

The threesome ventured about one block. Alarmed, Alderic noted the streets rapidly emptying from the day's activities. Most of the storefronts had already boarded up for the night. Down the avenue, he noticed a patrol of Rome's urban cohorts disappearing from view as they turned a corner.

The trio turned and ventured off the main avenue. They traveled about half a block, when he saw it—a furtive movement deep in the shadows ahead. It was barely discernible, but he was certain there was something there. Perhaps it was nothing, but he wasn't about to take any chances. He decided not to say anything yet. No point alarming his masters.

Alderic, out of caution, markedly slowed his pace. The couple, engaged in an intense argument about their visit, nearly collided with Alderic. Cilo looked up in annoyance. "Can we hurry up? It is getting late."

They arrived at the intersection of an alley; there seemed to be no one else in the vicinity. Alderic spotted movement within the shadows again. He tightened his grip on the stave, preparing to use it if the occasion arose. His eyes remaining fixed ahead as he spoke over his shoulder. "Beware, we have problem."

Without warning, three men stepped out of the darkness. The man in front of the other two smirked as he tapped the edge of his cudgel on his palm. Alderic spied no weapons on the other two, but they held their hands low behind their backs. He guessed they held daggers. There was a disturbance to their rear, and a pair of men suddenly materialized behind them, blocking any retreat. The street was empty, and they were alone against five street thugs. The senator grabbed his wife by the arm, holding her protectively.

Alderic sized up the situation, remembering his training at the ludus. *Strike hard, strike fast.*

The three men before them couldn't have anticipated what happened next. In a blazing attack of speed and ferocity, Alderic recklessly charged at them. He leveled the leader with a smash to the jaw with his heavy wooden stave. A few teeth flew out of the man's mouth as he collapsed with a groan. The second man to the leader's right managed to extend his right arm that held the knife. Alderic chopped at his elbow with the wood, breaking the arm with a resounding crack. The third figure, wanting none of this, turned around and fled.

Alderic averted his attention to the rear. One of the men charged at Cilo and his wife, knocking them to the ground. He was in the process of unsheathing his knife when Alderic intervened. Using his stave, he knocked the knife out of his hand. He speared into the assailant, leading with his shoulder, sending him catapulting into the cobbled street. The ruffian landed in an unmoving heap. The last of the assailants closed the distance and thrust at Alderic with his knife. He sidestepped quickly, blocking the thrust, but he could feel the familiar sting of a wound. In close quarters with the man, he dropped his stave and drew out his long dagger, viciously burying it to the hilt in the figure's chest. The man collapsed lifeless.

"Run," he yelled to the senator who stood petrified up the street. "I will see to your wife." In one fluid motion, he scooped up the fallen Lucretia and threw her over his shoulder like a sack of grain and began running after the senator. They sprinted the rest of the way home.

Alderic raced up the stone steps of the residence, through the massive doors, and gently lowered Lucretia to her feet once they were in the vestibule. The senator's face was ashen, shaken from their encounter. He ran up to Lucretia and held her in a tight embrace.

Alderic discarded his thin cape and slid up the sleeve of his tunic. A long shallow gash on his upper arm dripped blood onto the tile floor. "Alderic, you're hurt!" cried Lucretia.

"I see worse. I will have it bound. It not serious."

She ran over and embraced him, weeping profusely. "Alderic, you saved our lives."

Alderic was at a loss of what to do. He could feel the woman's softness against him. He kept his arms at his side, wondering what to do or say next.

Cilo spoke in a stern tone. "Lucretia, it is improper to hug slaves."

"Don't you tell me what is improper. Alderic saved our lives. If it were not for his efforts, we would lay like gutted fish on that filthy street. Besides, Alderic is more than a slave—he is a member of our household."

Alderic looked at the senator awkwardly, hoping to extract himself from the situation. By now, several other household staff had materialized at the scene. The senator turned to Martia, a heavy-set middle-aged woman who served as the keeper of the hearth and kitchen, and said, "Would you please get some fresh linen to bind Alderic's wound. He cannot do it by himself. Now, all of you, there is no need for alarm. Back to your stations."

The next day, Cilo sat with his wife in a small room off the peristylium, which afforded a pleasant view of the fountain and the garden. A worried frown creased his face. "My dear, there is no doubt in my mind," he spoke. "The attack was no random act. It was a premeditated attempt to take our lives."

"How can that be?" said Lucretia. "Why would someone attack us? Surely you are imagining the perils."

"There is no mistake. We were the intended victims. I have received whispered warnings about the danger that imperil many of us. At first, I ignored these admonitions. But I continued to hear such things, and last night confirmed that danger. Listen to me, Lucretia, and please do not interrupt. Rome faces great turmoil—a political upheaval— after Caesar's death. Antonius, Octavius, and Lepidus— the ruthless Triumvirate— are the new players on the scene, and they plot to make war against Caesar's assassins."

"But you were not part of that group. You—"

"Lucretia, please listen to me. You don't understand. The new rulers need money to finance their government and wage war. There have been whispers that they will employ proscription to seize the property and wealth of those who were allied with the Liberators. You have heard of proscription and what Sulla introduced years ago? It's a callous and brutal practice that ensnares the guilty and innocent alike."

Lucretia's face froze in fear. "But why us? We are only minor players in the political landscape."

"I am related to Quintus Antistius Labeo, one of the conspirators. He is my cousin. That's all the excuse they need."

"But what can we do? Surely, you can reason with them and pledge loyalty?"

"The harsh reality is that they don't require my loyalty, only my money," he declared. "We must flee Rome. Escape to one of the provinces." Cilo paused for a moment, deep in thought. "They would probably be watching, so we must flee at night." Cilo hushed down to barely a whisper. "I have a plan. I've been liquidating my various properties lately. We have money. Our chests are full and secured in this house. I will have Alderic and Diomedes move the chests by wagon to a safe location—the house of our dear friend Gaius Silvanus. His home is outside the walls of the city and en route to our escape. We can trust him. He is a loyal friend. You know the two of us have had many business deals together. He is a man of honor. After we collect our chests of coin, we can board a ship at Ostia to take us away from danger."

Lucretia nodded meekly, her face still in fear, deferring to her husband. A look of disquiet creased her face. "What about the slaves? What will become of them?" she asked.

Cilo put his arm reassuringly around his wife. "I've taken care of that as well. I have left instructions with Silvanus for their emancipation as well as a small sum of money for each of them."

Lucretia, shaken to her core, had tears glistening on her face. "I had no idea the political situation was this perilous. I will miss our home in Rome, but if we must flee, then so be it."

Later that day, Alderic was summoned by one of the slaves to the master's study. He was told that the senator was waiting for him there. A worried frown creased his face. *Had I done something wrong?* His only transgression had been taking Lucius to the brothel. Surely, they couldn't have discovered that. Lucius would have never told his parents about the episode. He reached the *tablinium* located in the front of the house. He had never been inside this particular space before; it was the senator's inner sanctum.

He knocked politely on the thin partition, and immediately, the senator's voice bid him to enter. Alderic entered to see the senator seated at his work table with Diomedes, his Greek freedman, seated to his right. Alderic had had little contact with Diomedes, but what he knew of him, he didn't like. He was balding and in his middle years. His demeanor had always been a bit haughty. Alderic supposed that since he had been granted his manumission some time ago, he felt superior to all the other slaves in the household. The other servants also appeared to share Alderic's sentiments, frequently offering a disparaging comment about the freedman. He knew that the senator trusted the Greek implicitly, delegating many household responsibilities to him.

Alderic was not offered a seat, so he continued standing. The senator addressed him: "I'm sure you don't understand much about Roman politics, being new here in Rome?" He continued without waiting for a reply. "Unfortunately, my family and I are in grave danger. I cannot explain the details at the moment, but suffice it to say, our lives are threatened. That attack on the street the other day was no random act of violence. We were targeted. We must flee the city, and you and Diomedes must help us."

"I protect you, wife, and son from harm. I keep you safe."

"Thank you, Alderic," Cilo smiled. A noble sentiment. "But you cannot defend us from the many people that might wish to harm us. You may continue to serve us in our new home, wherever that might be." He looked straight into Alderic's eyes, his smile fading. "Listen carefully. This is what we're going to do tomorrow. In the morning, Diomedes will bring a covered cart to the home's alley at the back, away from prying eyes. You will load my chests of coins into the cart, which you must note are quite heavy. You and Diomedes will drive the cart beyond the walls of Rome and exit on Via Ostiensis. Not far from the city limits is the home of my good friend, Gaius Silvanus. Leave the chests with him and the wagon. The two of you are to then return here by foot." He paused for a breath. "Tomorrow night, under the cover of darkness, my family and I, along with you and Diomedes, will depart and walk to Silvanus's home. From there, we will take the road up to the port of Ostia and board a ship. I believe that it would be safest to cross the sea to the eastern part of the empire. We will need to evaluate our options once we reach the port. Understood?"

"I bring weapons, yes?"

"Absolutely, arm yourself with a gladius, dagger, and a wooden staff. There is a lot of gold and silver you will be transporting. Guard it with your life. Tomorrow is going to be demanding, so try and get some rest."

Alderic turned to leave.

"Wait. One more thing," said Cilo as he came up to Alderic. "You are not to discuss with or tell anyone about this conversation, not even the other slaves. No one. If word gets out that we are planning to escape, we are all doomed."

"I understand."

The next day, Alderic huffed as he carried the five heavy chests down a long subterranean hallway that connected the senator's house to a rear alley, which was barely wide enough to permit a wagon to pass through. The wooden chests were banded with iron straps on the bottom for extra support. He deposited the containers next to the heavy oak door that was always barred from the inside. Like most Roman houses, this one had a large front entranceway and a side ingress for the slaves and the delivery of goods. Cilo's house was unique in that it had a third portal—a rear entranceway that almost no one knew about. It was rarely, if ever, used.

Alderic wiped the sweat from his brow, waiting in the passage for Diomedes to rap on the door, indicating his arrival with the wagon. A small oil lamp was the only source of illumination in the dark recess. Cobwebs hung from the rafters. It was still early in the morning, and Alderic had no idea how long it was going to take for Diomedes to arrive. His stomach was queasy. There was no mistaking the aura of fear that enveloped the senator when he had spoken to him yesterday. Alderic had little understanding of the politics, but there was no question in his mind that this was a precarious situation. He inhaled deeply to calm himself. He wished he had someone to talk to, to dispel his nervousness. He sighed. If he could face the fearsome Baladar, he could certainly handle this task.

He briefly mused about where they might go. He was ignorant about the other lands and peoples in the empire, except for his homeland, which he could only assume was one of the last places they might flee to. He chose not to dwell on the subject. It was beyond his purview of understanding.

Alderic released the heavy iron bar securing the door when he heard a rap from the other side of the door. He pushed outward, and the door creaked slowly open. Diomedes stood on the other side, the wagon parked several paces down the alley. "Hurry up and load the chests," he ordered. "The sooner we can get the cargo to the house, the safer it will be." With that, he turned and went to the front of the wagon, not offering to help Alderic load the treasure.

Alderic grunted as he loaded the last of the chests, and then climbed onto the wagon's seat with Diomedes. "Thanks for helping," he said sardonically.

Diomedes stared straight ahead, ignoring the barb. He jerked the reins and yelled at the mules. "Ha!" The cart moved slowly down the stygian alley to emerge into the sunlight as they entered a paved avenue. They moved slowly through the streets, already crowded with traffic. The wagon rumbled over the paving stones, with the mules' hooves clopping as they struck the pavement, as it journeyed westward. Alderic scrutinized the road ahead for any sign of trouble, but all he saw were mobs of people and other carts. Every so often, he would caress the hilt of his gladius for reassurance.

The cart neared the exit gate of the city. Several bored legionnaires and their officers stood guard at the gateway, observing the flow of traffic. Suddenly, the centurion of the guard stepped in the path of the wagon transporting hay immediately before them. He yelled at his legionnaires. "Search this cart."

The two legionnaires climbed aboard, poking about with their swords into the straw. One of the soldiers took his javelin and rammed it deep into the mound of hay. He turned to his centurion and shook his head. The centurion looked at the driver. "Why are you transporting this load out of the city? It should be coming in, not out."

The driver shrugged. "My master told me to deliver this load to the cattle yards of Marcus Pitulius. There was no one there by that name to take ownership of it. I waited, but no one appeared. My master will be most displeased."

The centurion looked at the load once again. "All right. Be on your way."

Alderic stared straight ahead. He knew there would be a lot of trouble if the legionnaires searched their wagon. Carrying this much gold and silver would raise a lot of questions. Glancing toward Diomedes, he saw sweat streaming down his face. The man was on the verge of panic. Alderic hissed, "Calm down. Loosen your grip on the reins and stare straight ahead. Act bored. This is a routine task. Understand?"

Diomedes nodded weakly. The centurion looked up at the two figures. He stared hard for a few moments, then motioned with his arm. "Go. Move it along. You're holding up traffic."

Alderic let out the breath he was holding as the wagon exited the city walls. They travelled several miles in the busy thoroughfare, although most of the movement was coming from the opposite direction into the city. They proceeded a bit farther where the traffic had halted completely. He smelled smoke in the air. Looking ahead, he saw a large, dark cloud swirling about, obscuring the landscape. Diomedes began choking on the acrid fumes. The traffic edged forward, stopping and starting repeatedly. Alderic saw bright orange tongues of flame shooting out of a large, stately dwelling, obviously the home of a wealthy person, on the right side of the road. He looked over at Diomedes, whose face paled, eyes wide in fright.

"What's the matter?"

"The smoke and the fire."

"Yes, what about it?"

"That's our destination. The home of Gaius Silvanus."

Chapter VI

Darus and his gang of ruffians, known as the brotherhood of the docks, controlled the wharves. "Brotherhood" was a rather charitable term. In truth, these men were a savage bunch of cut-throats and hooligans who would slip a dagger between your ribs for a single denarius. By most accounts, Darus, the leader, was a loathsome individual. He ruled his small empire of crime by fear, and those around him tread cautiously, for he was infamous for cutting people's throats simply on whim. He had a dark complexion with a mass of greasy cascading locks. He stood with his henchmen in the shadows, observing the home of Senator Cilo from afar. Two of his men, who had been stationed closer to the domicile, trotted up to him. "Everyone is at home and accounted for," they reported. "No one has departed the premises this morning."

Darus smiled. "Good. We are going to have a little party. Carve-up some rich people." His men grinned in anticipation.

Earlier this week, Darus was approached by two military men representing Marcus Antonius. They had requested his services in the looting and recovery of monies and treasures from certain families who were about to be proscribed and had been declared enemies of Rome. He and his men, as he had been informed, would be handsomely rewarded for their services. Antonius's two men had stressed that the blood couldn't be on their hands, which was why Darus and his thugs were being employed to do the dirty work. Darus couldn't have been more pleased. He was skilled in the use of violence, and that allowed him to enforce his will on the docks. The truth of the matter was that he enjoyed it. The fact that they were rich people made it that even more pleasurable. His first attempt to kill the senator on the streets had failed several evenings ago, but this time he was determined to succeed.

He waved for his gang, around a dozen equally repugnant men, to approach the front entrance of the house. Trailing behind the mob were two well-groomed men in cream colored tunics. They were set apart from the mob of unruly thugs by their appearance and demeanor. These were Antonius's agents.

The taller of Antonius's men seized the large, wolf-head iron knocker and rapped gently on the massive door.

In Alderic's absence, Rufus, one of the older servants, looked out the viewing slot and noticed the well-clad individual. Perceiving no threat, he slid the slot back and opened the door a hand's breadth apart. Two of Darus's men rushed out of their hidden positions and forcefully pushed the door wide open. A sword was rammed into Rufus's gut, silencing him before he could cry out a warning, while the remainder of the group entered and quickly slammed the door shut behind them. The band of thugs rampaged through the villa, rounding up the family and the servants of the household.

The terrorized Cilo family and their slaves huddled together in the garden toward the rear of the dwelling. One of Antonius's men unrolled a scroll. "Titus Junius Cilo, you have been declared an enemy of Rome and are now under proscription. As such, all of your property is to be forfeited and, if necessary, your lives."

The senator stood dejected, knowing he had waited too long to flee. His fate was cast. He summoned the courage to speak, and his voice came loud and ringing. "Do what you wish with me but spare my wife and son."

Darus rushed over and punched him in the face, drawing blood from his smashed lips. "You don't give the orders here. We do. Now shut your filthy mouth and only talk when asked."

Several of Darus's henchmen, who had been tasked with searching the house, filtered back to the gathering in the courtyard. Darus glared at them. "Well? What have you found?"

A dreadful looking figure with a misshapen face and a missing eye spoke. "We found no coin."

This infuriated Darus. "Where's the money, Senator?" he spat out.

Cilo shook his head. "What money?"

Darus pointed at Lucretia. "Bring her here."

Two of the men grabbed the cowering woman. Lucretia, screaming in terror, was dragged before Darus. "Maybe this will refresh your memory," he said. With that, he ripped the front of Lucretia's gown, exposing her ample breasts. He grabbed one in his grimy paws and produced a wicked knife. "What a stunning figure. Here's how it's going to go, Senator. You're going to tell me where the coin is or I will begin slowly sawing off one of her breasts. And then the other. Now, where is the money?"

Cilo answered quickly. "My freedman and one of the slaves took my treasure chests to the house of Gaius Silvanus this morning."

"You lie, Senator. I've had that house watched. No one departed this house this morning." He flicked the knife and made a shallow cut down her right breast. Lucretia screamed.

"Stop! Stop! It's true. Don't hurt her. My men used the back entrance in the alley. They loaded a wagon early this morning."

Darus paused, his knife still held against Lucretia's breast, then motioned to one of his men. "Check it out. See if there is a back entrance. And make it fast." He turned back to the senator, brandishing his dagger. "For your sake, you had best be telling the truth."

A short time later the man returned. "Darus, there's a back entrance that leads to an alley."

One of Antonius's men spoke. "Where did they take the money?"

"To my friend's house."

"And who is this friend?"

"Gaius Silvanus."

Darus turned toward Antonius's men. "Did you hear that? The senator was one step ahead of us … but not quite quick enough. What about my cut of the money?"

The taller of the pair replied, "You will get paid. We will have our men search for this wagon and Silvanus's house. As I recall, he is also on the proscription list, so there is nowhere they could go. I would suggest you post your men here, in the event that the two others return. I will have my colleague, Drusus, stay here with you. You can keep whatever treasure you find in this house."

Darus gestured with his arm. "What about them?"

"They are on the proscription list and have been declared enemies of the state. Do what you want, just wait until I leave."

"And the slaves?"

Antonius's man shrugged. "They are of no importance to us."

The tall man departed, but not before he heard the first scream reverberated through the house.

Alderic turned to Diomedes. "Keep the wagon moving past Silvanus's house. Don't stop. This isn't our affair. Eyes straight ahead."

Diomedes lurched at the reins, urging the mules onward. The wagon rumbled past the dwelling as smoke continued to spill out the windows and roof. A large crowd had gathered, and several bodies were sprawled by the side of the road. The blood stains on them indicating that they were certainly not the victims of a fire. The freedman inquired timidly, "But what are we to do now? We have a wagon full of gold and silver that we can't deliver. I assume we should turn around at the first opportunity and head back to the senator's house. He will know what to do."

Alderic concentrated on what the freedman was saying, so there was no misunderstanding. His suggestion was to turn around and go back to the city, and it seemed a reasonable course of action, probably even the easiest thing to do at this point, but something wasn't right. There was no mistaking the fear in the senator's voice last evening. Whatever had occurred at Silvanus's house was no accident. This wasn't a random act of violence directed at the good friend of the senator and certainly not a coincidence. It must be related to the problem that the senator faced. If this man's house had been attacked, Alderic reasoned, then perhaps the senator's dwelling had been seized as well. He pondered the situation, turning the matter over in his mind. He sat up straight, his eyes blazing. He knew what to do.

"Diomedes, we traveled this road several weeks ago when we visited the senator's family crypt, yes?"

"As a matter of fact, yes, we did. You have a good memory. But what does that have to do with our current dilemma?"

"This crypt is considered sacred, yes? What is name you call it?"

"It is a sepulcher, Alderic. A sepulcher."

"Last time you had the key to vault door. You still have it?"

Diomedes smugly patted the pouch hanging from his waist. "Yes, I have all of the keys to the senator's household in my possession. But what are we going—"

"We hide chests in the vault and lock the door. We can recover the chests when the senator says so."

"But why don't we take it back to the house."

Alderic glared at the freedman. "Those enemies of the senator may have attacked his family as well. Too dangerous to take the wagon back. Safer to hide the chests here. We must be careful when we return."

Diomedes wilted under his gaze. "I suppose you're right. The chests of coin should be safe in the crypt."

"I can conceal the chests in the unused part of the tomb. There is much empty space. It is close?"

"Yes, the family crypt is just ahead. You can almost see it from here."

They trundled farther down the road. The wagon slowed and pulled up next to the tomb. Other ornate vaults, belonging to the wealthier families in Rome, were clustered in the vicinity. The Cilo family crypt was a large, elaborate stone building. The thick walls of the structure stood some twenty feet high with an arched doorway and a vaulted roof. Diomedes dismounted from the wagon and produced the large iron key to open the massive door to the entrance. Both men looked about to see if anyone was observing them.

The pair crossed the threshold and entered the dim interior. An array of niches built into the wall held urns containing the ashes of the senator's ancestors. A large part of the crypt was not yet in use, reserved for future generations. Alderic wrinkled his nose at the musty odor and then wandered over to the empty section. There was an interior wall partially constructed to contain niches for future urns. The flooring slabs ended at around a foot from the rough stone exterior wall. This is where the plaster and frescoed wall would be constructed when needed.

Alderic bent at the knees and grasped one the stone slab sections used for the flooring. He heaved with all his strength, and slowly, the slab lifted from its brick support, revealing a crawl space between the flooring and the foundation of the tomb. He turned to Diomedes. "We put chests here to hide. No one will see. We must hurry."

Alderic carefully carried the five chests from the wagon to the subterranean space beneath the floor. He was in the process of placing the last chest when he stopped. "We take some money in case we need it in Rome. Give me key to chest."

"Are you out of your mind? That's stealing. The senator will have us crucified. I won't give you the key." He crossed his arms in petulance.

Alderic grabbed the freedman by the neck. "You will give me key now. You can say it was my idea. I made you. We can give money back to senator if all is well. But if there is problem in Rome, we must escape. To flee, we will need money. Men will look for us. They will want all of gold and silver. Once they know about location of vault, they kill us. You understand?"

Diomedes, clearly out of his element, reluctantly handed the key to the chest. "This was your idea. You forced me to do this."

Alderic gave him a hard stare. "Diomedes?"

"What?"

"You are ass pain."

"No, Alderic. We say 'pain in the ass.'"

"Same thing."

Diomedes sighed. "Learn the language, you ignorant barbarian."

Alderic's face filled with fury. He grabbed the front of Diomedes tunic and drew him in. He scowled at Diomedes, who cringed in fear, knowing he had crossed the bounds. "You listen to me from now, Greek, and maybe you get to live."

Alderic used the key to open the last chest. He scooped the gold and silver coins into the purse attached to his waist, not bothering to count it. He grabbed another handful and offered it to Diomedes. Reluctantly, the freedman dropped the coins into his pouch as well.

It was late afternoon by the time the two men approached the senator's house from the back alley. They had returned the rented wagon to its owner on the outskirts of Rome with the provision that they might return later in the day to use it again. If people were looking for them, they would be searching for a wagon with two men. They crept down the darkened alley. All was silent, nothing out of place. Alderic pushed the door. It emitted its usual groan. He drew his gladius from its sheath. "Stay with me. There may be dangerous men in the house. Stay by my side. Understand?"

Diomedes nodded, his pale face filled with dread.

The pair walked silently through the underground passage, Diomedes meekly following in his footsteps. They slowly made their way down the tunnel and into the garden. There were several hints for Alderic to know immediately that something was amiss. First, was the smell. A cloying odor he had experienced once before—the tang of blood and death in the arena. They slowly inched forward. The next hint was the stillness. There was no sound of any activity in the house. Nothing.

They moved into the open courtyard to see the senator's family and the servants, or rather, what remained of them. They had all been butchered. Great pools of blood lay stagnant everywhere. Alderic only needed a glimpse to know that their ending had not been swift. The senator lay amid the shrubbery, numerous cuts and gouges adorning his body. His wife had been stripped naked. Who knew what torments she had endured? Finally, there was young Lucius. He had a single gaping wound to his throat.

Eight figures emerged out of the shadows. A man with dark curly hair and a perpetual sneer on his face spoke. "We wondered when you might show up."

Alderic glanced at the bunch of gangsters before him. They wore grimy tunics, now splattered in blood and gore. He tightened the grip on his short sword, measuring his chances.

The leader continued. "Now drop that sword and tell us where the money is. We may even let you live. No use denying that you have the coin. They told us everything." He gestured to the bodies with his knife to make his point.

Alderic stared at the bodies on the ground and the gaping wound in Lucius's throat. A boiling rage enveloped him. Cilo's house had taken him in and showed him kindness. Lucius was like a younger brother to him. He wanted vengeance. His gladiatorial training took over. In a matter of moments, he had decided upon his plan of attack. Alderic calmed himself, keeping his facial expression impassive. He would eliminate the speaker first, obviously the leader of the goons. After that, he would destroy the two men on either side of him. Finally, beyond these men, there was the one wearing a cream-colored tunic. Although he appeared less threatening than the others, he was the one most likely responsible for this carnage. Pure and simple, he must die. With a roar, he charged.

The gang leader was first. Alderic slashed downward with the sword. The figure was surprisingly agile. He avoided most of the blow, but the tip of the sword cut a slice down the side of his face. Screaming in pain, he fell back, holding his head, blood leaking between his fingers. Alderic easily took out the other two thugs; first, with a forward slash that disemboweled one and then a backward slash to the throat of the other. He then charged at the figure in the fine tunic, thrusting his sword deep into his chest. He brutally twisted the blade as he pulled it out for maximum damage. By this time, the others had recovered. One of the ruffians took the opportunity to plunge his sword into Diomedes, who collapsed with a gasp. Knowing Diomedes was a dead man and realizing there was nothing more to be gained by continuing to fight, Alderic turned and fled back the subterranean chamber and away from the house of horrors.

Alderic bolted down the alley onto the main thoroughfare. Realizing he was conspicuous, running with a bloody sword in his hand, he sheathed the weapon and slowed to a brisk walk. His sole purpose was to put as much distance as possible from the senator's house. He walked aimlessly for some time, unaware of his surroundings. Soon, shadows cast their pall on the buildings and streets. He noted that it was almost twilight and people were beginning to exit the streets. At a crossroads, a patrol of urban cohorts abruptly materialized before him. The group of twenty men marched in formation in full armor, their expressions stern. The officer in front of the men gave Alderic a brief glance, then did a double take, his eyes wide in astonishment. "Seize that man!" he roared, "He is a fugitive and wanted for questioning."

In shock that the officer was pointing at him, Alderic momentarily stood frozen in place. But not for long. He deftly eluded the grasp of two of the guards, then fled down the narrow street, shoving people out of his path. He heard shouts behind him, but he dared not look back, lest it slow him down. Running hard, he made several turns down random alley-ways, following their twisting paths, before emerging in another lane. He stopped in the deep shadows of a tenement and bent over panting.

It was almost dark, which was good, for it would conceal him from his pursuers. He had no idea where he was. He didn't want to spend the night on the streets and knew he had best find a place to stay. A chill was descending with the darkness, and he was exhausted. There were many inns from which to choose. He fingered the heavy purse at his waist. He had a lot of money, courtesy of Cilo's treasury. He could afford to stay anywhere. He started walking, hoping to find one of the main avenues of the city. A good bed and a cup of wine would do him good. Besides, he was too noticeable on the streets, better to be secluded in a room somewhere.

Upon reaching a paved street, he turned left and approached a small establishment that appeared to be busy. Laughter and shouts reverberated onto the street. Good. He would blend into the crowd. It had a sign above the entrance, announcing itself as the "Grunting Boar." Noted underneath the logo were few words indicating that rooms were available upstairs. The aroma of food emanating from the doorway was enticing. Alderic entered and strode up to the main serving area. Behind the counter, amphorae of wine and large bowls of steaming food were set in recesses on a wooden plank. The proprietor turned toward Alderic, wiping his hands on a stained apron. "What can I get you?"

Alderic was about to point to one of the amphora, when the proprietor abruptly pointed at Alderic and shouted, "Milo! Narsic! It's him!"

Two figures, brandishing long daggers, erupted from the shadows. Fortunately, one of the patrons, alarmed at the clamor, chose that moment to get up from the bar, directly in the path of the two assailants. Their thrusts fell short of Alderic. He would have been skewered had the other man not hindered their lunges. Alderic dashed out the door and back into the night, running for his life.

Macro sat in his quarters at the gladiatorial school, finishing his meal. Two small oil lamps burned to provide the meager illumination. Sighing in contentment, he dusted some crumbs off his hand and rose from his chair. A slave burst into his quarters, a look of alarm upon his face. "Master, sorry for the intrusion, but armed men at the gate bearing the seal of Marcus Antonius are demanding to see you."

Macro scowled. "What kind of shit is this? Can't they see it's dark outside? This can't wait until morning? All right, let's go see what they want." He picked up an oil lamp and followed the slave into the night.

Macro arrived at the iron-barred gate where five individuals, tough-looking military men, were waiting for him. They had a certain look about them; erect postures and heavily muscled, with an aura of cruelty. A tall lean man with a thin scar down the right of his face stood at the helm of the others. Several bore torches, illuminating the night. Scar-face did not attempt an introduction. He glowered at Macro. "Are you Macro, the owner of this establishment?"

"Yes, I am the lanista here. What's so urgent that it couldn't wait until morning?"

The man snarled in reply. "It's not up to you to decide when we come. That's my choice. I come under the seal of Marcus Antonius. You will answer my questions right away or I will have you flogged or worse at this very spot. Understood?"

Macro knew these were powerful men and it would be prudent not to fuck with them or offer an insolent reply. "What is it you want?"

"You can let us enter for a start," he demanded.

Macro unfastened the lock and slowly pulled the cumbersome gate open. The men filed inside the compound.

"You had a gladiator here named Alderic?"

"Yes, we did. But he left us months ago. He is in the employ of Senator Titus Junius Cilo."

Scar-face snapped in reply. "I know who employed him. Is he here now?"

"Now why would he be here?"

"Just answer the question. Or would you rather have my companions here teach you some manners?"

Macro grimaced. He was not used to having people order him around. "No, he isn't here. What do you want with him?"

Scar-face nodded to one of his men. The figure stepped forward and smashed Macro in the mouth. Scar-face smirked as Macro wiped his bloody mouth. "For the last time, we will ask the questions. You answer them. Got it?"

The lanista nodded, dabbing his split lip.

Antonius's man continued. "Is there anyone here who might have contact with him?"

Macro nodded. "Yes. He was friends with one of our gladiators, Lothar."

"Have him brought here immediately."

Macro gestured to the slave cowering behind him. "Go fetch Lothar at once."

The men waited in silence, with only the guttering of the torches for company. A short while later, Lothar appeared out of the darkness. He looked inquiringly at Macro.

Macro spoke to Lothar with a warning glance. "These men are agents of Marcus Antonius. They are looking for Alderic. Have you had any contact with him?"

"As a matter of fact, yes. I saw him weeks ago. He came here to see me."

"What about?"

Lothar stared at Scar-face. "I don't see how that concerns you."

The leader gestured at his men. "Teach him a lesson in manners." The four men jumped the unfortunate Lothar and began pummeling him with their fists. When they finished, three men held him, while one of the men produced a dagger. He sliced a wound down the side of Lothar's face. The unfortunate gladiator screamed in pain.

"Are you ready to answer my questions now?"

Lothar moaned in agony and shook his head, indicating that he was ready. Blood streamed in rivulets down his face. "He came to see me about a brothel. His master's son wanted to go to one and needed a recommendation."

Scar-face snarled. "What did you tell him?"

"I mentioned a place I'd heard about."

"And what was it called?"

"The Palace of Venus, over by the curia."

Scar-face leaned in close to Lothar. "And of what else did you speak?"

Lothar, now released by the heavies, held his palm to his wound to stop the bleeding. "There is no what else. That's all we talked about. He promised to look me some time in the future and buy me some wine."

"He hasn't contacted you since?"

"No, I haven't seen him."

Scar-face turned to Macro. "Who else does this Alderic know?"

Macro answered. "His trainer was an ex-gladiator named Labenius. He was the one who arranged his sale to the senator."

"Do you know where this Labenius lives?"

Macro shrugged and held out his hands. "No. I'm not really sure," he lied.

Scar faced snorted. "No matter. We will find out." With that, the men turned about and exited the compound.

Macro stared after the departing figures. "Arrogant pricks," he mumbled. "What is Rome coming to?" He turned to Lothar and grasped the man's face. Holding it up to the light, he sighed. "Come on, let's get you stitched up."

Alderic shivered in the cold, as he huddled deep in the recesses of an alley that stank of garbage and feces. No one would find him here. After all, who in their right minds would venture into this filthy alcove? He understood that powerful people were searching for him, and it would be highly risky to attempt entering another tavern. He was safe for now, but had no idea what he was to do tomorrow. He could try to visit Lothar, his only friend, but that made no sense. By now, the lanista would have been informed that Alderic needed to be captured. He pondered briefly. What about Labenius? He tried to remember where Labenius lived. It came back to him. As Alderic remembered, Labenius had told him that it was at the base of the Viminal on a street … a street called Mercury. That was it. He also said that he lived above a store that sold iron pots and cookware. He would seek the dwelling of Labenius in the morning. He felt safe here. He closed his eyes, attempting to sleep.

The next day, stiff and bleary-eyed, Alderic ventured forth to find Labenius's house. There was a chance that his dwelling would be under observation, but that would be a risk he would have to take. If his reckoning was correct, he was near the base of the Esquiline, which meant he would need to move north. He kept a wary eye out for the urban cohorts, hunching over and blending with the crowd. He made a number of turns in the direction he believed Labenius's dwelling to be located.

Fortunately, with his excellent sense of direction, he found the residence quite easily. He traveled a short way up the street named Mercury and found a storefront with a crude sign advertising cooking implements and pots. He moved into the shadows of a nearby building and studied the surrounding area. He peered about, looking for something that was out of place, although he wasn't sure what that might be. He noted a man with a small push cart, standing idly by. But after a short while, he moved on down the avenue, slowly shoving the cart forward. A group of three men turned the corner, walking abreast of each other, talking in loud voices, who too soon disappeared down the road. Detecting nothing amiss, he advanced across the road and bounded up the wooden stairs. He tapped on the door above the shop several times, furtively looking over his shoulder to see if anyone was observing.

The door opened almost immediately. The craggy face of Labenius appeared in the opening. "Alderic! What are you doing here? Get in." He yanked his former acolyte inside and quickly shut the door behind him. "What have you gotten yourself into? There were armed men here last night asking if I had been in contact with you. They said you have killed one of Antonius's men and wounded one of the primary gang leaders in Rome. They are turning the city inside-out looking for you."

Alderic interrupted his former trainer with a sudden burst of words. "The senator and his family are all dead. Cilo ask me to transport his chests of coin to safe location. I hide money. Master was going to flee Rome next day. When I return to house in afternoon, I saw family and servants slaughtered and bad men waiting for me. I kill some and flee. I was pursued several times last night and—"

Labenius interrupted, "Practically the entire city is seeking you. Very powerful people are after you. I don't believe you understand the grave danger you are in. The soldiers and the gang members are combing the streets. Look at you. Your height is a curse. There are not many men in Rome as tall as you." He jabbed at Alderic's tunic and light cloak. "You look like you've been in the arena. Your clothing is stippled with blood splatters."

"I not understand why they kill senator and his family. This would not happen in homeland. And they call us barbarians."

Labenius sighed. "Alderic, the politics of Rome are extremely complicated and can be very brutal."

"But what should I do? Can I show them where money is? Then they stop looking for me?"

"Listen to me. Tell no one where the money is hidden, including me. They will torture you and kill you if they capture you. Get out of Rome any way you can and escape into the countryside. The farther away, the better. Go north, go south. It doesn't matter. Just get away. Don't try to board a ship. The ports will be watched. You must somehow blend in, which is going to be difficult given your size. Start by getting some new clothes. I have nothing here that fits you. Do you have any money?"

Alderic hefted his money pouch. "Yes, I have much money from the senator's chest."

"Good. Now you can stay here for part of the day and rest, but you must leave. I'm in extreme danger just for giving you shelter. They will come back here. I know it. These men want that money and your life. Once you depart from here, trust no one. Understand? No one. Have you eaten?"

Alderic shook his head.

"Let me get you some food. You're probably starved."

Chapter VII

Alderic ventured out warily in the late afternoon. He traveled southwest toward the Tiber, where the commercial district was located. The traffic was thickest there, and he figured he would better blend in that section of Rome. He avoided the main thoroughfares, which funneled the traffic from the Aventine to the markets along the river. Hunched over to shrink his tall form, he hurried through the back alleys before reaching his destination. His nose immediately informed him that he had arrived at Forum Boarium—the cattle markets of Rome. His first order of business was to buy some new clothes.

He noticed a small shop from across the avenue, with a crude, wooden sign advertising clothing for men and women. Seeing no suspicious persons in the vicinity, he quickly crossed the avenue and entered the shop to find that he was the only customer. The proprietors were an older couple of indeterminate age, who, thankfully, didn't appear alarmed to see him. Relieved that not everyone in Rome was on alert for his presence, he spoke quickly to alleviate any fears they might have, for he knew his size alone could be intimidating. "I need new clothes. I have stains from working in cattle market." He pointed to the blood splotches on his tunic and cloak. The couple nodded sympathetically.

The husband studied his height. "I have only a few garments your size. Come over here." He pointed to various garments hanging from pegs on the wall. Alderic toyed with the various apparel. The weave was rough, which suited him just fine. He wanted to blend in, not stand out like a rich man. The first two tunics were nearly white in color. That would not do when he would hide in the night. The last tunic was a dreary dark grey. He held it up. It appeared to be close to his size. *Perfect.* "I take this. I need new cloak too. Not too heavy."

"We have only one that would fit you," he said as he fetched it from a nearby shelf.

Alderic hefted the garment, which was also greyish in color. "I would like to wear these, if they fit."

The man gestured toward a curtained recess. Alderic changed his clothes there, making sure the new cloak concealed the sword and dagger strapped to his waist. The new clothes appeared to fit well enough. He exited the changing area. "How much?" he asked.

The wife stepped ahead, clearly the negotiator. "Because of your size, we will need to charge you extra. Six denarii."

Alderic frowned. *That is too much.* He realized he should have bargained first before letting them know he was going to buy the clothes; but it was too late for that now. He needed to negotiate some, but not excessively so. He wanted the clothes and didn't wish to linger in the shop, in case someone else entered. "The cloth is rough weave. I like the fit, but you are asking a high price. I will give three denarii."

The wife pouted. "How can we make any money at such a price? Five is a fair amount."

"I will pay four, and you can keep my old clothes. That is all or I will leave."

The women pretended to consider his offer, but hastily replied. "We will accept four. Thank you for the business."

Alderic smiled and counted out four denarii before handing them over the woman. It was probably too much, but he had other things on his mind. Without further ado, he departed. He wandered about, occasionally holing up in an alley or recess where no one was around. He moved along, at last noting the encroaching darkness. It was twilight, and the streets were beginning to empty. He chose the next small alley he saw and entered it without looking back. He made his way through the rubbish to a foul-smelling recess off the side street and hunched down with his back to a tenement's wall. Exhaustion was settling on him, and he decided to shut his eyes for a few moments. His right hand resting on the hilt of his sword, he drifted off into troubled sleep.

Shouts and running footsteps resounded in the night. Alderic bolted awake. It was pitch black. His heart pounding, he was instantly alert. Drawing his sword from its scabbard, he crept forward from the small recess and peered down the alleyway. He could discern the sound of hurried steps and panting breath. In the sliver of moonlight available, he spied a figure briefly hesitating before running down the alley toward him. In the distance, he saw men with torches moving in his direction.

The fugitive was leading the men in pursuit directly to his hiding spot. Alderic deftly stepped out of the shadows and grasped the figure around the torso, clamping his other hand over the mouth. With a heave, he jerked the person back into his recess. Looking at the figure's face and feeling the softness of the body, he was astounded to find he was holding a woman. He peered into her eyes that were wide with fright and whispered in her ear. "Don't make sound. I'll not hurt you. I take my hand away if you promise not to scream. Understand?"

The woman stared at him dazed, then nodded. Alderic slowly slid his hand away from her mouth. "Shh. No noise." There were more shouts. Alderic furtively peeped out of the recess to see the men at the head of the alley staring in their direction. Seeing nothing, they moved on. With the light from their torches gone, the backstreet was once again bathed in total darkness.

Alderic stared at the woman, his face close to hers. "What are you doing by yourself in this part of town? This is a dangerous place, full of thieves and murderers."

The woman spat back. "I could ask you the same question. Which one are you? A thief or a murderer? And while we are at it, could you please get your hand off my breast."

"Oh, sorry. It wasn't intentional." Alderic let go of his grasp. He turned his gaze back to the alley to see if there was any danger. Seeing no threat, he sheathed his sword. He turned toward the woman and was met with a sharp slap to the face. "What was that for?"

"That was for scaring the shit out of me a few moments ago."

He rubbed his throbbing jaw. "At least you're safe now. Why were those men after you? You must have done something."

He noticed the woman hesitate.

Alderic let out an exasperated sigh. "Oh, for Wodan's sake! What you think I'll do? Turn you over to the urban cohorts? "

"I'm a runaway slave," she blurted out. "My master was trying to get me into his bed. I resisted at first but knew that sooner or later he would have forced me. The worst part was that if his wife found out about it—which she would eventually, for nothing escapes that bitch in her household—I would be sold to the brothels. I had no alternative. I had to escape."

"Looks like you didn't get too far."

"I can't believe I'm telling you these things. I don't even know your name. I'm Bridin."

"My name is Alderic."

"Alderic? That's German. Oh, isn't this just bloody great. Now I'm stuck with a German barbarian. I have some nasty people chasing me and look what I have for a companion. Now tell me why you're here lurking in an alley. There are better places in Rome to spend the night. Come on. Out with it."

"It's a long story. I'm not sure you want to hear it."

"At the moment I have nowhere else to go. Tell me."

"I have many people searching for me—all of Rome. I am a slave like you, but I not run away. Bad people kill my master and his family, including servants. I escaped the house. Now they look for me. I do nothing wrong."

"Then why are so many people searching for you. There must be a reason."

Alderic stared into the darkness. Remembering Labenius's words about trusting anyone, he was silent. He mulled a reply, and at last he spoke. "You ask too many questions, Bridin."

"Out with it," she replied impatiently.

Alderic sighed. "If you really want to know, my master made me transport chests of gold and silver. He was going to flee Rome, because powerful men didn't like him. I hid silver and gold in safe place. When I come back to house, I found them all dead. Bad men were waiting for me. I killed some of them and fled. One of the men I killed was accomplice of some man named Antonius. The others were members of the street gangs."

"Let me understand this. You killed one of Marcus Antonius's men? Do you have any idea who he is?"

"I heard he is important man."

"Important man!" she exclaimed. "Yes, he is an important man, probably the most powerful one in Rome. So, he wants not only the money you hid but also your head on a spike."

"Yes, that sounds correct. I must get out of this city. I must flee where they can't find me. I have no friends who can help me. I must try something tomorrow, not sure what. You want to come with me? I have money." He hefted his purse as proof.

She stared at him, contemplating her next words. She hesitated, then took a step away from Alderic "I don't know if I should trust you." She wavered for a few moments. "Oh well, I suppose I have nothing to lose. They will catch me if I stay in this city. What do you suggest we do for the remainder of the night?"

Alderic extended his arm. "Welcome to my abode. We stay here. They have all the wine shops and inns under observation. I cannot go to public place. Come sit here with me. Think about what we can do tomorrow to get out of Rome."

The two moved deeper into the recess and sat down. It was a cold night, and he observed that the woman wore thin garments and was beginning to shiver. Alderic extended his arm, holding his cloak out so that they could share it. The two huddled there, waiting for the morning.

Alderic roused first in the grey light of early dawn and got his first real look at Bridin. She had a pretty face framed by ginger hair. She lay huddled against him, no doubt exhausted from her ordeal. He let her sleep, pondering how he was going to escape the city. At some point, he would need to exit through one of the gates. The walls were taller than six men put together, so he could not possibly climb to the top or jump over. He assumed all the traffic entering and leaving the city would be under great scrutiny. There had to be a way.

He was gazing at her face when Bridin awoke. She stared at him startled for a moment before she recalled the events of the night. She gathered herself. "I thought about your plight—well, perhaps *our* plight—before I went to sleep last night. I have an idea."

"I would like to hear it. I can't think of anything other than dashing through the exit before anyone can catch me."

"That would never work. Listen to me. This is what we must do. We need to stay out of sight until later in the afternoon. By then, everyone will be heading out the city or going home. We will blend in with the crowd. We'll go to the commercial district and look for a wagon with an overhead cover about to leave the city. You said you had a stash of coin, so I will request a ride in exchange for some money. You slip in the back while I bargain with the owner. It will be a busy time, chaotic with all the traffic. They can't search every cart that goes through the gate. At least I don't think they will."

Alderic was silent as he considered Bridin's plan. "What about you? If you're riding with the cart, you'll be visible to all."

"I will put my hood up to look like I'm part of the driver's family. They won't be expecting an escaped slave to be there." She beamed. "I think my plan has a chance of succeeding, don't you?"

"I have nothing better. If we're caught, it is bound to end in Hades for us. You are not just runaway slave anymore, you are with me. They will kill you too if we are captured. You understand, right?"

"I have nothing to lose. I'm willing to take that risk. Now enough talk about getting caught. We are going to succeed. I'm starved. I don't suppose you have any food?"

"Funny you should ask." Alderic produced a hunk of bread he had taken with him from Labenius's house and broke it in half with a grin. He tossed the stale bread to her. She nimbly snared it out of the air and bit a piece from it.

After finishing, she dusted the crumbs from her hands. "I'm going to take a look at the gates in the walls and see how heavily guarded they are. You stay here. Your height is too noticeable. I should be back by late morning or early afternoon."

As she rose to set out from their hiding place, Alderic grabbed her by the cloak. "Don't get caught. Be careful out there."

She regarded him silently. She twirled about while adjusting the hood of her cloak to obscure her features, then left. Calling over her should she said, "I'll be back."

Hours later, she materialized back in the alley, her face weary. Sighing, she collapsed in a heap next to Alderic. "Bad news. I walked half way around the city, viewed seven gates. They're all heavily guarded. No one gets in or out of the city without close inspection. I saw one tall fellow about your size; the guards rushed over to him and knocked him to the ground. Beat the crap out of him. They took him away for questioning."

"What's the good news?"

"There is no good news. We will attempt to exit through the Porta Esquilina. It is in the commercial district. Although it's guarded heavily like the others, the crowds will be the largest there. If we get through the gate, it will put us on Via Flaminia, heading north."

Later that afternoon, the pair mingled with the surging crowd. With Alderic hunching over as before, they headed to the commercial district. This was where produce, livestock, and other goods were traded. As they neared the cattle pens of Forum Boarium, their eyes watered at the stench. They wandered until they reached the farm markets, where the fall harvest was on full display. The wooden stalls were filled with baskets of leek, onion, cabbage, lettuce, grapes, plums, apricots, and pears. It was chaos as vendors shouted out declarations of the quality of their produce and buyers quibbled over prices. Teeming crowds jammed the streets. It was just what the fugitives had wished for. Alderic surveyed the scene and immediately spotted what he was seeking. Gesturing with his head, he signaled to Bridin that he was going to enter one of the wooden stalls that had already vacated for the day. He surreptitiously ducked into the booth and slid under the counter-top, hiding him from view. Bridin ambled off, continuing her search for a likely candidate for their transport out of the city.

The marketplace soon began to empty. Bridin sauntered near the stand Alderic was using as shelter. She pretended to examine the array of fruit for sale. Catching his eye, she gave him a slight nod and then walked off. Alderic followed, shuffling along with the crowd.

Bridin boldly approached an older man loading his wagon for the journey out of the city. He was clearly a merchant of some kind. He was an older man with kindly features and a bald pate with a fringe of grey hair. He methodically heaved the empty woven baskets and coarse sheets that the baskets had rested upon.

"Excuse me, kind sir. Do you think that you could provide me transport out of city on your wagon? I would be willing to pay."

The figure eyed Bridin suspiciously. You are not in trouble, are you? There is something going on and the guards are out in force looking for someone. Not you, I hope. I won't aid criminals. Why don't you just walk?"

Bridin sighed. "Do I look like a criminal?" Without waiting for a reply, she continued, "If you want to know, the truth is that I *am* in trouble. I'm fleeing from an abusive husband who beat me all the time. I'm done with him. The only way to escape him is to leave the city. My legs are tired. I have been running all day."

"Your husband beat you? Why would he harm a pretty lady such as you? I most certainly will assist you in your quest to escape. Hop on the seat and stay with me. I could use the company. No fee." With that, he tossed the last of baskets into the back of the wagon and moved toward the front.

Bridin embraced the old man to distract him. "Oh, thank you, kind sir! You're the answers to all my prayers. By the way, my name is Claudia."

"Pleased to meet you, Claudia. They call me Petrus."

Alderic dove into the back of the covered wagon and quickly buried himself under the old blankets and assortment of woven baskets. By the time the old man and Bridin climbed onto the front seat and she had put the hood of her cloak up to mask her face, he was completely hidden. The cart jolted forward, as the two large oxen pulled the wagon through the throng heading toward the city gates.

The carriage moved slowly, stopping frequently. The surging crowd funneled to the city gate, creating a massive jam. Alderic could hear the susurration of the throng and caught occasional fragments of conversation between the two occupants in the front. Above the din, he heard commands of the urban cohorts. "Move it along now. You there! Let me see what's under that bundle." Alderic gripped the hilt of his sword, expecting a soldier's face to appear, peering into the back of the wagon. But nothing happened. After a brief pause, more shouts followed. "Keep it moving."

Alderic gasped; his heart pounded. He waited expectantly for the fateful command for this cart to be searched, but nothing more was said. He felt the coolness of the shadow of the gate's archway as the cart moved through the massive wall. *Had they done it?* Apparently so, for the oxen plodded along, farther away from the city. He heaved a sigh of relief. He was out of Rome. They journeyed onward until it neared twilight.

Alderic heard Bridin speak. "I think I will get off here if you don't mind." The wagon halted. There was no one in sight. She had selected a good location to leave.

"Are you sure you want to get out here? My village is just ahead. You can find food and shelter there."

"No, I think here is good."

Alderic attempted to unobtrusively leave the back of the wagon, but the driver felt the weight shift. He glanced back and spied Alderic. "Who's that?"

Bridin spoke quickly. "He's my boyfriend. He's helping me escape my husband."

Alderic approached the old man, who cowered in fear at the size of the approaching figure. "I have little money, please don't hurt me," he pleaded.

Alderic grinned. "Don't worry, I won't hurt you. In fact, I reward you. Here are two silver denarii for your trouble. Thank you for helping us. You have saved her from a horrible fate. If you don't mind, please don't mention you saw us. We are forever grateful. Her husband is nasty brute and will hunt her down if he finds where she has fled to."

The old man offered a gratuitous smile, staring at the two silver coins in his hand. "Thank you for the coin. Your secret is safe with me. May the Goddess Fortuna always be with you."

The pair walked down the road, heading away from the city. There was a silence between the two, before Alderic abruptly spoke. "I guess I should thank you for getting us out of the city. I never could have escaped without you."

Bridin proffered a smug smile. "Trust a woman to get you out of a mess. I'm glad it worked. It saved my butt as well."

They hiked on, down the nearly deserted road, in silence, each lost in their own thoughts. Alderic broke the silence. "So, tell me, Bridin, how did you become a slave in Rome? Were your parents slaves as well?"

She scowled. "It's not a nice story. But since we're here and have nothing better to do, I'll tell you anyway. I grew up in the province of Gaul, far north of here. My parents lived in a prosperous village. We sold woven goods—blankets, rugs, shawls, capes. My father died of the plague that swept through our settlement, so it was just my mother and me managing the business. To cut a long story short, a new magistrate was appointed to our district. He was corrupt and only sought to line his own pockets. He doubled the taxes on the local businesses, driving most of them away. My mother tried to fight it, pleading for reason with the taxes. A short time later, she died—I think it was the worry that killed her—leaving me and a lien on our store. I was quickly sold into slavery to satisfy the back taxes. Now, your turn."

"Believe it or not, I've been extremely fortunate."

She tittered. "You call this fortunate? Half of Rome is searching for you and wishes you dead."

"Laugh if you will, but you need to hear the whole story. By all accounts, I should be dead. I was captured by Roman legionnaires. My clan crossed the river into Gaul to raid the local settlements. It was the first time I was allowed to accompany the warriors. Almost the entire contingent from my tribe was killed. Only a few were spared, including me. That was my first stroke of luck. I was sold to a ludus in Rome to be trained as a gladiator; the others, I believe, were sent to the big farms to be worked to death. After a few months, I was forced to fight a skilled gladiator, a secutor, named Baladar. It was my first fight, and I was just a novice in the arena. There were heavy odds against me, something like twenty to one, but in another stroke of fortune, I prevailed."

"Wait," she said, "are you telling me that you were the retiarius who defeated Baladar? Even I, a mere household slave, heard about that. My master talked about the bout incessantly."

"Yes, it was me. It gets better. Because of the severity of my wounds, I couldn't continue to serve as a gladiator. Again, the gods intervened on my behalf. My trainer placed me as a bodyguard for a rich senator, Titus Junius Cilo. Ever heard of him?"

Bridin shook her head.

"So instead of being sold to the mines, I defy death once again."

"You are fortunate, Alderic. So, what happened next?"

"I told you about hiding the treasure and arriving back at the senator's house. Although greatly outnumbered, I slew some men and escaped. I fled into streets. A patrol of the urban cohorts was searching for me. They recognized me and chased me, but I escaped them. That night I attempted to get shelter at an inn. Two of the gang members recognized me and attempted to skewer me. They would have succeeded if a patron at the bar had not chosen that moment to step back from the bar. And then, I had the good fortune to meet you, and you got me out of the city."

"Alderic, if that is your way of issuing a compliment, I hope you can do better than that."

Alderic frowned. "What is compliment?"

"Never mind. Now, where are we going to sleep tonight?"

"I don't think it's safe to go to any inns this close to the city. They might be watching them. We will need to travel farther away from here. I suggest we find the nearest stand of trees and camp there. It's getting dark and the roads are dangerous at night. There is a copse of evergreens in that direction," he said, pointing ahead. "Let's go there."

Upon entering the grove, Alderic surveyed his surroundings. A raven flew from its perch, squawking in admonishment at the trespassers. The small bit of forest was redolent of his homeland. They were in the middle of a thick patch of trees, their trunks iron-black in the twilight. He inhaled deeply, once again savoring the reminiscent scent of the forest. They were hidden from sight unless someone left the road and entered this patch. But why would they? There was nothing here.

He thought about building a shelter. He had done it many times before, back in Germania, when he had hunted with his comrades. He turned to the north and sniffed the air. If there was rain coming, it would be from that direction; or at least, that's how it was back in his forests. He sensed they would get no rain tonight. Further, the density of the trees protected them from the wind. So, no, he wouldn't build a shelter. It wouldn't be worth the effort.

Hungry and exhausted, the pair huddled at the base of a large oak tree. The twilight morphed into a long, cold night. They managed to get a little sleep, before they were awoken by the cold and overcast day. A blanket of frost covered the landscape. They set out once more, avoiding the main roads whenever possible.

It was now mid-afternoon; they had been walking non-stop since dawn, following the road north, covering many miles. Whenever the pair encountered a village or town, they circumvented the dwellings, preferring anonymity.

Despite their fatigue of the events of the past several days, both ventured farther away from Rome. But they had other problems. The weather was starting to turn ugly. Grey scudding clouds appeared overhead and the wind picked up, blowing in gusts. Before long, it started to rain heavily, soaking the two.

Alderic stared through the deluge, hoping some shelter lay ahead. Glancing at Bridin, he noted that she was shivering. Staying outdoors was not an option tonight. They needed to reach an inn and seek accommodations, notwithstanding the risk. They were in luck; in short while, they encountered several dwellings along the road, hopefully a herald for a settlement not too far away. Alderic grabbed Bridin by the arm. "Hurry. We must get out of the rain and get a roof over our heads."

Bridin looked at him, relieved. "You will not get an argument from me about that. I hope there is a nice cozy inn waiting for us ahead."

In about half a mile, they reached a town square, dominated by a two-story brick building with a red-tiled roof. A sign over the door proclaimed it the "Happy Rooster." They paused hesitantly at the door before entering the spacious main chamber. Alderic peered about. It was a quiet place. There were a few other patrons, minding their own business, and no military men as far as he could see. He double checked the dark recesses of the room but found nothing suspicious. Alderic approached the man behind the serving area, a tall, bearded figure who looked like he ran the place. "We are weary travelers and seek food and shelter for the night."

The bearded figure appraised their disheveled appearance. "You have coin to pay?"

"Of course, I have money. Give your best room for my wife and me."

"It will cost you three denarii for the room and food. Our rooms are clean. We change the mattress straw daily. The food is freshly cooked each night. Tonight, we have boiled eggs and a meat stew."

Alderic reached into his purse and counted out three silver coins. "Show us to our room, then we will come down and eat."

The proprietor greedily accepted the coins, examining them to make sure they were real. He grabbed a small oil lamp and led them up a winding staircase to an upper level. He opened the door to a room with a window looking out into the street below. There was a wide mattress on the floor and at its foot lay several rolled blankets.

Bridin examined the room and nodded to the owner. "This will be fine. We will be down shortly. Could we get a table by the fire?"

"Certainly. I will have the dinner ready for you." The innkeeper exited, closing the door behind him.

They dried themselves the best they could and then went down to the main room of the tavern. They sat at an unoccupied table, close to a crackling fire. Alderic and Bridin tore into the food. They hadn't eaten since they'd left Rome. Alderic waved for more wine, as he spooned another portion of the stew into his mouth. Bridin hastily tore off a chunk of bread from the loaf on the table, chewing noisily on it. There was little conversation, mostly eating. At last, their hunger was sated, and they rose and headed upstairs. Alderic shut and bolted the door.

"Alderic, please turn around while I take off my damp garments." A moment later, she was under the blankets on the straw mattress. Alderic quickly stripped his water-logged clothing and hung it on the rafters. He placed his sword and dagger beside him and lay beside Bridin, not touching her.

"Alderic, I'd appreciate it if you kept your other weapon sheathed."

He smirked. "Of course, but speaking of weapons, I do have something for you." He reached beside him and produced his sheathed dagger. "I have been meaning to give this to you. Who knows? It might come in handy in the days ahead. Please take it."

Bridin accepted the knife and placed it on the floor next to her. She turned on her side, away from Alderic, and fell asleep in moments.

Alderic awoke in the middle of the night to the sound of the pounding rain on the tile roof. Rumbles of thunder shook the air. He was conscious of Bridin's naked form curled up next to him. He stared at the rafters above, wondering how he had gotten to this place with this woman beside him. He was fortunate to have become associated with her. She had spirit and determination. She knew far more than him about the ways of Rome and was a clever thinker. It seemed so improbable, but yet, here he was. Would he survive this ordeal? If he had a future, would Bridin be in it? He certainly hoped so.

The couple awoke early the next morning and got into their still-damp garments. Thankfully, it had ceased raining. They descended the stairs to the main room of the inn again. Weak sunlight filtered into the room. Warm bread with olive oil and dried figs had been lined up on the countertop. A few other customers were already up. The two ate in silence. Alderic spoke in a hushed tone. "When we take our leave from here, follow my lead. We need to convey some misinformation."

Alderic approached the proprietor and spoke in a loud voice for the benefit of other patrons. "How far are we from Rome? It has been a long journey and we seek friends in the city."

"You will be there in two days' time. If you are coming back this way, be sure to stop here. I appreciate your business. I hope you found the food and accommodations satisfactory."

"It was more than satisfactory. Everything was excellent. We shall certainly recommend your establishment to our friends. Thank you for the wonderful hospitality. Good day."

As they exited the establishment, Alderic steered Bridin south—the opposite direction they wished to travel in. After a short distance, she turned to him. "Why are we going back the way we came?"

Alderic beamed smugly. "We will get off the road and reverse course in a bit toward north. I said those thongs back at the inn for everyone to hear and so there is no doubt about where we're heading."

"And where did you learn this subterfuge? Certainly not in the ludus."

"What is a subterfuge?"

"A trick. Now tell me."

"Back in my homeland, when we tracked and hunted game, sometimes the creatures would double back on their trail. We're doing the same. Well, kind of. The point is that if people come asking about me, they will be confused, and that is what we want. Up ahead is a good spot to exit the road and head north once again."

The pair ventured north on the thoroughfare for most of the day. If they saw other travelers approaching, they ducked into cover at the side of the road. Late in the afternoon, they approached a village. Bridin went into the settlement to procure a blanket and some food for the evening meal. People weren't looking for her; run-away slaves of her ilk didn't merit much attention. He, on the other hand, was a different story. The weather had cleared, so they would be spending the night outside and not risk discovery at an inn. Not the most comfortable alternative, but certainly the safer one.

Marcus Antonius sat behind a wooden table laden with documents. Before him stood Darus, the gang leader who had failed to capture Alderic, along with one of Antonius's men, Publics Suetonius. He had also been present at Cilo's house but had departed to inform his commander of the situation before Alderic's arrival. It was his associate who had been gutted by Alderic. There were no chairs, so the two men remained standing, waiting to be interrogated. The right side of Darus's face was completely swathed in a bandage, masking the injury delivered by Alderic's blade.

Antonius stared hard at the two men, his expression hostile. "What do you have to report to me? It has been three days now since a household slave defeated, what, eight armed men? Tell me you have captured this brute, and we now have the chests in our possession."

Both men remained silent. Finally, Publius Sentonius spoke. "He seems to have disappeared, sir. There have been no sightings in the last few days."

Antonius rose from the table with a murderous look. "Let me understand this. A common slave…what was his name?"

"Alderic, sir."

"Yes, this Alderic, confronts eight armed men, killing or incapacitating half of them, in the late Senator Cilo's house, and then escapes into the streets. We have all the urban cohorts and all the brotherhoods seeking this man, who I'm told towers above the rest of the population, and we still can't find him. How is this possible?"

There was no reply.

Antonius let the silence linger, and then spoke. "This slave has absconded with five chests of gold and silver coin. Do you have any idea how much money this represents?" Without waiting for a reply from the two, he continued. "I will tell you how much. It could pay for several of my legions. This slave has stolen my gold and silver. My money! I sense that he is no longer in this city. He has escaped. I don't know how, but he is gone and so is my coin."

Antonius walked from his position behind the table to stand before the two men. "This is what we're going to do. I want patrols sent outside Rome. I want them to scour every town and inn within one hundred miles of the city. He is out there. Find him. Bring him back here to be interrogated. Do you understand?"

Both men replied in the affirmative. Darus stepped forward. "I would like to have my men paid the agreed upon sum of money for the Cilo job. Furthermore, we will need to be compensated with additional coin for our services."

A look of unabashed fear came upon the face of Publius Suetonius. Darus had committed an unspeakable breach of protocol—he had spoken out of turn. No one was to talk to Antonius unless directed to do so. Moreover, he had demanded something of him.

Antonius was silent for a few moments, a cold fury burning in his eyes. "Sentonius, is there a second-in-command in Darus's gang?"

"I believe so, sir. His name is Pulchrus."

"Good. You may inform this Pulchrus that he is now in charge." In a lightning move, Antonius drew his gladius and expertly rammed it through Darus's chest all the way to the hilt. He savagely twisted the blade out for maximum impact. "Here's your payment. Spend it in Hades if you can."

Chapter VIII

Alderic and Bridin walked along the paved road. On either side, olive groves, wheat fields, and fruit orchards dotted the landscape. The weather remained favorable, with bright autumn sunshine warming their faces, as they tread north—constantly north and farther away from Rome. They had chatted little since they arose that morning after another cold night with little sleep, but at least they were dry this time. Their footsteps resonating was the only sound other than the calls of various birds nesting in the trees lining the thoroughfare. Bridin broke the silence. "Alderic, do you have any idea where we're going and what our destination ultimately is?"

He pondered her question at length before replying in a laconic tone. "No, I don't have any idea; except that I want to put great distance between us and Rome. Labenius, my trainer from the ludus, told me this is what I must do. In case you forgot, we're fleeing for our lives. If they catch us, they will kill us. And our deaths will not be pleasant. I have no idea what lies ahead. I know nothing of the cities and villages that we might cross. Do you?"

Bridin stopped in the middle of the road, forcing Alderic to halt. "No need to be so terse. I too know little of what lies ahead. I was just asking, that's all. Come on, don't be angry at me." She linked her arm in his, and they began walking again.

Alderic was elated by her show of affection. Her touch felt nice. It had been some time since he had experienced the warmth of another human. "Sorry. It's not my nature to be ill-tempered. You got me out of the city. It was a good idea. I shouldn't be annoyed. In fact, I'm grateful. You saved me."

Bridin drew him closer. "We saved each other. You rescued me in the alley. I would've been captured. As I was saying, my question wasn't intended to be critical of your judgement. I just thought that perhaps we should have a plan. You know, an endpoint. I understand we must put as much distance as we can between us and Rome. But how far, and then what? Will we ever be able to evade the long reach of Rome?"

"I not know all that. My focus has been on our escape. I agree we must have plan. Any ideas?"

Bridin contemplated for a while. "I'm trying to think of something."

Alderic smirked.

Bridin looked at him quizzically. "What's so funny? What did I say?"

Alderic smiled. "It's nothing to do with you. Our conversation reminded me of my master's son and his tutor."

"How so?"

"Sometimes I was allowed to sit in on his lessons. They would have these long-winded discussions about phil... phil..."

"Philosophy, Alderic. So? How was this humorous?"

"Well, they would talk about the meaning of life, about beauty, one's inner self, and this and that. They incessantly discussed the thoughts of these Greeks with funny names. My viewpoint is that the purpose of life is simple. One only needs food in belly and avoid having some arsehole from neighboring tribe or Roman legionnaire stick a sharp spear up your butt. These men whose words they study were obviously never in a German forest, battling for survival."

Bridin trilled in laughter. "Oh Alderic! That's precious and well said. What do those Greeks know anyway, right?"

"In my opinion, not much." He played with the heavy purse attached to his waist, jingling the coins. "Back to your original question—until we reach our destination, wherever that might be, we have lots of money. Food and shelter aren't a problem." The pair trudged along in the autumn sunshine, their final destination unresolved.

It was late in the afternoon. Alderic observed that Bridin was beginning to falter. He chastised himself for not realizing that not all people had his strength and stamina. He studied her again. Her face was weary with exhaustion, her feet were dragging, and yet, she hadn't complained. She must have taken his words about putting as much distance as possible from Rome to heart. Perhaps a little too much, for she appeared totally spent. Looking west, he spied ugly-looking dark clouds on the horizon. He didn't know a lot about the weather here, but it wasn't hard to guess that to guess that rain was coming this way. There was no question that they would have to seek shelter at an inn tonight, hopefully some place nice with good food and fine accommodation, like the last place they stayed at. He peered ahead, noting several houses by the side of the road. A wooden sign proclaimed that the village of Tredarius was one mile ahead. He breathed a sigh of relief. "Come, Bridin. We'll find an inn to stay in tonight."

She smiled back at him. "Oh Alderic, I sorely need a warm bed and some good food. Lead the way."

A short time later, they approached a small establishment with sign in front advertising good food and fine accommodations. It was called the Inn at Tredarius. The pair entered without hesitation. Alderic peered about for any possible threats. The main room was spacious and featured a hearth with a small fire. Scattered customers occupied some of the tables; none of them gave the newcomers a second glance. Bridin nodded in greeting to a man behind the counter she assumed to be the owner. "We would like a room for the night if one is available."

"Certainly," he replied. "We have four rooms, two of which are taken. How about the one at the rear? It's as comfortable as the others and has a measure of privacy."

Alderic replied, "We'll take it."

"Good!" exclaimed the proprietor. "Dinner will be served shortly. This way. I'll show you upstairs."

Later that evening, the couple entered into their room. Both lay on the thin mattress. Bridin snuggled up to Alderic and spoke. "Please hug me. It has been so long since I have experienced anyone comforting me."

Alderic slipped her arm around her waist, reveling in the warmth and touch of the woman. As he had anticipated, it had begun to rain. The drops hissed and pattered on the roof. Bridin abruptly rolled over, facing Alderic. "Have you thought any more about a plan? We'll need to decide how far to travel and what we are to do once we arrive at a destination."

Alderic grimaced. "Bridin, I agree we need a plan. But I still believe we're in grave danger. I can't put my finger on it, but somehow, I believe men are pursuing us. They will not give up. Once we feel we've put enough distance between us and Rome and stop running, we'll need to support ourselves."

"You know, we can't continue going north indefinitely. There's a limit."

He gave her a quizzical look.

Bridin grinned at his ignorance. "Eventually, the mountains will block our path at this time of year. The snow. As for supporting ourselves, I know the weaving trade. I'm skilled and knowledgeable," she said proudly. "It takes many years to learn. What about you?"

Alderic shrugged. "I did some farming and hunting. Not much help in this…what do you call it…a republic? I have skills as a gladiator. Not a worthy skill either."

She tenderly patted him on the shoulder. "You will find something. Let's not dwell on it for now." She snuggled closer to him. "I'm tired. I need to sleep."

With the woman cuddled against him, Alderic stared at the ceiling, wondering what he would do in his new life. Would he have a future? Where would their flight end? He had no answers. He slowly drifted off into uneasy sleep.

It was barely light when Alderic was awakened by the sound of horses, the whinnying echoing in the early morning air. It took him a few heartbeats to remember where he was. He looked at the slim form of Bridin curled up on the mattress, still dead asleep. He groggily rose and padded over to the window.

The four mounted men had clearly been riding all night. There was no confusion as to who these individuals were—Roman legionnaires. They wore their iron helmets and armor. They were big, tough-looking men. Their expressions were grim. They were splattered with mud and other offal from the road. The leader wearily dismounted. He tossed aside his cloak as he slid off his mount, revealing a leather cuirass and short military sword strapped to his side. Leading the three other similarly attired men inside the inn, Julius Quintus shook the droplets off his cloak. "Warm wine for the four of us," he roared at the proprietor. The innkeeper quickly filled four goblets and carried them, two in each hand, to the serving board. The men drank greedily from their cups. "Give us another round. Do you have any decent food here?"

"Yes, this morning we have warm porridge, bread, cheese, and some dried figs. Would you like some?"

Julius glowered at him. "No, I was just asking to pass the time. Of course, we want food. Now fetch more wine and the breakfast."

The men drank their wine in silence. Julius Quintus fumed. He was a member of Antonius's elite cavalry, and here he was—chilled to the bone out in the hinterlands, chasing some phantom thief. It was beneath his station to be doing this. He had earned the rank of decurion through blood, sweat, and tears and *this* was his reward? He gulped some more wine, but his ire refused to subside. Perhaps the most grating fact of it all was that there was nothing he could do to escape his current circumstances. He had been given a direct order by Domitius Cremetius, Antonius's second in command. He was to seek out and capture a tall escaped German slave, who held the knowledge of a vast treasure of silver and gold coin. He was to keep searching until recalled. It was an order he dare not disobey.

He wasn't alone in his discontent. Others of his rank, and even those higher, had been tasked with the same mission. Find the tall German and above all, bring him back alive for questioning. They were to fan out and ride as far as a hundred miles from the walls of Rome. He and his retinue were directed to proceed northwest along via Flaminia. Julius had been directed to use extreme caution when approaching the suspect. He was reputed to be an ex-glad-iator skilled in the use of arms. He was told that this fugitive had already wreaked havoc on those who had previously attempted to apprehend him.

The four men sat at a table, waiting for the inn keeper to bring their food and another round of warm wine. A serving girl appeared, carrying a tray containing a bowl of steaming porridge, bread, and cheese. Having heard the abuse that had been directed at her employer earlier, she tremulously placed the tray on the table and fled before any wrath could be directed her way.

Julius looked up as the girl hurried away. He felt remorseful. He was not ordinarily a man of ill-temper. In fact, given the low station he was born in, he was usually sympathetic to those of lesser means and birth. It was just his current mission that had put him in his current state of wrath. They had been riding for days, mostly in the cold and rain, seeking the tall man. They said his name was Alderic.

The proprietor cautiously edged toward the table with another fresh tray of warmed wine. He placed the goblets, and like the servant girl, attempted to escape quickly from their presence. "You there, halt." The inn keeper cringed at the command.

In a more mellow tone, Julius addressed the owner. "No need to fear. I did not mean to be so cantankerous. My companions and I are all tired from riding a long distance in bad weather. You wouldn't happen to have seen a very tall German fellow lurking about, would you?"

The proprietor blanched, his face frozen in fear. Julius jumped up. "By all of the gods and Jupiter's arse! Where is he?"

The owner spluttered. "I rented a room to a tall man who might be German. I couldn't be sure. His woman was with him."

"How long ago?"

"He's upstairs now, in the room all the way to the back."

The four men rose as one and drew their swords. They rushed to the top of the landing. Julius gestured to one of his men and spoke in a hushed tone. "Cassius kick the door down. We'll be right behind you."

Cassius charged down the narrow hallway and delivered a mighty kick to the door with his booted foot. The door splintered and crashed inward. The four men gazed at the open window and the empty room. Julius muttered a curse under his breath.

The four men piled down the stairs and rushed out to the rear courtyard. They looked about to see nothing but the misty rain.

Alderic and Bridin huffed as they rushed through the valley. They were off the road, traveling over rough ground. The landscape was a patchwork of timber and plowed fields. Alderic halted, waiting for Bridin to catch up with him. She trudged up to him, gasping for breath. "How did you know those men were looking for you? They could have been anybody."

"Would you rather we'd waited to find out? I don't know if they seek me, but my intuition said they were. No doubt they were military men. They will alert others. Soon the area will be crawling with men searching for me."

"What should we do?"

"We stay off the roads. Out of sight. If we see more mounted men, we'll know for sure."

She hugged him. "Oh, Alderic, I thought we were free of all of this. Let's get out of sight." They ventured toward a thicket up ahead on the trail and rested.

Sometime later, the pair walked onward, following muddied paths and game trails. The landscape changed from fields and stands of timber to dense woods. Alderic breathed in the heavy scent of the forest. He was back in Alderic territory—for him, this was home. He felt more confident of their safety back in his element. Employing the position of the sun, Alderic did his best to keep them headed in a northerly direction. It proved difficult as often the sun was obscured by the towering trees. They moved onward for several more hours at a swift pace.

A while back, Alderic had scrounged some late-season edible berries not yet devoured by creatures of the forest. The two popped the succulent fruit in their mouths as they advanced along a well-trodden path. A slight breeze ruffled the autumn leaves and the birds chirped from their high branches.

Bridin spoke. "I've never walked in a forest for so long. I must say it's quite beautiful. You appear so in harmony with your surroundings, as though you belong here. By the way, those berries were delicious. I hope you can find—"

Alderic abruptly held up his hand indicating silence. The two stopped. He'd heard a twig snap. It could be an animal scurrying to avoid them or perhaps something else entirely. Alderic peered intently at the foliage ahead, his senses alert.

It was silent, but Alderic remained vigilant. He smelled an odor that wasn't part of the forest. He drew his short sword out of the scabbard, holding it menacingly in front of him. Five scrofulous figures emerged out of the brush ahead. Their clothes were raggedy and dirty, their bodies emaciated.

The leader of the bunch stepped forward. He wore a filthy cloth cap and had a black eye patch over one eye. He leered at the two intruders. "Looks like you chose the wrong path in these woods."

He moved a step closer, although still some distance from Alderic. He drew small dagger from his waistband. The four others, following their leader, too produced an assortment of weapons. The figure with the eye patch spoke. "Make it easy on yourself. Drop your sword and give up your purse now. There is one of you and five of us."

Alderic remained silent. He stared hard at the ruffians and leveled his glistening sword unwavering at waist level.

The five men tentatively advanced a few more paces toward the intimidating figure before them. Eye patch spoke again. "What's the matter? Can't you speak?" He turned back toward his comrades and chuckled. "We have a silent one here."

As the leader diverted his gaze, something one should never do in an armed confrontation—even the dumbest of gladiators knew that—Alderic struck. He bounded forward slashing his neck, and then quickly striking the two men to his left. Bright arterial blood fountained into the air. He turned toward the men on his right, blocking one of their knife thrusts. He reflexively threw his shoulder back as he detected movement on his far right. He felt the heavy blow of a cudgel on this bicep. Ducking low to avoid another blow he twisted around and thrust hard with his gladius, skewering the man wielding the club through the torso. Withdrawing his blade, he backed off to fend off the remaining attacker, but there was no need. The man staggered back, grasping the hilt of the dagger Bridin had buried deep into his side.

Alderic met her gaze for a moment then shouted. "Go up ahead! I'll take care of things here."

She stared at him, unable to move. Alderic gestured with his arm. "Move. I'll meet you there." She numbly moved up the trail.

Three of the men were still alive, crawling on the ground, trying to hold their wounds shut. Alderic ruthlessly dispatched them. No sense having any witnesses to their presence here. Besides, their wounds were already mortal. He briefly searched the dead men but found nothing of any value on the pathetic creatures. He withdrew the dagger he had given Bridin from the man's side and wiped the blade in the grass. Without a second glance, he hurried to Bridin.

Alderic walked the remainder of the day with a comforting arm around Bridin's. The path they were following eventually led out of the forest and intersected a main thoroughfare. Not wishing to be exposed, they retired to a secluded thicket from where they had an unimpeded view of the road. After several hours of crouching among the bushes, they observed no suspicious activity on the thoroughfare. The traffic was sparse, and they witnessed only a few wayward travelers, no presence of bands of mounted men. Alderic was somewhat relieved, but his anxiety remained. He wasn't about to set foot on the road until he was certain the others weren't searching for him. The pair huddled under their blanket they had pilfered from the inn while escaping and settled in for the night. He hoped that tomorrow would be an uneventful day.

Alderic rose early to a fog shrouding the early morning landscape. He left Bridin and moved closer to the road, hiding in a heavy patch of thorn bushes. He peered out from his concealed position, observing the avenue before him. He was close enough to hear any loud conversations. He waited.

The sun burned away the mist. Mostly merchants and farmers with wagons of hay and wheat traveled on the road. There was a pause in the traffic and the avenue was empty momentarily. From the south, he heard the sound of many horses approaching. His heart sunk. A troop of about twenty horses cantered past his bush, the men talking in loud tones above the sound of the clopping of their steeds. He couldn't make out their conversation but heard the words "tall German" and "capture." He glanced to his rear and saw Bridin standing up, directing her gaze at him. From his concealed position, he frantically gestured for her to stay there and remain low. He turned back to the road and saw a second troop of mounted men approaching from the south. Alderic remained motionless. Over the course of several hours, he witnessed several more bands of mounted legionnaires on the road. The word was definitely out.

Despondent, Alderic returned to where Bridin was concealed. "There is no doubt. All of these riders are searching for me. They'll be combing the area for us." He stopped speaking, staring off into the distance. He searched for the right words for what needed to be said. He turned to her again. "We must separate. It's too dangerous for you to be with me. By yourself, you'll at least have a fighting chance to escape." He unfastened the cloth pouch, removing a handful of silver denarii for himself, he handed her the purse. "I want you to have this. Travel a bit farther north. Perhaps you can start a business in the weaving trade at a town in the north. You're a resourceful person. Find something."

Tears glistened on her face. She gave him a reproachful glance. "I thought you liked me?"

"I do like you and wish to stay with you, Bridin. But it makes no sense. I stand a better chance if you're not with me, slowing me down. Your odds are better too if you're alone. You're not recognized as an enemy of Rome yet. It's me they're after. Now listen. Someday, I'll come back for you after the danger passes. Is what I'm saying make sense?"

Stifling a sob, she nodded meekly. "But what about you Alderic? How can you survive with no money?"

"I'll make do. Now, what name will you choose to be known as, so I can find you again?"

Bridin sniffled. "I guess I like Claudia, the name I used when we escaped in the wagon. It has a certain Roman tone to it."

"Then I will search for Claudia, the weaver in the north country."

She managed a smile between her sobs. "Please come back for me. I'll be waiting." She kissed him and the two figures embraced for a long time before separating.

Alderic watched wistfully as the figure of Bridin slowly faded into the distance and out of sight. He began to second-guess himself—was he doing the right thing? Was it truly the element of doubt or was it just his desire to be with Bridin? Yes, he decided, it had been the best thing to do. The men seeking him were looking for a man and a woman. He wouldn't be staying at any inn, that much was certain. His plan was to get off the road and rapidly move north, away from any pursuers. Hopefully, Bridin could blend into a town without raising suspicion. Looking toward where Bridin had walked one last time, he turned around and jogged on the wooded path.

Two weeks later, in the early dawn, Alderic walked along the via Aemilia, still heading north. He was now several hundred miles away from Rome. He traveled mostly at night so no one would see his tall form. He had to be wary of bandits. Three men had accosted him late at night last week. Fortunately, Alderic had recognized the danger quickly and drawn his weapon in time. That combined with his menacing size had been enough to scare them off.

He was exhausted and almost out of funds. He still had no plan, other than to continue putting distance between him and Rome. He had come across no more mounted patrols, but that didn't mean they weren't still looking for him. He remained cautious. He thought of Bridin. He wished he could have stayed with her. She was smart and quick-witted. Despite his yearning to be with her, he had no regrets about his decision to part from her. It was the sensible thing to do. He hoped she had found a way to survive in a new locale.

He staggered on in the faint light of early dawn, hoping to find a place to rest. He warily peered ahead and entered the stand of trees. At once, he was assaulted by the smell of wood smoke. Which meant people, which meant danger. He gazed around but couldn't see anything in the vapor. Venturing farther into the copse to investigate, he spotted several moving figures in the mist. In blind panic, he darted to his left, only to see more people. Getting a little closer, he recognized them as Roman legionnaires. His heart dropped—trust his luck to have turned tail. What was he to do? If he fled, it would look suspicious, and someone was bound to see him. Anxious to get away from this place, he moved to his left at a fast trot, but not a run. Were the soldiers searching for him? *Unlikely.* Why would they be in this particular grove at this hour of the morning? He moved rapidly, only to find himself in a clearing amid a cluster of large tents. Darting forward, he moved past the tents and burst out on to the road. This was an even worse place to be. *Now what?*

Turning about in the mist, he decided to retrace his steps, anything but the road. He had advanced only a few steps when he collided with a solidly built individual. Both men grunted from the impact. Stunned, Alderic recovered first and looked at who he had crashed into. To his horror, he was staring into the face of a Roman officer—he believed they were called centurions. The man was massive. He wasn't as tall as Alderic, but his girth was impressive, and none of it appeared to be fat. He wore a leather cuirass over a grey tunic and marching sandals. From his armor hung several torques and brightly colored discs. Alderic knew little about military uniforms and badges, but he sensed these decorations were important, worn only by a select few.

The legionnaire rubbed his shoulder, and then grinned at Alderic. "Up awfully early, aren't you? By Jupiter's arse, you're a large one!"

In return, Alderic gaped, at a loss for words.

"So, you've come to see us about joining the legions?" he inquired.

It dawned upon Alderic, as he had suspected all along, the men surrounding him were not searching for him. "Joining the legions?" he asked.

"Yes, this is the recruiting station for the Fifteenth Legion. We are on the outskirts of Mutina, hoping to sign up new recruits for Octavius

Caesar's legion. I assume that is why you came bumbling through our camp, yes?"

By now, Alderic had recovered his wits. "Yes, could you tell me more about the legions? I have heard much but don't know what is true and what is not."

"Let me ask you some questions first. From your accent, I take it you are not a Roman citizen, but from one of the provinces."

"I'm from the north," Alderic replied evasively.

"You're not a runaway slave or anything, are you?"

"No, I was employed as a bodyguard," he replied glibly.

The centurion stroked his chin in thought, giving Alderic an appraising glance. "Well it's like this. Since you're not a Roman citizen, we can place you in the auxiliaries. They fight and train like the legions but don't get paid as much. Generally, we require a service of ten years. You get paid about one hundred and twenty denarii a year and are fed. If the army captures booty, you are entitled to a share. At the end of your term of service, you will be granted citizenship. By the way, what do I call you?"

Alderic paused, unprepared for the question. He couldn't use Alderic. He decided on a Roman name that was slightly similar. "Artorus."

The centurion grinned. "All right, Artorus, let me give it to you straight. You are not going to get rich in the legions, but it does offer an individual such as you a path to citizenship after a ten year commitment. Furthermore, you earn a living wage, get fed, and receive good medical care. The pay and benefits are better than most civilian jobs. Now, you might ask me, is it dangerous? Of course, it is. But life is dangerous. Plus, here, all your fellow legionnaires will have your back. I guarantee that you will make steadfast friends for life."

Alderic nodded, his thoughts racing. This could be his opportunity. He could blend in with the legions. Nobody would look for him there. "I think I might be interested."

"Good. We will need to examine you to ensure you have no physical deformities."

Alderic's heart sank. What would they say about his scars? They would ask questions.

The centurion shouted. "Medicus, come over here and take a look at this man." He turned to Alderic. "I need you to strip down to your undergarments so the medicus can take a look at you."

Hesitantly, he removed his tunic, shivering in the early morning cold. The medicus moved to his front, his eyes focused on Alderic's chest. He traced the angry red scar that traversed down Alderic's chest. "What have we here?"

"Disagreement with some bandits," he lied artfully.

"Do you have full function and range of motion in your arms?"

Alderic didn't want his flexibility and range of motion to be tested. In response, he grabbed the diminutive form of the medicus and lifted him up off the ground, twirling him about. "Does this answer your question?"

The figure gasped. "Yes, yes! Please put me down."

Alderic eased him down with a playful smirk.

The centurion grinned. "That's what I like to see. You said you were a bodyguard. Can you fight?"

Alderic's mind whirled. He couldn't brag about his prowess or even hint that he had been a gladiator. That would be a foolish mistake. He deftly answered, "I'll let you be the judge of that."

The centurion turned and shouted to an officer hovering close by. "Centurion Fulvius, we have a potential recruit here. I need to assess his fighting skills. Would you bring the training armor and wooden swords?"

The recruiting officer stood observing Alderic. "By the way, my name is Centurion Gracchus, commander of the second cohort, Fifteenth Legion. I'm in charge of this recruiting station. My second in command, Centurion Fulvius, is going to test your fighting skills."

A short, stocky legionnaire attired similar to the recruiting centurion made his way to them carrying iron mail, helmets, heavy wooden shields, and wooden swords. He dumped it unceremoniously in a pile at Alderic's feet. "Here, get kitted up with the armor and pick up a sword and shield."

The two centurions huddled while Alderic fiddled with his armor. Gracchus spoke. "He says he was employed as a bodyguard. He isn't a citizen. Looks formidable enough."

Alderic decided to be coy. He fumbled with the chain mail as if he was unfamiliar with it and hesitantly placed the iron helmet to his head. It fitted, but barely. If they only knew, he thought, that he could do this in his sleep.

Centurion Fulvius observed Alderic's fumbling attempts to fit on his armor. He snorted in derision and helped fit the mail over his shoulders. He spoke in a condescending tone. "Now strap the shield to your left arm and pick up one of those training swords. Have you used a sword and shield before?"

Alderic nodded in reply. "Some."

Centurion Gracchus said, "Alright, Artorus. I just want to warn you that Centurion Fulvius is a skilled sword fighter. He's almost as good as me. So, show me what you got. You ready?"

"I ready."

"Good. Begin."

Alderic eyed his opponent. He sensed that the centurion would attempt to bull rush him to end the match quickly and, in the process, humiliate him. He decided he would stay on the defensive and not try to beat the centurion, which might have disastrous consequences. Humiliating a superior was not a good idea. Just as he had anticipated, the Roman charged. Alderic nimbly avoided the rush and stepped to the side but didn't counter-attack. Fulvius quickly turned and resumed his offensive. Alderic parried the thrusts, keeping his shield in front of him. Next, the centurion attempted to reach over his shield and stab from the top. Alderic blocked the thrust and retreated. This was rudimentary stuff. Advancing once more, his opponent locked his shield with Alderic's, trying to wrench it from his grasp. Alderic had seen this ruse before in his gladiatorial training. He yanked his shield away, and then backed off again.

Fury clouded Fulvius's eyes. He was used to winning quickly. His every move had been stymied by this foreigner. He faked a full charge at the recruit, then quickly moved to his left, seeking an opening. He was startled when no opening materialized. Fulvius ran at his opponent once more, slashing and stabbing, stumbling in the process. As he moved past, he realized his entire left side was vulnerable, but strangely the recruit made no attempt to strike.

Fulvius stopped. He raised his arm signaling a halt to the combat. Turning around, he walked over to Gracchus. He spoke in quiet tone so Artorus couldn't hear him. "This man is good. In fact, he's damn good. He will do nicely in the legions."

Centurion Gracchus nodded in reply. He turned briefly away from Fulvius. "Artorus, very good. Do you mind if I confer with my colleague in private for a bit?"

In response, Alderic made a magnanimous gesture with his arms.

The two men huddled out of hearing distance from Alderic. Fulvius spoke. "I couldn't beat him. Furthermore, he could have defeated me. He deliberately held back. This guy is highly skilled. We need to sign him up."

Gracchus had a bright gleam in his eyes. "Fulvius, I want this man. Not only do I want him, I want him in my century, not the auxiliaries."

"But you can't do that. You told me he isn't a citizen."

"Who is to know? I thought I heard him say he was a citizen. Didn't you?" he remarked in a sly tone. "We'll lose his records. That man belongs in the front of my century when we move into an attack wedge. His skills weren't lost on me. He is fast and powerful. I'll sign him up for the legions. Hah! I knew the Goddess Fortuna would smile upon me today."

PART II

Chapter IX
The Legions

Forty raw recruits stood in attention facing Centurion Fulvius, the designated training officer and the one who had sparred with Alderic—or rather, Artorus—upon his recruitment. They were assembled outside the camp walls of the Fifteenth Legion. In the background, the mud parapets of the legionary fortress towered above the open plain. A cold autumn wind swirled around, freezing the lightly dressed legionnaires-in-training to the bone.

The centurion paced back and forth, rhythmically tapping his *vitis*—the wooden staff carried by all centurions, symbolizing their authority—against his right thigh. His optio, the second in command of the training century, Rufus, lurked to the side. In the legions, the smallest tactical unit was the century, usually of eighty men, commanded by a centurion. The officer immediately below him was the optio, who was expected to take command in the event the centurion was disabled or killed. Both Roman officers directed their steely gaze at the recruits, searching for any possible infraction. Fulvius spoke. "Listen to me, for I'm not going to repeat myself. We were hoping for more men to compensate for our casualties from the campaign last year against Antonius's forces, but the forty of you will have to do. When you have satisfactorily completed your training, you'll be assigned to one of the six centuries of the second cohort commanded by Centurion Gracchus."

He continued after a brief pause. "There are three things we're going to train you to do." For effect, he held up three fingers. "Only three you might ask? Yes. Only three. That's all. First, you'll learn to march. I'm not talking about that fancy parade ground stuff. We'll do that too, but that's easy shit. I'm talking about forced marches of twenty miles with full armor, weapons, and assorted gear. You see, in the legions, we carry everything on our backs, except the large tents you'll sleep in. The mules carry those. But believe me, the mules have it easier. If you can't march the twenty miles with full gear as all the other men in the legion, then you are of no use to us. And let me give you a clue—it's not easy. It's an ass breaker. At least you'll not have to do it in the heat; it's easier in the cold. So, consider yourselves fortunate that we're training at this time of the year."

The centurion paused to let his words sink in. He held up two fingers. "The second thing you'll learn to do is dig. Every time we break camp and march, we build a new camp; a fortified camp with earth walls and ditches. You will be responsible for building this camp. Again, it may sound easy, but it's not. It's tedious, hard, grueling work. At the end of your training, you'll have blisters upon your blisters. Do you think I adequately described the rigors of the digging, Optio Rufus?"

The figure smirked. "I believe you characterized it perfectly."

Fulvius grinned. "Good. Last, you will be trained to fight. You will be issued a short stabbing sword that we call a gladius; a javelin, known as a *pilum;* a dagger, *pugio;* and a *scutum,* what you call a shield. You will learn to fight with these weapons as an individual and as a century of eighty men."

The centurion maintained a hard gaze at his men. "I'm giving you the straight talk. The next eight weeks are going to be pure Hades. Make no mistake about it; we're going to run your asses ragged. You should know this upfront. I guarantee you it will be the hardest thing you've ever endured. When you're finished, you will be assigned to your centuries in the second cohort, Fifteenth Legion, where you will undergo additional drill and tactical training. There isn't much time. There is another war coming, and you will be in the thick of it. Let's begin."

He gestured to the optio to take over the formation and began exiting toward the side. He stopped suddenly. "Oh, and one more thing. Some of you may have questions. In the legions, there are no questions. You will obey every command given by Optio Rufus or me without hesitation. That's all you need to know." He nodded to Rufus and continued walking away.

130

Three days later, Alderic, now Artorus, gasped for air under his heavy load. The forked pole, to which his personal belongings and other assorted gear were attached, cut cruelly into his shoulder. He had discounted the centurion's warning about the hardship they would endure, and why wouldn't he? He had suffered the rigors of gladiatorial training, which hadn't exactly been a stroll through the woods on a sunny day either. But he was experiencing a massive pain throughout his body. His gladiatorial training and conditioning was long in the past. In retrospect, he realized he had led a soft life over the past few months compared to what was being demanded of him now. Everything hurt.

He couldn't believe the crushing weight he was carrying. His chain-mail armor, while protective, was the most burdensome of his gear. His military belt held his dagger and a pickaxe on the right. A leather strap over his left shoulder, reaching his right hip, held his sheathed gladius. His shield was slung over his left shoulder was supported by the baldric. His left hand carried two pila and his right the dreaded forked pole upon which an assortment of items was attached, including his personal kit. On his feet, he wore the standard military marching sandals, replete with iron hobnails on the bottom. On his head, he wore an iron helmet with protective flaps for the sides of his face and an angled flange at the rear that protected the back of his neck. Their equipment clanked and jangled as the forty recruits marched onward. By Wodan's fat arse, he was tired and ready to drop.

"Halt," commanded Fulvius. "You may take a short break on the side of the road now. We're half-way there."

Alderic dropped like a rock. Grabbing his goatskin water container, he drank greedily, as did the other inductees. Looking at them, he realized they were just as weary, if not more, as him. He was bigger and stronger than the others. How were the smaller men keeping up? Well, that wasn't his problem. The other recruits were locals who appeared to know one another. They seemed like a good bunch. He didn't sense another like Draxir from his gladiatorial school within the ranks. Nevertheless, Alderic pretty much kept to himself. As far as he was concerned, the less the others knew about him, the better.

He once again questioned the lunacy that had made him decide to join the legions. Too late for remorse. Besides, he reasoned, he didn't have a lot of options. If he had stayed on the run, he may very well have been captured by now. He loosened his *focale,* the scarf worn around the neck to prevent the mail armor from chafing. Wetting it with his precious supply of water, he used it to mop his face. He sat there wondering whether he'd be able to get up again. He directed his attention to his right shoulder, which bore the burden of the forked pole, and attempted to massage his shoulder. He gave up; it was impossible with the thick chain mail.

"Shoulder your gear. Let's mount up," Fulvius bellowed. "Don't worry, when we get there, there'll be a nice hot bath waiting for you." Some of the men smiled in anticipation.

The optio, Rufus, spluttered with laughter. "And if you believe that, watch me sprout wings out of me arse and fly the rest of the way there."

The smiles were replaced with embarrassed, sullen frowns. None of the recruits found the twisted humor funny. They had another ten miles of torture ahead of them.

Later that afternoon, they arrived at the destination for their night encampment. The mules carrying the tents had arrived earlier and were waiting to be unloaded. Fulvius pointed with his *vitis* at the small hilltop to their front. "That, gentlemen, is the location of your overnight encampment. I want everyone to get their pick axes out now. Leave your gear where it is. It's time to dig."

That night, Alderic stood guard on the recently constructed earthen wall made from the spoils of a deep excavated ditch immediately to his front. A frigid wind blustered over the plain upon which they were camped, sending chills through his cloak's flimsy protection. To him, it was stupid to stand watch. Nobody was going to attack them. So, why bother? But Centurion Fulvius had told the recruits that every Roman camp posted a watch, and it was serious business. If one was caught napping, the penalties were severe. First offenses would result in a flogging. Second offenses, death. He wasn't sure he believed the centurion, for the penalties seemed excessive, but he had no reason to doubt him either.

Hugging his cloak around himself for protection, he wondered where Bridin was; if she had made good her escape. He hoped so. She was a good person with many fine qualities. He wished he had gotten to know her better. He missed her, wondering if he would ever see her again.

His thoughts wandered back to his homeland. What had become of his mother and his sweetheart, Ealdgyd? They probably thought him dead. And although he wasn't, they might be in the land of shades. Villages didn't survive long when most of the warriors were slain. His musings leapt to the home of Senator Cilo, his wife, and young Lucius. Gone. All gone now. He had been content living at Cilo's house. They had treated him kindly, but that part of his life had been abruptly ended. There was so much violence in this Roman world—the street gangs, the arena, the legions. He was still trying to come to grips with it.

He chastised himself for his melancholy thoughts. Despite tremendous odds, he was still alive. So here he was—on a rampart guarding against the frigid wind. What other alternatives did he have, after all? In short, none. His musings were interrupted as he observed movement to this left. It was probably the optio, Rufus, attempting to sneak up on him to see if he was awake. Alderic chuckled. The optio was doing a piss-poor job of concealing his stealth. He straightened his posture to look more alert and issued the challenge. "Gladius," he roared. "Stab," came the reply.

Days later, the recruits were gathered around Centurion Fulvius. He had traded his wooden staff for a sword and shield. He walked before the recruits, presenting a menacing appearance. "Today you're going to learn to fight like Roman legionnaires. Listen closely, because your life and the lives of your comrades will depend on your ability to use these two weapons. First is the scutum." He held the large rectangular wooden shield close to his body. It covered the area from his neck to his knees. "This shield is not only meant to block the thrusts and jabs of your opponents but is also to be used as an offensive weapon."

He walked over to straw figure affixed to a wooden post. "The first movement in combat is to smash this shield into your foe. Like this." The centurion led with his left leg and delivered a tremendously powerful blow. The wooden post wobbled from the impact of the shield. "Punch the boss of the shield directly into your enemy's face. If you do it correctly, you will put him off balance or even knock him to the ground. Once you do that, the rest is easy. Finish him with your sword. That would be your second movement."

The centurion stepped back from the straw effigy. "So just think of this mantra: Punch and stab, punch and stab." He proceeded to perform a series of thrusts with the shield and jabs with the short sword.

He walked back to the men and held out the short Roman thrusting sword. "Oftentimes, when you're fighting barbarians, they'll have longer swords or spears. Not to worry. You only need the length of this sword to accomplish your mission, which is to kill the enemy."

He paused for a moment before continuing, holding up his gladius for all to see. "This sword is designed for stabbing. Always remember to stab and not slash. I'll say it again—stab, not slash. Why? First, if you attempt to slash at your opponent"—he raised his right arm over his head to demonstrate—"you expose your entire right side in the process, so it will be you who is skewered. Second, if you slash with this weapon, odds are you will not kill your foe and are more likely to just piss him off. If, on the other hand, you stab your man, he will go down and be unable to get up. When you thrust your gladius into your foe, twist the blade on the way out. This will kill your enemy while also making it easier to withdraw the blade. If your sword is stuck in someone's gut, you'll be dead too shortly."

He strode over to the straw figure on the post. "Now, you're probably wondering where you're supposed to stab your enemy. The short answer is, anywhere you can. But the best places are here, here, and here." He pointed with his sword to the throat, torso, and groin. "These are the vulnerable areas. You stab a man in any of these places, he will go down and be as good as dead. Now, let's get you in your armor along with the wooden shields and swords. It's time for some intense sword drill."

They practiced all day. Nothing escaped the attention of their instructors. Even the slightest flaw or lack of sincere effort was noted. Alderic was not exempt from their wrath. This was a new way of fighting for him. In his sword training at the ludus, slashing with the sword was an acceptable approach. Alderic felt the sting of Centurion Fulvius's vine-wood staff. "How many times have I told you today? Stab don't slash. Now for fucks sake, pay attention."

The hard regimen continued with no respite over the next several weeks. There were more forced marches, endless digging, and weapons training. From sunrise to sunset, the men labored, the arduous physical demands never ending. Oftentimes at night, men collapsed in their armors in the allotted tent spaces, too tired to take it off. But the forty recruits endured. They were becoming hardened legionnaires; tough men who could withstand the harshest of conditions.

Centurion Fulvius was meeting to discuss the status of the training of the recruits with his superior, the cohort commander of the Fifth Cohort—Centurion Gracchus, the officer who had recruited Artorus and wanted him in his century. They sat in Gracchus's tent at a small field table. A cold wind whistled outside. The senior centurion poured some wine into two clay goblets. Gracchus raised his goblet. "To Rome."

"To Rome," echoed Fulvius.

"So how is the training come along, Fulvius? I take it the recruits are measuring up?"

"They are rounding into shape. I had my doubts about a few of them, but they're all progressing."

"Good. That is what I like to hear."

Fulvius replied. "You know we only have forty of them. The cohort has more vacancies to fill than recruits. We need every single one of them. By the way, some of the other centurions have been nosing around my training area, no doubt seeking to snatch as many as possible when the training is done. Remember, you promised me twenty of them since my century has the most vacancies."

"Did I say twenty? I don't remember quoting that figure."

"Come on, Gracchus. I don't mean to whine, but I really need those replacements. You know I am the most understrength of all of the six centuries in the cohort."

"Look, Fulvius, I understand you have the most vacancies. While I appreciate you acting as their training centurion, I'm hearing from all the other centurions as well. I will keep my word. I promise that you'll get more men than the others."

Somewhat mollified, Fulvius nodded in affirmation.

"So, tell me Fulvius. How is my man, Artorus, coming along?"

"He's a man among boys. What an imposing physical specimen. Smart too. He picks up on everything real quick. Except the arsehole keeps slashing instead of stabbing with his sword."

Gracchus snorted. "Well he isn't the first recruit to make that mistake."

Fulvius replied. "No, he isn't. But he's just so good in everything he does except for that."

"Excellent. I look forward to having him in my century."

"I must say, at times, he seems a bit standoffish. All other recruits are from around here but him. He pretty much keeps to himself, doesn't say a whole lot." The centurion shrugged. "I'm not going to dwell on it, but it's almost like he's hiding something. I wonder what his real story is."

"As long as he can fight. That's all I care about," replied Gracchus.

Fulvius took another sip of his wine, then lowered the goblet. "So, what's the word on our deployment? I can't see the legion staying here doing nothing, and I know there is a war brewing."

Gracchus offered a wry smile. "Somehow, I knew that would come up. It just so happens that I met with the legate and his staff the other evening. There's going to be a war, no doubt about it. The way the legate explained it, the forces of Brutus and Cassius—they call themselves the Liberators—are massing in the east. Somewhere in Greece I think. A big force too. Some estimate as high as twenty legions. They have absorbed the legions posted to the east of Rome and recruited the rest from the populations there. Can't say they are seasoned fighters like most of the legions here, but still, that is a lot of legions. Antonius and Octavius Caesar are making plans to go there, sometime in the next six to nine months and avenge the murder of Caesar."

Fulvius whistled through his teeth. "Twenty legions. That's a lot. How many do Antonius and Octavius have?"

"Don't know, Fulvius, but I'm sure they'll attempt to match, if not exceed, the number that the Liberators have. So, my advice is to get your men ready. A big fight is coming. If we aren't on the winning side, our careers, our retirement, and our lives will be at stake."

Alderic grunted from the heavy burden on his back. This was the worst yet. It was a forced march with a full kit and load with no breaks. On all their other treks, there had been respites for them to catch their breath and drink water. To make matters worse, much of their journey was uphill, into the mountains. No talking was allowed, but that didn't matter. Speaking required too much effort anyway, and the men needed every last bit of their strength to see the journey through.

He shifted the forked pole containing his kit and other items. The only sounds were the grunts of the other recruits and jangling of their equipment and gear. They marched steadily onward. He mused briefly about his fellow trainees. They had formed their little cliques based off previous friendships. Many had enlisted together. He, on the other hand, remained reclusive.

A few miles on, one man collapsed. His name was Mellitius. Everyone stopped in their tracks. Artorus looked at the man upon the cold ground, unsure how he was supposed to react. Like a fish out of water, the man gasped for breath, his face pasty white.

It was not surprising that Mellitius was the one to collapse. He was the by far the smallest of the men among the forty recruits. Ordinarily, he would have been rejected as being too slight for the legions, but these were desperate times. The legions needed every able-bodied man. Besides, he had joined with a group of his friends. If Mellitius had been rejected, his comrades might have also decided negatively about entering the legion.

Alderic's gladiatorial training discouraged him from assisting the fallen figure. In the ludus, it was every man for himself. You relied upon your abilities and generally didn't make too many close friends, for odds were that they would not be around that long. For him, Lothar had been the sole exception. But underneath this recently cultivated veneer, there were his village roots, where you always helped each other. If someone was disadvantaged or in trouble, you aided them. His village origins overrode his gladiatorial creed. Without another thought, he rushed over to Mellitius. He pulled the small wiry figure to his feet and grabbed his forked pole. While gingerly supporting Mellitius, he shouldered the additional burden and began marching once more. The other men gawked in awe, wondering how someone could march with two forked poles.

Centurion Fulvius stood to the side of the formation and watched the entire scene unfold. A slight crease of smile appeared upon his face. "Come on. Let's keep the pace up. We have miles to go before we're done. You know the rules. No stopping. No talking."

The under-sized legionnaire proffered a grateful nod to the giant legionnaire. Unknown to Alderic, he had gained a friend.

Several nights later, back at the training encampment, Alderic sat outside his tent, sharpening his sword and dagger in a desultory fashion. He was both bored and exhausted from the recent forced march. The men were to be allowed to visit the local town as a reward for completing the field exercise. It was the first time they had been permitted free time outside the camp since their training had begun. A few small groups had already wandered out.

"Hey, Artorus, come with us. You going to sit here all night doing that shit?"

He looked up from his sharpening to see Mellitius with a group of friends, ready to venture forth into the town. "Where are you going?"

"What do you care as long as it's away from here? Come on. You need to get out." The others nodded their approval.

"I come. I need some good wine."

"Now you're talking."

The small group of six walked a short distance from the legionary encampment into the nearby settlement that featured an array of inns eager to sell their wine to the local legionnaires at inflated prices. They wandered up to a brick building with a tiled roof. Appearance wise, it was a cut above most of the other places they had passed. The wooden sign above the entrance read *The Legionnaire*. Artorus and his group of new friends entered the establishment to be accosted by a blast of raucous shouting. Amid the dim interior, the place was packed with veteran legionnaires from the Fifteenth Legion. Looking about, he noted that all the tables were occupied.

Mellitius elbowed his way through the throng crowding the serving area and displayed six fingers. The harried serving girl nodded and quickly thrust six goblets of wine before him on the serving board. Mellitius picked up the goblets and handed them to his thirsty entourage.

Alderic sipped the contents and winced. He had come to enjoy the fruitful, slightly sweetish flavor of the grape, and although he wasn't knowledgeable when it came to judging wine, he knew this stuff was pure swill. Even the potion they called wine at the ludus was better than this stuff. The wine served at the senator's house, even to the slaves, was ten times better than this. In unison, the six men raised their cups, toasting their survival of the legion's training regimen. Alderic grimaced as the liquid trickled down his throat. The men clustered together so they could hear each other talk. Mellitius shouted above the din. "So, Artorus, where you from?"

Alderic cringed inwardly. The last thing he wanted to discuss with other people was his past. He offered a vague response. "I originally from north in Germania. Leave there when young and become bodyguard."

Flavius, a tall thin youth, inquired, "Is that where you got your sword training? We all noticed that Centurion Fulvius exempts you most times in the one-on-one sword drills."

Alderic grinned in reply. "I have good teacher. Spent many hours on the drill field learning my craft. Before long, you all be as good as me."

"Why did you quit and join the legions?" asked Mellitius.

He hesitated slightly before answering, wishing they would stop with the questions. "Long story. Man who employed me got sick and died. Have trouble finding work. Needed steady employment, so I joined the legions. Bad decision."

The others chuckled in understanding. Alderic heaved a sigh of relief. They'd bought his story. Mellitius gestured to the serving girl for more wine. The men thrust their goblets toward the serving board.

Publius, a heavy-set fellow with dark curly hair, spoke. "I hope life becomes a little easier once we get through this madness. I'd heard the training was tough for legionnaire recruits, but what we've been put through borders on cruelty."

The others all nodded sagely, and then, like a budding rain storm, the bitching and complaining began. It went on non-stop for the better part of the evening. Artorus was content to just listen, occasionally offering a short comment. Any subject was more tolerable than inquiries about his past. He was feeling mellow, the wine buzzing in his head. It was getting late in the evening, and he was beginning to wonder when they would call it a night, when the trouble began.

A legionnaire with protruding lips and a perpetual sneer on his face wandered over to the group. He was backed by a bunch of his cronies. Artorus and friends had been so engaged in their conversation that they'd missed the derisive scowls directed their way. The leader moved to stand in front of Mellitius, so he was right in his face. "Never seen you here before? You new here?"

Alderic sighed. Intuitively, he knew this wasn't going to end well. These men were looking for a fight, and they outnumbered the six recruits. Of course, the leader with the sneer face had selected the smallest of their group, Mellitius, to instigate a fracas.

Mellitius, despite his drunken stupor, quickly realized that these men were seeking a brawl and handled the situation with aplomb. He puffed out his chest. "We are new recruits in training. So why don't you let us alone and piss off."

Alderic smiled. Good. He was not backing down to these veteran pricks. Just like at the ludus, being timid would be the worst thing one could do.

Sneer-face, turned to his companions. "Look what we have here. A bunch of raw recruits drinking in our establishment." The others now moved closer, ready to pounce upon Artorus and the others.

Alderic, who towered over the other legionnaires, acted decisively. He slid between Sneer-face and Mellitius. "Either you move away now or I'm going to toss you out." He didn't wait for the man to answer. He lifted Sneer-face off his feet and tossed the figure tumbling into his cronies, sending most of them sprawling to the floor. The brawl was on.

The veteran legionnaires recovered quickly, charging into the six recruits. Alderic was content using his long arms to keep his antagonists away. He wasn't trained as a street fighter and quickly learned that pushing people away wasn't enough. Several fists flew from behind him, connecting with his face. He began punching back. The battle didn't last long. Out of nowhere, the street patrol materialized. They swarmed into the establishment and having had extensive experience in bar brawls quickly restrained the offending parties. The six recruits were bound and escorted back to their training area. Alderic, looking back, observed that Sneer-face and his retinue were afforded better treatment. They remained behind, some bloodied, but smugly holding their drinking cups.

It was late in the evening. The six men stood in line, facing Centurion Fulvius and Optio Rufus. The six figures were silent, heads hung low, their faces swollen and blood-caked. Fulvius paced back and forth, smacking his leg with this wooden staff. "You men are a disgrace. I allow you your first taste of freedom from training and what do you do? You get in a drunken brawl with other legionnaires, some of whom I'm told require medical attention. What am I to do with you?"

Publius raised his head slightly. "Sir, we was just drinking when those bastards—"

"Silence," roared Fulvius. "Who gave you permission to speak?"

The recruits stood mute, their eyes downcast.

"Here's what's going to happen. You will all be restricted to camp for the remainder of your training and you will get extra shifts of guard duty. Your punishment could have been much worse, but since it was communicated to me that you did kick the shit out of those arse holes from the sixth century, I will show some leniency. Dismissed."

The men grinned, knowing they had been spared severe punishment and that Fulvius was not that angry with them.

Several weeks later, close to the completion of their training, the men were undergoing a final exercise. They would clash with an equal number of men from one of the other centuries of the cohort in mock combat. It was to test how much they had absorbed in their training and whether they could measure up to experienced soldiers.

Alderic stood among his new-found friends, waiting for their final instructions. Across the drill field an equal number of veterans were gathered, waiting for the exercise to commence. Alderic looked up and noticed the soldiers pointing directly at him. He wondered why they would be singling him out. It dawned upon him that these were the same men from the tavern brawl, the sixth century. "Look guys! It's the same bunch we tangled with at the tavern."

Mellitius, never at a loss for words, stepped forward. Cupping his hands near his mouth, he shouted at them. "Hope you arseholes can fight better than the last time we met." His words spawned whoops and shouts among the new recruits. Word had spread about the altercation with the sixth century, and as a result, Mellitius and his friends were looked upon as heroes.

His remarks were greeted by jeers from the opposite camp. The two clusters edged toward one another. Men brandished their wooden swords and shields.

Centurion Fulvius stepped between the two groups of legionnaires before things escalated. "Enough. Save your strength for the battle drill. Now, back off, all of you." For effect, he gestured with his wooden staff to separate. He waited for both groups to move apart.

"Listen up. Today's drill will feature unit combat, with two ranks of twenty men each in each force. You will put on a good show. Our cohort commander, Centurion Gracchus, is observing. So, don't fuck up. Men of the sixth century, you are expected to perform like the veterans that you are. Recruits, show me that the last eight weeks have not been a waste of my time. I trained you and my reputation is on the line. Now form up."

Artorus was positioned in the first rank, in the exact center of the formation. This is precisely where Fulvius wanted him to be. The recruits were expected to demonstrate several things today. First, they were to show that they were physically equal to experienced soldiers. Second, they were to act cohesively as a unit. Each man was to depend on the person on either side of him and behind him. If one of them fell or was incapacitated, another would take his place from the second rank. This was how legions functioned. Every man fought as an individual but was part of a larger unit that ebbed and flowed with the tide of the battle. That was how they had been trained.

Alderic looked to his left and right. Each man was attired just like him—chain mail, helmet, wooden shield, and wooden sword. One was Publius, the heavy-set recruit involved in the brawl. He wasn't sure he remembered the name of the other. Didn't matter. These men were the largest of the recruits. It was critical for the center of the line to be invincible.

The two opposing forces shifted into their final alignment and made minor modifications to their ranks. They were set. The distance between the trainees and the sixth century was about thirty paces. "Ready," roared Fulvius. "Advance."

Alderic rushed forward, careful not to get ahead of his comrades. There was a resounding crash as the two sides collided, shield on shield. Screams and grunts reverberated in the air as the men pushed forward with their shields and thrust with the blunted wooden swords. Alderic peered over the rim of his shield at the man opposite him. He faced a burly figure with a short beard. The man snarled and attempted to drive Alderic back. "Get ready to learn a lesson," he sneered. But his arrogance soon dwindled, as he grunted and heaved forward. It was like pushing a brick wall. There was no give. Alderic effortlessly blocked an attempt by his opponent to hammer him with the sword over his shield. Alderic countered with a tremendous

heave using his legs. The man became slightly unbalanced. This slight change of position was all Alderic needed. He drove the man into the ground. But his opponents were trained veterans. A legionnaire from the second rank of the sixth century leaped into the gap limiting any possible breach in the lines.

Alderic's companions to his sides hadn't displaced their adversaries. Both men were at a standoff. Realizing he was slightly in front of the others and his flanks were exposed, leaving him vulnerable, he grudgingly gave ground to be back in line with his mates. And so, it went. The two forces pushed and thrust back and forth, achieving little. A shrill whistle blew. The second ranks from both sides surged forward between the two men to their front, replacing the tired bodies with fresh troops.

Alderic gulped for air once back in the rear rank, waiting to surge forward if the need arose to replace a fallen man from the front ranks. He used his forearm to wipe the sweat trickling down his face. Glancing about, he noted that neither side had gained any ground. Relieved that they were holding up against the veterans, he readied himself for the next whistle. The man in the first rank to his front was struggling against his opponent from the sixth century. His feet slid slowly but inevitably back toward Alderic. He yelled encouragement to the man, a former farm laborer with massive arms. "Go after him, Sempronius. He can't get past you. I'm here to back you up. Smash his face with that shield boss."

After more grunting and bashing, the whistle sounded. Alderic charged ahead knocking over the man who had previously been mishandling Sempronius. The legionnaire from the sixth century had reacted too slowly to the whistle, and as a result was caught flatfooted. Sempronius, now in the rear rank and somewhat winded, recognized the opportunity to seek some reprisal. From the rear ranks, Sempronius, although spent from the recent action in the front rank, surged forward next to Alderic and flattened another man from the sixth. Suddenly, there was a large hole in the lines of the opposing century. The recruits surged forward to exploit the gap. To their credit, the veterans of the sixth regrouped quickly. The lines reformed about five paces behind their original position, sealing the breach. A second surge by Alderic's friends met stiff resistance. Alderic grimaced, disappointed they had not routed the men of the sixth. The whistle blew short trills in succession signaling a cessation of combat. Some men, out of anger and frustration, continued to battle. Fulvius blew the whistle again, with little effect. Then he waded into the fracas, separating the men, beating them about the head and face with his wooden staff to make his point.

Fulvius gathered the trainees away from the sixth century under the shade of a giant oak tree. A medicus stood nearby, but apart from a few bloody noses and some facial bruises, there were no injuries that required his attention. Fulvius proffered a wide grin. "Good show. You executed well. Of course, I expected it, since I trained you, and you made me proud. Centurion Gracchus, our cohort commander, observed your performance and was pleased. And if he was pleased, I was pleased. Tomorrow, you will be assigned to one of the six centuries in the cohort. Since I have the most vacancies, a good number of you will be coming with me to the second century."

Fulvius paused, a grin creasing his face, waiting for a reaction. "Well don't all cheer at once. How about a little enthusiasm for joining my century?" The men chuckled, then shouted loudly.

The next day, Alderic was given his orders. He was to become part of the first century. It was no surprise. Centurion Fulvius had informed him weeks ago that he was destined for the first and that Centurion Gracchus had wanted him to be part of his unit. There was one other recruit joining him—Mellitius. This was a surprise. The men had been told during their training that the first century usually had the largest and most experienced men. This was logical, for the cohort commander directed the first century and the unit usually took the lead in battle. So why was Mellitius posted to the first? He was by far the smallest of the trainees. Alderic was pleased that Mellitius was joining him but he couldn't figure out why, if indeed the first housed the biggest and toughest. Was it because Gracchus wanted to keep an eye on the under-sized man? Alderic was to soon learn that not all decisions in the legions made sense and one just had to go along with the flow of things.

The two men wandered over to the headquarters of the first. An optio, named Lucullus, indicated that they were to enter the tent of Centurion Gracchus. The officer was expecting them.

Gracchus was seated at a camp table, squinting in the dim light at a parchment. He looked up at the two men standing at the entrance to his tent. He appeared glad to see them. "Ah, my new replacements. Come in. Come in. Welcome to the first century. This is the part where I tell you to do your duties and obey all orders—which is precisely what you are expected to do. Your life and that of those around you may depend upon your following orders. Understood?"

Both men nodded.

"Good. Then we understand each other. And don't get too attached to your surroundings. We'll be leaving here soon. I'm not sure where we'll be heading, but the armies of Octavius Caesar, of which we are a part, will be marshalling in the near future. There is a war coming, and it will be fought against other Romans. Any questions?"

The two men remained at attention, silent.

"All right then. Optio Lucullus will take you to your new tent mates. Oh, and one more thing. You may be slightly harassed by the veterans, being new here and all. Don't let it bother you. I saw the way you handled the sixth century. Damn impressive. You're as good as any of them. A bit raw, mind you, but capable. Dismissed."

Lucullus guided them some distance away to the section of the encampment occupied by the first century. He gestured toward a large eight-man tent made of goatskin. "You will both be stationed at this tent. This is the first *contubernium*. You will eat and sleep with the other six men of this section. There are nine other contubernia in the first century. Each has their own tent. The other centuries of the cohort are tented the same way. We sleep like we're organized. Rank has its privileges. Centurion Gracchus and I have separate tents. The men are a good lot. You should have no trouble getting along with them. Get your gear stored. We will be performing drills this afternoon, so bring your armor and weapons, and not that wooden shit you've been training with." He turned and departed.

Alderic stood on the drill field in a cluster with the other seventy-nine men of his century. More than a few veterans examined the novices with inquisitive hostility. The two new men were outsiders. The veterans of the first century were unsure if the newcomers could be depended upon. Alderic had been expecting this sort of welcome.

He sighed. He guessed this was the way of things in the legions. He gazed off wistfully in the distance to the north and mused briefly of his home back in the woodlands of Germania, wondering how he had gotten to this point in his life. His past life across the Rhenus was lost to him now. He pondered briefly what his mother would think if she saw him now, dressed and armored like a Roman legionnaire. Men like these had killed her husband and captured her son. She would probably pass out. Turning about, he decided that he had best stop his reveries and concentrate on his current situation.

The other five centuries of the cohort aligned to the right of the first century. The men wore their cloaks to ward off the winter chill that had descended upon the drill field. They were armed with their shields and swords but no javelins. Practicing throwing the deadly spears was reserved for another day. Today was all about the battle drill of the centuries and the cohort. They stood in a closed formation, meaning they were grouped tight together, about three feet apart; enough room for each man to fight, yet close enough to protect the flanks of the adjacent comrades. The use of the open formation, where the men were about six feet apart, was employed when the ranks took turns flinging volleys of javelins at the foe. The drill began.

"Line formation," roared Gracchus. The other centurions echoed his command. Alderic found himself in the first rank of forty men. He sensed the second rank immediately behind them. The first five squads, totaling forty men, assumed their positions, shield held slightly forward, gladius in their right hands.

"Forward," commanded Gracchus. The two battle lines of the entire cohort surged onward across the drill field. They continued for some distance. "Rapid advance," bellowed Gracchus. At a swift pace, the cohort moved forward. This continued for a few moments before the next command was issued. "Wedge formation."

Alderic was lost. He had no idea where his place was and where to go. "That way, you dumb fuck!" yelled Optio Lucullus. Alderic hurried to catch up with the others. His place was at the very center of the wedge. He realized that he was the tip of the spear for the second cohort. They trotted quickly across the drill field.

"Testudo," commanded Gracchus. The century swiftly flowed into a rectangular group. The center of the formation held their shields overhead. The men at the front and edges of the rectangle held their shields, protecting the fore and sides. Once again, Alderic was in the front of the century, his shield protecting the group from any missiles coming from that direction.

"Line formation," growled Gracchus. His unit, as well as the other five centuries, smoothly transitioned into their double ranks. Artorus was impressed. These men were good; in fact, they were damn good. It appeared as though they could do this in their sleep. There were no missteps among the veterans. Everyone, with the exception of recent recruits, knew exactly where to go and what to do. It was so fluid. There was absolute silence in the ranks during the entire process. No curse, no wise cracks. They had been trained this way. There would be plenty of time for yelling and screaming once the fighting began. They drilled all day, back and forth across the parade ground, nonstop.

The men returned to the encampment, bone-weary and ass hurting. The evening meal was served on a cohort level, which was always a good thing. If they had been on the march, the rations, meager portions of porridge with biscuits, would have been prepared by each of squads. When meals were served on a cohort level, their bread and porridge rations were supplemented with boiled vegetables, cheese, and an occasional piece of meat. Alderic and Mellitius returned to their tent and began sorting out their gear. The pair continued to receive the silent treatment from the other six men of their squad. Their status as "new men" was reinforced during the day's drill, exposing every misstep and mistake.

Later that evening, a small campfire blazed in front of their tent, providing a bit of warmth on a cold evening. The men huddled around the fire sharing a jug of *posca,* a cheap sour wine. The ration of posca had been issued to each of the eight-man squads by Centurion Gracchus as a reward for their outstanding drill. No one offered any to Alderic and Mellitius. Alderic fumed. He went over, forcefully grabbed the jug from one of the startled legionnaire's hands, and proceeded to pour healthy servings into both their clay cups. Without warning, he tossed the jug back to the man, forcing him to drop his cup and spill his wine while trying to catch the container. The other legionnaires of the contubernium gave Alderic resentful looks.

Alderic spoke loudly. "Listen up, first contubernium. In case you haven't noticed, the two of us are part of your squad. My name is Artorus and this fellow next to me is Mellitius. I know you are distrustful of us, but don't you think it might be courteous to at least introduce yourselves. I believe that it's polite to introduce oneself, at least where I come from. You were new guys once too, in case you forgot. Or maybe you're just plain rude."

He paused before continuing. "The second thing I have to say concerns my friend, Mellitius. You might have noticed he's a bit undersized."

A few of the men smirked in acknowledgement.

Alderic continued. "That may be, but he completed his training and humped the same load as everyone else. Furthermore, some fellows from the sixth century decided to pick on him at a tavern a while back. He gave his all. Now, if any of you decide that you want to harass my comrade here, feel free to do so. But know this, you'll have to get through me first, and that is definitely not something you want to do."

With that, the pair walked away from the group into the night, holding their cups of posca, leaving the six veterans dumfounded. They were not used to having new recruits address them this way, but no one stepped forward to challenge Alderic's words. Intuitively they knew better than to risk confrontation with his intimidating bulk.

The next day brought more training. First on the schedule was javelin practice. The new recruits, owing to the time constraints of their condensed training schedule, hadn't received any instruction on heaving the lances. Throwing the deadly front-loaded spear required a good deal of skill, acquired through endless repetition. The wooden javelins were weighted with a heavy iron head to make penetrating armor and flesh more effective. The problem was that the missiles required a sufficient arc to reach their objectives. It took great repetitive training to achieve the desired accuracy. Too small an arc and the javelin would drive into the ground, killing nothing but worms and snakes. Too much loft and the spear would lose penetrating power or fly over the heads of the enemy. Today's exercise was made more arduous by their heavy cloaks. As a rule, the legions didn't go into battle wearing cloaks, but there was always the possibility that a marching column might be ambushed when the men were adorned with the garments. They prepared for all eventualities.

It took a while for Alderic to adjust to the heavier javelins. Back in his homeland, the spears were light, not intended for piercing heavy armor. The shaft was wood, upon which an iron point was affixed.

The German spears could be heaved farther because of their light weight but could not match the front loaded Roman *pila* with regard to penetrating power. Like most of the other recruits, his throws fell short of the intended target. The new men were subjected to numerous mocking comments from the veterans on the quality of their throws.

After javelin practice, they hacked at a wooden post with their swords to increase their stamina. The men detested this particular exercise. Not only was it tiring but it nicked their blades. They commonly spent several hours of what was their free time polishing and sharpening their blades with a grindstone to repair the damage. Last on the day's training schedule was more unit drill. Alderic and Mellitius fared a bit better the second time around on the unit drill, as they were now familiar with the what's and the where's.

It was late in the afternoon and the men were gathered around for the evening meal. Alderic had wandered apart from the others, enjoying a moment of solitude, something rare in a legion encampment. His musings were interrupted by strident voices to his left. He observed a rather large legionnaire, a bull of a figure, holding Mellitius's mess tin high in the air, out of his reach. The tormentor was not from their squad, although he seemed vaguely familiar. As he observed the antics, his anger began to boil with rage.

Alderic strode over and ripped the mess tin from the man's hand. He then shoved him away from Mellitius. "You want to pick on someone, try me. I'm more your size. What do you say, big man?"

The legionnaire was too startled to speak, which incensed Alderic even more. He pushed the figure again. This time, the man retaliated, pushing him back. A crowd quickly gathered, some shouting words of encouragement.

"What in the fucking Hades is going on here?" Centurion Gracchus waded into the middle of the altercation. "You know the rules. No fighting. Corvinius, what do you have to say for yourself?" The soldier shook his head and remained mute. "What about you, Artorus?" He didn't wait for an answer. "You're not tired from today's training? Fine. You both are assigned guard duty, double shift tonight. You'll be paired together in the guard tower at the camp gate. I suggest you get to know one another a little better."

Gracchus stared at the small crowd that had gathered. "Now listen up, all of you fuckwits. There is a major shit storm brewing across the sea and we're going to be part of it. I'm going to say this only once. There is to be no fighting among yourselves. Save it for the forces of men who murdered our beloved Caesar. Next time there's even the smallest infraction, I will come down hard on you, and not just with guard duty like these two. Now get in formation for the evening meal." He shook his head in disgust and wandered off.

Later that night, Alderic and Corvinius stood in the high wooden guard tower, staring off into the night. A frigid wind blew from the surrounding plain, buffeting the two men. There was an awkward silence between them. Alderic glanced at his recent antagonist. He was a big man. No doubt the reason he was in the first century. His hair was a light brown, almost blonde, cut short. He had high cheekbones framing a handsome face. He was older than Alderic, perhaps in his mid-twenties. From his corner of the rectangular platform, the figure spoke. "I was only having some fun with the little man. Nothing mean-spirited about it. There was no need for you to overact."

Alderic hesitated, unsure of what to say. "He a new recruit like me. You all think he isn't worthy because of his size. I don't like that."

"Listen, I'm sorry. I was just trying to get some laughs. I'm not a bully." He walked toward Alderic. "My name is Corvinius." He reached out his arm to shake hands.

Alderic believed the man to be sincere and decided to respond to the gesture. "Call me Artorus."

"I can tell from your accent that you are not from the Italian province. What's your background?"

"I from Germania. Work as a bodyguard, but my employer died. I seek more permanent work, so I join the legions. What about you?"

"Germania, heh. Welcome to the legions, Artorus. I'm from the Italian province in the mountain district. I enlisted eight years ago. Couldn't stand farming. We mostly grew rocks and barely survived. This legionary life is hard, but where I came from, it wasn't much better."

"What did your parents say about your leaving?"

"They were glad to be rid of me. I ate too much. One less mouth to feed."

Alderic chuckled. He decided he liked the man. He was forthright. "So, Corvinius, was joining legions good idea?"

"I guess. A little good, a little not so good. I get fed, have some money to spend, and made good friends. If I live long enough, I get to retire with some land and money, but the fighting is hard. We tangled with Antonius's forces last year. I lost some good comrades fighting, fellow Romans no less. Now, we're supposed to be joining forces with Antonius to fight other Roman legions. I don't understand it. I hope we'll be rewarded with a large bonus, assuming we win. At least that's the rumor."

There was brief silence between the pair. Corvinius asked, "Have you been in the fighting before?"

Alderic hesitated, attempting to cobble together a response. "Some. I fight as bodyguard. I get paid for that. I never fight as part of an army like you."

"Fighting is fighting. Dangerous business, no?"

Artorus nodded. "Yes, dangerous business."

Corvinius smirked, his tone a bit lighter. "You should know that Gracchus can be mean as a snake sometimes. He never lets up on us, but when we get in the thick of it and the swords are out, you want someone like him in command. He knows his stuff. So, my advice is to suffer his discipline but follow him blindly in combat. That way, we all have a better chance at survival. Most of the men feel the same way. They despise him but will do anything he says without question."

"I kind of got that impression. It is good to have strong leader in the thick of it."

The silence resumed between the two. Alderic attempted to break it. "I'm curious why stand in this tower, staring into the dark. You have years of experience in the legions; tell me, why?"

"You don't know? We are to serve as sentries in case the barbarian horde from the north—no offense Artorus—cross the mountains and decide to attack this encampment."

Alderic chuckled. "You have sarcastic wit, Corvinius. I'm a barbarian from the north and wouldn't spend a minute of effort to cross the mountains to attack this place. Loot some villages in Gaul, maybe, but here, I think not."

"Ah, so you were a raider, were you?"

"I didn't say that. Only that if I was one, I wouldn't come all of this distance to strike here."

The two men talked on into the darkness about everything, yet about nothing. They were finally relieved in the middle of the night and staggered back to their tents to grab a little sleep. Days in the legions started early.

The next morning, the centuries of the cohort were engaged in one-on-one individual combat training. The men cheered and yelled for their tent mates, as the pair of fighters traded sword and shield blows in the make-shift arena. It was individual combat between different squads. Lucullus refereed one bout, and Gracchus mediated the other. The men loved this kind of training. It was fun to root for your squad mates, and best of all, you spent most of the time standing around. When one was actually in the ring fighting, well, that was a different story. It was a draining and often a dangerous endeavor, even with the armor and wooden shields and swords, but this ranked high above the endless repetitions of battle drills and forced marches that normally characterized their days.

The first bout ended in a draw. The man in Artorus's squad, Barilius, had given a good account of himself despite being matched with a bigger, more powerful opponent. Gracchus shouted out the next pair. "Artorus, first squad, versus Corvinius, third squad. Get out here and show us what you got."

Corvinius strode into the ring, brandishing his sword. "Come out, Artorus. Show me the skills you learned as a bodyguard." He missed Gracchus's silent smirk.

Alderic trotted into the small arena bordered by the wooden logs that lined the perimeter. He realized that Gracchus had deliberately paired them up after their altercation the previous evening, unaware that the two had patched things up. *Sorry to disappoint you, Centurion.*

Corvinius stuck out his chest. "I'll show you what an experienced legionnaire can do. I won't be too hard on you."

Alderic replied blandly, "If you say so."

Gracchus looked at the two combatants. "Ready. Begin."

Corvinius immediately charged at Artorus, only to not find him there. He had moved to his left in a lightning-quick dart. Startled not to have found his opponent where he had expected, he advanced again. He came in close, attempting to hook his shield with Alderic's and wrench it out of his grasp. This ploy of his was quickly foiled as well, as Alderic easily slid his shield out of the way.

Alderic, separated from his opponent, grinned mockingly at Corvinius, beckoning him to attack. He lowered his sword and shield, appearing defenseless.

With a growl, Corvinius charged, attempting to bull rush Alderic and knock him down. He was rewarded with a painful slash to his back as Alderic side-stepped the rush and dispensed an attack of his own. Corvinius bit back the urge to cry out. Even with the armored mail, the strike had hurt like Hades. It dawned upon him that Artorus was a skilled fighter, much better than him. Artorus could have taken him down during any of his previous maneuvers, and yet he had held back. *Now what?*

Corvinius edged forward warily, less eager now. He delivered a series of sword thrusts that clattered harmlessly off Artorus's shield. He decided to retreat and let Artorus do the hard work. He got his wish. Artorus attacked Corvinius with a fury, his shield thrusts and sword strikes a blur. Corvinius recoiled, desperate to get away from the menacing figure. Despite his rapid retreat, several blows penetrated his defenses.

"Enough," roared Gracchus. He turned to address the crowd of legionnaires who watched the fighters, most of whom were in awe of the fighting skills displayed by Artorus. "Those of you who think you're good fighters may want to challenge Artorus. He is one of the best I've ever seen. Next pair, front and center."

Corvinius wandered over to Alderic. "Thanks for going easy on me. You could have really embarrassed me out there. I never faced anyone like you. Where did you learn your skills?"

"I have good teacher. It is long story that I would prefer not to dwell upon."

"Good teacher, you say? It was like fighting one of those touted gladiators."

Artorus gulped. "Some say I have natural talent. Gracchus likes the way I fight."

"That bastard Gracchus deliberately paired you with me."

Artorus laughed. "You should choose your enemies more wisely."

"Thank the gods you're not still mad at me. I would be a crippled man on the ground otherwise."

Chapter X

Several weeks later, the men of the first century, second cohort of the Fifteenth Legion stood in formation—a ten-man front, eight ranks deep. A bitter wind from the north blew their cloaks about. Centurion Gracchus paced before them, tapping his staff against his side. "We have our marching orders. This should come as no surprise to you. I told you this was coming. So, here it is. Next week, we will march the entire legion, including all baggage carts and supplies on a south-westerly course from our base here near Mutina and proceed on via Aemilia to Ariminum and then due south to Ancona."

He paused to let the eighty men in front of him process the news. He continued. "The going should be easy on this initial stretch. We will be on a Roman paved road. There will supply points along the way to refurbish our food stores. After we reach Ancona, the second leg of our journey gets a bit nasty."

The men let out involuntary groans in unison. There was always something that would conveniently present itself in the legions to fuck up their day.

"SILENCE," he roared. "Did I give you permission to speak? Enough of your whining." A quiet settled over the men. "That's better. Now, as I was about to say, to remain on the paved roads, we would need to head southwest toward Rome and from there, move southeast toward our destination in Brundisium—the coastal town and home of the east-coast fleet. The problem is that the Triumvirate has decided that no legions are to approach within fifty miles of Rome. Therefore, from Ancona, we will proceed due south along an unimproved dirt track. I'll be blunt. This route is shorter than going through Rome but will prove to be far more difficult. We will face major obstacles with baggage trains on this dirt trek. So, prepare yourselves for some tough humping. Once we reach Brundisium, we will begin training with the other legions under the command of Octavius Caesar. Dismissed."

Alderic heaved a sigh of relief, perhaps the only man in the century, or the cohort for that matter, to do so. If he had to march back into Rome, he was certainly going to be recognized. That would most likely be the end. He didn't give a fig about the dirt trek and the hardships that would befall the legion. It would keep him away from Rome. That was all he cared about.

Alderic grunted from the load he was carrying. He shifted the forked pole holding his gear to a spot on his shoulder that hurt less than the other places. His current world consisted of the view of the man directly in front of him and the two men on his either side. The sounds of clanking armor and jingling equipment resonated up and down the legionary column. It was a discordant sound, yet, in some ways, melodious to the ears of the marching soldiers. Scudding clouds from the north obscured the sun, casting a perpetual grey over the landscape. Periods of gusty rain pummeled the column of marching soldiers, who gritted their teeth, hunched their shoulders against the cold, and trekked onward.

Alderic glanced to his right, noting the struggling form of Corvinius. Despite the frosty conditions, sweat streaked down his face. The two men had carried on a conversation for the better part of the day's march, but nearing the end, the pair was too tired to speak. Normally, talking would be forbidden while marching but given that this was not a tactical situation and there was no threat of an enemy attack, the restrictions had been relaxed. The pair had bonded even more over the past three days, marching, sharing stories, and partaking meals with each other. One might even call them good friends.

In the late afternoon, the column halted. Alderic observed Centurion Gracchus walk ahead to the ranks of the first cohort where the legate and his staff were located. A short time later he returned and pointed with his vine-wood staff. "We camp just ahead."

Several hard days later, they were bivouacked outside the town of Ariminum. The Fifteenth Legion had completed the first leg of their journey but had much farther to go. The legate decided to stay there an extra day to take on additional provisions and rest the pack animals. The next day, troops were given the freedom to venture into town and enjoy the pleasures being offered. It wasn't an especially large town, but it had a large number of taverns and brothels to satisfy the sudden influx of men.

Alderic and Corvinius ventured out of the encampment. Fortuitously, they selected a place called *The Lucky Dice*. It was a good choice, with a mixture of both townspeople and legionnaires. The atmosphere of the inn was somewhat subdued compared to the other raucous establishments, now flooded with legionnaires. In the Lucky Dice, one could make conversation without having to shout. There was a sense of civility in this tavern. The two men had just devoured several smoked sausages and were on their third cup of wine, when Corvinius wiped his mouth on his sleeve and said in a hushed tone, "So, do you want to have a go in the back room with one of the women? I hear they're not too bad."

A distant look clouded Alderic's eyes. "No, but feel free to do so yourself. I'll wait for you here."

Corvinius backed away from his friend in surprise. "What's this? A legionnaire who doesn't like whores? I hope you're not one of those men lovers, are you?"

Alderic shook his head. "No, it's nothing like that. I would prefer not to be in the company of whores. It's a long story."

"That's the second time you've said that to me."

"What?"

"That it's a long story. You said that about your fight training also."

"Well it really is a long story. I'll tell you about it someday, but not now. Can we change the subject?"

Corvinius mockingly backed away again. "Aren't we getting a bit touchy? All right. Some other time. You remain a man of mystery."

Alderic drained the contents of his goblet and slapped it down on the counter. He signaled to the bar maid for another round. He was beginning to feel a bit mellow, the wine numbing the various aches and pains in his arms and legs. He sighed in contentment.

Another legionnaire stumbled into their midst. Alderic recoiled to avoid colliding with the figure. Upon recognizing the man, he frowned. The man's name was Quintus. He worked for the quartermaster at the legion level. Most of the men despised him. He was obnoxious, even more so when he had been drinking. He had quite a racket going on at his quartermaster position. It was rumored that he often issued the men substandard equipment, probably destined for the scrap heap, which soon fell apart after limited use, and yet charged the legionnaire the full value of the equipment as if it were brand new. He was a loathsome-looking person, with a round body and a moon face with fat protruding lips.

Corvinius didn't attempt to mask his dislike. "What do you want, Quintus? Don't you have some other place to be?"

The drunken man ignored the acerbic welcome and pointed his finger at Artorus. "Heard about you," he slurred. "They said you were one of the best fighters around. Don't know how that's possible. I mean, a fucking German is one of the legion's best?" He sniggered at his own remark. "You think you're some hot shit, better than us Romans?"

Alderic paid the bothersome man no heed. He turned his back on him and picked up his goblet, which by now had been refilled.

Not to be deterred, Quintus continued. "Well do you? Fuck, how can we fight the barbarians when we got them in our ranks?"

Corvinius interceded. "Quintus, why don't you piss off? You're insulting Artorus for no reason other than that you're a nasty drunk."

The man sniggered. "I can say what I want." Swaying slightly, he pointed his finger at Alderic. "You look familiar. I never forget a face. I've seen you somewhere before. I know I have. It'll come to me. Where have you served?"

Alderic glowered, now facing Quintus. "You're mistaken. Let us alone. Now piss off." Both men turned their backs on Quintus and retreated to a corner for privacy. Thankfully, Quintus didn't follow them.

They drank several more rounds. Corvinius raised his empty cup and looked at Alderic inquiringly. Alderic shook his head. "I've had my fill. I'm going out back to relieve myself. My eyeballs are floating. Then we can depart."

Alderic returned, issuing a satisfied sigh. The pair exited the tavern and ventured into the night. They hadn't gone far when Quintus reappeared, chasing after them. "Shit," Corvinius muttered, "Can't you take a hint?"

The drunk staggered up close to Alderic. "I know where I saw you before. You was in the arena in Rome, a retiarius. You beat that secutor, killed his ass at the end. It was you. Big fucking hero. Now, a bloody gladiator in the legions. Wait till they hear this."

Alderic looked up and down the street to ensure they were alone. They were. In a swift move, he withdrew his dagger and savagely drove it to the hilt under Quintus's chin and into his brain, killing him instantly. Blood splattered on Alderic as he withdrew the dagger. Quintus collapsed.

"Let's get out of here," said Alderic, his voice shaking. He began to move but realized Corvinius was frozen in place.

"Jupiter's ass, you killed him!"

"Yes, I killed the fuck and for good reason. What's the matter? Never seen anyone slain before? Now, can we get going?" He grabbed Corvinius's arm, half dragging him down the road. The two men moved rapidly away from the scene.

"Artorus, do you have any idea what the legions will do to you if they discover you slew a fellow legionnaire? It will not be pretty."

"I'm aware of what they can do, but it will be no worse than if they find out who I am."

Corvinius slowed down. "Is this part of your long story?"

"It is. If the legions find out who I am, I'm a dead man, and by most unpleasant methods."

"So, it's true? You were a fucking gladiator? No wonder you kicked my ass out there on the drill field."

"Yes, I was a gladiator, and it is a long story, one that you don't need to know. If they discover my identity, they will kill me and my friends, including you." He pointed with his finger for emphasis.

"What kind of shit have you gotten yourself into?"

"Listen to me, Corvinius. I'm not going to tell you much. I was a gladiator, then a bodyguard. My master who I was paid to protect became a political enemy. Powerful men killed his entire family and his slaves, except for me. It's best you not know the details."

"All right, Artorus, I will trust you. But we need to get our stories straight and wash off any blood you might have on you. Sure as shit there's going to be an inquiry about the murder of Quintus, despicable as he was. Now wipe down your dagger. Make sure there is no trace of blood. Let me look at you."

Corvinius squinted at Alderic. "Fuck, I can't see a bloody thing. Not much moonlight. We're going back into the town. Wash off any traces of blood in the fountain. Then we go to another tavern as if nothing happened. Got it?"

"Fine. Let's go."

The legions broke camp and were on the road the next day. Like most of the other men, Alderic and Corvinius were hungover from the night before. The weather was cloudy and cold. The long column, stretched over several miles, made its way down the road. The conversation was muted, given their conditions. Alderic and Corvinius had both agreed the night before that under no circumstances were they ever to mention the killing of Quintus to one another in case their words were overheard by others.

Corvinius turned toward Alderic. "The inside of my mouth tastes like dried mule shit from all that cheap wine last night."

Alderic continued striding forward under his heavy load, then looked at his friend quizzically. "I've never tasted dried mule shit. What's it like?"

Corvinius spat back. "It was only a figure of speech."

"What is a figure of speech?" asked Artorus.

Corvinius thought for a few moments. "I don't know how to explain that. Wait a minute. If I said, for example, that a woman was hotter than Venus, that would be a figure of speech."

"Why, does the woman have a fever?"

"Artorus, you are trying my patience. Stop messing with me."

Alderic let out a mighty chuckle, knowing he had bested his friend."

The Roman column marched all day before mercifully stopping for the night. The troops constructed their usual fortified encampment. Both men kept their ears open for any word about an inquiry into the death of Quintus but heard nothing.

Their relief didn't last long. Two days later, the pair was summoned to the tent of Centurion Gracchus. They reported, trying not to look apprehensive. Both men stood before their centurion. Next to the centurion stood another officer. Gracchus began. "Artorus, Corvinius, this is Tribune Flaccus from the legate's staff. He has been charged with investigating a crime within the ranks of the legions. It seems that there has been an unfortunate development. Three nights ago, back in Ariminum, a man named Quintus was found dead with a knife thrust to his throat."

"Aye, we've heard. The whole legion's heard about it," replied Corvinius.

"It has been reported to Tribune Flaccus by others that you were seen in the company of Quintus at The Lucky Dice. Is that true?"

Corvinius took the lead. "We saw him there. He was drunk. He made several nasty remarks to Artorus about his nationality. I told him to piss off."

Tribune Flaccus interrupted, "So, you don't deny meeting him at the tavern?"

"No, we were there. So was Quintus."

"And you got into altercation there," he said accusingly.

Corvinius replied, "Sir, I would hardly call it an altercation. He had had too much to drink. He was being a bit of an arsehole. We told him to go elsewhere."

Flaccus responded. "What about you?" he said pointing at Artorus. "Can you speak?"

"Of course, sir. As Corvinius said, the man was being obnoxious. We told him to piss off."

"What did you do after you left The Lucky Dice?" inquired Flaccus.

Corvinius jumped back into the conversation. "We went to another tavern, the Three Sisters."

Flaccus frowned. "Did Quintus follow you or go with you?"

"No, we didn't see him again?"

There was a period of silence. Gracchus looked toward the tribune. "Sir, are you satisfied with their answers?"

The tribune glared at the two men before answering. "I guess so. But I intend to press this matter to the fullest. The legate has directed me to find the man responsible for this villainous act and mete out the appropriate punishment. They can go for now."

Gracchus nodded, giving them a jaundiced eye. "Go on and get some rest."

The pair exited the tent. Once they were out of hearing range and no one else was around, Alderic spoke through the side of his mouth. "You think they believed us?"

Corvinius replied in a guarded tone. "I do, but we're still under suspicion. Until they have something more solid, we are a connection to the man who was murdered that night. It could be that others will be identified who had words with the unfortunate Quintus in The Lucky Dice, but as of now, we are suspects. If I'm reading Gracchus correctly, he wants this thing to go away, so let's not give him any reason to cast further doubt upon us. As we agreed previously, we are not to speak of this event ever. They have no real link of us to Quintus, and the man had the reputation of being an arsehole. Agreed?"

"Fine by me. Let's get some food. I hope this Tribune Flaccus does not pry too deeply into my past and look into my recruiting records. One thing might lead to another, and then I will be truly fucked."

Days later, the Fifteenth paraded through the streets of Ancona, the next town on their journey south. The streets were lined with people. They cheered and waved brightly colored cloths as a mostly full-strength legion marched down their avenues, through the forum in the town center, and past the shops and inns. Ordinarily, there would be festive garlands and flowers, but this was the dead of winter and there were no flowers to harvest.

The busy harbor—filled with many merchant vessels and fluttering pennants—sailed the waters of the Mare Adriaticum below the town. Gracchus stood to the side, observing his century, all in step, file through the twisting streets. He smiled inwardly. By the gods, they looked good. He was proud of his first century and the second cohort that he commanded. He dropped a bit farther back to watch the other five centuries parade past.

Alderic stared straight ahead, making sure that he was in step with the others of his century. They were in a tight formation, ten abreast and eight men deep. He was positioned on the outer right side of the ranks, so he was visible to the entire crowd. He happened to glance up to see people standing on balconies one floor above the street level, applauding as the legions proudly strode past. A jolt traveled through him, almost causing him to stumble—an act not lost on Corvinius, who shot him a puzzling glance.

Alderic was fixated on a figure straight ahead on one of the upper tiers. Clad in a pleated, flowing stolla and waving a colored cloth stood Bridin. There was no doubt, it was her. Her golden-brown hair, cut short, shimmered in the afternoon sun.

Alderic continued glancing upward, hoping she would direct her gaze at him and recognize him beneath his iron helmet. She turned her head and looked straight at him. His heart thumped in his chest, but her gaze wandered to the next batch of legionnaires coming into view, and then he had passed her. He turned his head back toward her as the century continued marching, but to no avail.

After the parade, the legion established camp, complete with a palisade and ditches, on outskirts the town. By the time they had finished their preparation and the pitching of tents, it was nearly twilight. Corvinius wandered over to Alderic, who was finishing pounding the last tent stake. "Do you mind telling me what that was about?"

"What?"

"Don't give me that 'what' crock of shit. You know what I'm talking about. I saw your eyes just about pop out of your head when you saw that woman on the balcony. I thought you were going to break rank."

"Corvinius, as I've said before, it's a long story."

"Not that again. C'mon, tell me."

Alderic looked around to see others in the vicinity, so he waved Corvinius to an isolated part of the camp. "She is part of my past. It would be dangerous if the legions discovered she knew me or was with me. That's all I can tell you for now. Maybe later I'll tell you the entire story. Don't let anyone know."

Corvinius sighed. "Alright mystery man, are you going to try and see her? You know we're all restricted to camp. No passes into the town except for the officers. I guess you heard the legate was most displeased after the liberty granted in Ariminum. Too many soldiers puking by the side of the road on the march the next day, plus the murder of Quintus."

"I'll find a way to exit the camp and come back in without detection."

"And how are you going to manage that? Do tell."

"I have a plan," he announced proudly, "and you are going to assist me. I'll tell the guards I'm on a detail for collecting wood for the night fires. I'll make several trips, then not come back after the last one. Be gone maybe a few hours. I bring wood to gate. You take it from there."

Corvinius stroked his chin in thought. "Not bad. It has a chance. Just don't get caught."

Later that evening, Alderic, clad in his gray tunic and heavy cloak, approached the sentries at the northern gate, the one closest to town.

"I'm charged with the wood gathering detail for the century. I be bringing in wood. Permission to leave the camp?"

The two guards looked at one another quizzically. One of the guards stated sternly, "No one is to leave camp. Those are our orders."

Alderic shrugged his shoulders. "Fine by me. But my centurion will be very displeased."

The other of the two guards spoke. "How far are you going?"

Alderic replied glibly. "Not far. Probably in sight of the palisade."

"I guess we can make an exception. Go ahead then. Don't get lost out there. By the way, how did you get that shit detail?"

"I not follow orders well. This my punishment. You know how it is; the crap we have to put up with in the legions."

"Aye, brother. I've had enough of those details myself. Don't be too long out there."

Exiting the camp, Alderic waved his arm in acknowledgement to the guards and then entered the wooded area outside of camp to collect firewood. He hastily gathered pieces of wood of various sizes up in his arms and took them back inside the gate, handing them to Corvinius, who transported the bundle to the tent area of the first century. He made another trip so the guards would get used to his coming and going. On the next excursion, as soon as he was out of sight of the guards, he sprinted in the direction of the town. Once within the walls of the town, he slowed to a walk, attempting to find the place where he saw Bridin. He made several false turns before finding the main avenue. Then, he began looking for a merchant shop that sold woven goods. That would most likely be the place Bridin would be.

Walking slowly so that he could carefully scrutinize the various store fronts, he found what he was seeking. It was a storefront with a modest facade. A small wooden sign declared that this was the place for Ancona Woven Goods. Most merchants lived above their shops. He hoped this would be no exception. He also remembered that Bridin would go by the name of Claudia. He climbed the creaky wooden stairs to the second level and rapped on the door.

A muffled female voice echoed from behind the wooden door. "It is late. What do you want?"

"Claudia?"

"Yes, who is it?"

"Bridin, you don't recognize my voice? It's Alderic."

The door cracked open a hands-breadth. She peeked out into the darkness then flung the door open. She leaped into his arms, embracing him tight. She tilted her face to his and kissed him deeply, then broke apart. "Oh, Alderic, I had given you up for dead." She dragged him into her abode, closing the door firmly behind him. She eyed him up and down, her mouth open. "You're a legionnaire? How did you manage that?"

"To cut it short, I wandered into a legionary recruiting camp by accident. I was kind of trapped, but the more I thought about it, the more it seemed like a good idea. I mean, who would look for me in the legions?"

Bridin grinned knowingly. "It's perfect. You're right. Who would ever think to look for you there?"

"Oh, and by the way, my new name is Artorus."

She raised her eye-brows curiously. "Artorus? I like it. It's such a proper Roman name."

He grinned in return. "We are restricted to camp, but I managed to exit unnoticed. I only have a few hours at best."

Bridin replied, "I know just what I want to do in those few hours." With a cry, she leaped into his arms.

A while later, Bridin clung to Artorus, as he adjusted his uniform in preparation for leaving. She whispered in his ear. "Promise me you'll come back to me. I thought you were dead. I don't want to lose you again."

"I don't know how, but I will make my way back here. For now, there's a war coming and I'll be part of it. I will survive." He hugged her tightly. "I have something to live for. I vow to return."

Bridin wiped a tear from her cheek. "I'll be here waiting. Now back to your camp, and don't get caught sneaking back in."

Carrying a bunch of wood that partially obscured his face, Artorus approached the camp by the west gate, a different one form the one he exited. He reached the point where the sentries were stationed. "Halt," they commanded.

He stopped, still holding the pile of wood. An optio strode over to him. "Where in Hades have you been? The legate's order was for everyone to be restricted to camp."

Alderic grunted under the heavy load. "I been gathering wood all night, leaving by the north gate. Pickings were getting slim there so I moved in this direction. I found a lot out here."

The optio was silent, trying to decide what to do next. Alderic shifted the wood in his arms. "Listen, if you not believe me, go to north gate. They will tell you. I need to get back to my century. This shit is getting heavier by the moment."

"All right. Go ahead, but I'm going to check with them. What's your name and unit?"

"Artorus, First Century, Second Cohort, Centurion Gracchus commanding." He smiled inwardly as he moved toward his tent area. After the few hours he had spent with Bridin, any punishment he might receive was worth it.

The legion broke camp before daybreak the next day. They angled off the Aemilia road, which headed southwest toward Rome, and onto a dirt track that headed directly south along the coast. Alderic marched with his heavy burden, with Corvinius next to him. There were few complaints. The road was dry and compacted, easy to march upon. Alderic had a spring in his step. He had found Bridin. She was alive and well, prospering in the town of Ancona. He had no idea when he might be back, but he now knew where she was.

She had told him the previous evening that when they had departed months ago, she had wandered some distance before stumbling upon the village of Ancona. She had taken a liking to it at first sight, noting the small harbor that would assist her in the trade of her woven goods. The large cache of coin that he had given to her had made it easy to set up a small business, which began thriving almost immediately. It had been like a dream come true.

She had been worried about his fate, wondering what had become of him, and whether he had managed to avoid capture by the many soldiers sent to find him. She told him how she had listened to the town gossip for any news about him, but there had been little information to be gleaned from that avenue.

Corvinius gave him a side-long glance. "You want to tell me why you have that silly grin on your face? No, let me guess. It has something to do with your disappearance last night. I assume it was worth it?"

"No one has said anything. The optio at the gate took my name and unit. Hopefully, he forgot about."

Corvinius smirked. "You are a relative novice in the ranks. Let me give you a little advice. No one forgets anything in the legions. Don't let me say, 'I told you so,' later."

Alderic grunted under the load as a bitter gust of wind swept over the marching column, chilling the men to the bone. "It was a minor transgression at best. Even if they discover my ploy, it will be of little consequence."

"If you say so, brother. But in the legions, there is no such thing as a minor transgression." The century continued marching south, the winter sun weakly glinting to their right. After a brief period of silence, Corvinius spoke again. "I'm thinking of a nice warm fire tonight with some hot porridge and posca to go with it. I can feel my bones getting warmed even at the thought."

That night, the eight men from Alderic's contubernium sat huddled around a roaring blaze, eating their rations and drinking posca. The men sat close to the fire, frequently shifting positions so that the other portions of their body could be warmed in the frigid night. The seven other squad members included Barilius, Felix, Marcus, Livius, Silvius, Petrus, and Mellitius. The veterans of the contubernia had finally warmed up to the newcomers and accepted them into their ranks. Perhaps it was because the imposing presence of Artorus. None of the men wanted to cross the giant of a man.

Corvinius sauntered over to the group from his tent of the third contubernium. "Move your arses and make room," he growled. The men made a space so Corvinius could join them. He had no sooner squatted with them, than Optio Lucullus suddenly appeared.

"Corvinius and Artorus, you are to report to Centurion Gracchus's tent immediately." The other men breathed a sigh of relief, thankful it was not them. It wasn't a good thing to be bidden to the centurion's tent under any circumstances. The group looked up as the two men departed with Lucullus, wondering what in the Hades it was all about.

The two men entered and stood at attention before Gracchus, who was seated at his camp table studying some documents by the feeble light of an oil lamp. Lucullus stood behind the two men, observing them. Gracchus spoke. "Do you mind telling me what kind of shit you were pulling last night?"

Alderic shifted uncomfortably, trying his best to maintain a calm demeanor. "Not sure what you mean, Centurion. Pulling what shit?"

There was an uneasy silence, as Gracchus glared at the two men. "The optio of the guard reported to me that you entered the encampment through the west gate with a load of wood in your arms. He stated that you exited the north gate in search of wood for the fire."

Feeling relaxed and emboldened that this wasn't about Quintus, Artorus spoke. "That is correct, sir. I did indeed gather wood last night. Once inside the gates, I handed it over to Corvinius to take back to our century. As I told the optio, I exited the north gate, but moved to the west because there was more wood to be found there. I made several excursions out of the encampment."

Gracchus wasn't buying any of it. "The optio told me he talked to the guards at the north gate. They said you went out much earlier in the evening. You brought the wood in and Corvinius here carried it back to the camp site. Something is not adding up. I know you two are thick as thieves."

Artorus adopted an innocent expression. "The men at the north gate must be mistaken, Centurion. I'm not sure what all the fuss is about."

Gracchus picked up his vine wood staff and tapped it lightly on the table. He mimicked Artorus in a whiny voice. "The men at the north gate must be mistaken." He glowered at the two in silence; the oil lamp guttered and flickered in the quiet of the tent. He pursed his lips, coming to a decision. "All right. I'm not wasting any more of my time with your false accounts. You know that yesterday Tribune Flaccus asked me about both of you concerning that murder investigation of Quintus. I defended you. Told him you were two of my best legionnaires and were not possibly involved in that killing. He accepted what I said. But this. You two pulled some kind of scam last night. I don't want to hear any more of your professed innocence. For the next five nights, you both have guard duty on the middle shift, so it totally fucks up your sleep. Consider yourselves fortunate I'm not in a bad mood. Now get out of my sight."

The pair executed an about turn and walked off into the darkness. When they were out of hearing range, Corvinius guffawed. "That went well. So much for minor transgressions. We got off cheap. And Artorus...?"

"What?"

"Promise me you'll never be a politician. You're a lousy liar."

"Says you."

"No, you fool, says Gracchus. He wasn't buying a single word you said."

"At least we are in the clear of Quintus's murder. What is additional guard duty? Ha! Consider ourselves fortunate."

The relative easy-going on the dirt road ended several days later. The army was pounded with a deluge of cold rain, soaking the men and making everyone miserable. But being cold and damp wasn't the worst part of it all. The path leading south had been transformed into a quagmire. Their progress slowed to a crawl as the men slugged their way through the morass. The viscous mud oozed over their marching boots and coated their legs with slime. By the end of the day, most couldn't feel their feet. The journey, which was rumored to be over two hundred miles, was rendered a lot longer. The men made camp that night in a field of mire. Mercifully, the legate—recognizing the men's exhaustion and ill temper—had ordered that ramparts were not to be constructed that night. By the light of feeble fires, the men huddled around and glumly ate their cold rations.

The legions were up before dawn the next day and were on the march once more. Again, they struggled for hours in the glutinous slime, with an icy wind blowing off the sea to their left. Tempers frayed. Corvinius, in his usual spot of the first century next to Artorus, noting his placid expression scowled at his marching mate. "Do you want to share why you look so content with me? I mean these are not idyllic conditions."

Alderic adopted a puzzled expression. "What does idyllic mean?"

Corvinius glowered, his frustration mounting. "It means pleasant. Damn you!"

"No need to be hostile. I happy because I found my woman. I thought she might be dead."

"And when are you going to tell me about her and how you met. We have no secrets in the legions."

"Later. It's a long story."

Chapter XI
Spring

Brundisium

Many hard weeks later, the Fifteenth completed their month-long trek to the outskirts of Brundisium harbor—the main Roman naval base on the southeastern side of the Roman republic. It had been a long and bitter march, replete with wind, rain, ice, and snow. The ever-present mud, clinging to their clothes and equipment, inhibiting their movement, had sucked the spirit out of the men. Now, winter had morphed to spring, and the legion was encamped with the other forces of the Triumvirate. There were two armies: one belonging to Antonius and the other to Octavius. It was a massive military camp— or rather two camps—sprawled over a wide plain. The two armies each comprised ten legions plus auxiliaries. The forces had not been integrated, and each army maintained their own bivouac area. It was enormous in scale and totaled about a hundred thousand men for the combined army. Below the plain sat Brundisium harbor, now bursting with ships preparing to move the army across the narrow Mare Adriaticum to the land of Greece, where the army of the Liberators under Brutus and Cassius had gathered.

Alderic stood next to Corvinius in the ranks, both attired in full armor with their swords, shields, and javelins. The ten Octavian legions, each with about 4,500 men each along with numerous auxiliary forces, slowly maneuvered upon the commands of their respective officers and heralding trumpets. Gracchus bellowed. "Form a double line." The men of the first century smoothly shifted from their column formation, eight men wide and ten men deep, to a line formation two ranks deep. This was the typical formation deployed during an assault.

Up ahead, Alderic spotted the first cohort performing a similar maneuver. The bright morning sun blasted down upon the armored figures, causing them to sweat in buckets. Artorus glanced to his rear. In the distance, on a slight rise of ground, he spied a gaggle of senior officers on horses, no doubt including Octavius Caesar. *Wonder how their day is going compared to mine.* His reverie was broken by Gracchus bellowing new orders. "At the quick time, move."

The ranks broke into a slow trot, the men careful to stay in a straight line over the undulating landscape. The ten legions were tactically arrayed in a checkered formation. As a huge wave, the ranks trotted forward. Of course, from his limited vantage point, Artorus could see little of this grand design. He concentrated on staying in line. Huge clouds of dust rose from the arid plain, the particles sticking to the men's sweat-soaked faces and finding every nook and cranny in their armor. The line continued advancing forward, through the vast dust cloud generated by the legion in front of them.

The signal horns sounded. Again, Gracchus pointed with his arm and yelled above the pounding of many boots, "Oblique left." The formation shifted to the left, continuing to advance. Chaos ensued. With no visibility, the men of the first century collided with a century from another legion, which had shifted to their right instead of their left at the sounds of the trumpets. Alderic stopped dead in his tracks, cursing those he had bumped into. Centurions bellowed orders, separating the two forces. Gracchus yelled. "Form on me over here."

The century gathered. Obscenities reverberated through the blanket of dust at the offending century. "Dumb fucks," one man cried. "Don't know their arses from a hole in the ground," uttered a second. Some started laughing. "What kind of cluster fuck is this?" muttered another. Corvinius added to the din. "Your other left, arseholes."

"SILENCE," roared Gracchus. "Stand in place."

The men stood quiet amid the swirling haze of dirt, some coughing, others spitting out the grimy contents from their mouths. Alderic turned about and, through a break in the brown pall, witnessed the officers on the hilltop slowly turn their mounts and depart. He smirked at the absurdity of it all and fervently hoped that the army of the Liberators wasn't well trained. If they were, Octavius Caesar's army was in a lot of trouble.

It was twilight, and cooking fires blazed in the massive Roman encampment. A thin haze of smoke enveloped the men of the legions as they wolfed down their serving of porridge. They were on half rations. The required food supply hadn't materialized to feed the huge accumulation of forces. Most were too tired or too bored to complain. Every day was the same—drill and more drill. First, they maneuvered as a century, then at a cohort level, and at the end as a legion. Once that was completed, the legions drilled as an army. When not performing tactical movements, the men were assigned ceaseless camp maintenance chores—reinforcing the palisade, collecting water, digging latrines, guard duty, and sharpening weapons.

The barren plain upon which they were camped offered little in the way of amenities, and the men were restricted to camp. No exceptions. Alderic, his appetite only partially sated from the evening rations, sat staring into the fire, his thoughts wandering to Bridin. He had hope. He wondered again whether the search for Alderic was still active. It had been many months since he had disappeared. Now, all he had to do was to survive this upcoming battle. Romans fighting Romans. *They're as bad as the German tribes back in the homeland. Always at each other's throats for some reason or another.*

Alderic ate the last of his biscuit, crunching it between his teeth. He pictured a life with Bridin in the sea coast town of Ancona. It appeared peaceful enough with little threat of a foreign invader. From his brief stay there, it had seemed like a prosperous place. What was that word that Corvinius had used on the march? *Idyllic.* That was it. He would lead an idyllic life with Bridin. His musings were interrupted by Gracchus, who suddenly materialized to his front along with Lucullus.

"First century, gather on me. I have some important news," bellowed Gracchus. He waited as the men hurried from their tents and from neighboring camp fires. Lucullus began counting the men present using his index finger. Satisfied, he nodded to the centurion.

"The good news is we're leaving here." There was an audible sigh of relief among the men. He continued. "I know you're tired of this place, and frankly, so am I. We will depart some time over the next week and will sail on those small transport ships you see anchored at the wharf in the city below. This is where it gets a bit dicey. I'm not going to mince words. Our enemy, the murderers of our beloved Caesar, own the seas from here to the Greek coast. It is rumored that they have over a hundred war galleys at their disposal. They will attempt to intercept and sink our ships while we cross."

There was a disturbed chatter among the men as they absorbed the latest news. "SILENCE! Did I give any you permission to speak?" he yelled. The group immediately became quiet. "Now as I was saying, our foe has the advantage on the sea, but with the winds at our back, the transports are faster and more maneuverable than their warships. I'm told our enemy has an assortment of vessels, including biremes, triremes, and quinqueremes. For those of you unfamiliar with naval terms, and I guess that's most of you, that means double, triple, and quadruple banks of oars. They are large and ungainly ships in comparison to our smaller transports. So the strategy is to outrun their galleys. We will not embark without a favorable wind. If the breeze dies while we're at sea, so do we. The enemy warships will be able to overtake us with their banks of oars. Let's hope that doesn't happen. Once we get to Greece, we will march inland in an easterly direction. That is where we will find the enemy. They have gathered their forces at a place called Philippi. Dismissed."

Several days later, the men in Alderic's century sat around in the early morning sunshine, staring dimly at the transport ships docked at the wharf. They had broken camp while it was still dark, eagerly packing up their gear. No persuasion had been required. They were glad to leave this place of constant drill and boredom. The squat vessels tugged slightly at their mooring tethers, their bright pennants flapped sporadically in the half-hearted breeze—which, precisely, was the problem. There were enemy galleys beyond the horizon, lying in wait. The single-mast transports, which would hold a cargo of about eighty men—an entire century—had to rely on their speed and maneuverability to escape death from the prowling war ships. To do that, they needed a favoring wind, a strong one, which had not yet materialized.

Alderic and Corvinius sat beside each other, studying the harbor, glancing at the pennants attached to the main sail. The entirety of the Fifteenth Legion sat waiting at the docks, their supplies already loaded aboard the ships. They had been informed that when the ship banners began rippling with the wind, it would be time to depart. "Corvinius, do you know how to swim?"

"Just a bit."

"I'll take that as a no. Either you can or you can't. I'm fortunate," he declared proudly. "I learned to swim in my youth. If we get rammed, at least I'll have a chance."

Corvinius snorted. "You think so. I hate to be the bearer of bad tidings, but if you get flung into the sea, you are going to sink like a stone with all that armor and drown with the rest of us. Just hope we make it through the blockade these rogues have set up."

Alderic sat there puzzled, contemplating a response, when the morning peace was shattered by Gracchus. "Everyone up. We have wind. Get ready to load now. No time to waste. Move. Move!"

Alderic glanced up and sure enough, the ships' pennants were whipping with the breeze. He quickly gathered his load and followed Gracchus and the rest of the men to a transport almost directly to their front. In a matter of moments, the centuries and cohorts boarded their assigned vessels. Alderic staggered up the boarding plank under the weight of his gear. Optio Lucullus directed him to his assigned spot. He dropped his load and leaned against the ship rail. Glancing up, he observed a person in a worn tunic with a heavy sea cloak fastened about his shoulders. He was an older man with a weathered complexion and a face like tanned leather. He wrung his hands in nervous anticipation, all the while chewing on his lower lip. Alderic nudged Corvinius with his elbow. "That must be our captain. He doesn't exactly inspire confidence, does he?"

Corvinius frowned, then shook his head. "No, he doesn't."

Gracchus stood in the center of the deck. He watched as the mooring lines were cast aside. He shouted above the wind. "Whatever gods you pray to, best do it now. Me, I'm praying to Neptune to keep this breeze up. Oh, and try not to do anything stupid like fall overboard."

The crew of the ship raised the single sail, and the ship knifed through the waters of the harbor. The rest of the flotilla, perhaps fifty ships, raced along with them. They were one of the first legions to embark across the narrow passage to Greece. A second wave of ships would also sail later in the morning. It was hoped that over the course of several days, the entire army could be transported to the Greek shores.

Alderic turned to face the breeze, the sun shining on his face. He reveled in the sensation of the wind blowing through his hair. "I could get used to this. I mean, I'm not walking with weight on my shoulders that would hobble a mule, and I'm sitting here enjoying the sunshine. No mud. No cold. No snow. Tell me, Corvinius, why did I join the legions when I could travel in style like this in the navy? No humping under heavy armor and heavy packs."

"Good question. Maybe the centurion will let you transfer. Go ask him."

"Even I'm not that stupid." He pulled a skin of wine from his belt and took a long swig before handing it to Corvinius. "Here's to your god of the sea, Neptune, or whatever his name is."

The ship sailed through the waters unopposed for hours. Lulled by the rhythm of the boat as it cut through the sea, some of the men fell asleep. The taut ropes creaked and groaned as the sail filled with wind, pushing the vessel steadily eastward. Artorus glanced up at the lookout stationed near the top of the mast. The man shaded his eyes with his hand, scanning the waters ahead. Abruptly, the figure rose to his full height and screamed a warning. "Sails to our front."

The captain ran to the prow of the ship, seeking confirmation, then ran back to the crewman manning the rudder. He looked to the left and right at the other vessels in the flotilla. They were waving red flags. He turned to the man at the rudder, and commanded, "Turn to port." The rest of the flotilla was also turning to port.

Everyone on deck was staring in the direction of the reported enemy ships, but they weren't visible. For the next several hours, the ship sailed north east. The lookout continued scanning the horizon. The captain, his expression anxious, moved beneath the lookout and shouted. "Anything?"

The man perched high on the mast shook his head. The tension in the captain's shoulders seemed to ease. He even proffered a slight grin. It seemed that they had evaded the enemy vessels with their speed. Now mid-afternoon, the men broke out their cold rations of bread, turnips, onions, and sour wine. Most of the soldiers were relaxed, thankful they had escaped the enemy galleys. Muttered conversations filled the air punctuated by an occasional laugh. Several dice games broke out on the pitching deck. Few noticed that the breeze that had carried them along had diminished. No one paid attention to the captain's apprehensive pacing.

Alderic and Corvinius leaned back against the gunnel, enjoying some rare leisure time. Alderic dug through his pack and produced a large biscuit. He broke it in half and offered one of the portions to Corvinius.

Alderic munched on his portion. "I've never been in a battle before with so many soldiers. What's it like?"

Corvinius scratched his chin in thought. "It's kind of terrifying. You never get used to it. I just fight like I trained and follow Gracchus's orders. I'm sure it's no more frightening than what you experienced as a ... you know ... in what you did before the legions. Your heart pounds and your mouth gets dry. Don't let your fear overwhelm you. Just fight like the rest of the men in the century. They have your back."

Alderic pondered the words for a few moments. "I'll fight like the men of my century. There is strength in numbers. These men are all—"

"Sails!" screamed the lookout. Everyone stood up once more.

The captain yelled to the crewman, "Where?"

The man pointed to the rear, angling his arm slightly to the right.

The captain looked at the position of the sun, and then the sail, which was now only partially inflated. He scanned the horizon once more, then back to the sail. He trotted over to Gracchus. "They're gaining on us with their oars."

"Will they catch us?"

The captain replied, "Aye, unless the wind picks up." He then turned his back on Gracchus to study the flag signals from the lead ship. He turned back to face the centurion. "They are signaling for us to move closer together so that we present a unified force to the enemy vessels."

Gracchus thought for a moment. "What would you have my men do?"

"Be prepared to repel boarders should they seek to come along our side."

"I see. How will they attack us? I'm a stranger to naval tactics."

The captain snorted. "If I were them, I would ram as many ships as possible or use the catapults to destroy our vessels. On the other hand, if they wish to capture us and add the ship to their fleet, they'll attempt to board us. Get your men ready, Centurion. This situation could get ugly quick."

Alderic watched in grim fascination as the giant war galleys, now visible to all, gained on the flotilla. He counted five of them. Meanwhile, the numerous transports had bunched into a tight rectangular formation of perhaps twenty-five ships. The wind remained slack, the seas calm. In the space of an hour, Alderic could now make out the figures manning the war galleys. Their oars stroked through the water, edging them closer.

Suddenly a ball of fire streaked through the air, fired from a catapult of one of the enemy ships. It was followed by additional missiles as the war machines aboard the enemy galleys advanced within striking range.

"Greek fire!" screamed the captain in fear. A blazing container smashed into the water near the port side of the ship. A raging inferno spread over the surface of the sea where the missile had struck, the flames hissing in anger. More flaming pots were launched from the five enemy ships. Two struck an unfortunate transport, sending the shrieking men over the side. The blazing ship then collided with another transport, lighting it on fire as well.

The captain muttered to himself. "What a goat fuck." He stared at the other transports as the signal flags waved once again. He screamed to the helmsman. "Right rudder. They want us to separate now." The ship heeled away from the formation. Other ships performed the same maneuver. A war galley bore down on one of the slower transports, ramming it in the side. The shuddering impact of splintered timbers could be heard across the water. The oars reversed course, as the enemy galley withdrew from the ram. The doomed transport slowly began to sink beneath the waves. Sailors and legionnaires dove from the sinking ship, and they too disappeared beneath the sea.

The same enemy galley, one of the smallest of the enemy fleet—a bireme—which had rammed and sunk the troop transport attempted to strike another. The captain of the transport managed to avoid the ram with some deft maneuvering of the vessel. Instead of hitting head on, the transport slid along the side of the galley, splintering some of the oars. Not to be deterred from their prize, the enemy vessel threw grappling hooks, drawing the transport to its side.

Gracchus swore an oath. "Fuck me! That's one of my centuries. I believe it's the third. Captain, bring this ship along the other side of the enemy vessel. I intend to board her."

"Are you crazy? Now is our time to get away. I am in command. This is my ship. We will sail away from this carnage."

Gracchus bounded over to the captain and withdrew his gladius, pointing it at the man's throat. "I'm now in charge of this ship. Do as I say."

The captain, glancing at the tip of the centurion's gladius poised near his throat, his face wide in fright, motioned to his helmsman to maneuver alongside the enemy ship. Gracchus bellowed to his men. He pointed with his sword. "That ship under attack belongs to a century from our cohort. Prepare to board the enemy vessel." The men drew their swords and prepared their shields. Because the transports sat so high in the water, the ship's railing was almost even with that of the much larger enemy vessel. With a satisfying crunch, the two ships slammed together, the impact disabling more oars on the enemy ship.

Alderic was thrown to the deck by the violent collision. Grappling lines flew over the rail. He quickly got his feet again and following his centurion, leaped over the railing on to the deck of the other vessel. The sailors and marines on the warship were in the act of capturing their prize when the first century slammed into them.

With a snarl, Alderic rushed at the first man opposite him. He smashed his shield into the marine sending him flying ass over heels. The next man opposing him was braced for the impact, but it did him little good. Alderic rammed into the man, sending him off balance. He then stabbed the man in the neck, killing him.

Glancing to his right, he noted Corvinius engaged with a large sailor wielding a pike. Corvinius was stymied by the long reach of the weapon. Alderic attacked the man's flank and stabbed the man in the torso. The wounded man stumbled to the deck. Looking about, Alderic realized that he was part of vanguard of about twenty men. They had destroyed the initial resistance from the crew of the bireme. He observed pockets of men engaged in hand-to-hand fighting. Turning to the aft, he saw a line of men guarding the catapults, and the amphorae of oil used as the projectiles. He headed in that direction.

The enemy was disorganized, surprised that they were the ones being attacked from both sides of their ship. The legionnaires of the first century swarmed across the deck towards the catapults. The line of men defending the catapults held their ground briefly before they were savagely dispatched. Alderic tipped over several amphorae of black thick oil, which slowly flowed out of the containers and across the deck. He saw Corvinius grab one of the torches and throw it at the oil. It immersed the deck with a whoosh.

Thick black smoke curled into the air. Recognizing that his own forces were in peril, Gracchus screamed above the din. "Everyone back to our ship. Hurry, before it is too late." The men needed no urging as the fire spread along the deck and on to the sides of the enemy ship. The rest of the century disengaged and leaped back over to the transport. Legionnaires and crew frantically hacked at the grappling lines, desperate to get free of the burning wreck. At the same time, the damaged transport of the third century on the other side managed to free itself, cutting the grappling lines. Seeing their ship ablaze, some of the crew of the war galley panicked and jumped into the sea. Others attempted to hopelessly extinguish the inferno. Gracchus roared to the captain. "Get us out of here."

Their transport followed by the ship of the third century glided away toward empty waters, gaining separation from the war galleys. The gods were with the Fifteenth today. Abruptly, a wind blew out of the west, filling the sails of the smaller ships. The transport ships knifed through the water, away from the danger of the Republican warships. After several hours, the enemy ships were only distant silhouettes.

Gracchus glanced to the rear at the enemy vessels. "I assume they'll continue to follow us?"

"Yes, they'll try. But this wind will keep them at a distance. My intention is to lose them in the darkness. There will only be a quarter moon tonight, and visibility on these seas is often compromised by mist. We must have no lights and no noise. Please inform your men. Our survival may depend upon it."

The transport sailed into the twilight. Off to their left and right, other transports were visible, seeking to lose their pursuers. The darkness deepened. There was total stillness among the troops. The captain pointed ahead into the mist and spoke in a hushed tone. "Look Centurion, there's our friend."

Gracchus glanced forward, seeing only a large wall of mist. He whispered to the captain. "How can you see in that soup?"

"You can't, Centurion. We risk colliding with another ship or running aground on some shoal, but it's better than facing a Roman war galley. I'll happily make that trade any day."

The remainder of the voyage to the Greek mainland was uneventful. The winds continued to be favorable, and the enemy war galleys gave up in their pursuit of the Fifteenth Legion's transports. Overall, some of the vessels and their crew had been lost at sea, but the bulk of the Fifteenth Legion had survived. The real battle was only about to begin.

Chapter XII
The Plains of Philippi

Marcus Antonius and Octavius Caesar, each with their respective retinue of officers, crowded into the command tent of Antonius. There was enough gold- and silver-plated armor to fund Rome's treasury outlays for a month. The two generals had separate camps about a mile apart. The stated purpose of today's meeting was to develop a military strategy to defeat the forces of the Liberators, more commonly referred to as Caesar's murderers. It was mid-day, and the tent flaps were rolled up to escape the suffocating heat.

Antonius, wearing a resplendent silver breast plate, was clearly the superior figure with respect to military affairs. He stood before a wooden table upon which had been heaped sand and dirt that had been molded to reflect the topographical features of the Philippi plains. Various wooden pins with attached flags, denoting friendly and enemy forces, dotted the model landscape.

Antonius walked over the table and began his discourse, almost as a lecture. "You can see," he began, pointing with a straight wooden rod with an affixed ivory head, "the army of Cassius and Brutus are entrenched upon the high ground, putting our forces at a distinct disadvantage. Our intelligence estimates the army of Brutus and Cassius at over one hundred thousand, about equal to our forces. Cassius commands about half of their forces and is on our right flank. Brutus and his forces are on our left. You will note that the road, the via Egnatia, bisects the plain almost along the center. Far to the rear"—he pointed to a marker on the sand table—"is the town of Philippi. It holds no strategic importance. A large swamp protects Cassius's flank, and mountainous hills Brutus's flanks here and here."

Antonius glowered at Octavius, his tone disdainful. "Understand so far?"

Octavius nodded. Controlling the tone of his voice, he responded. "By all means, please proceed."

Antonius continued, his tone increasingly patronizing. "Our army is positioned on this flat plain. The plan is to draw up our legions for battle and approach the enemy lines. Hopefully, they will take the bait and abandon their high ground to engage our forces. But my guess is that they will do nothing, no matter how much we provoke them."

Octavius appeared confused. "Why would they not engage our legions? Brutus and Cassius hate us and want to see us destroyed."

Antonius snorted. "Because they can afford to wait us out. They have supply lines that are open and secure. They control the Aegean and the Adriaticum seas. We, on the other hand, must live off the land and scrounge from the local populace. Brutus and Cassius can wait for us to approach them on their high ground."

Octavius shot a quizzical look at Marcus Vispanius Agrippa, his general and military strategist. Agrippa, a large figure with a martial bearing, nodded in acquiescence, then whispered into Octavius's ear.

Octavius turned to Antonius. "So, what's the plan?"

"My plan," he emphasized the word *my*, "is to draw them off their high ground. It would be unwise to have our forces attack up that slope occupied by our foe. The outcome might be disastrous. So, we will present our legions for battle far enough away from their archers and artillery pieces. If they don't come off their summit—and I certainly wouldn't if I was in their boots—we'll need to reconvene and come up with a plan B."

Octavius stayed silent, trying not to look intimidated. He had little military experience while Antonius was a seasoned general. He kept reminding himself that Antonius was his ally, which was true to a certain extent. There was an uneasy peace between them. He knew Antonius despised him and, if given the opportunity, would depose him and his family. But for now, Octavius would continue to look upon Antonius as a friend because he needed him and his forces. There was no way his legions could defeat the Liberators without the army of Antonius. After they vanquished the Liberators and Octavius had the political upper hand, he would strike. But for now, he would maintain a peaceful façade and act grateful for Antonius's military leadership.

Smiling, Octavius said, "I agree with your plan. Your military acumen will see us to victory. I'm confident of that. Your strategy appears sound. When do you suggest we draw up our legions for battle?"

In a derisive tone, Antonius replied. "How magnanimous of you. I'm so glad you concur with the battle plan. As to the when, I think the day after tomorrow would be an auspicious time. Tomorrow, we'll need to plan the order of battle and decide which legions will be at the forefront and which in reserve. So, consult with General Agrippa, and be ready to advance against the Cassius and Brutus. Oh, and try not to piss your pants." He laughed heartily at his own humor

Octavius, still maintaining a polite demeanor, replied in a neutral tone. "I look forward to leading our legions to victory." With that, he turned and exited the tent, followed by his retinue.

Several miles away, the opposing commanders met in the joint headquarters tent. The two men, Gaius Cassius Longinus and Marcus Junius Brutus, were experienced military leaders and the consensual choices to direct the military campaign against the Triumvirate. A retinue of other military officers and exiled senators, who had participated in the assassination of Caesar, filled the tent with idle chatter, waiting for the strategy session to begin.

Cassius broke away from his conversation with Brutus. "Gentlemen, I would like to bring this meeting to order." He paused, waiting for the conversations to cease, before beginning. "As you are aware, the armies of Antonius and Octavius have finally reached our shores. Our naval blockade didn't prove to be much of a deterrent. We captured and sunk some of their fleet, but the bulk of their forces reached the shores of Greece. They are camped but a few scant miles from here. Our estimates are that their forces are approximately the same size as ours. We believe they will present their legions for battle within perhaps a matter of days. Our forces don't have numeric superiority, but we have other advantages. First, our legions hold the high ground. It will be a tough go for them to displace us. Second, our legions are well supplied with food, water, and fodder for the horses. They, on the other hand, have no secure supply lines."

Muttered words were exchanged among the staff. Cassius held his arms up for quiet. After the noise faded, he continued. "Brutus and

I agree that Antonius and Octavius will adopt a strategy that will seek to lure us off the summit to battle. We will not engage them, for the advantage lies with us. We can afford to wait here indefinitely; they cannot. Therefore, when they approach our lines for battle within the next few days, we will do nothing. My sense is that they will not be foolish enough to attack us up here on the acropolis. They're too smart for that. It will be challenging for them to assault us in our elevated position. But if they do, be prepared to take advantage of our position, and throw them back. Our javelins should wreak havoc within the enemy lines. We will be able to arc them so that the spears rain down on them. Victory will be assured if they are impulsive enough to attack. So, hold your ground, and if they should attack our positions, we shall destroy them in battle. Once again, don't, under any circumstances, move off your positions. Any questions?"

The next day, Gracchus assembled the other five subordinate centurions who commanded the second through fifth century. The officers stood in a relaxed semi-circle around him. "Listen up. I've just returned from the legate's briefing. The order of battle has been established for tomorrow. The Fifteenth will be on the left flank in a reserve position."

The veteran centurions smiled widely and issued a collective sigh of relief. Nothing worse than being in the front ranks. That's where the killing and dying occurred. Nasty business. "Now listen carefully. These instructions are for the entire army, especially those in the front ranks. Under no circumstances are any of our forces to attempt to advance up the slope upon which the enemy is entrenched."

"Then why are we going out tomorrow, Centurion?" Centurion Fulvius inquired.

"The plan is to lure them to battle on a terrain where the advantage does not lie with them. Now, if they don't come off the perch, we'll withdraw to our encampment in an orderly fashion. Are we clear about everything?"

There were mumbled assents from the assembled men. "Good," said Gracchus. "Try and get some rest. We'll begin assembling before dawn. Who knows what awaits us tomorrow. I know you will all do your duty because that's what I've trained you to do. Dismissed."

Corvinius and Alderic sat alone by the campfire. All the other men had retired for the night. Both men were silent, staring into the sputtering flames. The fire crackled as Alderic fed some more dried tinder into the blaze. Corvinius looked up, "Are you nervous about tomorrow?"

"No, it's just another day of wine and fine food. What kind of a dumb question is that? Of course, I'm nervous."

"No need to be so sarcastic."

Alderic countered. "Well it was a stupid question."

"Were you nervous when you first entered the arena?"

Alderic scowled, looking over his shoulder for anyone within hearing range. "I thought we agreed never to discuss that subject," he hissed.

"Oh, sorry. I forgot. Just trying to make conversation."

"To answer your question, yes, I thought I was going to wet myself. Once I got out there, I let my training take over."

Corvinius guffawed. "This is no different. You'll see some wet tunics out there tomorrow. As I told you before, fight as you're trained and listen to Gracchus. He'll tell you what to do."

"Gracchus led you when you fought Antonius's forces two years ago?"

"He did. The man knows how to fight. Our centurion never put the century or the cohort in a bad position. He is smart and resourceful. I fought as I was trained and listened to Gracchus." With that, he rose. "See you tomorrow."

The next morning Alderic marched beside Corvinius and the rest of their century toward the enemy position. In the distance, Alderic could make out the hill top and the massed legions occupying that terrain. He squinted slightly against the bright morning sun. It was going to be another hot day. The dust rose in a heavy thick cloud behind the advancing legions to their front. The fine powder coated everything. The horns sounded and shouted commands resonated among the ranks. Abruptly, the legions to their front halted some distance from the enemy position.

Gracchus turned from his position in front of his century. He gestured with his arm. "The legions to our front will advance no farther. Any closer and they would be in range of the archers and the *ballistae* perched upon that summit. We will wait here and see if there are any developments. You may rest your shields and pila on the ground if you wish."

Alderic carefully placed his two javelins on the earth beside him and lowered the shield from his left arm. He absently reached for his goatskin water container, forgetting that they had been ordered not to bring them along. Too cumbersome when engaged in battle, they had been told. So they waited. The two forces stood perhaps four hundred yards apart, staring at each other. Nothing happened. The sun continued beating down, roasting the men in their heavy chain mail and iron helmets.

Some of the men complained about the heat, cursing the legions and their fate to have been thrust in their current circumstances. Gracchus turned from his position facing the enemy, an angry scowl upon his countenance. "Silence," he roared. "By order of the legate, there is to be no talking. Shut your yaps."

Silence pervaded the ranks. Corvinius turned toward Alderic and spoke from the side of his mouth. "Can you believe this shit? Here we are baking in this heat, and for what?"

Alderic grinned, his face now powdered in dust. "You Romans have a strange way of doing battle. What is purpose of this?"

Gracchus turned about once more, his face in a fury. "Did I not make myself clear? I said no talking. Who was speaking?" He glared at the men. His gaze settled upon Artorus and Corvinius. "If I had to place a bet, it would be on you two. Extra guard duty for both of you tomorrow night."

Corvinius raised his voice in protest. "It wasn't us, Centurion. It must have been someone else."

"Shut up before I give you further punishment. In my mind you were guilty, so that is the end of that. No more talking and that applies to all of you." He turned back, facing the front. Several legionnaires smirked at the pair.

The men continued standing in the heat, waiting for something to happen. After some time, two men dropped to their knees, their gear rattling as they collapsed. Gracchus turned about alarmed. "Listen up. I want all of you to take your helmets off now and let them rest on your chests by the chin straps. Do not lock your knees. Keep them flexed. Pick up a pebble and suck on it. Think pleasant thoughts."

The men willingly followed his advice and shed their helmets. Almost at the same moment, a slight breeze blew over their faces, providing a bit of cool relief. The men who had buckled under the heat were carried back toward the rear. The brief respite brought by the cooling breeze didn't last long. It became still once more; the merciless sun beating on the unfortunate legionnaires.

The legate of the Fifteenth, Gaius Quintus Calvinius, approached on his horse. Staring at the men of the second cohort, massed in formation, he spoke to Gracchus. "Centurion, did I give the order for the men to remove their helmets?"

"No, you didn't, sir. I lost a few men because of the heat. I deemed it prudent to have the men remove their helmets before I lost others."

"I gave specific orders that the men were to be attired at all times with full armor. As for losing some of your men, perhaps you need to toughen up your men so they won't collapse when faced with adverse circumstances. Have them put their helmets back immediately. Understood, Centurion?"

Gracchus gritted his teeth. *Arrogant prick.* Not only was his commander uncaring toward the men, but the legate had dressed him down in front of his legionnaires. "Yes, sir. Right away."

The legate turned on his horse and trotted away. Gracchus turned toward his cohort. "The legate insists that you all put your helmets back on. Please do so immediately."

Before long, the heat took its toll and more men collapsed under the blazing sun. The stretcher bearers couldn't keep up with the number of heat casualties. Artorus grimly observed the fallen legionnaires. He could feel the effects of the sun too, roasting inside his armor shell. He didn't understand the logic behind the legion's maneuvers and why they couldn't remove their helmets. It all seemed so pointless.

Several hours later, the trumpets blared and orders were bawled from the legion to the cohort and then to the century. They were going back to their encampments. The men grumbled and picked up their gear. They were relieved there had been no combat yet dispirited from standing in the grueling sun all day.

That night, the men sat morosely around the fire. Not much was said. Artorus poured some olive oil on his hands and rubbed it on his sun-burnt face. He felt drained from the day's activities. They had not done much physically, but the sun had sapped their strength. He tore off a chunk of bread with his teeth and chewed noisily.

Corvinius followed Alderic's example and began chewing on a hunk of bread. Speaking to no one in particular, he began. "Rumor is we're going to do the same thing tomorrow. Another day of fun in the sun."

Before Alderic could respond, Gracchus materialized in front of them. "Gather round everyone." He waited until all the men had clustered near him. "I've just returned from a meeting with the legate. Tomorrow, you are permitted to bring half a skin of water with you. No more than half. Otherwise, you will become burdened with the weight if we fight. Pass the word on to the others. That is all."

After the centurion departed, Mellitius spoke. "I'm not ashamed to say I almost passed out today. Not sure I can hack another day of roasting in the sun." Other heads nodded in agreement. A voice from the shadows echoed Mellitius's sentiments. "No shame in admitting you were almost done in. Same for me. That was brutal. I heard our cohort lost about forty men. Some might not recover. At least Gracchus cares about us. That fucking legate has his head up his ass."

Alderic grunted as he rose from his squatting position by the fire and headed toward his tent. "I'm bushed. See you all in the morning."

That night, he tossed and turned with feverish dreams. First, he was facing the fierce Baladar once again. His thrusts and casts were easily blocked by the secutor at every turn no matter what maneuver he employed. His antagonist slowly carved him up. He felt the stinging cut of every stroke. Finally, he could no longer stand and collapsed. He woke briefly, relieved that it was only a dream. After tossing and turning for a while, he fell asleep once more, but his imaginations returned to haunt him, this time even more vivid. He dreamed that he was in a wide field. A large eagle flew down and perched next to him on a small tree. Then dozens of angry-looking birds, all with bloody beaks, attacked the eagle. Alderic defended the eagle, striking the fierce looking fowls down with his sword until there were none left. The eagle flew into the air, soaring through the sky. He woke again, dazed and confused, wondering why he was being visited by such strange visions. *Must have been the sun from the previous day.*

The next morning, Alderic stumbled about, his mind still fogged from lack of sleep and the vivid dream with the attacking birds. He slid his head into the iron mail and grabbed his weapons and helmet. He started forward to the assembly area when Corvinius stopped him in his tracks. "Forgetting something?"

"No, I don't think so."

"Your water bag? Remember last night? They said we could bring our water bags, but only half filled. What's the matter with you this morning? You look unsettled."

"I'm disconcerted. I had this vivid dream last night like nothing I've ever experienced. I was surrounded by these evil birds with blood dripping from their beaks. They were attacking a large eagle that had perched next to me for protection. I slew the attacking birds with my sword."

"You know, Artorus, we Romans believe there is a message from the gods behind every dream. Not sure what the meaning of your dream is, but perhaps when you get the opportunity you should visit a seer. Maybe they could shed some light on it."

"Bah. I don't believe in that stuff. Besides, where am I going to find a seer around here?"

Corvinius shrugged. "Good point. C'mon, get your water bag and let's hustle to formation before we're late."

The legions of the Triumvirate marched once again in proximity to the enemy lines of Cassius and Brutus. The two forces were close but remained out of range of the fierce artillery machines that could throw arm-length bolts and huge hunks of rock. It was as the day before. The two sides stood and stared at each other. Alderic took a swig of his water, then turned to Corvinius. "This is bizarre. I can't believe we're going to stand here all day again. If we not fight, why bother with these theatrics?"

In response, Corvinius, his face bathed in sweat, emptied some of his water over his head. "Ah, that feels really nice. Why are you asking me these questions? I'm just a simple legionnaire as you. I follow orders."

Alderic and Corvinius stood among the ranks of the massive army. As with the previous day, nothing happened. The dust swirled about, obscuring sight farther than fifty paces. Beside the coughing and hacking of the legionnaires, all was silent. After several hours, the recall was sounded on the signal horns. Orders were shouted. The massive army slowly wheeled about and moved away from the enemy forces back to their encampment.

The generals of the Triumvirate and their staffs stood in the command tent discussing the day's events. As usual, Marcus Antonius had the floor. "The actions of our foe aren't surprising. They are not budging from their position on the escarpment. I would do the same in their place. So, what are we to do?" He let a few moments of silence pass in the crowded confines of the tent and then smirked. "I'll tell you what we're going to do."

He walked over to the large sand table and using his ivory tipped pointer, he tapped the spot representing the swamp on the enemy's flank. "My forces are here on our right flank. Beyond our camp and protecting the enemy's left flank is a large swamp, a rather disgusting piece of real estate. I have personally explored this particular terrain, and it is formidable. For the past several days, my engineers have been secretly constructing a narrow causeway extending along the enemy's flank. The reeds are so tall that the construction of the walkway is hidden from our enemy's view. Upon completion of this road, it is my intention to funnel my forces along this walkway and turn their flank. That'll get them off their fucking hilltop."

Octavius Caesar stared at the sand table. "How long before it'll be completed?"

Marcus Antonius rubbed his jaw. "Not long. My engineers are on it. It is almost complete."

Octavius frowned. "What are my forces expected to do when you attack their flank?"

Antonius laughed. "Fight, boy. That's why we came here. Once we turn their flank, you must attack. It isn't necessary for you to take the summit, just hold their forces in position. They'll retreat quickly enough when they realize I'm crawling up their arse."

Octavius fumed at the condescending tone but kept his voice level. "Do we continue to march forward each day, offering to do battle, until the passage is ready?"

"Most definitely. The presence of our forces will keep them occupied. Plus, the dust clouds raised by our forces helps obscure the construction of the ramp. When the time is right, you must engage the enemy forces on their right flank. Pin them down. Once we've rolled up their left flank, their resistance will crumble, and we will rout their legions. Victory shall be ours."

That evening, Corvinius and Alderic walked aimlessly through the massive bivouac. It was nearly twilight and a refreshing breeze had sprung up, cooling the air after another blistering hot day. They wore only their tunics. The absence of their heavy mail armor added a spring in their step. The military camp was like all other Roman encampments—rectangular in shape with two main avenues running the length and width of the camp. Where the two intersected, the *praetorium,* the commander's headquarters, was located. Each legion, cohort, and century had its designated place within the ramparts.

Alderic stared at the banner fluttering along the tented avenue. It read *Legio IV* and had the figure of a bull on it. He vaguely recalled seeing that vexillum somewhere before but couldn't recall where. He had the uneasy sensation that someone was staring at him. He turned about to see if his instincts were correct.

Centurion Gnaeus Cattallus of the Fifth Cohort, Fourth Legion, watched the tall legionnaire strolling through the encampment accompanied by a second man. He had seen that tall figure before. The centurion had his faults, but he never forgot a face, and this one was somehow familiar. His mind raced, attempting to unravel this conundrum, when it hit him like a bolt of lightning. Germania! He was one of the men who had been captured and sold as a slave. That was it. Now he remembered. He had gotten extra coin for the man. He was sold to the slave trader. What was his name? Balbus, yes, that was it. He chided himself for not remembering the captured German sooner. How could he forget that tall frame and the physical confrontation that had ensued when Balbus had his restraints removed? But what was he doing in the legions? Slaves were not permitted to join the legions. The punishment was death.

Alderic directed his gaze to his left, then his right. There. A centurion was eyeing him. Somehow, he looked like someone from his past. Then, it all came flooding back to him. The Fourth Legion banner was from Germania. The man appraising him was the Roman officer who had sold him to the slave merchant.

Trying to be nonchalant, Alderic returned his gaze to the front. He spoke in a hushed tone. "Corvinius, we must leave this area quickly. Don't ask me why. Just pick up pace and move into the crowd with me." The two men blended into a host of other legionnaires and disappeared down the road.

Centurion Cattallus watched the two men vanish from sight. The tall legionnaire had met his gaze. There was no doubt about the hint of recognition on his face. The man had tried to hide it, but the centurion had seen the flicker of comprehension. Now, what was he to do? He would approach his commander, Marcus Verres, and tell him about the fugitive. Not now though. There was a battle to be fought. This could wait until after they had achieved victory. Perhaps, he gloated, the army of Cassius and Brutus would take care of this problem for him. After all, he expected there to be mass slaughter once the legions engaged in full combat.

Corvinius slowed his pace. "Do you mind telling me what got your pee so hot? I thought we were out for a leisurely stroll?"

"A man was staring at me back there."

"So what?"

"The man watching me was a centurion. He was with the unit that captured me in Germania and sold me as a gladiator. It was the Fourth legion. There was no doubt he recognized me. What am I going to do? If they recognize me, they will kill me. They will nail my ass to a cross. It is impossible to escape this encampment. It's heavily guarded. I have no options."

Corvinius frowned in thought. "You're correct about that. You can't escape. We can't do anything now. Let's wait until after the battle and see what happens. Assuming we win this fight, things should slacken up. For now, just lie low and be a soldier. The man who observed you might do nothing."

"When I pulled that stunt with the wood gathering, I remember you telling me that nobody forgets anything in the legions."

Corvinius snorted. "I did, didn't I? Listen to me. As I said, you can't do anything about it right now. I'm sure that centurion has other things on his mind—like surviving the upcoming battle. Let's see what develops. Assuming we are victorious, we can make plans. If we are not, it won't matter anyway. And as for us, no more leisurely strolls."

Two days later, Antonius's causeway had almost extended to the left flank of Cassius's army. Most importantly, its construction had passed unobserved by the forces of Cassius and Brutus. The narrow road was paved with wooden planks. It was a slightly elevated path that rose above the muck of the swamp. When completed, it would allow the rapid deployment of forces to the vulnerable flank of Cassius's army.

Meanwhile, the legions of Octavius and Antonius were once again forming up to confront the army of the Liberators. The via Egnatia ran straight through the middle of the plain, directly into the town of Philippi located in the distant rear of the Liberators. The road bisected the armies of the Triumvirate, Octavius on the left and Antonius on the right. The combined strength of twenty legions marched out of the encampment directly toward the entrenched army of Brutus and Cassius, only this time, a portion of Antonius's army was clandestinely making its way along the newly constructed causeway, toward the enemy's flank.

Alderic stood next to Corvinius, as they witnessed the legions deploy on the plain of Philippi. Once again, the cohorts of the Fifteenth legion were held in reserve. The forward legions were placed in three lines, each line ten men deep. Alderic could not fathom what was going on to his front. All he could see was a huge dust cloud, with occasional glimpses of massed legionnaires slowly maneuvering into position. He heard the sounds of the trumpets but had no idea what in Hades the horns signaled. His centurion would tell them what to do.

Gracchus huddled with the five other centurions in front of the cohort. The group broke up and the other centurions hustled to their units. Centurion Gracchus turned about to face the first century. His face was powdered with the fine brown dust. "First century, we are standing fast here. We will not advance any farther. We are the reserve force again. There are no other units behind us. Stand by for orders. We may be requested to move at a moment's notice in either direction. You may stand down and drink your water now."

Meanwhile, Antonius sat on his mount along with his officers on the far-right flank of the battlefield. He watched as his troops advanced, raising a thick cloud of dust. A rider approached, galloping his steed at full speed before abruptly pulling up in front of his general.

Antonius fixed upon him with a flinty gaze. "Yes, what is it Tribune Sulpuchius?"

"Sir, I'm to report to you that the enemy has discovered our causeway. As we speak, they are rushing reinforcements to the area and are building a transverse wall to our road through the swamp."

Antonius's face filled with fury. "So, the gods decided to shit on me today. It was almost complete. Well it's not an event I did not anticipate." He turned to his retinue of officers. "We knew this might happen, so let's go ahead with our contingency plan. I want my four reserve legions on that causeway now. They are to move at the fastest possible pace. I want six legions deployed here—the Eighth, Ninth, Twelfth, Thirtieth, Thirty-First, and Thirty-Second—to attack Cassius's force in a frontal assault on the Liberator's left wing. This will give him second thoughts about sending more reinforcements to block my causeway. Make haste and do it now. I'll leave you gentleman to manage this part of the battlefield. I am going with Tribune Sulpuchius into the swamp. I'm going to envelop their flank today and achieve victory. Send a messenger to Octavius that he is to advance against the summit when he sees our forces attack." With that, General Antonius departed with the tribune.

Antonius arrived where his troops were massing near the blockade established by Cassius's forces. He leapt off his horse and approached General Caesilius, with whom he had served for many years. Caesilius spoke, his tone uncertain. "Sir, we were waiting for orders from you."

Antonius snarled. "We're going to attack the enemy blockade right now. I didn't expend all that effort to build this road just to have it obstructed. General Caesilius, I want your men in formation immediately. My reserve legions are coming down the road to assist us, but we aren't waiting for them. We must attack. Now, get moving."

With Antonius leading from the front, the Roman cohorts, although outnumbered, assaulted the hastily erected fortifications. The incomplete breastworks, made of timber and earth flung perpendicular to the causeway, proved to be only a minor impediment. Nevertheless, it was a bloody battle. Legionnaires on both sides fell in clusters. Antonius's forces prevailed. They stormed the blockade and overwhelmed the forces of Cassius. As they swarmed over the palisade, and the men began pulling down the timber walls. A second relief force from Cassius's army arrived to stem the advance, but it was too little too late. The surge by Antonius's men along with the timely arrival of Anthony's four reserve legions turned the tide. The flank of Cassius's legions was now under siege.

General Lucius Calpurnius Biblius of the Liberator's force stood on the escarpment, studying the movements of Octavius Caesar's legions approaching his position. He could make out that their legions were deployed in triple lines in open formation, which meant they occupied twice the front of a formation in closed ranks. If he were their commander, he would have ordered closed ranks. There was much better control that way. His general, Brutus, had ordered that under no circumstances were they to leave their elevated position. It was too advantageous to abandon. As with the previous days, he expected the forces of Octavius to halt slightly beyond the range of his archers and artillery. Another uneventful day, he thought.

Peering intently at the forward progress of the opposing forces amid the huge dust cloud, he was astounded to see a huge gap in the lines on the left flank. Several of the legions appeared to be moving to the side rather than forward. Was this some ruse by his opponent? Excitedly, several of his aides pointed at the huge breach. What in Hades were those legions doing? It appeared they were attempting to advance but amid total chaos. Could they possibly be that disorganized?

Biblius was a good soldier and understood that one must follow orders, but a tactical opportunity such as this couldn't be ignored. He turned toward his subordinates. "We are going to attack that gaping hole in their left flank. I want the cavalry to expand the breach. We are going to turn their flank, rout their forces, and strike at the heart of their encampment." There was no time to request permission. He needed to seize this opportunity immediately. He turned to one of his aides. "Find Brutus and tell him we're attacking a huge gap in their lines. Ask him to come forward with the reserves to exploit our thrust."

Disregarding the strict orders to remain in position, the cavalry and infantry lines of Biblius surged forward toward the huge gap between Octavius's legions.

Centurion Gnaeus Cattallus of the fifth cohort, Fourth Legion, the man who had recognized Alderic from his capture in Germania, looked to his cohort commander, Centurion Marcus Verres for orders. None were issued. The battlefield was a mass of confusion. Gnaeus could hear the clash of arms and the screams of the dying. *We're fucked.* He heard a thud and saw a javelin embedded in the ground three feet from his position. He couldn't see the enemy, but he knew intuitively that they were near. The noise of combat became louder. His men stood ready, their shields in position and their short swords in hand. What his men couldn't anticipate was the overwhelming force that smashed into both their flanks.

The shield walls of the fifth cohort collapsed in a matter of moments, overrun by a numerically superior force. The legionnaires of Brutus's army savaged the men of the fifth cohort, killing most of the legionnaires and their centurions as waves of the opposing army swept over them. Unknown to Alderic, the centurion from Germania who had helped capture him and later questioned his identity, had died from several sword thrusts to the neck and groin. His revelation about Alderic died with him.

Centurion Gracchus stood in the front of his beloved second cohort, attempting to peer through the thick cloud of dust. He didn't need to see what was happening to realize that something was terribly wrong. A rider came storming up to his position and halted in front of him. "Centurion Gracchus, I have a message from our legate, Gaius Quintus Calvinius. The front lines have been breached. The Fifteenth is falling back. You're to take your cohort to the rear where the command staff is located. You are to escort General Octavius back to the encampment. Protect him with your life. Understood?"

Gracchus dismissed the messenger. He quickly sent his own messengers to the cohorts on either side of him, with the explanation that his cohort would be vacating this area and moving to the rear to protect the commander. That way, they could consolidate and not leave a breach between the adjacent units.

Young Octavius sat on his horse conferring with his military advisor and confidant, Marcus Agrippa. The bulky figure of the general stood in stark contrast to the painfully thin Octavius. "Sir, you must retire from the battlefield now and go back to the encampment. It is too dangerous here, now that Brutus's army has breached our lines."

Octavius would have none of it. "My place is here. I am the commander of this army."

Agrippa shouted above the din of battle. "Sir, if you perish in the clash, then all is lost. Everything you have worked for will be for naught. I beg you to reconsider. You must leave at once. The situation is becoming untenable. You must go back to the encampment with the cohort escort. You will live to fight another day."

"Antonius will think me a coward. My place is here."

Agrippa exhaled in frustration. "Sir, he will not think you a coward, and since when did you care about what that fuck thinks. Please, your place is back at the encampment. Look there," he said pointing. "There is the second cohort. They have been charged with protecting you and taking you back. You must withdraw now or face the real risk of being slain."

Without waiting for a reply, he gestured toward the officer leading the six centuries chosen to protect Octavius. "Centurion, please escort our commander back to his command tent. If we are overrun here and the enemy attacks our camp, take him and flee to the swamps. He must be protected at all costs."

Centurion Gracchus glanced at the turmoil to their front and sides. "Right away, sir."

Gracchus took the initiative and boldly seized the bridle of Octavius Caesar's horse. "Come sir, we need to make haste." Within moments, Octavius and his small retinue of servants and bodyguards were surrounded by the six centuries of the second cohort. They moved at a fast trot back to the base camp over a mile away.

Upon reaching the ramparts, the gates opened wide. The cohort surged inside the gates of the empty fort and advanced down the main avenue to the commander's tent near the center of the stronghold. Gracchus directed the cohorts to deploy facing the main avenue they had just trekked. The centurion sent a few others to the walls as lookouts in case the camp came under attack.

Alderic stood among the ranks of his century, now deployed as a blocking force across the avenue. He waited with the others of his unit, unsure of what was going to happen next. He didn't wait long. He heard shouts from the distance. Peering down the main avenue, he observed legionnaires sprinting frantically toward him. Observing more closely, he saw that they were being chased by other Roman soldiers. He looked toward his centurion. Gracchus had seen them as well. He pointed with his sword and shouted. "Move down the avenue, away from the legate's tent." The centurion then hurried into the tent of Octavius Caesar.

Gracchus entered the tent and pulled aside the flap, interrupting a conversation between Caesar and his personal physician, Marcus Batorius. Caesar glanced up in anger. "It is impolite to enter my quarters unannounced. You should know better, Centurion."

Gracchus spoke rapidly. "This is no time for niceties, sir. The walls have been breached. There are enemy troops streaming down the avenue. We must evacuate immediately."

Octavius huffed. "Then we will take a stand. We are Roman legionnaires, brave and skilled—"

The physician and confidante of Octavius interrupted. "Sire, perhaps you should listen to Centurion ... "

"Gracchus. Centurion Gracchus of the Second Cohort. Sir, please, based on my many years of combat, it is best, no, it is imperative that we leave now. Our situation is perilous. We are vastly outnumbered by the approaching force." He looked beseechingly toward the physician for support.

Batorius wasted no time in following up. "Please sir, we must vacate the camp now. Listen to Centurion Gracchus. He knows what to do in these situations."

His face flushed with anger, Caesar stomped out of the tent, followed by his retinue.

Gracchus exited the tent. Peering about, he was alarmed at how close the advancing forces were to Caesar's quarters. He guided Caesar down the road and into the protection of the ranks of the first century. "Listen up, second cohort. Here's what we're going to do. First century, I want a shield wall across the thoroughfare, protecting the withdrawal of Caesar. He must be defended at all costs. I want the second through sixth century in a column formation to our rear ready to relieve the first century upon my command. We will conduct a fighting withdrawal. Now, out the rear gate and into the swamp."

Alderic stood in the middle of the avenue. The century was deployed into two-men-deep lines. Caesar, despite Centurion Gracchus's insistence, stopped immediately behind Alderic to observe what was happening. Alderic glanced at Octavius. He had never been near a general before. He wore a shining breast-plate and a red cloak. His helmet featured a large black plume. He steadied himself as the enemy approached closer. Suddenly, javelins whistled in the air, hurtling toward the ranks of the first century. Alderic raised his shield high above eye level exposing his torso to incoming pila. Two javelins thumped into the wooden shield. If he had not acted quickly, the missiles would have impaled Octavius Caesar, who was standing right behind him. The shaken commander, his face pale, gave Artorus a grateful smile.

Gracchus had seen enough. "Optio Lucullus, make haste. Escort our general away immediately."

Gracchus had no sooner spoken than the initial charge of the enemy slammed into the shield wall. Fortunately for the first century, the opposing force was a disorganized mob, incline more toward plunder than fighting. Despite the efforts of their officers, the Republican legionnaires broke ranks to plunder the command tent. Alderic withstood the initial charge, then stabbed his opponent in the neck over his shield, killing him instantly. The next legionnaire charged into him. He fared little better. Alderic raised his shield high, stabbing his foe deep in the leg. The wounded man shrieked, then collapsed like sack of grain, disappearing beneath the next wave of enemy forces.

The battle raged on, as the opposing forces surged again and again at the shield wall of the first century. Just as he had been trained, Alderic thrust with his shield, then stabbed with his sword. Some of the men of his century's first rank fell and were immediately replaced by fresh legionnaires. Alderic's arm ached from the constant stabbing, but he remained in the first rank. He knew his presence was an anchor for the other men. Alderic understood it was important that he, as the best fighter, be in the front ranks despite his fatigue. He smashed an assailant with his shield, knocking him silly. Another man leaped into the gap, snarling at Alderic. He blocked his foe's sword thrust, then slammed his shield down on the man's unprotected foot. He fell down screaming in agony.

More of the legionnaires who had charged at the first century began to divert from the assault to loot the command tent. Soon, it became a mass exodus. Perhaps they would have acted differently if they knew it was Caesar they were pursuing. Gracchus took advantage of the temporary lull. He screamed at his men above the din of the battle. "Fall back. Slowly. Do not break ranks or we will be slaughtered. Nice and easy now. Move back."

Alderic stepped back, keeping his pace measured with the rest of the men. Several crumpled forms littered the ground. He recognized the figure of Mellitus, a gaping wound in his throat. He gave his fallen comrade one last glance and continued moving.

Gracchus, who seemed to be everywhere, bellowed out his next command. "Centurion Fulvius and the second century move up and replace the first century." The second century surged forward through the ranks of the first, allowing the first to move back through their lines. Alderic's arms sagged in weariness. He realized he should have vacated his position earlier. His fatigue might have killed him.

The first century retreated in good order down the avenue to the rear gate. Gracchus positioned two more centuries ahead of the first, knowing his men were spent and had incurred the most casualties. Alderic looked about and couldn't see Caesar. He assumed he was safely in the rear by now.

Despite the pressure from the enemy forces, the men of the second cohort continued their withdrawal in a leapfrog manner, taking turns relieving each other at the front. They made their way back, then exited the rear gate. Gracchus looked about and pointed to their right. "That way. Into the swamp. Go into the reeds. If you are followed by the enemy, kill them. First century, you're up again. Stay here with me. Form a double line right here at the edge of the reeds. We're going to provide the discouragement if they choose to pursue us."

General Lollius Faustus of the Republican forces rode his steed, urging his Twenty-Second Legion forward through the camp of Octavius Caesar. He had been startled by his orders to leave the summit and attack the legions of the Triumvirate. It was the last thing he had expected today, but once his legion had been deployed and plunged through the huge gap in the enemy's lines, it appeared to be a good strategy after all. His forces had exploited the breach, driving through the opposing ranks toward the rear. Other units had deployed to attack the exposed flanks of the opposition. It had been a rout.

His focus was the praetorium. He wanted the head of Octavius Caesar. What a coup that would be. He could see a small force of

Octavius's men close ahead, probably no more than a cohort, blocking the avenue; nothing his forces couldn't handle, even though the men under his command were a mixture of units from other legions alongside some of his own forces. It had been a chaotic clash with the forces of Octavius. Legions and cohorts were scattered everywhere. His forces contained the ranks of at least three other friendly legions.

As the vanguard of his forces met the opposing enemy, many of his forces began to disband and loot the command tents. Their progress was stymied by the stiff resistance of the foe. Because of the desertion of many of his men, the numerical superiority he had once enjoyed had substantially eroded now. His face purple with rage, the general screamed for his centurions to maintain order. The officers attempted to organize the men, but in vain. Many of the legionnaires were in an uncontrolled frenzy, seeking booty from the empty tents. In frustration, he watched as a high-ranking officer with a bright red cloak, perhaps Octavius himself, escape down the avenue. He cursed at his legion. In retrospect, he should have known this might occur. His legion was newly formed, the men recruited with the promise of a generous bounty and all the loot they could capture. They were not seasoned legionnaires and lacked disciplined. He hung his head in defeat, knowing he had missed an opportunity to capture Octavius Caesar.

The tall reeds devoured the five centuries of the cohort, making them invisible to their pursuers. The first century stood resolute, waiting for the pursuit by the enemy. Gracchus knew the first had devoted more than their fair share of time battling the enemy forces at the front ranks, but they were the best he had, and he had faith in their abilities. A disorganized band charged at the first century. There was a resounding boom as shield met shield. The two sides stabbed at each other amid a scurry of screams and groans.

Alderic and Corvinius stood side by side, issuing death and mayhem. A pile of dead men formed before the pair. A centurion from the opposing force shouted for his men to push forward. Leading the way, he charged directly at Alderic. He did not get far. The centurion attempted to strike Alderic high in the face. The German parried the blow while simultaneously stabbing low at the man's leg. The man collapsed with a groan. Alderic then dispatched him with a stab to the throat. Abruptly, the opposing forces lost heart and retreated toward the camp, no doubt to seek loot like their comrades.

Gracchus surveyed the retreating enemy and smiled at his men. "Good show. Now let's enter this marsh before these crazy bastards change their minds and attack us again."

Alderic warily eyed the area in front of him to establish he wouldn't be attacked with his back turned and then entered the morass. The watery mud was ankle deep and threatened to suck his marching boots off his feet. He gingerly made his way forward, not wanting to fall head-first into the ooze. It was not long before the air was filled with curses from the men as they advanced through the bog. The men of the first century followed in the path created by those that went before them. Clouds of insects rose and feasted on the exposed flesh of the legionnaires as they struggled through the mire.

Chapter XIII

Back on the plain of Philippi, Gaius Cassius Longinius, co-commander of the Republican forces, looked around himself in panic. His left flank had been turned as a result of the causeway through the marsh. The reinforcements he had dispatched to counter the flanking maneuver had been insufficient to contain the breach by the opposing legions. *Damn that Antonius. How could he have possibly constructed that path through the swamp without being detected?* Cassius had been forced to turn his army away from the high ground to avoid being flanked by enemy forces and to keep pace with Brutus's forces, who had unexpectedly abandoned their position on the summit to attack the enemy. The Triumvirate forces were pressing his disorganized legions back. It was close to a full-scale rout. He knew that his legions were not as strong as those of Antonius. His men were not half as experienced or well trained. His perceived advantages were the high ground and the favorable logistical supplies—which had both now been negated. Why had Brutus's forces disobeyed their standing orders to remain on the summit? Cassius turned to his faithful aide and confidant, Titinius. "Plant the flag here. We will make a stand on this ground and repel the enemy."

"Yes, sir."

Cassius, looking to fortify his present position, grabbed several messengers. "Go find the legates in our left and right flanks. We will consolidate our forces here." He watched as the men dutifully mounted their horses and galloped away toward his flanks.

Cassius was perhaps the most capable commander of the Republican forces. But today, things weren't going well. The huge dust cloud that had enveloped the battlefield obscured the reality of the situation. He was unaware that his present location was untenable; the forces of Antonius had already penetrated the surrounding terrain in several spots. If he could have an aerial view of the developing battle without the dust cloud, he would have realized that his current position was indefensible and that he would have been better served to establish a rally point farther back from the encroaching legions of the Triumvirate.

More confusion followed as the lines of his friendly forces collided and mingled. There was no cohesion anywhere. Cassius's personal bodyguards formed a ring around him, as more of the hostile forces pressed toward the command. They were getting close. Two legates from the Twenty-Seventh legion and the Thirty-Sixth legion joined Cassius, and like him, peered through the dust, attempting to make sense of what was happening. The clash of arms and the screams of the dying increased in intensity and number.

The opposing forces swarmed his left flank. It didn't take long for Cassius to realize that his present position was compromised. His rally point was under tremendous pressure and threatened to give way any moment. He needed to act fast and decisively. He gave the order. "Retreat back to the acropolis. We will set up a defensive position there. I hope Brutus's forces were successful in their attack, but I've heard no word of their fate."

Cassius and the Republican forces began to retreat once more in an orderly fashion. They moved a fair distance, putting space between themselves and the forces of Antonius. It was as good a withdrawal as he could hope. The pressure on his lines slackened. The surviving army of Cassius slowly ascended the summit. Cassius and his retinue of bodyguards and advisors hurried up the hill, hoping for a better to view so they could determine the magnitude of their defeat.

From his elevated position on the summit, Cassius looked at what remained of his army on the hilltop and observed six legionary standards. He had no idea of what had become of the other four but assumed they had been destroyed. He watched in horror as a huge dust cloud rolled toward his right flank. His army, in the heat of battle, had rotated to the left to avoid Antonius's men. He had no idea what forces, friend or foe, lay within that cloud of powder. If those were Octavius's forces, he was doomed, for that meant that Brutus had been defeated as well and both armies of the Triumvirate were approaching this summit. He would be squeezed like a grape.

He turned toward his trusted aide, Titinius. "I will attempt to organize our forces up here on the summit. I want you to ride down toward that approaching dust cloud and see who it is. I hate to be a pessimist, but I fear that the legions of Brutus have been overwhelmed by Octavius. Hurry now so we can prepare ourselves."

"Right away, sir." He turned his horse about and galloped toward the cloud on the plain below.

Cassius watched the receding figure move down the slope while simultaneously observing the oncoming mass to his front. He was shocked at how rapidly they were advancing. Could Brutus's forces have been completely overcome? It wouldn't be long now. The horse and its rider disappeared into the cloud. Even from this distance, he could hear the resonating cheers and bellows of men. That could only mean one thing—Titinius had been slain or captured by his foe. The commander hung his head. All was lost. Everything he had strove for with the resurrection of the republic was no more. He grimaced. He refused to be taken alive to be executed like some criminal.

Cassius looked about and found the eyes of his freedman and main bodyguard, Pindarus. "I want you to take my head. All is lost."

Marcus Porcius Cato, one of his fellow senators, walked up to him. "Cassius, surely you must wait. It's not over yet. Who knows what might happen."

"Can you not see, Cato?" Cassius replied. "They have either captured or killed Titinius. You can hear it in their cheers and the way they are so full of themselves. Listen to them. No, I will tarry no longer. Now is the time." He turned to his legates. "Thank you for you devoted service. Make the best you can. Chances are you will fare better with Antonius than that unpredictable Octavius. He is a ruthless young man who is not inclined to show any clemency as Caesar did. I bid you all farewell. Pindarus, come with me. We will do this in private behind our lines."

Pindarus and Cassius retreated a hundred yards to the rear. Cassius dismounted and discarded his cuirass. With no delay, he knelt and extended his neck forward. "Let's get this over with. Strike hard and true. I ask this final favor of you. Please proceed."

Pindarus, a large hulking figure and ex-gladiator, drew his razor-sharp gladius and approached Cassius. Tears glistening in his eyes, he hesitantly stopped before Cassius.

Cassius looked up in anger. "Do your duty, Pindarus. My final order."

Pindarus raised his sword and struck hard, severing Cassius's head in one stroke. Blood sprayed into the air, coating the executioner's armor. The figure dropped his sword, as tears ran freely down his face. His commander was dead.

Back on the summit, the legions of Cassius braced for the attack. Men gripped their swords, preparing for the onslaught. Out of the dust cloud, rode a triumphant Titinius, surrounded by the forces of Brutus. Cassius's retinue gasped in shock. As one, they turned to the rear and galloped toward Pindarus, yelling for him to stop. But they were too late. The weeping men crowded the headless body of their leader.

Titinius thundered through the surrounding throng to see his leader's body. "No, it can't be!" he screamed. He walked slowly to the corpse and hung his head. Without a word, he stripped off his armor, withdrew his gladius and fell on it, impaling his torso. He whimpered briefly, then was still, his eyes glazing over.

The next day, the command tent of the Triumvirate army had been emptied, save for a handful of the most senior officers. Marcus Antonius, his eyes glistening with malevolence, sat across Octavius. "Well, what do you have to say for yourself, boy? It seems Alexander the Great has nothing to fear from the likes of you." He chuckled at his own rhetoric. "The fucking war would be over and the Liberators dead if you had done your part. I collapsed the left flank of Cassius's army. I came this close"—he held his thumb and index finger nearly touching each other—"to destroying Cassius's legions. All you had to do was hold the forces of Brutus in position, and I could have done the rest. Instead, we are right back where we began. What did you lose, three eagles today?"

Octavius stared coldly at his antagonist, saying nothing. Interpreting this as his sign to interrupt, Marcus Agrippa began to speak. "We faced some adverse developments on the—"

Octavius held up his hand. He glared at Antonius, while maintaining a mellow tone. "We lost some of our legions today, it's true. We shall do better next time. My legions became disoriented in the dust cloud and ran into each other, resulting in a wide breach in my lines. My men are well trained and shall do better henceforth."

Antonius was far from finished with his mocking repartee. "I heard they chased your ass into the marsh. You had to hide in the swamp like an escaped slave to evade the pillaging legions of Brutus as they destroyed your camp. I wonder if you're up for the task of defeating our Republican foe."

Octavius decided to issues some barbs of his own. "As I recall, my legions defeated yours back in Italia and forced you to retreat into Gallia."

"So? You got lucky, boy."

Octavius remained cool and collected. "So you say, and today my legions were unlucky. It is but a temporary setback. As I said, we will do better the next time and defeat their forces. Our legions will prevail. Can we put aside our enmity and concentrate on defeating the Liberators. What do you suggest we do now?"

Antonius, his eyes unmoving from Octavius's, reached for his wine goblet and chugged half its contents. He wiped his mouth on his sleeve. "First, we will need to consolidate our respective forces to adjust for the losses we each suffered. After that, I suggest we ensure we have adequate provisions for the men and horses. Once we've accomplished that, we can relaunch our next phase of tactical maneuvering."

"How long will this take?"

"Perhaps a week, maybe two," replied Antonius.

Octavius turned to his military commander, Marcus Agrippa, who nodded in acquiescence. Octavius rose from his seat. "Fine, we will do as you suggest. I will have my forces ready to fight again in the near future." Octavius exited the tent followed by his four generals.

Gracchus stood in his tent facing Artorus. "Well Legionnaire Artorus, it appears fate has smiled upon you. Octavius Caesar is grateful to our century, and especially you, for saving his life yesterday. I saw what you did. Your shield took two javelins that would have skewered our esteemed commander, had you not intervened. He lives to fight another day. He wishes to thank us personally with a little ceremony in his command tent."

Alderic stood there, saying nothing. His mind whirled at the implications of entering Octavius Caesar's quarters. Visions of being arrested and executed flashed before his eyes. They would rejoice at finally having captured the infamous Alderic, the one who killed one of Antonius's men and hid a vast treasure.

Alderic continued standing before his centurion, mute. Gracchus growled. "Artorus, say something."

"I not want to go and meet this Caesar person. I'm only a lowly legionnaire. I just did my duty, nothing more. It is best if I stay here with my mates."

Gracchus frowned. "Listen to me, Artorus. It doesn't work that way. You're going whether you like it or not. That is an order. Your presence has been requested by Octavius Caesar. One does not say no to his summons. I suggest you polish your uniform and look parade-ground ready. If you're intimidated by the high command, well, so am I; but we are ordered to go and be recognized, so we are going. All you have to do is be presentable and stand tall. Just follow my lead. You say 'yes sir,' 'no sir,' and 'thank you, sir.' Got it?"

Alderic cast his eyes downward and replied. "I go if ordered."

Gracchus looked at him for a moment before responding. "Good. I will have someone fetch you at the appointed hour. It will be close to dinner, so spend your available time looking presentable. No need to be so nervous about this. Our general is honoring your bravery. Now go. You are dismissed."

Later that day, Alderic stood outside the command tent of Octavius Caesar along with Centurion Gracchus, waiting to be called inside. With the help of Corvinius, he had cleaned his armor, painstakingly removing all the splattered blood, dust, and grime, and then polishing the leather and iron links to a high luster. He had shaved and looked somewhat presentable. He paced back and forth, his clenched hands nervously held behind his back. Gracchus looked on calmly. After a time, the centurion could take it no more. "Artorus, stand still. Enough of this pacing. Calm down. We will be called soon. I've never seen one so nervous to meet a general. They're like us. They put their marching boots on one foot at a time."

Alderic stood next to his centurion, staring at the sky, wondering if this was to be his last bit of freedom. He clenched and unclenched his fist in nervous anticipation. He inhaled deeply to dispel his angst. A stern-faced tribune exited the command tent and approached the two men. "He is ready for you. Once you enter the tent, you will approach the table where Caesar is seated. Come to attention five paces in front of him and be silent. Answer only when spoken to. Got it?"

Gracchus replied for both of them. "Lead the way, sir." The flaps were held aside by servants. The two men entered the tent.

Alderic, his gut rumbling from anxiety, followed his centurion's lead. He stopped the requisite five paces in front of the table and stared at a spot several feet above their seated commander's head. Upon closer inspection, he was taken aback at how young Octavius Caesar appeared without his helmet. He was a slim figure with a handsome countenance that featured blazing eyes. Alderic continued staring above his piercing stare.

Octavius gazed at the two soldiers before him. "Aha! The two heroes who saved my life. Centurion Gracchus and Legionnaire Artorus, your efforts and heroism were duly noted in those hectic moments yesterday. I'm extremely appreciative of your military prowess." He gestured to one of his aides who produced two sacks of coin. "I'm not going to give you a decoration, as I think a sack full of coin would be more valued." He smiled smugly. "Don't you?"

He gestured with his hand for the men to approach. An aide handed Gracchus the larger cloth bag and then deposited the smaller sack in Alderic's hand. "Thank you both for your heroics yesterday. You're a credit to the legions, and I, for one, venerate your bravery. You saved my life. I thank you."

"Yes, sir," replied Gracchus. Alderic blurted out a "Yes, sir," at the same time.

Octavius directed his gaze at Alderic. "You know I could use a man like you as part of my personal guard. A man of your size and martial capabilities would be a valuable addition.

Alderic cringed. *Isn't that just fucking great. Now I'm truly fucked. Just kill me now and get it over with.*

The general returned his gaze to Gracchus. "What say you, Centurion?"

Gracchus, stunned by the recent pronouncement, scrambled to compose the right words. "Sir, if that is your desire, so be it." He added in a deferential tone, "Artorus is by far the best warrior in my cohort. We would hate to lose him."

Octavius Caesar laughed. "I got your not-so-subtle message, Centurion. You shall continue to have Artorus under your command, at least until we have defeated the Republican forces. We can discuss his future duties at a later date."

Octavius smiled at both of them. He was about to continue, when another aide entered. "Sir, sorry to interrupt the proceedings, but General Antonius has arrived with several of his staff."

Octavius frowned. "They are early for our meeting. No matter, please show them in. I'm almost finished here." He turned his gaze back to the two men. "It seems we will have to cut this short. Again, you both have my profound gratitude."

With that, Antonius swept into the tent with his retinue of officers. Alderic shot a quick sideways glance at Antonius, sweat beading his forehead. He stiffened even more, if that were possible. His mind swimming with calamitous thoughts, he felt the arm of Gracchus guiding him out of the tent.

Antonius gave the pair a curious parting glance, dismissing them as no one of importance, and then turned to Octavius.

Gracchus and Alderic exited the command tent and walked back in silence toward their cohort area. They reached the bivouac of the first century. Artorus eagerly broke away from the centurion to venture toward his tent. Gracchus grabbed his arm. "Not so fast. You are coming to my quarters. We are going to have a blunt discussion. You have some explaining to do."

The pair entered the tent of Gracchus. The centurion sat behind his table. He didn't offer Alderic a seat. "Legionnaire Artorus, would you explain to me why you were so petrified to meet Octavius Caesar? Furthermore, you nearly jumped out of your skin when General Antonius entered. Unlikely as it may seem, do you have a history with either of them?" His queries were greeted by silence. Gracchus continued. "You know, Centurion Fulvius told me there was something odd about you. He couldn't put his finger on it. I'm getting the same feeling. Please, do tell."

Alderic bit his lower lip and nervously fidgeted with the sack of coins given to him. He knew his life hung in the balance. If inquiries were made about his past at a higher level, the truth would eventually come out. "Centurion Gracchus, my past is my past. I would like to keep it that way. If I told you the entire saga, you wouldn't believe it, because it is so improbable. What is it you call her, the Goddess Fortuna? She has been both kind and cruel to me."

The centurion gazed at Alderic. "You won't elaborate?"

"No, Centurion. For my sake and maybe yours. But all you need to know is this. I am and will continue to be the fiercest warrior of the first century, second cohort, Fifteenth Legion. That is why you chose me to be in your century, because I can fight. I owe my loyalty to the first century. I promise to serve and defend my fellow legionnaires to my last breath. That is what is important to me. When I joined the legions, I swore an oath to obey my officers and pledged my loyalty to Rome. I intend to uphold that oath."

Gracchus stared daggers at Alderic, the period of silence extending infinitely between the two men. At last, he pursed his lips and spoke. "You are correct. I selected you for the first century because I have never seen a skilled fighter of your size. Your actions in the recent battle confirm my faith in your abilities. I would love to know your story, but something tells me that there are some unsavory parts that will stand in severe violation of the legions' regulations. I have my suspicions, but I will put them aside for now. So for all concerned, it is best that I not know of your history. Our conversation about your past will remain in this tent. I'm pleased you are with my century. You are dismissed."

Alderic heaved a sigh of relief and exited the tent. Reaching the tent area of the first century, he found Corvinius sharpening his sword. Alderic spoke in a brusque tone. "I'm back. Let's take a walk."

Corvinius rose and sheathed his weapon. As the pair walked away to find some privacy, Corvinius spoke. "I've been thinking. Remember that dream you told me about, the one about the eagle and the attacking birds?"

"What about it?"

"If you will recall, I said that you should consult a seer. Romans believe dreams have meanings and are not to be ignored. The gods are speaking to us. In your case, your dream foretold the saving of

General Octavius, our esteemed commander, from the enemy. The eagle that you rescued in your dream was Octavius Caesar, and the birds with the bloody beaks were the legionnaires of the Republicans. Don't you see?"

Alderic stopped walking and turned toward his friend. "No. I don't see. What a stretch that is. A dream about birds reflects on our current fight among Romans. In Germania, we don't believe in any of that crap. I mean, really? The gods talking to us in dreams?"

Corvinius shrugged his shoulders. "No need to get irritable about it. I was just offering my perspective as a Roman. I still say you should think about it a little more. It all fits together so nicely. So, how'd it go? You know, the ceremony and everything?"

Alderic continued walking, waiting until they were out of hearing range of others and let out a sigh. "I was rewarded with coin." He held up and displayed his sack of money. "Not that I have anywhere to spend it."

Corvinius smiled. "First, you can buy me some wine, you cheap bastard. If it were me, I would purchase some fine gifts to present to your woman back in Italia when you return. What was her name again?"

Alderic grimaced. "Bridin. Her name is Bridin. Listen, it's been a trying day. Gracchus noted my reluctance to meet with Octavius Caesar. Then General Antonius entered during the ceremony. On top of all that, Octavius mentioned he would like to have me as part of his personal bodyguards. Gracchus took me back to his quarters and asked me some pointed questions."

Corvinius gasped. "Wait a moment. Are you telling me you have a past with General Octavius Caesar and General Antonius?"

"I have not met either, but yes, there is a link," replied Alderic. "It's a long story."

Corvinius looked on Artorus in disbelief. "You're shitting me? In your past, you somehow crossed purposes with the two most powerful men in Rome, and yet here you are. Someday you're going to tell me this long story of yours. I need to hear this. So, what did Gracchus want to know?"

"He guessed there was something in my past. I turned it back on him. I let him know that he was the one that selected me to be in his century even though I not a citizen. I said that I was the best warrior by far in the first and would continue to serve faithfully. He seemed satisfied with that. He kind of agreed not to inquire into my past as I'm such a fierce warrior." Alderic chuckled. "I live to see another day."

Corvinius smiled. "Yes, you do, and I have some even better news for you."

"What would that be?"

"That little scrap we got into the other day was a big scrap for some of the other legions. Apparently, the Fourth Legion, the one with a certain centurion who might know of your past history, was destroyed. I heard that all their officers are dead and the surviving legionnaires are being reassigned to other legions. You live a charmed life, Artorus."

"Indeed, I do!"

Chapter XIV
Two Weeks Later

The Plains of Philippi

Alderic marched alongside Corvinius as the army of Octavius Caesar advanced across the plain toward the enemy forces. Absent were their javelins. After the debacle two weeks ago, when units had collided with each other amid dust clouds, the generals had decided to forgo open formations, which were required when the legions hurled volleys of javelins. Now, it was strictly closed ranks, which allowed for greater command and control. Today would be restricted to swords and shields and tight formations. Of greater importance, their legion, the Fifteenth, was no longer in reserve. As a result of the consolidation owing to the losses two weeks ago, the Fifteenth, a relatively full-strength legion had been shifted from the reserves to the head of the deployment. They were in the front lines, where the fighting and dying would occur. In fact, there were no reserve forces. Even the units used to guard the camp had been stripped. The combined forces of the Triumvirs were to engage in a brutal frontal assault; their purpose, to breach the lines of the Republican army and achieve a final victory.

Alderic peered to his left and right. Long lines of advancing legionnaires filled his vision. As far as he could see on both flanks, the forces of the Triumvirs advanced upon the broad plain. Already, huge clouds of fine powdered dust had risen into the hot air. The first series of coughs began, the men hacking to rid the disgusting contents from their throats and lungs.

The enemy commander, Brutus, sat upon his horse, nervously watching the advancing lines of the opposing legions. The previous

213

strategy of occupying heights and not attacking was no longer available to him. A portion of his forces, perhaps five thousand men, most of them previously under the control of Cassius, had deserted to the opposing army. Today, he would attack. He had no choice. He needed a decisive engagement. If he tarried, more of his legions might change sides, leaving him at a distinct numerical disadvantage. He had stripped some of legions from the center of his army to fortify both flanks. There would be no repetition of their previous battle, where the left flank of the army had been turned. He was certain his enemy would deploy a similar strategy—maneuver their forces to envelop one or both flanks. Today was to be the day of reckoning.

As they approached closer, Alderic could make out the faces of the Republican forces. He was wondering whether their foe will attack when he got his answer. Suddenly, a wave of opposing legionnaires swept off their hill toward him. He braced himself. The two lines crashed together. A charging legionnaire slammed into Alderic. The impact drove him back several feet, but he was not put off balance. He recovered quickly. He stood behind his shield, punching it forward, then stabbing with his sword. He grunted and pushed forward but made little progress. The ranks of the two forces moved back and forth over a small area, with neither side making any headway. The killing began. Large heaps of bodies mounted on both sides.

Alderic lost all sense of time. The savagery was beyond imagination. Everything was a blur, as men on both sides screamed and died. His only focus was the man opposite him, clashing sword and shield. He lost count of the men he killed. His shield and armor were splattered with blood.

Alderic and Corvinius backed away as the second rank moved forward to take their place. Alderic lowered his sword, his arm aching painfully. He panted with exertion. He needed to drink some water, but he dared not let his concentration lapse for even a moment. In the event the man in front of him was overcome by the enemy, it would leave him vulnerable if he chose that particular time to quench his thirst.

Before long, Alderic and Corvinius stepped forward in the front ranks again, punching with their shields and thrusting with their swords. Little by little, the lines of the Triumvirs began to push back the lines of the Republicans. The distance they had pushed the enemy forces was perhaps forty paces, and it was all traveling in one direction—the Republican army was retreating.

The advancement of the second cohort was suddenly halted as the Republicans appended their reinforcements. The standstill was temporary. Slowly and inexorably, the centuries of the second cohort advanced yet again. Gracchus appeared next to Corvinius and Alderic. He pointed with his sword at the Republican lines and growled. "Now is the time to strike. It appears they have committed the last of their reserves. We have them. They are wilting." He waved additional men forward from the rear to increase the pressure. Several men from the opposing forces fell, leaving a gap. Alderic spied the opening in the enemy lines and surged forward. Others followed his lead. The breach grew larger. The men of the first century pushed forward, leaving a trail of dead in their wake.

To his front, Alderic observed a large group of enemy legionnaires rushing from the flank in a desperate attempt to plug the breach. Alderic found himself and several others surrounded by Republican legionnaires. He lunged forward knocking down several men. More of the first century came to his aid, but they were still outnumbered. Alderic sensed a movement to his right. Glancing out of the corner of his eye, he saw a sword descending toward his head. Corvinius used his shield to block the blow, but the life-saving effort left him vulnerable. A sword thrust from the left pierced his leg. Corvinius moaned in pain and collapsed.

Seeing his friend fall, Alderic rammed his shield into the man whose thrust Corvinius had blocked. He delivered a stab to the assailant's neck, sending the figure crashing to the ground. Several other members of the first fell under the onslaught of the enemy reinforcements, but others took their place, maintaining the pressure on the Republicans. Alderic stood protectively over Corvinius stabbing and slashing like a wild man. A sword strike smashed into his helmet, making him woozy. Everything became a blur, his vison clouded. Another foe stabbed Alderic in the shoulder. Luckily, the blow was deflected by his armor and didn't affect him. From his left, a sword struck his unprotected leg. He collapsed next to Corvinius, waiting for the fatal strike, but nothing came. Instead, he sensed more of his century advancing forward, driving the enemy back. Then all went black.

The breach in the Republican lines initiated by the first century turned from a trickle into a gush. Thousands of legionnaires, under the command of Octavius, charged forward, killing any opposition in their path and enveloping the rear of the Republican forces. It was a slaughter of incomparable proportions. The forces of Triumvirs turned the battle into a rout. Victory would fall to the Octavius and Antonius today.

Marcus Junius Brutus sat upon his horse on the acropolis, looking down at the destruction of his legions. The surviving units, perhaps four partial legions, had retreated to the summit where their commander pondered his next course of action. Brutus frowned. The view was terrifying. He was now heavily outnumbered with fifteen thousand survivors at most. He slowly dismounted and signaled for his subordinate commanders to join him in a council. He eyed his six senior commanders, but none would meet his gaze. They appeared ragged and bloodied, weariness etched upon their faces. He wondered briefly if he looked as worn as them.

"This is no time for oratory, gentlemen. Our forces have been decisively defeated today. Our situation on this hilltop is precarious. I am going to ask a single question of you. I want you to respond in yes or no. That is all. No equivocating. In your military judgement, does our current force of four legions have any chance of defeating the Triumvirs?"

He turned first to his most trusted commander, Lucius Calpurnius Biblius. "I will start with you, Biblius." Biblius was silent for a moment, then uttered a single word. "No." The other five commanders followed, responding in the negative.

Brutus sighed. "Gentlemen, that was my conclusion as well, but I wanted to be absolutely sure. The Triumvirs want my head on a spike. I will not give them that pleasure. Shortly, I will end my life. What I want you to do is arrange for the best terms possible, for yourselves and the men. Approach Antonius. He is an experienced military commander and more likely to accept your surrender. Do not deal with young

Octavius if you can help it. I thank all of you for your service. This defeat was my responsibility alone, so don't blame yourselves for any of it. I will not tarry. I am going to end my life now. Good luck. May the Goddess Fortuna smile upon you."

With that, Brutus gestured to his servant to accompany him and walked away from his commanders, not looking back.

Alderic awakened to the familiar sting of a deep wound. His skin felt inflamed and tightened around the crude stitches that bound the wound in his leg. He blearily shifted his gaze about to see where he was. He noted that he lay in a tent and that there were about twenty cots, all of them occupied. He could smell the vinegar in the air, but underneath it there was the familiar cloying odor, redolent of blood and death. The tent flaps were open to permit ventilation. He had a terrible thirst that made his throat ache. "Water," he croaked feebly to whoever might be around.

A slave materialized at his side holding a clay cup of water. Artorus drained it greedily. "More," he said and drank again.

Gracchus appeared in front of him. "Ah, you're finally awake. We won. The field is ours. The Republican army is routed. I heard that their General Cassius has committed suicide."

Alderic stared numbly at his centurion, trying to contemplate what had just been said. He was glad it was finally over and really didn't give a crap about this Cassius fellow. "Corvinius? He lives?"

Gracchus grimaced. "Just looked in on him and talked to the medicus. He is alive, but they are unsure about his survival. His leg wound was very deep. He lost a lot of blood. We will have to wait and see. Hope for the best. You, on the other hand, are expected to fully recover."

Alderic closed his eyes and sank back on his cot. "He saved my life, perhaps at the cost of his own. I owe him."

Gracchus replied. "That's what legionnaires do. I've seen many such acts of bravery. You should know that it was because of the efforts of both Corvinius and you that we achieved victory today. Ours was the first cohort to break through the Republican lines. You know, you're developing quite a reputation. I was summoned again before Octavius

Caesar owing to the feats of my cohort. When I mentioned your exploits in today's battle to Octavius Caesar, he was most impressed. He asked about you and told me to keep him apprised of your condition." He turned to leave. "I'll look in on you again."

Alderic spoke. "Wait. Did the general mention anything about me becoming part of his bodyguards again?"

Gracchus paused briefly. "As a matter of fact, he didn't. Let's hope for both our sakes that he has forgotten about it." The centurion turned and departed.

Days later, Gracchus entered the medical tent once more. Alderic and Corvinius sat propped up on their cots next to each other. The pair was still under the care of the legion's medical corps. Miraculously, both men had survived with no mortification of their wounds. They could even hobble about with the aid of a walking cane.

Gracchus pulled up a stool next to their cots and eyed both men. "Glad to see you're both on the mend. I came by to let you know that we have our orders. In five weeks, the Seventh, Eighth, and Fifteenth legions are returning to Rome to march in a triumph, celebrating our victory over the Republicans. So gentlemen, get ready to travel. Antonius and his legions are staying here in the east. The other legions of Octavius are being deployed elsewhere on the frontiers."

Corvinius replied. "But Centurion Gracchus, we can barely walk right now."

Gracchus responded, his tone gruff. "The triumph is still a ways off. You both should improve by then. You are part of this legion and you will therefore take part in the ceremony. Next subject. Now that we are at peace, the standing legions will be consolidated and the number of legionnaires reduced." He turned toward Corvinius. "I'm sorry as Hades about this Corvinius, but the medicus told me you'll never fully recover the full use of your right leg. Therefore, in all likelihood you will be medically discharged."

Crestfallen, Corvinius replied. "That makes no sense. I'm expected to march in the parade, but I'm judged medically unfit, a cripple?"

"You're one of my best legionnaires. I don't want to lose you, but the medicus said that your leg cannot endure those forced marches. You wouldn't be able to keep up. The powers that now rule are looking to any excuse to cut the roles of the army. It is called a reduction in force."

"But what am I to do, Centurion? Soldering is my livelihood. Besides, how does the medicus know such things. They're wrong—"

Gracchus held up his hand. "Stop with the whining. Now, before you equate yourself with a beggar, there will be a generous donative for each legionnaire as a result of our victory. Several hundred denarii from what I'm told."

There was a brief silence among the men. Gracchus turned toward Alderic. "And what about you? What are your thoughts?"

Alderic looked at Gracchus. "I can leave if I want to?"

Gracchus frowned. "You are my best fighter. I don't want to lose you. But, yes, it's your choice. The ten-year commitment you and others signed up for has been voided by order of Octavius Caesar."

Alderic grunted. "Then I go with Corvinius. It is good time to leave the legions. I have done my duty."

Corvinius looked perplexed. "Don't leave on my account. This is your livelihood."

"I go with you, Corvinius. Together we will find work. I owe you. You saved my life."

Gracchus rose from his seat. "Think about it some more. You don't have to make a decision now. Once we get to Rome, let me know." He turned and departed.

Alderic turned to Corvinius. "Come. We need to go somewhere to talk in private about our future. The two men picked up their canes and painfully made their way from the medical tent toward the corral where the horses were penned. Once they arrived, Alderic looked about to make sure no one was around. "I can't risk going to Rome. If I'm recognized, I will be killed and so will you."

"What are you talking about, Artorus? I believe it's time you told me this long story of yours. You have shared tantalizing bits and pieces, but never the entire saga."

Artorus stared off in the distance in silence contemplating his words, then he began. "First of all, my name isn't Artorus. It's Alderic. I belong to the Tencteri tribe." And so Alderic recounted his tale of how he came to become Cilo's bodyguard once again.

"You were a German raider, a gladiator, a bodyguard for a rich senator, and now a legionnaire?" Corvinius asked, incredulous.

Alderic spoke in a wistful tone. "Yes. The senator's family took good care of me. I was a slave, but it was like I was part of their family. He had a beautiful wife and a son who was slightly younger than me. The boy's name was Lucius. He had just begun his training as a future tribune. We used to practice mock sword fights. He adored me for my fighting skills. He was a good lad, not some little snot."

"Sounds nice. What happened?"

"The senator and his family were on a, what is the term … a proscription list. The senator had some inkling of this. It was his plan to flee Rome in the evening. He entrusted me to take his hoard of coin to a friend's house, with the expectation that he and his family could somehow escape Rome that night and pick up the chests of money on their way out. The friend's house was under attack when I arrived, so I hid the coin elsewhere. When I came back to the senator's house later that afternoon, the whole family had been brutally murdered. The assassins of the senator's family were waiting for me. I took my revenge on some of them, including one of Marcus Antonius's men. Killed the fuck, then fled."

Corvinius interrupted. "You're shitting me. You've got to be making this up."

Alderic shook his head and continued. He told him about meeting Bridin in an alley and about how she was a runaway slave. He proceeded to talk at length about their flight to the north and the men looking for them. He then described the incident where he had accidentally wandered into the legionnaire camp.

Alderic continued. "The problem is this. About a year ago, half of Rome was looking for me because I knew where the money was—a bloody fortune. I was a fugitive. Because of my height, I was and am easily recognizable. Thankfully, Antonius and his henchmen are in the east, but there are still those who would like to get their hands on me. The street gangs in Rome might identify me. The other bodyguards of the senators knew me and those from my gladiatorial school would know me too. On top of all of this, General Octavius Caesar wants to recruit me as part of his personal bodyguard. If that were to occur, I will surely be recognized by someone in Rome. I must leave the legions. This march in Rome will be my last duty."

Corvinius gulped. "About the parade, my suggestion would be to keep your helmet on at all times and stay in the center of the formation if possible. There are other tall legionnaires in the ranks, nearly as big as you. Not many, but some. Be one within the mass of soldiers. No one would be looking for you among a century of legionnaires, even if they knew your face."

Artorus responded. "I agree, but if I am identified as Alderic, it will end badly for me. I must not let my past catch up with me."

Corvinius shook his head in wonderment. "And this treasure trove that you hid, it's still there, intact?"

Artorus grinned in response. "How would you like to be a rich man?"

Chapter XV
Rome

Five Weeks Later

Alderic stood, mingling among the thousands of other legionnaires in the assembly area outside Rome's walls, waiting for the parade to begin. He reflected on his plight. *After my incredible escape from these walls and my flight north, the trek to Brundisium, the harrowing journey across the sea, and fierce battles fought in a foreign land, I am back where I started. Surely the gods are toying with me.*

Three legions—nearly ten thousand men, only about twenty-five percent understrength owing to the battle—stood poised to march down the main avenues of the city. Despite the pleasant autumn warmth, Alderic shuddered slightly at the sight of the towering stone walls. The last time he had been here, he was concealed at the bottom of a cart, hoping to escape the guards of the urban cohorts and the street thugs seeking him. Yet, here he was, about to enter the bear's den once more. There was little he could do about it. He couldn't plead illness or say his wounded leg was too weak to march. But any excuse would kindle the centurion's suspicious of him. Gracchus had chosen not investigate his past, and Alderic wanted to keep it that way. Perhaps, he guessed, the centurion had some vested self-interest as well, since he was the one who had decided to recruit Alderic into the legions, ignoring the fact that he was not a citizen. Gracchus wanted him to march in the triumph, and thus, that is what he would do.

Alderic would be in full kit, replete with his armor, helmet, and sword. The legionnaires had spent the last two days laboriously cleaning and polishing their equipment. With any luck, he wouldn't be identified as Alderic the gladiator or the bodyguard of a now-dead senator. He intended to find a spot deep within the ranks of the century so that no one would see much of his face.

Corvinius, hoping to dispel his friend's anxiety, approached him and slapped him on the back. "Are you ready for this?" Corvinius was still a bit hobbled from his wound, but he would march as ordered by his centurion. Corvinius wondered if anyone was still looking for the missing bodyguard who had hidden a fortune. It had been a year, based upon what Artorus had told him. Was that enough time? For Artorus's sake, he hoped so.

"Artorus, listen to me. I know you don't want to spend a lot of time in the city, but I need to visit a woman. I have that heavy feeling, you know what I mean? I understand that you're remaining faithful to Bridin, but I have no attachments. So, if you don't mind, I'll stay for a bit in the big city."

Alderic grinned back. "Fair enough. I'll even accompany you in your quest. I know a place, high quality, perhaps the best girls in the city. It's mostly nobility who frequent the place. It'll cost you extra coin, no doubt. It's probably safe for me to venture there, so I'll go with you. In return, you go with me afterwards to visit a friend who saved my life. He trained me for the arena. I seek his advice about what to do with ourselves once we are discharged from the legions. I trust his judgement."

Corvinius's face brightened. "Of course, I'll accompany you. If you know a good place without a hundred legionnaires standing in line, I'm all for it. What's the name of this place and how much is it going to cost me?"

"It is called the Palace of Venus. I took my young master there to lose his virginity. He paid twenty sestertii."

Corvinius whistled. "That is steep, but I can afford it." He fingered his heavy purse for effect. "Where is this place?"

"Conveniently, it's near the forum area where the parade ends. I believe I know my way there. If we're fortunate, it'll be absent of other legionnaires."

Suddenly, commands were issued throughout the mingling mass of soldiers. Gracchus, his armor sparkling in the sunlight, strode to the front of his century. "All right, first century. Let's form up. You know the drill. I want ten across, eight men deep."

Alderic and Corvinius walked casually toward the middle of the century, hoping to blend into the center of the formation. Meanwhile, others eager to show off to the crowds hustled to the front. Gracchus observed the men for a few moments. He spoke loudly above the din. "Wait. I want Corvinius and Artorus in the front ranks. They were the ones primarily responsible for our success. You two"—he pointed to two of the legionnaires in the front—"go to the back and let Corvinius and Artorus take your spots. They are heroes of Rome." Artorus and Corvinius reluctantly did as they were told.

The men of the century settled into place. Gracchus walked across the front, down the side, around the back, and then back to the front of the formation. A smile creased his lips. "Looking good, first century. Listen up. This is how it's going to go. We will march into Rome, down the main avenues and past the reviewing stand. Listen for my commands. Stay in formation. There will be large crowds cheering for you. Don't get distracted. When we come to the end, you will be dismissed for the day. This is not your typical triumph parade. There is no booty to be displayed or any captives in chains. I'm told this cavalcade has two purposes—to demonstrate to the people of Rome that the civil war is over and that Caesar's murder has been avenged. I'm sure there is enough wine and women in the city to make you happy. Keep those swords in their sheaths. I don't want to hear of any of Rome's fine citizens being skewered by my men. There will be harsh punishment for any altercations. You didn't survive the battle at Philippi just to have your ass punished here in Rome. So, stay together and be sensible."

The encampment of the legions was on the via Appia on the south side of Rome, fairly close to the city walls. They began marching toward the city. As standard practice, talking during a formal march was prohibited, but this was a celebratory event, so the rules were relaxed. Alderic, with Corvinius by his side, watched the distance shrink between them and the walls. Shortly, the towering walls were looming above them. He turned his head slightly toward Corvinius. "How's your leg holding up? Once we enter the city, the distance is not far, perhaps a mile at most."

Corvinius responded, his tone light. "It hurts like Hades, but I guess I can make a mile on it. Besides, something hurts worse than that, but that pain will soon be soothed once we go to this Palace of Venus of yours."

Alderic gave him a knowing grin. "That's what I call motivation. Listen, just so you know, I'll be keeping my eyes straight ahead once we enter the streets with the cheering throngs. I don't want to catch the eyes of anyone staring at me and risk them recognizing my face. So, don't think I have a stick up my arse. I don't want to make eye contact with anybody."

"Fair enough," replied Corvinius. Shortly, they passed through the shadows of the arched entrance and into the city. Masses of people lined the road, cheering and throwing flowers. Bright garlands of flowers were strung above the street, welcoming the conquering legions.

"Here we go, first century," shouted Gracchus. "Let's look smart; show them why we won."

Alderic marched straight and tall, his eyes focused directly ahead. The parade route was the same everywhere. Cheering masses applauded the troops as they advanced down the avenue. Their beloved Caesar had been avenged. The three legions strutted onward, block after block, displaying the military might of the new regime. The Fifteenth Legion was last of the three units. Rank after rank of soldiers paraded down the paved streets, the iron studded boots of the legionnaires ringing out a clamorous cadence, the lines straight and true. Eventually, they arrived at the forum area and marched past the reviewing stand on the via Sacra.

Octavius Caesar stood in full uniform, his armor glistening in the sun. He was accompanied on the raised platform by his military commander, Marcus Agrippa. Off to the side was Lepidus, an equal no more. Octavius's chest swelled with pride. Smirking, he turned to a group of senior senators standing behind him, gesturing at his marching centuries. "Aren't my legions magnificent?" he proclaimed, emphasizing the *my*.

The senators looked at each other, then offered tremulous smiles, realizing that they had traded one dictator for another. There was no more Republic.

When the parade was over, Alderic guided Corvinius down the twisting street past prosperous shops and fine homes of the Capitoline district. Corvinius rubbed his wounded leg. "How much farther? You said it was not too distant from the forum, and we are now well past that area."

"Just a bit more," replied Alderic. "It'll be worth the journey. Do you see any other legionnaires around here?" He answered his own question. "No, and you'll be glad. No standing in line. Only the best women. Would I steer you wrong?"

They moved steadily down the narrow avenue. It looked familiar to Alderic, but it had been a while, and he had only been here once. He advanced past Corvinius, peering ahead. There it was. He recognized the hanging sign. He heaved a sigh of relief. He had found it. "There you are my friend," he said pointing.

Corvinius proffered a wide smile. "It looks like a nice place. Are you coming in with me?"

"Why? Have you never been in a brothel before? You go in. I will wait out here."

Corvinius sulked. "There is no one around. I feel awkward. I've never been in a high-class place before. C'mon. Just go in with me, then you can leave."

Alderic sighed. "All right. Just for you. I sure hope you enjoy yourself."

The pair entered the establishment, Alderic leading the way. He looked about. It was just as he remembered it. Same sense of cleanliness, same smell of incense wafting through the room. He recognized the madam of the house right away. She was the same woman who had greeted Lucius many months ago. She was dressed similarly, her bodice overflowing. Hard to forget that. She stepped forward and greeted the two. "Ah, the conquering heroes. The avengers of Caesar. Welcome to my establishment. How may I serve you this afternoon?"

Alderic highly doubted the sincerity of her words. He could sense her unease at having lowly legionnaires in her establishment. He stepped back. It was up to Corvinius from here. His friend stuttered, a bit overawed by the exclusiveness of the place. "Ah … my friend here recommended this place. Said it was the best in town."

"Yes, indeed it is. My name is Freida. This is the best brothel in Rome. Wait until you see what we have for you." She clapped her hands three times. With that, a bevy of girls, all beautiful and scantily clad, paraded out into the spacious vestibule.

Corvinius's jaw dropped. These women were many grades above what he was used to. He stared at them all, rubbing his jaw in nervousness. He stood there for what seemed like a long time. "I'll go with her." He pointed to a buxom blonde.

Freida spoke. "A fine choice. Her name is Helsa. The fee will be twenty sestertii. She will take you back to her room."

Corvinius nodded numbly and fished in his small purse for the correct amount of coins. He handed them to Freida.

Smiling, Helsa walked over and hooked her arm with Corvinius's. The pair moved down the hall.

Freida turned to Alderic. "I thank you for the recommendation, sir. Are you not going to enjoy one of our women yourself?"

Artorus grinned. "No, not this afternoon. Thank you. Maybe some other time." He turned to depart.

"Wait, you've been here before? You look familiar. I never forget a customer."

Artorus replied, his response vague. "No, I heard about this place from a friend of mine. I'll be outside waiting for my friend to finish. "With that, he exited the establishment.

Freida welcomed several other customers, all previous clients, and went about her routine of displaying the women. The men selected their consorts and were off to the back rooms. After a while, she looked up and observed the beefy legionnaire with the limp walking toward her. Helsa was hanging on to his arm. This was the customary practice when seeing clients out. It added a personal touch to the engagement. Freida peered up at him from her seated position. "Everything was satisfactory? Helsa treated you well?"

Grinning like a fool, Corvinius responded. "She was the best."

Helsa leaned in and kissed his cheek. Before Freida could continue the conversation, four more clients walked in, wealthy ones judging from their attire. The aristocrats scowled at Corvinius. This was supposed to be a place for high-class clientele and not the riff-raff from the legions. Relieved to see him leave, she quipped a hurried goodbye to Corvinius. "Thank you for your patronage. Please visit us again."

Freida dealt with the new customers, seeing to it that each had the woman they wanted. When the foyer was empty once more, she attempted to recall where she had seen the tall legionnaire, who had accompanied the one with the limp. She had certainly seen him before. Who was he? She thought back. It had been a while since she'd seen him, but when? It was strange. He never took his helmet off when he entered her establishment. Why wear that heavy gear in this warm weather? There was something about him, not right. Suddenly, it all came together. She remembered. He came accompanying the senator's son. The virgin. Yes, that's where she'd seen him. She had been questioned, none too gently, by Antonius's men. They had linked her and the Palace of Venus to the bodyguard. Then there was that alert to capture him at all costs. There was a price on his head. The gangs and Antonius's thugs were after him. In fact, all of Rome was seeking him. She beckoned one of the guards. "Aulus, I want you to take a message to Pulchrus. Remember him? He's the leader of the brotherhood that rules the wharves. He replaced Darus last year."

Aulus, a hulking ex-legionnaire, nodded. "I know who he is, and I think I know where to find him."

Freida replied in a laconic tone. "Don't think, just find him. I want you to tell him that it is urgent I speak to him on an important matter. Tell him he should meet with me immediately."

Alderic lounged against the corner of the building, relieved to take some of the strain off his wounded leg. At last, he spied Corvinius approaching. His friend had a silly grin plastered across his face. "Well? Was she worth it?"

Corvinius chuckled. "Best I ever had. Thanks for that recommendation. Now, where are we going? You said you wanted to visit your mentor from your arena days."

"Yes, follow me. His name is Labenius. He's an ex-gladiator. He trained me for the arena and saved my life. I believe I can find my way there. If we're going to rescue that treasure and live out our days in luxury, I want some advice from him, so my past doesn't catch up with me. He may not be the most knowledgeable person to ask, but I have no one else I can trust. Let's go. It's getting late."

Alderic led Corvinius through the streets and narrow alleys. On occasion, they had to turn around at dead ends. Alderic kept a wary eye on his friend, for his limp was getting more pronounced by the minute. At last, they came to the street called Mercury with the rug shop. He went up the rickety stairs and tapped lightly on the door. There was no answer. He knocked harder, rattling the frame. The door opened a crack, and the face of Labenius appeared. "Yes, what can I do for you?" Suddenly, recognition dawned on his face. "By Jupiter's hairy arse, it's you, Alderic! Didn't know it was you in the legionnaire uniform."

Labenius opened the door wide and gestured for the two men to enter. He grasped Alderic's arm, a wide smile creasing his face. "I thought you dead, although I never definitively heard that you'd been captured. By the gods I'm pleased you're still with us."

"It's good to see you again, my friend. Oh, and I'm now known as Artorus. The man who was Alderic is gone."

"Then, by all means I shall call you Artorus."

Alderic gestured toward Corvinius. "This is my best friend and comrade, Corvinius. We served together in the legions of Octavius Caesar. We've recently returned from Greece. Corvinius knows my history. I told him you were the one that saved me in the arena with your instruction."

Corvinius spoke. "Yes, and he used to beat my ass regularly in sword drill thanks to you."

Labenius cackled. "Alderic... I mean Artorus was one of the best. I have never seen a fighter like him." He looked at Alderic. "You must understand that your circumstances have not changed. These men have long memories. If someone recognizes you and reports back to Antonius or Octavius, they will surely come after you. How did you manage to get yourself in the legions? A strange choice for a fugitive."

"I know. I had little choice. Like a fool, I accidentally wandered into a legion encampment in northern Italia, but then I figured no one would look for a former gladiator named Alderic in the legions."

Labenius grunted. "I'm impressed. You're right. No one would think of looking in the legions, especially one posted in Greece. There's an old saying that goes, 'Go to the heart of danger, and there you will find safety.' You appear to have adopted that strategy. But now that you're here, it's still dangerous."

Alderic replied, "I had to come to Rome and parade with the legions. If I could've avoided coming here, I would've. My centurion is suspicious of my past, so I couldn't protest too much. I came to see you for two reasons. First, to let you know I was alive and see you again. I owe you a lot. The second to seek your advice. Corvinius and I are seeking discharge from the legions. As far as I know, my buried treasure is intact. My plan is to recover the hoard of coin and then disappear, hundreds of miles from Rome."

He was careful not to say where he was going. If Labenius was questioned under torture, he would have no response.

He looked at Labenius eagerly. "What do you think?"

Labenius was silent, pondering how to respond. "I fervently hope you succeed. If it were me in your place, this is what I would do."

The two legionnaires leaned forward in anticipation.

"Again, I can't emphasize enough how grave a danger you are in, here in Rome. If someone recognizes your face, and you are memorable because of your height, they will come after you hard. Trust me about this. I know a little something about the workings of the Roman government. They visited me repeatedly when you escaped Rome a year ago. I thought they were going to kill me—nasty brutes—and they could have easily disposed of me without anyone raising a fuss. Therefore, get out of the city and out of the legions as quickly as possible. Next, disguise yourselves as humble merchants. Get a wagon with mules and dress shabbily. That means no legionnaire trappings. Have you thought about how you're going to transport your chests of gold and silver?"

Alderic shook his head. "That is why I came to you."

Labenius nodded. "Listen to me. You need at get a wagon and some pack animals to pull it. There is a large depot on via Appia, which travels south from Rome. You can get a wagon and mules there to satisfy your needs. In your new identities as merchants, you must eradicate all traces of your past, so change your names. Legionnaires Artorus and Corvinius no longer exist. Finally, assuming you recover the treasure of coin, when you arrive at your final destination, don't draw attention to yourselves. You must not spend lavishly. Buy a home, not a villa. Purchase some slaves, but only a few. No extravagant dinner parties. Understand?"

Labenius rose and retrieved a jug of wine. He generously filled three clay cups and raised his flagon in a toast. "To your successful endeavor. I hope you retrieve the gold and live a long and happy life."

Alderic gulped the wine. "I owe you, Labenius. You helped me a year ago, and you're aiding me now. I will get a message to you. I need friends like you. Maybe you could even visit me in my new home." Alderic raised his goblet. "To good friends."

It was early the next morning when Pulchrus, the gang leader, arrived at the Palace of Venus. He tried the door, but it was locked. The establishment was not open for business at this hour. He angrily knocked on the door with his fist. Still no answer. He banged even harder. A disheveled Freida opened the door, blinking at the sun light. Pulchrus scowled. "You wanted to see me on a matter of utmost importance. This had better be worth my trip."

Freida opened the door wider, letting him into the cool dim interior of the brothel. "Come with me," she said, leading him down a narrow hallway toward her quarters. Pulchrus followed, admiring her swaying ass. The pair entered her private chambers. "Sit," she said, gesturing to the single chair in the room. She sat upon her bed. "I have important news that I think you will find valuable. Remember last year when you and the others, including Antonius's men, were searching for the bodyguard of that senator who was proscribed?"

Pulchrus nodded. "Aye, Antonius killed my boss, Darus, because of his impertinence and failure to capture the rogue. It was good for me because it made the leader of the gang. So what does that have to do with you wanting to see me?"

Freida puffed out her ample chest and beamed. "I saw him again."

Pulchrus's jaw dropped. "You're joking. Don't fuck with me, Freida."

The madam held up her hand to silence Pulchrus. "He was here yesterday afternoon after the parade. He was in the uniform of a legionnaire."

"You're sure?"

"Yes, positive."

Pulchrus rubbed his jaw. "Freida, I want you to do me a huge favor. I assume no one knows about this fugitive reappearing."

She nodded in acquiescence. "That is so."

"Don't tell anyone that you have spoken to me about this. And I mean strict silence."

Freida held out her upturned palm in response.

Pulchrus reached into his tunic and withdrew a small purse filled with coins, handing them to her.

She fingered the sack of coins, weighing its contents, then let out a force cough, keeping her arm extended. Pulchrus pulled another larger purse from his tunic and dropped it in her hand.

Freida smiled back at Pulchrus. "You have my assurance that no one will know of this mysterious legionnaire but you and that our conversation will remain private."

Chapter XVI

Alderic stood before Gracchus, who was seated at his field table. He looked up at the legionnaire. "So you've decided to leave the legions after all? Are you sure you won't change your mind? You know you are a valuable member of this century. You're a born fighter if ever I've seen one. You have a future here you know. You are promotion material. I could see you as an optio and then a centurion."

"Thank you for those kind words, Centurion. But I think I've had enough of the killing and dying. No more. I've decided to leave with Corvinius. Besides, I have a woman waiting for me."

Gracchus snorted. "You're trading one centurion for another."

Alderic proffered a wide grin. "Perhaps." He paused a moment, gathering his thoughts. "Listen, I want to thank you for leading us in battle and keeping us alive. You know, when I first joined the century, the men said that you could be a real prick, but once the shit started to fly, there was no better centurion to lead us. I'm sure you know this, but the men respect you immensely. Also you said to me when I first joined that I would make life-long friends and understand the meaning of the word loyalty here. Everything you said is true."

"Thank you for those words, Artorus. The legion is my life. The men of this century and the second cohort are my family. That is who I am. I know this life isn't for everyone." He paused, his turn to gather his thoughts. "Now that we've traded kind words, I would love to know your story. Actually, on second thoughts, maybe it's best I don't know. Someday in the distant future when I'm retired from the legions, we can share a cup of wine and you can spill your guts then."

"I would like that. I'll even buy the first jug of wine. All I can say to you is that there is no evil in my heart. Circumstances have cast me upon an improbable and precarious path, which I have somehow managed to survive, in no small part, thanks to you."

Gracchus smiled. "You have piqued my curiosity, but it will have to wait for another day. If you ever change your mind and want to rejoin the legions, there is always a place for you here. Good luck and good fortune. Dismissed."

Corvinius and Alderic exited the legionary encampment outside the walls of Rome. Toying with their heavy purses tied at their waists, courtesy of the large donative granted by Octavius Caesar to the victorious soldiers of his army, they grinned at each other. They were rich, at least for the moment, and free of all obligations.

All of their armor had been left behind. They wore their legion-issue drab tunics and heavy cloaks to ward off the autumn chill. If they had other garments, they would have turned out in them. Their standard weapons, the short stabbing sword and the razor-sharp dagger, were strapped to their sides, hidden by their cloaks. Each man carried a small satchel, which included a change of clothes and various personal items. At the first opportunity they got, they would trade their military cloaks for something more civilian.

Their first order of business was to proceed down via Appia a few miles to the large depot that served as a hub of transportation. Following Labenius's instructions, this is where they would make their first purchase with their newly acquired funds—a wagon and a span of mules. The two men were in high spirits, and why would they not be? They had money, survived a brutal battle, and were embarking upon a quest that might make them rich beyond all imagination. What they didn't know was that their movements were being shadowed by individuals who would rob them of their dream and wished to see them dead.

Pulchrus, leader of the wharf gang, had his right elbow planted firmly on the filthy table, supporting his head with his outstretched forearm, his expression one of bored indifference. He casually picked up his cup with his left hand and sipped his wine. He was surrounded by his four lieutenants, their poses reflecting a similar lassitude. They were in a tavern called *Toast of the City,* which it was anything but. *Tavern* was a rather generous description. The place was a dive, a gang bar.

Why anyone would want to frequent a dump such as this was beyond anyone's guess, but some did. The place offered cheap wine, unsavory women, and the lurking prospect of violence. It smelled of stale vomit and piss. A few other patrons had passed out; their heads resting on the table, some sprawled out on the floor in various stages of repose. Several small windows allowed some meager light, exposing motes of dust in the dingy interior. Several whores in a state of half undress lounged near the gang members, hoping to earn some coin.

The door to the tavern, hanging half off its hinges as a result of a brawl the previous night, burst open. A figure entered. He squinted in the dim interior, then spied his boss and hurried to the table in the back.

Pulchrus perked up immediately. The man was Nolius, one of the three men he had dispatched to observe the legionary encampment outside the walls of the city. The figure approached the table, breathless. Pulchrus glared at him. "What have you to report?"

The panting figure gulped some more air. "The tall legionnaire you described was seen leaving the encampment in company of a second man, both no longer in their uniforms. They were heading south on via Appia."

Pulchrus jumped up and shouted at his subordinates. "Get off your asses, we have work to do. This is our opportunity." The four others jumped to their feet and followed their leader out the door of the tavern.

Alderic and Corvinius approached the place that had been described to them by Labenius. It was a large establishment, well off the side of the road, featuring numerous pens filled with mules and oxen. A small crude hut guarded the entrance of the business and off to the side were parked a number of empty carts and wagons of various sizes and dimensions. A large wooden rack with three rails had leather reins and traces draped over the top.

The pair glanced around, appraising the wagons and animals. Alderic, with a baffled expression, stopped dead in his tracks and turned to Corvinius. "Do you know anything about wagons and animals?"

Corvinius scratched his head. "No. Do you?"

Alderic was annoyed. "What do you mean no? You told me you grew up on a farm. How can you know nothing about wagons and animals?"

Corvinius shrugged his shoulders. "We mostly grew wheat, some turnips and some figs. The only animals we raised were hogs. We never had a need for a wagon. We hired someone to take our crops to the market." He paused in thought. "How hard can it be?"

Artorus looked over and noted two men hitching up a team of mules to a boxy wagon. He observed them for several moments. "I've no idea what they are doing. It looks complicated. How are we going to do this?"

Corvinius played with the stubble on his chin as he thought. "We'll have to figure it out. Look, other people do it. So can we."

A rotund figure in a tan tunic separated from the men with his newly purchased wagon and mules. Dusting his hands, he approached the two men. "How may I help you today?"

Alderic spoke. "We're just out of the legions."

"I never would have guessed that," said the proprietor in a sardonic tone.

Alderic ignored the man's acerbic comment. "We're looking to buy a cart with some mules to haul it but know nothing about it. Can you find us something not too big that won't cost us too much?"

The proprietor answered. "What are you interested in hauling?"

Alderic improvised. "We're not exactly sure. Thinking about going into the transport business."

The proprietor frowned in skepticism, not believing a word the legionnaire had said. "Come around back with me. I'll show you what's available and tell you the animals that you will need to haul it."

After looking at an assortment of wagons, they settled on a boxy-looking cart that would suit their needs. It came with a large tarp to cover the cargo hold. There was room for two people to sit in front and adequate storage area in the rear. It would require four mules to haul it. The owner gestured at the pair. "Come into my abode. We can finalize the transaction."

Alderic and Corvinius entered the shed. The proprietor examined his tally on a wax tablet and then spoke. "That will be sixty denarii for the cart and eighty for the mules. Would you like to purchase some fodder?"

Alderic asked, "What for?"

The man sighed in exasperation. "In case you two get hungry. Why, to feed the mules of course. They have to eat too, you know."

"Oh, I forgot about that. Yes, include some fodder for several days as well."

"That'll be an additional two denarii."

Artorus counted out the coins from his stash and placed them on the counter. The proprietor greedily scooped up the pile and stuck them in his coin pouch. "Alright, come on with me, and I'll show you how to hook up the beasts so you can be on your way."

After a couple lengthy hours of instruction, the two ex-legionnaires drove away in their recently purchased cart. They had no idea that armed men were closing in on them.

The six gang members rushed along via Appia, hoping to catch-up with the two ex-legionnaires. Nolius was slightly ahead of the others. He turned his head slightly back in the direction of Pulchrus. "Do you think the six of us, plus the two men shadowing the soldiers, will be enough to overcome the soldiers? They appear to be awfully big men."

Pulchrus scowled at his words and swiftly advanced next to Nolius. He savagely punched his subordinate in the face. "Don't you dare question my decisions. It'll be eight of us against only two of them. I have limited the number of men for the purpose of secrecy. If word ever gets back to those who hired us last year that we absconded with their treasure, our lives will be forfeited. Understand?"

Nolius cowed beneath the fierce gaze of Pulchrus. "I just thought—"

"You don't think. I do the thinking here. Now let's pick up the pace. I want to conclude this business today."

He had no sooner spoken, when one of the lookouts came hurrying toward them. Breathing heavily, he gasped, "They're on the move. They purchased a wagon and bunch of mules. We questioned the proprietor. He said the pair that purchased the wagons asked about the best way to reach via Ostiensis without going through the city. They're moving slowly."

It took several long hours for the two men in the wagon to traverse the outskirts of Rome to the via Ostiensis. The roads exiting Rome were like spokes coming out of the hub. They were forced to move in a circuitous fashion from the south, where they had purchased the cart, to the northwest where the via Ostiensis ran toward the sea. This is where the family crypt of the late senator was located. A second option would have been to go through the city. It was the more direct route but much more dangerous. It just increased the odds of someone recognizing Alderic.

Corvinius, taking his turn at driving the cart, jiggled the reins to increase the pace the four mules were plodding at. Alderic half-stood, half-crouched peering ahead. He pointed. "I see the first of the crypt buildings lining the road. We should be there soon."

Corvinius glanced about, observing the lengthening shadows tone, he replied in a laconic tone. "I hope so. We've wasted most of the day getting here."

They neared the stone tomb. Alderic turned to Corvinius. "Halt right here." Alderic leapt off the seat and moved towards the entrance. He reached the door and his heart sunk in despair. The iron lock on the door had been busted open, hanging on one of its metal hinges. His heart pounding, he opened the door. It emitted a loud screech. He pushed it as wide as possible to provide the most amount of light. Corvinius was directly behind him, peering over his shoulder.

"Is it here?"

"I don't know. Someone's broken the front lock, but the inside of the tomb appears undisturbed. He rapidly moved deeper into the musty interior where the unfinished wall had been under construction. He moved to the edge of the stone flooring slabs. "Corvinius, help me lift this."

The two men grunted and heaved the heavy slab aside. Alderic peered into the gloom. At first, he saw nothing but then remembered that he had shoved the chests deep back so they could not be seen directly if the slab was lifted. He peered underneath and back into the shadows. There! He spied the outlines of a chest. He hopped down into the sub flooring area and hefted one of the coffers out.

"What's in it?" asked Corvinius.

In response, Alderic drew his military dagger and gently jabbed the point into the opening for the key. He gave the knife a slight twist and the lock sprung. He slowly lifted the lid, revealing a pile of gold and silver coins.

Corvinius was speechless. At last he blurted, "Jupiter's balls. I've never seen so much coin."

Alderic offered a smug smile. "We're rich. There are four others like this hidden below."

Alderic relocked the opened chest. The two men hauled the five chests into the wagon and covered it with the tarpaulin. By now, the sun's rays were hitting them sideways. Dusk was approaching. Traffic on the roadway had ceased. Alderic was about to leap up onto the wagon when eight armed men converged upon then in a loose semi-circle. They stopped about ten feet away, brandishing their weapons. Alderic and Corvinius edged back so the wagon protected their rear.

A figure in the middle of the group grasped a long-bladed dagger. He was obviously the leader. "So you hid the loot in the crypt? Clever man. I want to thank you for loading up my chests of coin." He eyed the sword hanging from the belt at Alderic's side. "If you drop your weapons, I'll let you walk away."

Alderic viewed the menacing group before him. He knew that if he disarmed, his life would be snuffed out in a matter of seconds. In all likelihood, this was part of the same group of thugs that had butchered the senator's family. Mercy was not a term they understood. He remained silent, hoping to unsettle the ruffians before him. They had made a major tactical mistake by not attacking immediately when they had the advantage of surprise. Alderic drew his sword from its sheath. It made an ominous hissing sound as it cleared the scabbard. He then retrieved his dagger with his left hand. Corvinius did the same.

Artorus continued to glare at the gang of thugs surrounding him. At last, he let out a few terse words. "Come and take it if you can."

The group hesitated, looking toward their leader for guidance. Without warning, Alderic charged at the figures on his right. Corvinius followed Alderic's lead and attacked the four on the left. Alderic's sword descended in a diagonal slice, opening a huge wound in one of the men's shoulder and then followed with a strike to the leg of a second man. Both men collapsed, writhing on the ground. Corvinius chose to deliver a straight thrust with his sword into the throat of another, killing him instantly. Now, there were five remaining.

Wasting no time, Alderic swung a savage backhand slice catching another figure across the face. The man cried out in anguish, dropping his knife and holding his hands to his head to stem the bleeding. Ignoring the last man on his right, Alderic charged into the men now engaged with Corvinius.

A heavy club descended toward Corvinius's head from his right. At the last instant, he spied the strike and twisted his shoulder to block the blow. The club struck Corvinius's shoulder instead with a solid thump. He grimaced in pain but held on to his sword. Alderic witnessed the strike but arrived too late to block it. He eliminated the man with the cudgel seconds later with a thrust through the torso. Three remained now.

As he withdrew his sword, he felt the slicing pain of a cut along his arm, inflicted by the leader of the gang. Alderic blocked the next thrust with his own dagger. By this time, he had cleared his sword from the other man's guts. He savagely pounded the pommel of the sword into the face of the boss, breaking his nose and cheek bone with an audible crack. The figure sunk to the ground, moaning in pain.

Meanwhile, Corvinius had dispatched a second man with a thrust through the ribs. The last man standing dropped his weapon, turned about, and ran. Alderic chased the ruffian for a short distance before drawing even with him. Knowing that he could not afford to have any survivors tell of his whereabouts or that he now had the treasure, Artorus sliced his neck with his sword, nearly decapitating him.

Alderic returned and motioned with his sword to the badly wounded men on the ground. "Finish off those two. I'll deal with this one. He appears to be in charge."

Alderic savagely kicked the dagger out of the leader's hand, breaking several bones in the process. He grabbed him by the front of his tunic and lifted him up. "Who else knows you're here?" he demanded.

The bloodied face leered back at him. "Fuck you."

Alderic rammed his dagger into the soft flesh of his stomach and ripped it upwards toward his chest. The man gasped in horror. Alderic withdrew the dagger, letting the man's entrails spill out of him. He whimpered once, and then died.

Alderic looked toward Corvinius. "Are you alright?"

In response, he rubbed his right bicep. "Hurts like fucking Hades. What about you?"

Alderic glanced at his left arm and saw a small trail of blood. "Nothing mortal. I've had worse. Are they all dead?"

Corvinius nodded. "I thought I was finished with the nasty business of dispatching the wounded, leaving the legions and all. But yes, they're all on their way to Hades."

Alderic replied. "Good. Nobody will miss that lot, that's for sure. Now let's get out of here."

The two jumped onto the wagon. Alderic gathered the reins, then shook them. "Ha!" The mules began plodding forward.

Corvinius stared ahead. Without turning his head, he asked, "Do you think others have been alerted to our presence? Will more men come after us?"

Alderic contemplated the question. "Don't know. It's strange that only the gang were after us, but no one from the higher-ups. If it were you, would you entrust that lot to secure a cache such as what we have?" He continued without waiting for a reply. "It might be that the gang wanted to keep all the coin for themselves. They were in the employment of Octavius and Antonius. One of them might have recognized me. It has been so long since the soldiers of Rome searched for me that this bunch of criminals may have decided to abscond with the treasure and not inform their masters."

They drove the wagon into the approaching dusk, moving into a side road that connected them to the via Flaminia, heading north. They stopped briefly at the intersection of the two roads, then wended their way into a field between several nearby houses. They fed the mules and then, just like in the legions, took turns standing watch for the evening.

The night was uneventful. They set out the next morning at dawn, traveling into the early afternoon without incident. With each mile they journeyed, Alderic breathed a sigh of relief. His guess that the group of ruffians had gone rogue and not informed their masters about their discovery might be true after all. He turned to Corvinius. "We should be reaching a town soon. We can spend the night there at an inn. We can get accommodation and someone can look after the mules."

Corvinius looked at him confused. "What about the chests?"

Alderic replied, "We bring them inside with us." The wagon executed a slight turn on the road. The view ahead that greeted them held an unpleasant revelation—there was a roadblock. A line of several wagons waited to be inspected by a group of uniformed legionnaires. They couldn't turn around, for they were already in sight of the soldiers manning the inspection point. Besides, there were several wagons behind them. *After all I've been through, it's going to end at a roadblock.* He slowly urged the mules forward. He had no alternative.

They were third in line. The legionnaires appeared to be questioning the occupants of the wagons ahead of them and inspecting their cargo. Alderic spoke quietly to Corvinius. "Keep yourself together. Act natural. Our story is that we are two legionnaires recently separated from the legions. Our first job in our new business is to transport these chests from our client in Rome to his patron in the town of Tredarius farther north of here. Bridin and I stopped there on our flight from Rome. We don't know what's in the chests or have the keys to open any of them. Let me do the talking."

Corvinius replied. "I hope they buy it."

"If things go sideways, be prepared to attack."

Their wagon was next. Alderic yanked on the reins. "Ave brothers. I thought I was done seeing the likes of you," he chuckled.

The decurion who commanded the detachment walked up next to the wagon. He eyed Alderic and Corvinius suspiciously. "What unit were you with?"

"The fighting Fifteenth, although we sometimes called it the farting Fifteenth."

The other legionnaires spluttered with laughter. The decurion cracked a wide smile. "So now you're haulers?"

Alderic proffered a wide smile. "You could say that. Me and my friend Corvinius here just separated from the legions. We marched in the big triumph in Rome, then said our goodbyes. Corvinius was badly wounded at Philippi and was medically discharged. The medicus said his leg would not withstand any more forced marches. I had the option of staying or leaving. I decided to join him. I had one too many close calls at Philippi. Know what I mean?"

The decurion nodded sagely, then turned his gaze to Corvinius and spoke in a gruff tone. "Turn up your cloak, so I can see your leg."

Corvinius complied, exposing the jagged scar of his wound, then dropped the cloak back down.

The decurion whistled. "Now that's a nice one. Sorry, I had to check. Make sure you're not deserters. What are you transporting?"

Alderic shrugged. "Don't know. My client requested I deliver these five chests in the back of my cart to his patron in Tredarius. The chests are locked, and we have no key. Corvinius, show him the chests."

Corvinius peeled back the tarpaulin exposing the chests. The Decurion peered inside the wagon, examining the five chests and the iron locks.

He then looked at Alderic. "Don't you think it's a bit unusual to be transporting goods and not know what they are?"

Alderic assumed an expression of naive innocence. He replied sheepishly. "Don't know. This is our first job. We were informed that if any of the locks were broken, we would not be paid when we deliver the chests."

The decurion looked at the pair with a bewildered expression. "What did you say your name was?"

"I'm Artorus and this is Corvinius."

"Well listen up Artorus and Corvinius. My suggestion to both of you is to find another line of work. Now, get your wagon out of here."

Epilogue
Ancona

Two Weeks Later

The two men and their cart had traveled for the last two weeks without incident. Alderic pointed up the road at the town ahead. "There's our destination. Those are the walls of Ancona. We were here before with the Fifteenth. Remember?"

Corvinius tightened the reins, keeping the mules on pace. "Aye, I remember marching through the town and building an encampment outside the walls. I also remember that, unlike some other people, I did not get to enjoy the pleasures the town offered."

"I was gathering wood for our century. I just happened to stray a bit farther."

"Yes, you did," replied Corvinius with a wink. "And I was equally punished for your transgression. You owe me for that."

"I think I have the means to more than compensate you for your sacrifice. Now get those mules moving. We're going to surprise Bridin. I can't wait to see her again."

They entered the town center late afternoon. As directed by Alderic, Corvinius pulled the wagon up to the shop selling woven goods. "Wait here." Alderic leaped off the wagon and ran to the door. He shoved it open. A small copper bell tinkled, announcing his arrival. Bundles of cloth were stacked on all the tables and shelves.

Bridin emerged from the back of the shop. "How may I help—" She stood speechless at the sight of Alderic. She ran and leaped into his arms. "You've returned!"

"Even better," he replied. "I'm back for good." He hugged her tightly before breaking away. "I want you to meet my friend, Corvinius, from the legions. He is outside with the wagon. We have some cargo I think you might like."

Alderic led her outside and introduced her to Corvinius. The two men carried one of the chests into the shop. Alderic knelt by the container. "Remember I told you I hid the senator's hoard of coin before his family was killed and I forced to flee?"

Bridin nodded. "Certainly, I remember your story."

Alderic produced his knife and sprung the lock on one of the chests. He opened the lid. "Well, here it is."

Bridin gasped. "Sweet Minerva's ass, that's a lot of coin."

Alderic grinned. "We're rich. There are four others just like this one. Of course, Corvinius gets a share. I'm going to have to change my name again to something other than my legionary name of Artorus, but that should be easy enough. We can talk later about our future. If you don't like it here, we can go anywhere else."

Bridin ran and hugged Alderic. He broke apart from his embrace. "Corvinius, what was that word you used that day when we were on the march? The one that meant pleasant?"

Corvinius frowned in thought, then his face brightened. "Idyllic."

"Yes," exclaimed Artorus. "We shall lead an idyllic life."

THE END

Author's Note

A *Barbarian in Rome's Legions*—and its central character, Alderic—is a work of fiction. Nevertheless, as in my previous novels, *Legions of the Forest* and *Return of the Eagles*, the story is set during the historical events of Roman antiquity. In this work, the time represented is the turbulent aftermath of the assassination of Julius Caesar. The novel includes a host of historical figures, including Octavius Caesar, Marcus Antonius, Gaius Cassius Longinius, Marcus Junius Brutus, Marcus Lepidus, and Lucius Biblius.

The unfortunate Tencteri tribe, from which Alderic descends, suffered a number of misfortunes. They were forced out of their ancestral homelands by more powerful neighboring tribes. Seeking new lands, the Tencteri crossed the Rhine into the territory of Gaul, recently conquered by the Romans. They sought to parlay with Caesar, but he would have none of it. The Tencteri were set upon by the Roman legions and vanquished, with the survivors retreating back across the Rhine.

With respect to Alderic's tenure as a gladiator, I have attempted to describe the weapons and armament of one of the more famed pairings—the retiarius and the secutor.

The harsh practice of proscription first carried out a generation earlier by the dictator Sulla had been employed by the Triumvirate to swell the coffers of the treasury for the upcoming war against the Liberators—it was used as an expedient means to rid themselves of political foes. Whether or not the rulers engaged the various brotherhoods to assist them in their brutal endeavor is a matter of speculation on my part; however, not an unrealistic supposition.

The shield I described in the book—and the one displayed on the cover—was known as the Augustan shield. It was extensively used during the reign of Augustus Caesar. At some point during the Republican era, the shape of the shield transitioned from oval to rectangular. Only speculation exists regarding exactly when this occurred.

After the battle of Philippi, I described a consolidation of forces. Again, there is only speculation that this might have occurred. I inserted this in the book to allow an honorable means of Artorus's discharge from the legions. What is known is that there was a huge consolidation of forces after the defeat of Antonius by Octavius, around ten years later. The standing army was cut almost in half, to twenty-eight legions.

The battle of Philippi occurred in 42 BC in Greece. It was actually fought in the month of October, but I took the liberty of having it take place during the hotter summer months. As noted in the book, there were two separate battles that took place two weeks apart. Marcus Antonius did indeed construct a causeway through the swamp on the left flank of Cassius's army. Octavius suffered the ignominy of having his command tent captured and looted by the enemy.

The second battle of Philippi was decisive: the surviving commander of the Liberators, Brutus, could no longer afford to sit upon the high ground and wait, as some of his forces were deserting his cause; and both commanders of the Liberators, Brutus and Cassius, committed suicide rather than facing the humiliation of capture and their probable execution.

I have described how the Republican forces ruled the seas in the scene where the war galleys of the Liberators attacked the transports of Octavius Caesar. Historically, on the day of the First Battle of Philippi, Domitius Calvinus of the Triumvirs sailed from Brundisium into the Adriatic Sea with over two legions to reinforce the armies of Octavius and Antonius. The transports sailed out of port in an effort to run the gauntlet when the wind suddenly failed. The Republican galleys swooped in and sank or captured the entire force.

With respect to the engagement at Philippi, never had two such large Roman armies opposed one another. Estimates put the Triumvirs' forces at nineteen legions, or about 110, 000 men, while the Republican army was estimated at seventeen legions, or 100,000 men.

The relationship between Antonius and Octavius was, at best, strained. Eighteen months earlier, the two men had been at each other's throats, their armies fighting each other. Out of political expediency—or for a better word, survival—the two joined forces; and the union of unlikely partners came to be triumphant at Philippi. Antonius married Octavius's sister to further strengthen their ties. Of course, this relationship unraveled years later, and ultimately, Octavius prevailed over Antonius and his ally, Cleopatra, at the battle of Actium in 30 BC.

—Mark L. Richards

Coming Soon in 2019

Tribune Valerius and Centurion Marcellus from *Legions of the Forest* and *Return of the Eagles* are back in a new adventure. The two retired Roman officers, now civilians, are engaged in a prosperous business, trading goods on the German frontier. It has been years since they served under the eagles. Life is good. The two men are wealthy and have settled into family life. Their tranquility is shattered when both men are abruptly recalled into active military service by Emperor Tiberius Caesar and his henchman, Lucius Aelius Sejanus, prefect of the Praetorian Guard. Trouble is brewing once again on the German frontier and Valerius and Marcellus will be smack in the middle of the impending storm. The emperor demands the two officers assist the Empire in quelling the nascent rebellion. Valerius and Marcellus will face extreme peril, both on the home front and with the rebellious German barbarians on the Roman border. They will need to utilize all their experience, guile, and fortitude to accomplish their mission. Will they survive once more amid desperate circumstances?

About the Author

Mark L. Richards is a graduate of Pennsylvania Military College (now Widener University) and had served in the US Army as an infantry officer before entering the healthcare industry. He was employed as a chief financial officer at a large academic health center. Now retired, Richards resides in West Chester, Pennsylvania. He is married with two daughters and five grandchildren.

A lifelong historian of Roman antiquity, Richards was inspired by his favorite subject to write his debut novel, *Legions of the Forest,* and its sequel, *Return of the Eagles.* He can be contacted at legions9ad@aol.com

Made in the USA
Las Vegas, NV
24 May 2021

23608480R00142